SHOOFLY PIE TO DIE

A Granny Hanny Amish Country Mystery

By

Barbara Workinger

Barbara Workinger

authorHOUSE™

1663 LIBERTY DRIVE, SUITE 200
BLOOMINGTON, INDIANA 47403
(800) 839-8640
WWW.AUTHORHOUSE.COM

First published by AuthorHouse 10/05/05

ISBN: 1-4208-6738-5 (sc)
ISBN: 1-4208-6739-3 (dj)

Library of Congress Control Number: 2005905885

Printed in the United States of America
Bloomington, Indiana

This book is printed on acid-free paper.

For my wonderfully supportive friends, each one is a great gift and deeply appreciated.

ACKNOWLEDGEMENTS

With sincere thanks to the Old Order Amish of Lancaster County, Pennsylvania, many of whom I am privileged to know. As one of them has told me, "We don't mind being written about, but we like it when the author gets it right." I have tried to accurately, within the confines of the mystery, do just that. Over ten years of ongoing research into the Amish culture has gone into the Granny Hanny series. Unfortunately, for I would love a friend like Hannah Miller, there is no real Granny Hanny. What is real is the fondness and respect I have for the people and traditions of Lancaster County.

Thank you to my agent and friend, Sara Camilli, and to Michelle Camilli, for their patient proofreading and suggestions, to my children and husband who put up with a writer in the family, and my Hershey writing critique group.

I appreciate the guidance of many research sources for answering innumerable questions and supplying endless information, most especially to the wonderful facilities at Elizabethtown College and the People's Place in Intercourse, The Lancaster County Prison for information and the tour of their facilities, and The Quilters' Heritage for the information gleaned from their wonderful yearly event.

Last, but never least, thank you to my readers who are a joy to know.

For more information on mysteries, quilting, recipes, please visit me at: www.barbaraworkinger.com

PROLOGUE

The stream, thawed by recent warm weather, meandered around a bend in the gully. Spring grass poked up along the bank and willow branches, burgeoning with buds, hung low over the water. Under a covered bridge, water splashed and gurgled onto stones and rocks, and picked up speed as it spilled downhill. Boulders lined the uphill side of the creek bed. It was there that a large wooden barrel was wedged on its side, caught between two of the largest boulders. Its contents were visible to anyone who focused on it. A body of a man was stuffed in, head first, half in and half out of the barrel; one leg, clad in tan trousers, was bent at an unnatural angle, and stained with the unmistakable red color of blood. The man was as still as Hannah's breath.

"Gott im Himmel, not another dead body," she gasped, and dropped her sketchpad. Then she felt a blow, and crumpled to the ground, her charcoal drawing stick still clutched in her hand.

CHAPTER ONE

It was the second week in April and the last half of the two "Quilt Weeks" in Lancaster County, Pennsylvania. No one enjoyed the week more than well known Amish quilt maker, Hannah Miller. She had already spent two days at the Heritage Quilt Show, an annual event, which this year drew over 10,000 quilters and quilt lovers. Hannah liked to see what wonderfully inventive designs the quilters came up with; she never ceased to be amazed at the ingenuity and craftsmanship. She seemed to gravitate to the designs of groups who celebrated their heritages with quilts. She had always loved the Hawaiian quilts with their designs reflecting the beautiful flowers and fruits of the Islands. This year, Hannah was delighted to see so many African-American quilts. The Amish heritage was represented by a collection of crib quilts, which Hannah particularly enjoyed. Her 21 grandchildren not only each had a crib quilt made by Hannah, but the older ones also had a full sized quilt put away for their future homes.

This spring there was added incentive for Hannah's enthusiastic attendance at all the events connected with the celebrations. Hannah's formerly Amish granddaughter, Caroline, was being married in a few weeks and Hannah was deeply involved in the festive preparations for the wedding. Among the reasons for attending so many auctions, was to help Caroline find a few authentic old pieces with which to furnish her new home. The two-week event would top off the unofficial start of the spring and summer antiques and collectibles season at a gigantic flea market with over a thousand dealers present.

Though Caroline had never formerly joined the Amish church, she was accepted by her Amish family despite their disappointment in losing her to what they referred to as the "English" world. Caroline had gone to college, then law school and was now practicing law in the city of Lancaster. Having an attorney so closely connected with the Old Order Amish had proven to be a boon. Despite the reluctance of the Amish to deal with matters of the English laws and regulations, they often found a need to do just that. Caroline Miller was their bridge, their guide and their advocate in the confusing world of jurisprudence.

Hannah was ready to go. She stood in her *grossdotti* house, a smaller home attached by a long porch to her larger, original house, which was now occupied by her son, Daniel, and his family. The Old Order Amish of Lancaster County cared for their grandparents as treasures, not burdens. When parents retired from farming, a new house was built for them and the original home usually went to the oldest son and his family. The grandparents remained close by to help as they could or wished. One would never find a "retired" Amish person in an institution. Hannah often thought that particular "English" custom more than a shame. It was a waste.

The two shoofly pies Hannah was donating to the food concession were neatly packaged in their own plastic containers. The containers would be returned, unwashed as the Plain sects' women who ran the kitchen, and whose proceeds went to charity, would be much too busy to do dishes. The food prepared for the auction was one of the reasons people came. Like the county fair, each cook sent her specialty.

Hannah looked at walls filled with her handmade quilts. Despite the Amish reluctance to be prideful, Hannah was proud of the quality and artistry of her own work. She wouldn't be heard boasting, but her private opinions were her own. She didn't have to say anything; the quilts spoke for themselves.

Spread out in front of her and stretching up to the exposed rafters over the second floor was an array of quilts worthy of any gallery or exhibit. Mixed in with the jewel toned quilts -- traditional examples of her Amish heritage-- were dozens of examples of Hannah's own original and imaginative designs.

Hannah was waiting for Caroline to pick her up for the most exciting of the auctions. Many of the items were donated and would be auctioned off, with the proceeds going to a relief fund to help "in need" families who had suffered some misfortune. Since the Amish did not have either medical or home insurance, the fund would help cover hospitalization, refurnishing homes and restocking livestock after fires. If an Amish family member needed hospitalization, the fund and supplemental donations paid the bill. When a family lost a building, usually to fire, the Amish and non-Amish neighbors helped rebuild structures in an amazingly short time. That was a new beginning, but the contents of the buildings had to be replaced and the fund was often depleted by those needs. This year, Hannah had donated two quilts to the auction. They were patterns she had stitched many times. Decorators snapped up the traditional Amish quilt patterns, so Hannah's contributions were a vibrant colored "Nine Patch" and a subtle pastel colored "Sunshine and Shadows." Hannah's name signed discretely on the back gave the contributions added cachet and brought top dollar. Like a lot of Amish women, Hannah felt uncomfortable drawing attention to her work by signing it, but she had learned to overcome the reluctance as her reputation and fame grew.

So far, the week had been blessed by beautiful weather. All during the Quilters' Heritage Exhibit, the temperatures had hovered around an ideal 65 degrees with silken breezes and cloudless skies. Today, the weather had changed. The sky looked like buttermilk, overcast and clotted with clouds. Hannah hoped the rain would hold off until after the main part of the auction. Sometimes, being without an up-to-date weather forecast was not a good thing. Caroline could turn on her computer, her television, or a radio and get the latest report. Hannah's best weather prognosticators were her animals. Her three cats, staid, four year-old Daisy, and busy kittens, Qwill and Arch, slept more when the weather was changing and moved from the outside screened porch to the glassed in porch off Hannah's kitchen, where the window seat was Hannah's favorite place to spread out and read the newspaper. More often than not, when Hannah read, one cat could be found under the paper, another on top of the paper and still another precariously balanced on Hannah's lap. Today, all three cats slept in one large multicolored ball on the window seat. The birds and the squirrels, all of whom Hannah fed, were especially busy before a storm was expected. Today, they were scurrying and darting to gather food. Not a good sign at all, Hannah thought. She hoped the bad weather would turn as fast as it seemed to be arriving. It would make for an awful mess on the gravel -over -dirt parking lot at the auction if it rained for long. The only paved parts of the lot were reserved for Amish carriages and for handicapped parking.

Hannah had always read everything she could get her hands on, including her favorite mysteries from the Lancaster County library system, supplemented by paperback whodunits from Scholman's used book store. Hannah had read her way through the so-called "Golden Age of Mystery" to the present sub-genre of the cozy mystery, cat mysteries.

"Can't beat cat mysteries," Hannah told Caroline. Hannah preferred her mysteries with the violence occurring off stage. She didn't mind mild swearing as long as it wasn't gratuitous.

Basically, she read gentle mysteries where the puzzle was the point. Much like quilt making, she mused. Unfortunately, that Hannah herself kept stumbling over dead bodies in rural Chelsea Township was odd and unlucky. But, that she knew a lot about both murder investigation and puzzle piecing was fortunate. She had helped solve three murders and that, she prayed, would be all.

Hannah had always read voraciously, even in the midst of raising her large family. She found time to read her way through hundreds of books, even developing her own speed-reading system. Luckily for Hannah's schedule, she functioned very nicely on four hours of sleep a night. .

She heard a car pull up in the driveway. It was Caroline, accompanied today by recent bride, Jennet Adams Hunter. Jennet was in the area to sell her sister's house, and try to find a buyer for her sister's business. Neither would be an easy sale. Annette had been killed in her own house.

Hannah had known Jennet since Jennet and her late twin, Annette, were babies. Hannah, at barely five feet tall, had to stand on tiptoe to hug Jennet. "Well, Jen, you are looking very happy, already," Hannah said. Not surprisingly, Jennet looked better than the last time Hannah had seen her, after the murder of her twin sister. Always a beautiful woman, she was looking radiant. "Ian didn't come with?" Hannah asked, lapsing into an informal mixture of English and Lancaster County colloquialisms sprinkled with an occasional Pennsylvania Dutch term. Jennet was treated like family. With the English, Hannah spoke quite formally, even eschewing contractions in unaccented English. "Tired of marriage, already, so soon, Ian is."

"I hope not," Jennet said, smiling. "He had something to finish up in London, but he'll be here next week Of course, both of us will back for the wedding."

"I should hope," Caroline said. "I want everyone I love there. Stephen is telling me I love a lot of people. We have invited 200 and no one is declining."

"Wohl, no one declines weddings 'round here," Hannah commented. "Despite it being spring with the planting going on, your wedding is set for late enough in the day that everyone should be there. And it is not an Amish wedding, so it will not go on for hours."

"It will be the perfect wedding," Jennet added. "You seem to have every contingency prepared for."

"I hope so," Caroline said. "Everything except rain." Hannah noticed Caroline had quickly crossed her fingers. Next the girl would be knocking on wood, Hannah thought. Very un-Amish, to be so superstitious. Of course, Caroline was no longer Amish. Hannah was thankful, however, that both Caroline and Stephen believed in God, and were members of a church. It would have to satisfy her. They could be running off to have a justice -of –the- peace wedding in Las Vegas. Perish the thought, Hannah said to herself, trying to attribute that quote. Was it from the Bible? The way her mind was fixated on rain today, it probably referred to the story of Noah.

"The Lord will take care of it," Hannah said. Still, she couldn't help saying a quick, silent prayer and trust this time the Lord's way would be Caroline's way, too.

CHAPTER TWO

"I had forgotten how big this thing is," Caroline said, looking around the auction room at the array of merchandise filling the barn-size space. "It's been at least ten years since I was last here." The parking lot was full; people were parking on the grassy areas and into the graveled areas which bordered pastureland and fields. The barrels Caroline remembered as cordoning off the picnic area between the parking lot and the creek were still there. She wondered if they had been cemented into place to keep them from being stolen. When she got closer, she saw the barrels were filled with bricks. They'd be even easier to steal. But who would want bricks? They were not old, and found everywhere. These days, everything old, no matter how disreputable-looking, was being stolen. Even cemetery gates and figures from outdoor nativity scenes were now fair game for thieves.

Best-Stoltzfus was the largest auction house in Lancaster County, and had an unblemished reputation. Jonah Stoltzfus started the business in the 1930s as an offshoot of a mud auction. Mud auctions were sales held in late winter to benefit local volunteer fire companies. A little bit of everything from livestock to food might be purchased at one of the sales. Jack Best married into the business when he wed Jonah's daughter, Laverna. Jack, a born businessman, changed the name to Best-Stoltzfus Auctions when Jonah died. The name sure couldn't be beat for memorable, as the Amish might say. Word had it that Jack and

Laverna wanted to retire to Florida, and as they were childless, Jack was looking for a buyer for what had become the Best Empire.

Caroline looked around at the people who were at least as interesting as the items for sale. The five auctioneers, who would take turns with the gavel, were neatly dressed in white shirts with marine-blue, patch pocketed nylon jackets and matching ties. They mingled with the crowd, ready to answer questions about the merchandise. The crowd milled around inspecting items. Many of them were busily taking notes. Caroline knew a lot of the customers were dealers and decorators from New York and other big cities. A few people had reserved seats by leaving signs or boxes on chairs. In addition to the main room, there were three anterooms, all stuffed to the rafters with items to be sold that day and the next. And no junk, she thought. Perish the thought of junk at Best-Stoltzfus. It would never happen.

"Some of these people look vaguely familiar", Jennet said. Sometimes Caroline forgot Jen had grown up in the area. Jennet seemed eons away from rural Lancaster County, both in distance and sophistication. Today, she wore denim, like many of the people at the auction, but Jennet's denim jacket and pants fit like the tailor-made designer outfit Caroline knew they were.

"Wohl, Jen, all the usual suspects are here," Hannah said, in a stage whisper.

"Still reading mysteries, Granny?" Jennet asked with a smile.

"Mostly at night, when I cannot see to quilt. And, of course, I always have a paperback in my bag," Hannah said, patting her black bag. "My worst fear is to be caught somewhere without something to read."

"That would be awful. Do you ever relax?" A minute is a terrible thing to waste.

The irony wasn't lost on Hannah. "Very funny, Jennet. I relax when I quilt. As a matter of fact, today I intend to make some sketches of the covered bridge. I have an idea to use it in a quilt."

Caroline knew her grandmother was a proficient sketcher and often made drawings of landscapes, animals and Amish children. She did not sketch the faces of Amish adults as most felt drawings or paintings of them were graven images, as forbidden as photographs. Children and young people were not officially church members, and thus exempt from the ban.

"I see Dorcas and Swayne are still going to auctions," Caroline said, nodding her head toward a couple who were inspecting one of the tables of "smalls," the term for anything small enough to be on a table. "They haven't changed much since I was a little girl."

The couple in question was obviously elderly. The man, Swayne Hess, was quite pleasant looking. He had abundant white hair, neatly combed, and wore crisp, beige trousers and a long sleeved blue plaid shirt. He carried a highly polished, gnarled wood walking stick. Dorcas was very slight with platinum blond hair piled five inches above her head in a 1960s beehive style. Word had it she slept with her head wrapped in toilet paper to protect her elaborate hair-do. She wore what looked like stirrup pants tucked tightly inside high heeled, red patent leather, knee high boots. She had encased what Caroline would say was an admirable chest for any woman, in a white, ribbed turtleneck. Her face poked out from the sweater's top. Her heavy makeup was another homage to the sixties, complete with theatrical false eyelashes and neon orange lipstick. It was startling.

"My," said Jennet. "They would be memorable. Hannah, how old are they?"

Caroline knew Hannah was fiercely loyal to friends, so she didn't comment on Dorcas Hess.

"Ninety-something," Hannah answered, sounding distracted. "Do not look it, for sure." She handed her sketchbook and the chair cushion she had brought to Caroline. "Would you like to find us some seats?" In Central Pennsylvania, orders were often phrased as questions. When someone said: "Would you like to get out of the car here"? One did not answer no. It meant get out here.

"Remember, I am too short to see if we do not get on an aisle. Right now, I need to get rid of these pies."

Caroline knew better than to offer to take them to the kitchen. Hannah would miss the gossip, a worse thing than wasting a minute.

When Caroline and Jennet had found the perfect seats on an aisle, a few rows back from the front, Jen said. "Tell me about some of the other people you know, Caroline."

Caroline glanced at the crowd milling around the tables. One man she recognized as Denny Brody, with a note pad and a pen in his hand, and a pencil tucked behind his ear, stood out despite his short stature. He seemed to bristle with impatience and moved with nervous energy, darting in and out around the more leisurely inspectors. His hair was close cropped and reading glasses jiggled on his nose. He wore a tight white tee shirt and light colored pants. Caroline could imagine him in his youth with bad skin, a duck-tail haircut and a pack of cigarettes tucked in a rolled-up sleeve like a character from "Grease." Caroline and her fiancé, Stephen, had tickets for that play's revival when they honeymooned in London next month. One of the best things Stephen had ever done for Caroline, besides loving her, was to introduce her to the arts. She wondered how she ever did without music or the theater. Granny seemed to do just fine without either, but she got her education by reading about everything outside the Amish world. So far, her out-of-state travels had been confined to visits to her family in Ohio and Kentucky. Many Amish did travel, some even to Germany and

Switzerland, where their ancestors came from. The only restriction concerning travel was that they could not go by airplane.

Denny's jaw was moving at a fast clip, chewing something. Caroline remembered that he ate on his feet, and when he wasn't munching on a piece of pie or a cookie, he was chewing gum. Small wonder Denny has such a bulldog chin, she thought. He exercises those jaw muscles enough.

"That guy is Denny Brody." Caroline nodded towards Denny. "Ever heard of him?"

"Nettie used to talk about him. She didn't have too much good to say about him. Look, his arms are longer than his legs." Jennet, who was used to watching long-legged models strut down fashion house runways, would notice that.

"Better to reach in and grab merchandise away from the other people trying to see it," Caroline said.

"Isn't he a hoarder or something like that?"

"I guess you could call him a hoarder, or a dog-in-the-manger. It's not the stuff he gets that others don't want which makes him so disliked; it's that he outbids everyone on the stuff they do want. The guy has tons of money- 'Deep Pockets,' some people call him. That is probably the nicest nickname he's given. Most dealers, and even some collectors, can't outbid him. More than hoarding, Denny's problem seems to be greed or control, or some other unpleasant issue. Of course I'm not a shrink, just playing one at an auction."

Jennet laughed. "Actually, it is kind of fun to practice pop psychology. I get plenty of opportunities to do that in the fashion business. What does he do with the merchandise?"

"Stuffs it in one of three barns, or three garages on his property. He sells some at his shop in Reading, but no way he could sell even a fraction of what he buys. The one thing he never bids on is textiles or quilts. Good thing. Granny would read him the riot act if he bought valuable quilts, or any quilts, and stored them in one of those musty barns." Caroline had seen people who received what Hannah called: "A lesson in what is the right thing to do." It was enough to make Caroline feel sympathy for the recipient of her grandmother's lecture.

"Who's that couple coming in? There's something vaguely familiar about them," Jennet said.

Like two well-rehearsed soldiers, a middle-aged couple marched along the aisle past Jen and Caroline, moved to the second row of seats, removed the two boxes marking their places and sat down. There was nothing remarkable about their appearance. Both their faces were pleasant enough looking, albeit set in bland, poker faces, Caroline thought, although she could not imagine the woman playing poker. Sartorially, they were not a matched pair. The man was dressed in a loud Hawaiian print sports shirt worn over white pants. His head was very bald and shining brightly under the glaring lights. His body was more out of shape than actually fat. He wore one gold earring and a watch, which even from a distance, sparkled with a diamond-studded face. The woman was of medium build and what Caroline always thought of as pillowy. All her curves had fluffed into a shapeless mass from chest to thighs. She was dressed like many of the Mennonite women at the gathering, in a high necked, pastel printed dress with three quarter length sleeves and a modesty panel over the chest to keep her breasts from showing. The hemline brushed her ankle socks. Her gray hair was pulled tightly into a bun covered by a cupcake shaped prayer cap. Amish women would wear a larger, heart shaped cap and would never wear a printed fabric.

"That's Copious Clay and his wife, Matilda," Caroline said quietly. "Believe it or not, he's a jeweler. He's not Mennonite, but she is. Copious doesn't speak to Denny Brody. He says Denny is driving him out of business because Denny bids up everything Copious wants."

"That could make an enemy in a hurry. She's Mennonite? How odd! I suppose a Mennonite isn't forbidden from marrying a jeweler, right? It is a bit ironic since, as I remember, Mennonite women, like Amish, don't wear jewelry- not even wedding rings. Does he only sell old stuff?"

"No, he handles new and vintage, and he redesigns things, even broken jewelry, into really interesting pieces. As a matter of fact, he's designing our wedding rings. He has a shop in Doylesview," Caroline added. "Matilda still dresses like a Mennonite, but I've heard she doesn't attend church anymore. Not since her first husband died and she married Copious."

"How strange," Jennet said, "that she still dresses so conservatively. Mennonites can't be excommunicated or shunned for marrying out of the faith, can they?"

"I actually don't know that much about the restrictions, other than that there are all degrees of Mennonites from liberal to conservative. The Amish left the Mennonites because the Mennonites were too liberal. Most people think it was other way 'round, that the Mennonites left the Amish because the Amish were too conservative." Caroline lowered her voice. "The Clays are coming this way. Jen, we're gossiping as much as Granny." Caroline was smiling when she spoke, but she felt sorry for Matilda. Like Caroline herself at one point, Matilda Clay was a woman torn between two cultures and not belonging to either.

"You start looking at the auction offerings. I'll go drag Granny out of the kitchen," Jen offered, knowing Caroline was furnishing her new house and needed to get a good look at the items up for auction. "Besides, I want to take a few photos of the food area. I think this event would make a super story for one of the magazines I freelance for. It

13

sure is the flip side of haute couture. I really want to concentrate on the quilt auction, but I might be able to use some crowd photos as part of the article."

"Good idea! If I went into the kitchen, I'd get caught up in congratulations and never get out of there. Better remind Granny why we're here. She's supposed to play expert. She can always catch up on gossip later."

Caroline watched as Jennet expertly threaded her way through the ever- increasing crowd. She had plenty of experience moving in crowds. Jennet covered every major fashion show and opening from Milan to New York.

The trick wasn't getting to where Hannah was; it would be getting Hannah to leave. Granny would come back when Granny was ready, Caroline thought, smiling inwardly. No one hurried Hannah Miller unless she was into a murder investigation. Fortunately, those days seemed to be over, and Granny had promised nothing would spoil Caroline and Stephen's wedding. In the unlikely event of another death in Chelsea Township, under no circumstances, Hannah vowed, would she get involved. Caroline and Stephen's wedding would go off without a hitch, Hannah assured them. It would be the perfect ceremony, a reception to celebrate and a time to remember.

CHAPTER THREE

When she thought back about that segment of the day, Hannah would have said she had been in the kitchen just a few minutes, only long enough to say hello. But, saying hello to seventy women took a while, even Hannah had to admit. When a person had to top the hello off with a sentence or two asking about each family (with the average number of children each woman had being eight), it took a few more minutes. There were Amish women along with the Mennonites and even a few English, as the Plain people referred to anyone other than Amish or Mennonites. She noticed Denny Brody's former wife, Petula, was among them. Today, Petula was scurrying around with the other kitchen volunteers to ready their wares for hungry auction-goers. Pet Brody owned a small antique consignment business nearby. She didn't handle Denny's merchandise. He wouldn't want to pay someone to sell his stuff anyhow, Hannah surmised. He was too cheap, despite all his family money. Living in the same area and in the same business, the Brodys were bound to run into each other. They had reached an accommodation; they completely ignored each other. Hannah never thought the Brodys looked like a couple who would have a mutual attraction. Physically, they looked like an odd couple. Petula was a head taller than Denny and her brassy blonde hair was cut in a wild Afro-style. As seemingly calm as Denny was frenetic, Pet's small, brown eyes managed to take in everything going on around her. She knew everyone's name and was unflaggingly friendly. Hannah had always liked Petula, who was also Copious Clay's sister. In Chelsea Township, everybody was related in one way or another. Hannah could hardly keep track of them all. Hannah greeted Petula as warmly as the other women in the room. One place Hannah didn't hurry was when greeting folks. It seemed downright unfriendly to dash in and dash out of a gathering of any kind. In actuality, Hannah had been in the kitchen well over an hour.

One section of the kitchen was devoted almost entirely to sweets. Pie after pie and almost as many cakes, had been sliced and displayed in their original containers with the name of the cook prominently displayed. And that was only half the number of sweets donated. The other half would be held back for the second day.

Mattie King made the best lemon sponge pie in town, and experienced auction gourmets wanted only Mattie's pie. The same went for Lizzie Light's strawberry pie and Hannah's shoofly pie, to name a few of the favorites. Good cooking was one of the things no Plain person minded being proud of. Hannah thought of how fast her shoofly pie would go. She had seen one person buy a whole pie, and thought it a bit hoggish. After all, more than one person or family should have a chance to enjoy it. On the other hand, Hannah reminded herself, the idea was to sell the pie, not to allot it.

By the time Jennet arrived, the kitchen was about ready to open and a line of hungry customers was forming outside the long room. Hannah noticed that right at the front of the line, as he usually was when he wanted something, was Denny Brody, munching on a candy bar while he waited.

"Where does that man put his food?" Hannah whispered to Jennet. "He is always *fressing*, but he is as skinny as a hard working farmer. Not a spare ounce on him."

"Maybe he only sleeps four hours a night," Jennet answered, looking at Hannah who should know all about burning calories with activity. "I heard you prowl around at night."

Hannah didn't answer, but wove through the crowd until she spotted Caroline waiting in front of a beautiful hand painted trunk in the furniture section. Hannah looked it over carefully, and, with help from Caroline and Jennet, tipped it up to look underneath.

"I would give maybe $1,500 for it. That would be a bargain. It has some age, but it is not real old, maybe 1900," Hannah said, in an undertone. "It is a real nice piece, and out of Lancaster County, I think. Can never be positive; these things get faked. You would need some of those *Antique Roadshow* fellows to be sure."

Jennet didn't look surprised that Hannah knew about a television show. The Amish often saw television at the homes of non-Amish relatives and friends, or in stores. Even if they hadn't seen it on television, the *Antiques Roadshow* was like elections. You didn't have to vote to know about them.

"I would say leave an absentee bid; that way you will not catch auction fever and overbid. Besides, we might be here until tomorrow by the looks of this crowd. This area of furniture does not go up for bid until 7 tonight."

"Sounds like a good plan, Granny. I have my eye on some small stuff and I'd like to stay long enough to bid on those pieces. I'd appreciate your thoughts, and Jennet's, on the smalls."

An hour later, Hannah glanced out of one of the long windows towards the parking lot. "That sky wants rain," Hannah said. "It is getting *uckly*. I would like to make a sketch of the covered bridge a while. You and Jen stay here and bid. It should not take long for me to draw it." Hannah picked up her large black umbrella and her bag. "I will be back in a bit."

17

"You sure you don't want me to come?" Jennet asked.

"Nope," Hannah said in the direct way the Amish often have. "You would be bored, and maybe distract me. Nice of you to ask," Hannah added, aware she sounded less than appreciative of Jennet's concern. Hannah had always been independent and was not about to be anything less until someone had to hold her up or wheel her around. Hopefully, that was some years away.

As Hannah made her way to Spooky Nook Bridge, she glanced warily at the sky. It was darkening by the minute, but Hannah reckoned any storm was a half an hour away at least. It would be a good time for sketching the bridge against a lowering sky. Hannah envisioned the quilt she could make- a painting in stitchery. She would appliqué the pieces in grays and browns with the contrast of spring green. Then there was that odd color in the pale April sunset, beginning to streak the sky to the west with an almost tangerine-colored hue. The combination was almost too surreal for Hannah's tastes. Maybe she would just incorporate the surging stream, making the boulders stand out with a trapunto technique, stuffing them to be slightly more three-dimensional than the other elements in the quilt. The covered bridge with its weathered wood and shingled roof was in desperate need of repair. Lancaster County had more covered bridges than any other place except for Indiana, and many needed reconstruction. It was a long list and Spooky Nook wasn't at the top. For purposes of Hannah's quilt, depicting the structure wouldn't need more than appliqué using several textures and weights of fabric to make it look realistic. She would leave off the sign at its entrance that said: "Bridge Out. Do Not Cross." Bordering the quilt in a vivid sky blue would set it off nicely, she thought. As she always did, she could see the finished product clearly in her mind's eye. It already pleased her.

By the time Hannah had made her way to the stream and walked down to where the old covered bridge spanned the water, the hint of color in the sky in the distance was being replaced by a tarnished silver wash that was darkening faster than Hannah had hoped. Soon, the sky would be the color of Hannah's charcoal drawing stick. She was beginning to think she had misjudged the speed of the storm. Not to be *lobbich*, she chided herself. It was silly to worry about getting wet. Her commodious umbrella would keep her and her drawings safely dry. She found a good vantage point and took her sketchpad and charcoal stick out of her bag. Placing both the bag and the umbrella at her feet, she propped the pad in the crook of her left arm and quickly began her sketch.

She had caught most of the elements she wanted on the paper when it became too dark to see properly. She had a flashlight with her- one of the indispensable "modern" conveniences Amish were allowed to have. Good thing I do not have to deal with a kerosene lantern, Hannah thought. I'd need another hand, maybe two. She smiled, enjoying the ludicrous mental picture of herself as an octopus-like creature in Amish costume.

The sun, trying to get through the dark sky, broke through the clouds for an instant. It was then she spotted something. She blinked, not believing her eyes.

The stream, thawed by recent warm weather, meandered around a bend in the gully. Shoots of grass poked up along the bank. Under the bridge, burgeoning willow branches hung down to almost brush the water, which splashed and gurgled onto large rocks, and picking up speed, spilled downstream. Boulders lined the uphill side of the creek bed. It was there that the large wooden barrel was wedged on its side, caught between two boulders. Its contents were visible to anyone who focused on it. The body of a man was stuffed, head first, half-in and half-out; one leg, clad in tan trousers, was bent at an unnatural angle, and stained with the unmistakable red color of blood. The man was as still as Hannah's breath.

"*Gott im Himmel,* not another dead body," she gasped, dropping her drawing pad. Then she felt a sharp blow to the back of her head, and crumpled to the ground, still clutching her charcoal drawing stick.

CHAPTER FOUR

Caroline had placed an absentee bid for the trunk and won the bids on the several small items she wanted for her new house. The time had seemingly flown by. She looked at her watch, then out the window. It hadn't begun to rain, but it was almost dark. "Have you seen Granny?" she asked Jennet.

"No, but maybe she's back in the kitchen, or visiting. There are so many people here, and I was so absorbed in the auction. She must be here somewhere." Jennet's words belied her concerned expression.

"No, Jen, that isn't like her. She would have come back here to see how the bidding was going, or at least to leave her umbrella with us. We need to find her, Jennet."

Thirty minutes later, they had searched the building and discovered no one had seen Hannah recently. Caroline found Laverna Best at the check-out booth. Jack, who rotated auctioneering with the four other auctioneers, was not in sight.

"Where is Jack?" Caroline asked.

"Taking a break, or in the other room," Laverna, said. "He has a lot to do. Is there something I can do to help you?" Laverna, was regally overseeing the check-out booth, and was, as usual, overdressed. Caroline only perfunctorily took in her highly sprayed hair and tight-fitting black dress. Jack's wife looked more like she should be at the symphony in New York, than working at an auction in Central

Pennsylvania. Laverna had to be close to sixty, Caroline knew, yet there was hardly a line in her face. Caroline was too focused on Granny's whereabouts to think more about Laverna.

"You want Hannah paged? For heaven's sake, why?" Laverna's annoyance was plain. "We really don't like to page people; it breaks the momentum."

Caroline's mouth was half open, ready to protest, when Jack appeared from the office behind the check out. He looked hot and tired, and had shed his blue windbreaker. "I heard you," he said. "I wouldn't worry about Hannah, Caroline," Jack assured her. His once pristine white shirt was wilted and showed dirty smudges from handling so many old objects. "You know folks are always getting separated. This is one big crowd; biggest we've had, as I reckon. Hannah can take care of herself better than most folks. Small, but mighty," he finished with a thumbs- up sign. "But sure, I reckon we can page her if you want," he added.

"I've already told them we don't like to page," Laverna said.

It was Jack's turn to look annoyed – at his wife. "I heard you, Laverna. We will page for Hannah, of course," and he did so, interrupting the current auctioneer. Jack's strong voice boomed out over the intercom: "Attention, please! Will Hannah Miller come to check-out? Hannah Miller, meet your party please. Come to check-out."

Ten minutes passed with no response.

At least we know where she was going, Caroline thought through increasing worry. The last time Hannah went missing, they didn't know where to look, nor could Hannah help them find her. Thanks to her grandmother's resourcefulness, it had turned out fine. It would turn out fine this time, too, she thought positively, but said a quick prayer for insurance. "Should I call Stephen, or your father?" Jennet asked.

"Not yet," Caroline answered. "I'm probably overreacting. First, let's try to find her ourselves." If Caroline ever wished the Amish would embrace some modern conveniences, it was now. If only she had given Hannah her cell phone. Hannah would tell her what-ifs and worrying are a waste of time, Caroline thought. Trying to stay calm, she thought of one of Hannah's humorous maxims: "Don't borrow trouble. The interest is too high."

"We will find her!" Jennet added, patting Caroline's hand. "Jack's right. Hannah is pretty good at taking care of herself."

When Caroline asked to borrow a couple of flashlights, Jack Best supplied them with the powerful lantern-type flashlights he kept for emergency power failures. It would be nearly bright as daylight when they searched for Hannah.

"You sure you don't want me to go with you to the bridge?" Jack asked. How 'bout I ask for some volunteers to go along, too?"

"Thanks anyway, Jack. If we don't find her right away, then we'll come back, and organize a search party. Granny will be fit to be tied if we cause a commotion unnecessarily. She's probably on her way in now." Caroline realized she had said "fit to be tied," an exact description of what had happened to Hannah at Nettie's house when a murderer had left her to die. She mentally shook off the disturbing image. She had to try to keep her focus and go look for her grandmother.

Caroline's back was to the double-door entry, but she heard the doors swing open, followed by a collective gasp. Caroline spun around to see Hannah, eyes wide, and looking disheveled, with bonnet askew and bits of grass and dirt clinging to her black Amish cloak. To Caroline's relief, she looked more mad than hurt.

Everyone spoke at once, making it hard to hear anything.

"I am fine!" shouted Hannah, in a surprisingly loud voice for such a small woman. Honed by years of shouting over the din of her nine children, her voice cut through the murmur of the crowd like a gag, effectively silencing them. "But, there is a fella stuffed into a barrel by the covered bridge! He looks dead. Somebody better call 911."

The din started up again, and then abated enough to distinguish a collective word from the crowd: "Who?"

CHAPTER FIVE

Hannah shrugged her shoulders. Rumors would spread fast enough. Even though she had a pretty good idea as to the identity of the victim, it was more important to attend to him. If he wasn't dead, he needed medical attention in a hurry. She could not have reached him across the creek, even if she wanted to. The floor of the bridge was so rickety that it was dangerous, even to foot traffic. And, after getting hit over the head, Hannah wasn't about to give her unknown attacker another chance to come after her. Cowardice was the smarter side of bravery, or there very well might be two dead bodies at Spooky Nook Bridge.

Emergency vehicles wasted no time in getting to the auction house. With pulsing and screaming sirens, police cars, fire trucks and ambulances converged within minutes on the Best-Stoltzfus Auction House. The loading zone and parking lot aisles were soon filled with emergency personnel from Chelsea and neighboring townships.

An EMT looked Hannah over and pronounced her almost as good as new. Her heavy Amish bonnet and thick hair covered with a prayer cap had dulled the blow to her head. Hannah adamantly refused to go to the hospital to have a doctor check her. She had been to the emergency room once or twice and regarded the long wait as adding insult to injury.

"You might have a slight headache, Mrs. Miller, and I'd like someone to stay with you tonight to wake you every hour or so, but I don't expect any long-term effects. See your own doctor in the morning." The EMT didn't wait for Hannah to say more, but dashed out to join a group headed for the creek.

"You are coming home with me tonight," Caroline ordered.

"Please do not tell me what to do, Carrie." Hannah looked indignant. Even her late husband, Eli, didn't try to give Hannah orders. Nor did the Bishop; he made suggestions, and Hannah did not always take them, either. Her feeling was God gave her free will and she intended to exercise it, albeit with His guidance.

"If you are worried I might be attacked again, you are wrong. Whoever hit me could have killed me at the creek if he had wanted me dead. He, or she, just wanted time to get away. I have Bear barking at home, and dead bolts on all the doors." Bear was Hannah's very large mixed-breed dog. He was as gentle as the proverbial lamb, but strangers didn't know that. He had a bark loud enough to scare away a real bear.

Even before 85 Amish quilts were sold for a million dollars to a local museum, thieves had begun to steal older Amish quilts. They usually struck on the two Sundays a month when the Amish left for all-day church services. Many Amish had to abandon their trusting ways of leaving their doors unlocked and began to secure their homes. Some Amish actually put their valuable antique quilts in large lock boxes in banks.

"I agree with your theory, but you are not going home to stay alone!" Caroline backed off. "Jennet offered to stay with you tonight. Head injuries can have after effects. You need to be quiet and get some rest. Someone needs to check you to make sure you haven't passed out."

"Oh, all right," Hannah said. "You have a point, Carrie. "It is reasonable to take care of one's health at my age." Hannah grudgingly agreed that Jennet could stay. Although she didn't want to say so, Hannah thought Jen would not take over like Caroline might. Caroline was visibly relieved that Hannah had agreed without much of an argument. Hannah liked to pick arguments she could win, and right now, she didn't much care if she won or not. She was more distressed by the violent death she had discovered.

All the while the dramatic scenario was being played outside, the auction inside went on unabated. Some of the dealers and collectors had come from hundreds of miles away and they couldn't care less about a matter of murder. They were there to bid, and would stay until the evening's items had been offered and sold. Others, mostly locals and casual auction goers, were much more caught up in the high drama playing out in the parking lot and off towards the creek. Sheriff's cars and other emergency vehicles completely ringed the parking lot and no one was leaving until they were interviewed and released. This was the best two- ring show in Chelsea Township. It would provide fodder for the gossip mill for years. Little did anyone realize the show was just getting started.

Caroline paced the small office. Its walls were hung with framed photographs of past and present Best-Stolzfus family members and auctioneers. Hannah thought how sad it was that the dynasty would end in the second generation. Awards from the community services the family had performed were spotlighted. Hannah did want to get home, too, but there was no way they could circumvent the sheriff's deputy who had been given orders to get Hannah's statement before he let her leave. Once she had been checked by the EMT team, the deputy, who introduced himself as Wayne Lee, was at Hannah's side, clipboard and recorder in hand. They were shown into an anteroom adjacent to the auction office, which had been turned into a command center.

"This is just a preliminary statement we want from you, Mrs. Miller. By tomorrow, you might have forgotten important details. It happens." Hannah narrowed her eyes. She did not suffer from either a faulty memory, or an excess of patience with people who considered she might have either. He spoke slowly and loudly, as if Hannah had a hearing problem. This caused a further narrowing of Hannah's eyes. Caroline glanced at a point over her grandmother's head. Hannah knew by glancing at Caroline's twitching lips that her granddaughter feared she would do something inane like laugh, as much from relief that Hannah was acting so normally, as from observing Hannah's annoyance at being patronized.

The deputy didn't seem to notice. He looked about twenty, although Hannah thought he had to be a bit older. She wondered where the acting chief, Kiel Benton was, but couldn't say she was sorry he hadn't appeared. His people skills were worse than Lee's and a whole lot more irritating to Hannah.

The Chelsea Police Department had been in terrible shape since their Chief, Ted Rowland, had died from a heart attack. Crime in the Township was low and consisted of traffic tickets, an occasional robbery, but rarely violent crime like murder. Since Rowland's death, the township was struggling to find a new permanent chief.

Wayne Lee was Asian, a rarity in this part of the county. He was very neat and trying to look professionally cool, Hannah observed. Maybe she could overlook the patronizing attitude. He was a kid, and she would give him a chance.

Without waiting for him to start questioning her, she preempted him, and launched into a statement. This wasn't the first time she had given a statement and her years of mystery reading made her very adept at knowing what questions would be covered. The deputy's surprise was obvious.

"I think you've answered all the questions I was supposed to ask for tonight. When we recover the vic, we may be back at you," he said, casually. "We'll print out a copy and bring it by tomorrow, for you to sign."

"Call first," Caroline said. "Here's my card," she added, pulling one from a card case.

A surge in volume came from the crowd milling outside. "It sounds like our guys might have the vic ready for transport," Lee observed, leaving without another word.

"That Lee is a touch too casual," Caroline observed. "He sounded like he had seen a few too many episodes of *Law and Order*. I prefer at least a modicum of formality when interviewing a witness."

"He is young," Hannah said, shrugging her shoulders.

Hannah was torn between getting home and making sure she had guessed correctly as to who the dead man was. After all, she hadn't been close enough to determine for sure.

"We are not going until I find out for sure who was in that barrel." She stood up and adjusted her skirt. Grass fell from its folds.

"The police may not want to share that information until a positive identification has been made," Caroline said.

"The police will not have to share anything. Half of Chelsea Township was out there with them," Hannah countered. "The first person that we see will know."

As if on cue, Jack Best came into the office. His lanky frame filled the narrow doorway. "Denny Brody, and he's dead," he announced, tersely.

"Just what I thought," Hannah said. "What killed him?"

Jack knew Hannah and her knowledge of crime investigation, so he did not soften the news. "Looks like a double whammy- a whack to the head and, he smells like almonds."

"Almonds? Maybe cyanide, already?" Hannah observed. "Or maybe it was real almonds. He ate lots of snacks. Cyanide is a bit hard to smell even when you are looking for it."

Jack shrugged his shoulders. "Maybe someone wanted to make doubly sure Denny died. The cops will know more as soon as the coroner sees the body. They took Denny away."

"Any sign of the person who hit Granny?" Caroline asked.

"Nope," Jack said. "But, they are still out there searching, and the whole area is secured. "I need to get back to the auction. Knew you would want to know since you are involved," he said, including all of the women in his glance. "Get yourselves a good rest. As I said before, Thank God Hannah's okay." He reached down and awkwardly patted Hannah's shoulder.

Hannah had heard two things Jack Best had said, as if they were underlined: "Thank God Hannah's okay" and "You are involved."

On the trip back to her house, Hannah sat quietly in the back seat, mulling over the day's amazing events. Jack didn't seem too upset at Denny's demise. There were not too many people at the auction who would be volunteering to give eulogies at Denny Brody's funeral. Still and all, not liking Denny was far from killing him. Wishing he would go away was a far cry from making sure he permanently did. If Denny was poisoned, why also hit him over the head? Why put the body in a barrel and shove it down the creek bank? They must have been in a powerful hurry to hide the body. If whoever put Denny in a barrel expected that the barrel would float downstream, he did not know much about the creek. Or about barrels; Denny wasn't even all the way inside it. Boulders and rocks all along the creek would soon hold up the barrel, especially with Denny's feet hanging out, making it more likely the barrel would catch on something. Even as intimately as she knew the countryside, Hannah wasn't sure how far it was before it merged into a larger creek. There were all kinds of houses upstream, but none downstream. The trees were too dense and the water too close for houses. Maybe the killer was just figuring to buy some time, but Denny's truck would still be around. Sooner or later, someone would wonder why. Hannah's mind was leaping from idea to idea. Maybe whoever killed Denny was coming back for the truck? It might be one long time before anyone noticed Denny himself was missing. Pretty sad situation that nobody would notice, and nobody would care where Denny was.

"That deputy was a bit inexperienced, didn't you think?" Jennet asked, breaking into Hannah's reverie. "Where was Chief Benton?"

"I wondered that myself," Caroline said.

"Wohl, I did not miss him. That Benton feller is an idiot. I once felt sorry for him, but not after we had to solve his last case." The minute the words were out of her mouth, Hannah regretted them. The last case was the murder of Jennet's sister, and although it was never likely to be forgotten by any of them, Hannah tried not to keep bringing it up in front of Jen.

Jennet turned to look at Hannah, "Thank heavens you did solve Nettie's murder. How awful and how dangerous it would be to have it hanging over us forever. Of course it will always be with us, but don't worry about bringing it up, Hannah. The rawness is gone. Ian and time have helped."

And the good Lord, Hannah thought.

"Okay, Granny," Caroline said. "You must have some ideas on this case."

"I do, Carrie. Mainly I wonder why the over-kill, and I am not trying to be amusing. Was there one person or two involved? Or maybe more? Sounds so dramatic that there could maybe be more than one killer. Whoever did this to Denny was no professional. No, the killer was a real amateur. What is puzzling me, is why kill someone somewhere with so many potential witnesses? If it was poison, it must have been premeditated. It is not exactly like folks carry a vial of poison along saying, 'Wohl, guess I slip some poison in Joe's coffee today.' Then go and hit the victim to make sure. Then drag him off, where folks might see it.

"Now, then again, assuming whoever did this, knew Denny well enough to know his habits, they'd know he would go eat in his truck, that he always parked way at the end of the lot, right next to the trees..."

"Granny, let's not get into speculation. Please. This time we have no reason to be involved. We can't. I'm getting married and if nothing else, you promised me, and I promised Stephen, we would stay out of anything even slightly dangerous. We got out of this one with only a bump on the head for you. The next time, we might not be so lucky."

"Course you are right, Carrie. We will let Benton do it; he can muddle through. This does not really concern us. This time we will not get too late *schmart.*"

That night, although she thought she would be tired from her ordeal, Hannah found herself unable to sleep at all. She showered in the very modern bathroom, which she had installed when the *grossdooti* house was built. At the time, she was prepared to justify its relative modernity as necessary for a woman of her advancing years, but no one asked her to. It featured a large skylight, a soaking tub, a separate shower, and sleek blue and white tile on the floors and walls. The ceiling was painted pastel blue and Hannah herself had added a few painted clouds, which she could admire from the tub. It also boasted a greenhouse window, so Hannah could grow plants in the humid environment and away from the quilts which needed a drier atmosphere and no direct light. At this time of year, the window was filled with three rows of primroses, their cheery colors in shades of red, yellow, purple and pink, providing a bright punch to the room's quiet serenity.

After an hour of trying to sleep, and finding it impossible to even close her eyes, Hannah got up, put a robe over her white gown, picked up a flashlight, and quietly padded past her guestroom where Jennet slept with the door open. Normally Hannah read when she couldn't sleep, but she had her own mystery to solve and tonight she needed to do something, which would provide her a little thinking time. She first thought about working on the almost finished quilt, which was on its frame in the great room. Bear, asleep on the braided rug near the front door, opened one eye, and seeing Hannah, thumped his tail a few times before falling asleep again. Hannah had covered the quilt in progress, to keep it from any possible harm. The cats never climbed on Hannah's quilts. The quilt framed moved and the animals preferred their surfaces stable. Hannah still covered the quilts. In the daytime, the bright light coming through the windows in the great- room, wasn't good for quilts. Hannah only uncovered the work on the fame when she was working on it. Now, with Jennet in the house, Hannah was glad the quilt was hidden. Hannah wanted it to be a surprise; she loved surprises. The quilt on this frame was to be a belated wedding present for Jennet and her husband, Ian. The creation was unusual in both pattern and material. Normally, Hannah did not produce such bold, modern quilts. When she had started sketching ideas, it came to her as having components of both delicacy and sophistication, a description which fit Jennet perfectly. The pattern was vivid and dramatic, although its individual pieces were small and delicate. Hannah had chosen silks and velvets and combined them into a continuous spiral, worked outward from the center of the quilt. Colors of the appliquéd, rectangular pieces of material ranged from the palest of pink silk to the deepest red velvet, the darkest in the center and the lightest at its outer edges. It gave the appearance of a giant, unfolding rose. A heavily quilted background in cream perfectly suited the design. Deep red velvet was Hannah's choice for the narrow binding. It served to ground the design. Just looking at it, made Hannah more tranquil. She planned to give it to Jennet and Ian when they came for Caroline's wedding. Hannah looked at it and then thought better of working on it. It would take too much light and there was a chance Jen would see it.

Hannah lit the kerosene lamp over the kitchen table, took her bag from a nearby chair, and sat down. It was then she realized her sketchbook had been left at the crime scene. In fact, it was the last thing she had remembered happening at the creek. She saw the body and dropped the drawing she had been doing. The police must have found it, along with her umbrella, so if it hadn't been ruined by rain, she guessed it would be returned to her. She rummaged deeper into the cloth bag. Everything else was still in place, even the charcoal stick she had been using for sketching. She didn't remember how the stick got back in the bag. The bag had been over her arm and she had been using it to provide stability for the sketchbook, so it would not be so wiggly. The charcoal stick must have just tumbled into the bag. She tried to reconstruct what she had done after she came to, but it was a blur. The first thing she remembered was heading back to the auction house, almost instinctively, like a dog returning to the safety of home.

Hannah knew she shouldn't get involved in this case, and she wouldn't, yet she couldn't help thinking about it. After all, as Jack Best had said, she was involved. Telling herself not to think about it was like trying not to taste the food when you were cooking. Hannah went to a drawer in her kitchen and took out a large ruled pad of paper and a pen. Sometimes a person needed to think on paper.

She tore out six pieces of paper and lined them up in two rows. She neatly headed the top row: Facts, Questions and Suppositions. The next row was printed with the words: Motives, Means and Opportunity.

She hoped she had enough paper. The Questions and the Motives pages would be lengthy indeed.

CHAPTER SIX

When Caroline returned to her condo after dropping Hannah and Jennet at Hannah's house, she was met at the door by her grim-faced fiancé, Stephen Brown.

"What the hell is going on?" he asked without any other greeting. "Tell me you and Granny are not involved in any of this." He didn't need to explain how he'd already heard. Stephen owned the biggest independent hardware store in the county; word traveled as fast as a summer storm. "My phone has been ringing off the hook. I finally switched on the answering machine and started screening calls. When I started to get faxes, I closed up and came home."

Caroline was more than a little annoyed at his reaction, although she realized he was probably worried and his attitude was prompted by experience with Caroline and Granny's past history of close calls.

"You and Granny are going to leave this one to the professionals. For God's sake, Carrie, we are getting married in two weeks. Two weeks! We don't have time to do the stuff we need to get done now. I'm not even going to mention how dangerous this could get. Granny has already been hit over the head," Stephen said. "That she is okay is damn lucky," he finished, flopping onto Caroline's couch. "She is okay, right?" His handsome face was flushed and his hazel eyes were dark with emotion.

"She's fine, but Jen is staying with her and Bear is standing guard."

"Did anybody tell your folks?"

"I'm going out there in the morning. They were already in bed. Mom had been up all night the night before, so she went to bed early. Dad always goes to bed early."

"Yeah, and 'gets up with the cows,' as he likes to tell us."

From long experience in defusing his anger, Caroline decided to address his concerns head-on, as soon as she knew one thing. "Where is Molly?"

"Our daughter is staying the weekend with her friend, Emily," Stephen answered, formally. "She and Emily are wrapping almonds with flowers, or whatever, for the wedding. You do remember the wedding?"

She ignored the jibe. "Okay, Stephen, let's calmly talk this over. I understand you are worried. I had a few frightening moments myself when we couldn't find Granny and then she staggered into the auction, covered with dirt and grass.

"I promise you, Granny and I are not going to get involved. It was a fluke. Granny happened to find the body and unfortunately, she got hit on the head. She didn't go looking for trouble. I don't think Granny has any inclination to play detective this time. Other than her required statement to the police, we have no intention of doing anything even vaguely connected with an investigation."

Stephen stood up and put his arms around Caroline. "I don't know what I'd do if anything happened to you," he murmured into her hair.

"Nothing is going to happen," she said, in what she hoped was a resolute tone. "Now, let's talk about the wedding. I..." she began, but the rest of her sentence was stopped by Stephen's passionate kiss.

After he left, Caroline was too restless to sleep. She remembered her first meeting with Stephen.

Then his father, Gilbert Brown, owned Crossroads Hardware. Gil Brown was a long time friend of the Millers. He had been raised on the farm next to theirs. The hardware store had been in Gil's family since the turn of the twentieth century. With the advent of the mega chain hardware stores, business for the independents fell off, and they were quickly disappearing. Crossroads was an exception, mainly because they catered to the Amish need for the non-electric. Being a tourist draw didn't hurt either. Visitors reveled in the ambiance of what they perceived as a bit of the past, an authentic, old- fashioned hardware store. Behind the scenes, Gil utilized the latest technology, but tourists didn't see that. Gil hired Amish teens to add authenticity to the store as well as for their honesty and efficiency. With increasing frequency, Amish young people needed to find work away from the farms. There were too few farms and too many mouths to feed for the Amish to be able to support the entire family by farming alone. One of the draws of Crossroads to tourists was the abundance of Amish who frequented, and worked in, the store. And for once, the relationship of Amish and tourists was complementary.

From the time of his parents' divorce when he was a small child, Stephen had lived with his mother in Philadelphia, but spent summers with his father. As Gil's son, Stephen was in the store most of the day. Like Gil, he teased the Amish girls his father hired to work during the busy summer tourist season. Unlike Gil, whose teasing had a good natured, joshing quality, Stephen's teasing took on a flirtatious bent, which discomfited the straightforward, yet ingenuous girls. Although they knew the facts of life from growing up on farms, they were naive when it came to the kind of bold flirting the "English" in general, and Stephen in particular, engaged in. It had an edge. Although he didn't dare incur Gilbert's wrath by touching the girls, his leering looks were almost as bold. The more the girls blushed and looked uncomprehending, the more intense Stephen's attentions became.

From the first time Stephen saw Caroline, the summer she was seventeen and he two years older, he couldn't take his eyes off her. Knowing her family and Gil were long-time friends, Stephen treated her with more respect than he did other girls. In fact, his behavior was beyond reproach.

Caroline, unused to being singled out as special, fell in love. Stephen's attentions, as much as her intellectual curiosity, were compelling reasons to learn more about the unfamiliar English world. The more she learned, the more determined she became to stretch the borders of her world and go to college. She kept her feelings for Stephen secret. No one, not her family, not Gil, and especially not Stephen, had any idea how she felt. It wasn't until she entered the University of Pennsylvania, where he was a student, that they began dating.

They married during Caroline's third and Stephen's last year at Penn. Caroline graduated early, magna cum laude, and followed Stephen to law school at New York University. Again, as had been the case at Penn, she was at the top of her class, while Stephen coasted along, refusing to spend the time she did studying. Even though he was married, he wasn't going to forgo what he referred to as "the last, best years of my life." Occasionally, Caroline wondered if Stephen regarded her as more jailer than wife. She felt foolish at parties when Stephen delighted in introducing her as his Amish wife. She spent the uncomfortable evenings explaining the Amish way of life to strangers.

Eventually, she refused to join him, pleading the need to study. Even before Molly was conceived, Caroline felt them drifting apart. Her only ties to her family were Hannah who wrote regularly and Gil who called routinely. When Caroline became pregnant, Stephen was enraged. He told her he wasn't ready for fatherhood, they couldn't afford a child, and knowing she would never consider an abortion, suggested Caroline put the child up for adoption. Caroline wasn't sure if she threw him out of their apartment, or he walked out. But he left without a backwards glance.

That was eight years ago. The Stephen of today was miles from the callow youth of yesterday. If Caroline hadn't been positive of that, she wouldn't be remarrying him.

At six o'clock the next morning, Caroline was up and dressed, ready to go to her parents' house to explain what had happened at the auction before they heard it via the Amish gossip mill. By the time she reached the Miller farm, wisps of pastel streaked the eastern sky. From the shine on the pavement, it had rained steadily during the night. Caroline knew her father's routine. It never varied, not even on Sundays. She pulled up in front of the dairy barn where she knew she would find him. The cows were already milked and grazing in the vast pasture beyond the barn. Daniel Miller would still be in the barn attending to the many chores which were required in the life of a dairy farmer. Caroline got out of her car, and inhaled the pleasant fragrance of her mother's hyacinths born on the damp air.

Caroline let herself in through the small side door to the barn. Even at her age, and despite her professional history of battling real hardheads in court, she was not looking forward to confronting her father. He hadn't communicated with her the entire time she spent in New York, not even when Molly was born, and when she returned to help clear her brother, Josh, of a murder charge, her father had remained impassively formal. The family needed her expertise, and she had not been shunned, but had left the Amish before she was baptized, so her father had to grudgingly accept her help. Lawyers, who also knew the Amish ways, were not easy to come by. It had been Molly, Caroline's nearly eight year-old daughter, who thawed Daniel Miller. Now, he was warmer, but still a formidable presence. With his massive size and his curly, red-gold beard and hair, Caroline's childhood impression of thinking her father was a lion incarnate remained. Seeing her father in his territory had seemed as terrifying as bearding the lion in his den. Childhood impressions are not so easy to shake off.

The barn was warm from the cows' recent presence. Caroline called out, "Daat."

"I hear you, Carrie. I am coming a while," her father answered in English. Once he would have spoken to her in Pennsylvania Dutch, but not now. She was forever English in his eyes. More than once, Caroline wondered how a couple like her grandparents produced a son like Daniel. Most Amish were direct, but Daniel was past direct; he was brusque, and seemingly insensitive. When Caroline was growing up, it was only with her mother, Rebecca, and animals, that she saw a glimmer of patience or tenderness from her father. He was very hard with his children, expecting instant and complete obedience. Caroline had never heard him say he was sorry for anything, but she had seen him with Molly when he didn't know he was being observed. He was patient and relaxed. She wished he had shown some of those qualities to her, Josh or her sister, when they were growing up. Had Caroline judged her father too harshly? As Stephen was so fond of saying, "The jury was still out." Look at how Stephen had changed, Caroline told herself. This time, she was marrying him, not only because she loved him, but because she trusted him, something she had not consciously considered the first time.

Her father appeared from the barn's interior. He must have been stacking hay along the aisles as bits of the stuff clung to his black "broadfall" trousers, which were constructed with a button front closure and held up by suspenders. Amish men of all ages wore similar work clothes, with only the color of their shirts providing variety. Today, Daniel's was a deep green.

"So early you are here. Why?" he asked without preliminaries. Other than a few wires of silver protruding from his bushy beard and a deepening of lines around his blue eyes, Daniel's appearance was little changed from the time Caroline had departed ten years earlier. At least he was now meeting her glances directly, a sign to Caroline he was softening towards her.

So he hadn't heard about last night. She explained as succinctly as she could.

"Denny Brody, eh? Wohl, he sure was not liked by anybody at all, but killing him? It is a terrible thing. As for Granny being right there..." He shrugged his broad shoulders. "I tell her she should not be into all that murder and investigation business. It is those books she is always reading. Bad business. When I say something, she treats me like a kid. Tells me she is able to do yust what she wants. When my Daat was alive, she did what he wanted. I guess it is God's job to influence her. She would not listen to me, for sure. Never has; never will"

Caroline thought he sounded like a Victorian. Maybe there wasn't much difference between a Victorian patriarch and an Amish male. Caroline's relationship with her father was still too tenuous for her to defend Hannah. Besides, Hannah didn't need defending. She was a match for anyone, male or female, Amish or otherwise.

"What is Stephen saying about this?" Daniel asked. "Guess he is not too happy with what is going on, already, with the wedding being so close."

"Granny has promised me and I have promised Stephen we will not get into this..." Caroline answered a bit too quickly.

Her father tipped back his black hat and said, "Yah? Best not to make a promise in the first place, than break one."

42

Bit late for that advice, Caroline thought. Despite her determination to refrain from becoming entangled in this murder investigation, she had an ominous feeling it might not be avoidable. Bridal nerves, she chided herself. There wasn't any reason to think she would be drawn in.

When Caroline let herself into Hannah's house she found Hannah and Jennet ready to go to the auction. Hannah told her she had seen Caroline's car in front of the barn and knew Caroline was telling Daniel about Denny Brody's murder.

Caroline confirmed she had done exactly that when she came into Hannah's kitchen where Jennet sat, with a cup of coffee and a sticky bun. The animals sat expectantly at her feet, hoping for a crumb from her plate.

"They do not eat people food," Hannah assured Jennet. "But, they sit there looking interested anyway. Hope it does not bother you."

"No, of course not," Jennet answered. "It is funny. Perhaps I can use that somewhere in my quilt article."

"Writers," muttered Hannah. "Everything is fodder for the page."

Jennet shrugged and laughed.

Caroline sat perched on the edge of a chair "We need to get to the auction. The parking is going to be horrendous. After last night, there will be looky-loos and rubber-neckers and the morbidly curious as well as real customers. We'll never get a parking place."

"We could take the buggy," Hannah suggested, then immediately thought better of the idea. "No, we will be there too long. Clara would not like it." Clara was Hannah's horse, and no colt. Like a car with many miles on the odometer, Clara was best used for short trips.

As Hannah gathered her things, she asked, "How did Daniel take the news about Denny's murder?"

"Fine," Caroline said, anxious to go and avoid a long discussion about the killing.

"Carrie, you know 'fine' is not an answer I accept. It is a word like 'interesting.' It means nothing. I want specifics."

"Okay, okay. He reacted like I thought he would, but a bit milder, considering the gravity of the subject."

"Hmm," Hannah said, letting further discussion drop, or at least hover, until a later time.

By the time the three women arrived at the auction, the lot was almost full, and there was a line to get in the door. They had reserved their seats last night, so finding a place to sit would be quick, providing Hannah wasn't swamped with people wanting to hear all the details about finding the body and being attacked.

Luckily, Jack Best was standing outside and he spotted them. He quietly motioned for Caroline to park in the staff parking lot and follow him in through the office. "Might be a little less trouble to sneak in," he said jovially. "How are you doing this morning, Hannah? Any pain from that bump?"

"I am fine, Jack. I have a hard head."

"That you do," Jack said heartily. Caroline thought for someone who had a body turn up on his place just last night, he seemed oddly upbeat. "Most of the folks here this morning are for the quilt auction, so you shouldn't be hassled with questions. Course, there are bound to be some. Folks are nosy around here. But you already know that," Jack added.

Jack Best had lost one of his biggest customers when Denny Brody turned up murdered. Maybe Jack was relieved he wouldn't be hearing any complaints about how greedy Denny was, and how he ran up the price so no one else could get an item, and why couldn't Jack do something about Denny? The Bests didn't need buyers who were as much of a pain as Denny was. He was more trouble to Jack than he was worth. Still and all, Caroline thought, Denny was a human being and he was dead.

As if Jack could read her mind, he said, "No one is saying a whole lot about being sorry Denny is gone. It is almost like, out of sight, out of mind."

Caroline looked at Hannah. She could imagine her grandmother's thoughts. It was a sorry turn of events when the only thing folks thought about Denny Brody was that there was a fella no one would miss.

Caroline thought Hannah's lasting impression of Denny would always be seeing his broken body stuffed in that barrel like discarded refuse. But there was nothing anyone could do to erase it. Murder caused indelible impressions.

"Carrie, I forgot to call you. Things were so upset last night. You won the bid on that trunk. For sure, it won't fit in that car of yours. You're gonna need a truck to put it in. That sucker is heavy," Jack said.

"I won the trunk?" Caroline asked. "Super! What is the win going to cost me?" "Seventeen hundred, plus the 10% buyer's premium."

A bit more than Hannah had suggested paying, Caroline thought, but she suspected Hannah would not mention it now. It was still a bargain, or would be in time.

"Where is it?" Caroline asked.

"Loading dock area," Jack said.

"I'll call Stephen and ask him to pick it up after the quilt auction. I'll let him pay for it."

It was getting close to the time the quilts would be auctioned and, despite having previewed them, all three women wanted to take a last, close-up look. The quilts hung from lines in the largest auction room. It was breathtaking in scope and color. The collection consisted of sizes ranging from wall hangings through crib coverlets, and up to bed-size.

As usual, queen size was the most prevalent. Measurements were noted on tags carefully pinned on the corner of each quilt. Each contribution was either signed or the name of the donor was listed on the tag. Some quilters were well known and their pieces were sure to bring top bids. Due to the use of fluffy polyester batting, the quilts floated and dipped slightly with the air currents from the fans over them. Even though there was a variety of techniques used in construction, these quilts were nowhere as elaborate as the ones at the Quilters' Heritage show, nor was there such an unusual variety of artistic quilts as was exhibited there. These quilts were for sale and although the beauty was evident and their stitchery expert, the main idea was to sell, not particularly to display unusual techniques and original subject matter.

"There is one I would not mind collecting," Hannah said, admiring a long wall hanging The background was composed of vintage batiste handkerchiefs, each embroidered with a motif of blue flowers and bordered with blue satin ribbon. The quilting was confined to the ribbon and the border. The backing was blue velvet. "Would make a pretty runner on the table — chust for nice," she said, using the common Pennsylvania Dutch term for special occasion items. "Course I could make it; just need some handkerchiefs."

"And some time," Caroline added. "You could try sleeping two hours a night."

Hannah's answer was a raised eyebrow.

"I'd be afraid someone would spill something on it," Jennet said.

"Oh, I would not let anyone with food get near it," Hannah said. "I would put a nice, big sheet of thick plastic over it."

Caroline saw Jennet's eyes widening at the thought of combining plastic with the beautiful hand-worked runner.

"Just joshing, Jen. I knew that would give you a start," Hannah said, giggling.

At least three-quarters of the pieces up for bid were appliqué. Some of the designs were modern patterns, some more traditional motifs. Many were based on the patterns seen in antique Pennsylvania Amish quilts. These were currently very much in demand, and ever pragmatic, the contributors used the rationale, "Sought is bought." What Hannah called The "Big Five" were the most sought after, and thus, amply represented. They were Sunshine and Shadows, Ninepatch, Diamond in a Square, Lone Star and Bars. None of these donated quilts was vintage, and most were made with modern fabric, not wool like many of the originals. Still, they were starkly beautiful in their simplicity.

Once the auction started, action was fast and furious. Caroline didn't really need another quilt. Besides the ones Hannah had made for her and the few Caroline had quilted growing up, she had already received several for wedding gifts. She enjoyed watching the frenetic bidding, and was pleased for the Relief Society when the quilts brought such high prices.

Hannah, having seen her own quilts going at the top of the auction and for amounts which exceeded her estimates, went to the kitchen to "Wave Hello," as she put it. Caroline figured she would be gone for an hour.

While Hannah was in the kitchen, the blue handkerchief runner went up for bid. Jennet bid on it, and won. "I'm going to give it to Hannah," she confided in Caroline. "Don't tell her the price I paid."

"She'll never find out from me." Caroline laughed. "Are you going to present it wrapped in plastic?"

"Of course; that's the whole idea," Jen answered, with a pleased smile.

Caroline felt her cell phone vibrating in her pocket. She pulled it out and glanced at the caller ID.

"It's Stephen," she said to Jen. "I'd better go out and call him back."

Out in the parking lot, Caroline punched in Stephen's number at Crossroads Hardware.

"Morning, Love," she said, when he answered. "Anything new?"

Stephen's voice was so loud; she had to pull the phone away from her ear. "You might say so. The police called me. They want to talk to Granny. Now! Her pie was the one, the only one, which had traces of cyanide. Carrie, they seem to think Granny poisoned Denny Brody!"

CHAPTER SEVEN

The minute Hannah entered the auction kitchen area, she was aware of the difference in the atmosphere. To begin with, all heads turned towards her. At first there was silence and then it seemed everyone was talking at once. She felt like a prowling cat venturing into woods full of birds' nests. At least she hadn't yet been attacked by defensive jays.

There was another change. All the home baked pastries were gone. Instead, commercial packages and boxes lined the counters. Three, uniformed sheriff's deputies were stationed in the room. Hannah wondered what, if anything, they were supposed to be doing. Maybe they were serving as official tasters. By the look of their bellies, all three had plenty of experience with *Krispy Creme* donuts.

She approached the counter manned by Pet Brody. Hannah was not the slightest bit surprised to see her there, even though it was the morning after her ex-husband's murder. Pet had little reason to mourn. This morning her frizzy hair was spiked and matted, making her look like Molly's much- chewed -on Big Bird puppet, but without its benign expression.

"Oh, Hannah," she said in a sour voice, "the police took away all our baked goods." Not a word about Denny.

"So I see," Hannah answered.

"Do they really think some crazed poisoner has been at everything? That is so...dumb. Why weren't lots of folks poisoned? We sold out yesterday, even after the... accident. Nobody mentioned tainted anything, so we just keep selling food. At least they brought in this store-bought food this morning. Suppose it is better than nothing. But compared to the home baked things, it is awful stuff. Stale, even. They even made the coffee. Tastes like mud."

"I do not think we could call what happened yesterday an accident, Pet." Hannah was trying not to get into the all the literal gory details of Denny's death. Obviously, no one else had told Pet about the complicated condition Denny's body had been found in. Hannah sure wasn't going to either.

"Oh, well, I guess not," Pet said. "They are probably eating all our beautiful food."

"They? You mean the police?"

"They are just using the excuse that it might be tainted to pig out. I bet they are all at the police station eating it."

Hannah wondered if Denny's murder might have affected Pet more than it first seemed. She had thought Pet had more sense than to pose such a ludicrous idea, but decided no amount of logic was going to convince Pet otherwise. The confiscated food was evidence. By the time samples were taken of all the food, and they were tested, the food wouldn't be fit to eat even if it was still at the police station. It wasn't funny, but Hannah couldn't help the bizarre mental picture running through her mind of one deputy after another being sickened and dropping like flies from tainted pies. Pet's nonsense was affecting her. When a paying customer approached, Hannah walked away.

Hannah said hello here and there, and, thankfully, no one asked her for a recounting of last night's events. By appearing and looking well, she would allay anyone's concerns about how she fared after the blow to her head. Today, most of the people in the room were not among the previous day's antique auction crowd. Hannah recognized many of them, but she didn't know anyone well enough that they were likely to say anything about last night. It was as if everyone who was there would likely be wanting to put it behind them, she thought. Especially me, all I want to do is think about Carrie's wedding.

As she reentered the main room, Hannah almost walked into Caroline. The minute she saw her granddaughter's face, Hannah knew something had gone wrong. Caroline looked grim.

"Granny, I have to talk to you. Outside! Now!"

"Wohl, sure." Hannah would find out soon enough what the problem was.

Caroline whipped around and headed for the door. Hannah followed as quickly as she could through the milling crowd in the auction room. Jennet was nowhere in sight.

Caroline led the way to the car. "Let's go."

"How about Jen?" Hannah asked.

"Stephen will pick her up."

"Carrie, I am not going anywhere until you tell me what is wrong." Hannah was beginning to be seriously concerned.

"We have to go to the prison," Caroline answered.

"What? Where? Why?" Hannah asked, sounding like a journalism professor.

"Deputy Lee wants us to meet him there."

"The deputy said he was going to call me for my statement," Hannah protested. "What is the rush now?"

"He called Stephen. I'll explain on the way," Caroline got in the car and started the engine.

Hannah had little choice but to meekly get in and fasten her seat belt.

They negotiated the traffic jam of the parking lot and were on their way to what locals referred to as Lancaster City to differentiate it from

Lancaster County. Although Chelsea Township had its own small station in the township offices, prisoners were held in the County Prison in Lancaster City. It wasn't unusual for small police departments within the county to conduct interviews and take statements there.

Caroline repeated what Stephen had told her.

Hannah's response was to laugh, long and loudly. "Me, poison anyone? That is the silliest thing I've ever heard, Carrie. That they even are looking my way when the real killer is still on the loose. Unbelievable *dumassels*!"

Now it was Caroline's turn to laugh. The tension had eased, as had her tight grip on the wheel. "You swore, Granny. I'm shocked!

"They couldn't really think you have anything to do with it, but if it was your pie... they have to question you. I agree Deputy Lee was pretty naive to tell Stephen you are a suspect Stephen was seriously pis, uh ...annoyed at Lee's posturing."

"I hope that deputy is not big dealing this all over town. The bishop would tell me to put a stop to any investigating. Even if I am not thinking of investigating," Hannah hastened to add.

"I am putting a stop to Lee. If necessary, I'll get a court order. The sheriff's office can compromise a case by irresponsible talk, and Lee is ruining your reputation."

"Ha! That is the last thing I'm worried about. One of the good things about being my age is, as long as your conscience is clear, you don't much care about your reputation. Besides, I'd sell more quilts if I was at least mildly notorious. 'Hannah Miller, Killer Quiltmaker' has a nice ring, already. It would be unforgettable."

Twenty minutes later, they pulled up in front of the prison. The prison was undeniably the most unusual complex in the city. The original prison building was a squat, silver, painted box, topped with turrets. It looked like a medieval castle flattened by a giant's boot. Close behind it was a modern, multi-storied office building.

Once inside, Hannah and Caroline were greeted by a guard who said they were expected. Wayne Lee had at least thought of that much. They passed through the security system easily, and were given visitors' badges. At Caroline's suggestion, they had left most of their belongings in the trunk of the car. Hannah was not happy to leave her bag behind and would not part with the mystery she was currently reading.

"They will not have anything to read. I know," Hannah said. She had read about what jails looked like inside. Her mental picture did not include the presence of magazines in a jail.

"Okay, Granny, take it. We may have to wait, and I know you hate to be without reading material."

Inside, the building was nondescript, government-shabby from overuse. They were ushered into an outer office with uncomfortable plastic chairs and a dented metal desk that looked as if many an irate fist had pounded it. The decor consisted of two sagging file cabinets and a heavily screened, high window that was too small to use for escape, and too dirty to allow much light to come in. Florescent lights glared above them.

"Just like I expected," Hannah said in a whisper. "This is an interrogation room. Careful what you do or say. They probably have it bugged."

"Don't be so dramatic, Granny," Caroline said. "This is not an interrogation room. They don't have file cabinets in interrogation rooms. We are not here to be grilled into a confession. And where is the two way mirror?"

Hannah giggled. "Could not resist. I figured you were not buying, but you could have played along a little."

"Sorry, Granny, unlike you, I take this as a serious matter."

"The idea that someone even thinks I'm involved is so ludicrous as to be humorous. You, Carrie, need to lighten up...be more like me."

Just then, the door opened and to Hannah's surprise, Wayne Lee was accompanied by Acting Chief Kiel Benton. Inwardly, Hannah groaned. In her previous dealings with Kiel Benton, she had been unimpressed. Hannah regarded his intellect as lackluster, and his intractable belief in his marginal deductive powers as annoying. His attitude was another problem, Hannah decided. He was sure she, or just about anyone else, couldn't or shouldn't, have an idea how to solve a crime. Small wonder he was still acting chief. The township council wasn't about to hastily make his appointment permanent.

Neither Caroline nor Hannah rose when the two men entered. Benton was a good six inches shorter than Lee and already was showing a bulge over his waistline. Probably been eating too many of those doughnuts, Hannah thought.

Benton nodded to the women. "Good morning," he said, brusquely. "Ms. Miller, I assume you are acting as Mrs. Miller's attorney, right?"

"I thought Mrs. Miller was here to give a statement," Caroline said. "Why would my grandmother need an attorney? Are you charging her with something?"

"No, no, of course not," Benton said.

Hannah noticed Lee watching Benton with a slight smirk. Luckily for Lee, Benton was focused on Caroline. Hannah felt a little sorry for Benton if even his deputy thought he was inept. Lee would do well to act a bit more professional himself. Best not let Benton see him, or he wouldn't be around long.

A light knock on the door announced the arrival of a police stenographer. She settled herself into the last remaining chair and using her ample lap as a desk, expertly began typing, her fingers working so deftly they were a blur.

Benton first asked all the preliminary questions concerning the discovery of Denny Brody's body. Why was Hannah at the stream? How long was she there? Did she notice anything before seeing the body? Did she have any idea who hit her? Hannah's answers were crisp and to the point.

Then he got to the subject of Hannah's opinions. Did she know anyone who disliked the victim? That was just about everyone, but Hannah was prepared with an edited copy of her own list. She had left off anyone she didn't think had the opportunity or a real motive to want Denny Brody dead. No point in stirring up trouble for anyone with conjecture. Benton was a professional; he could do his own investigating, but he had asked her opinion, so she handed him the list from her pocket. Besides, she was trying to stay uninvolved.

"Oh, yes, one of your famous lists, Mrs. Miller," he said, with a fleeting glance at the list. "We'll probably have more questions about it later."

Hannah was a bit annoyed. Why didn't he ask her now? "You must know, no one liked Dennis Brody. You will not be lacking for suspects. The killer must have been after Denny, and I only got hit so he could hide his identity. He could have killed me if he wanted to."

The police chief changed the subject. "Why do you use 'he?' The murderer could be a woman," Benton said.

"She would have to be a strong woman, already, to haul a body across a rickety bridge and dump it in a barrel."

"He could have still been alive," Benton said. "Well, maybe," he added.

He is hopeless, Hannah thought. She thought back over the sequence of events. Denny was alive and well in the kitchen. Then very quickly after consuming the pie in his truck was dying from a quick-acting poison, probably cyanide from the description of the almond odor. It would have to be plenty strong to be smelled so easily. No way was he going to walk to the creek and cross the bridge on his own, even with someone forcing him with a gun or other weapon. Denny had to be hit either in the truck or at the creek. The weapon has me mystified, Hannah thought. We need to know what it was and when Denny was hit. Was it before or after he ate the pie, and why hit him at all? He was dying from the pie already.

"Mrs. Miller," Benton broke into her reverie. "The pie, Mrs. Miller? I need to know the location of the pie from the time you baked it to the last time you saw it. Its path? Where it went; who was with it?"

Hannah stifled an urge to laugh. How ridiculous! He was phrasing the question like the pie was an animated object. Hannah could see it with long cartoon legs sticking out from its container. She took a breath, and tried to be serious. That required not looking at Caroline, who probably had similar thoughts. "There were two pies," Hannah said.

"Yes, but the second pie was clean."

"Could I have a drink of water?" Hannah asked. She had to get hold of herself. This was serious. Maybe it was the tension; maybe it was Benton's ineptness; but she was feeling way too giddy for the occasion. Muttering a small prayer for patience and fortitude, she sat back and sipped the ice water Lee had brought.

Benton resumed. "About the pie. You know we found traces of cyanide in the pie container we took from Denny Brody's truck. From the preliminary autopsy report, there was also cyanide in the deceased's system and crumbs caught in his moustache showed traces of the poison. They are still analyzing the head wound, trying to determine what weapon was used. Whatever it was, there was no sign of it near the body. The blow to his head was not the cause of death; the poison was, or so it looks."

"Would you like me to have the stenographer repeat the question about the pie?"

Oh, no, Hannah thought. I will break up if I hear that again. "No, I remember," she said quickly, and launched into a description of how she had made the pies, what ingredients she had used, how she baked them, how she packaged them, transported them and even where she last saw them. When she got to naming who was in the auction kitchen, Benton stopped her.

"You're telling me at least forty people were in that room?"

"Those were only the ones I knew. There were even more milling around once the food sale began. Maybe sixty or seventy folks by then." Hannah sat back and took a gulp of the water.

She had gotten past her giddiness and was beginning to feel some empathy for Benton. He was going to have to interview everyone in that room, and that was only the beginning of his investigation. He sure could use her help. No, she silently vowed. No, no, no. If he wants her help, he will have to ask for it. He knows he's in over his head when he has to deal with anything concerning the Plain people, but he figures this has nothing to do with the Amish or the Mennonites. More than likely, he is right. Violence is not the way we solve problems, that is for sure, Hannah thought.

When Hannah's statement had been typed up, Caroline read it over, then with a nod, handed it back to Hannah, who signed it. After Caroline asked for and received a copy, Benton stood, and with Lee, who had been standing in the corner, walked out with the women.

"I may need more information as the investigation proceeds," Benton said. "How should I get hold of you?"

"Call me," Caroline said, handing him a card. "My office, my home and my pager are all on the card."

Hannah noticed Caroline did not offer him her cell phone number, and then remembered she didn't answer it in her car or in public places. Good idea, she thought. Those English gadgets are getting out of hand. A person could have an accident talking on one. Lancaster County had way too many Amish buggies hit by cars as it was, and way too much traffic with tourists who did not know where they were going. Adding a telephone yet was dangerous. There was enough trouble, already.

CHAPTER EIGHT

Retrieving her bag and Hannah's from the trunk, Caroline felt a palpable sense of relief. She hadn't seriously thought anyone would think Granny responsible for poisoning a pie. But her experiences with the Chelsea police force hadn't instilled a sense of confidence in her. Granny didn't need to be encouraged to delve into amateur crime investigation, now or ever. One of Caroline's worst fears was that the police would actually ask for Granny's help. Then Granny would have an excuse to jump in with both feet.

Caroline had asked Stephen to pick up Jennet and the trunk at the auction, but Granny wanted to return, too, so they drove back to Best-Stolzfus. Hannah was unusually quiet during the trip back. Perhaps she was unwinding from the effort to keep a straight face when she was confronted with some of Benton's questions. Granny did not suffer fools well at all. The ludicrous questions were enough to test Granny's resolve to remember the gravity of murder.

Caroline almost lost it herself with the questions about the pie.

When they arrived back at the auction, Caroline spotted Stephen's van in the loading zone, but there was no sign of him. They found him in the office, deep in conversation with Jack Best. Jennet was carrying a shopping bag and chatting with Laverna. Today, Laverna was looking a bit frazzled; her eyes were bloodshot and her hair flattened at the back. Poor thing probably didn't get much sleep, Caroline surmised, thinking of how early the Bests needed to be at the auction house.

When Stephen saw Caroline come in, he turned and gave her one of his irresistibly loving smiles. Caroline responded with a quick kiss. "Everything okay?" he asked.

"Hi and yes," she said, still hesitant to show affection in public. Her Amish childhood taught her to reserve such gestures for private times, and it wasn't always easy to become completely "English", even after all these years. Caroline didn't want to discuss Hannah's interview in front of the Bests. There was enough gossip around as it was. Laverna was not the problem, Jack loved to gossip. "Did you get the trunk yet?" Caroline asked.

"No, got talking with Jack," Stephen had inherited his father's loquaciousness. It was an important trait for a businessman. Jack had it, too. The two of them could talk for hours, as Caroline had seen many times. "But I paid for it. It better look good," Stephen said with a wink.

"I'd like to see it again before you load it. With all that happened last night, I've almost forgotten what it looked like".

"Sure," Jack said. "Hannah knows where the dock is. Go ahead. I need to spell Frank, who's auctioneering now. Can't have anyone losing his voice. Even with a mike, it is hard on the old voice box.

The trunk's right by the door, should be easy enough to load, but if you need help in getting it in the van, Frank can give you a hand."

Hannah led the way down an inside hallway and into a storeroom adjacent to the loading dock. High, somewhat dusty windows illuminated the room with slanting sunlight. In the morning light, they could see the trunk, sitting on a pallet. The mellow wood glowed even from a distance.

"Oh, it is even lovelier than it looked yesterday," Jennet commented. "What beautiful painted decorations!"

"I guess!" Hannah said, admiringly. "It is a fine piece, Carrie. Good eye."

Caroline didn't answer. She was busy admiring her purchase. "It's the first real thing I've actually bought for the new house. Let's look inside again. Wasn't there a narrow tray and a key?"

"As I remember there was," Hannah said, moving over to look as Caroline and Jennet tugged at the lid. Is it locked?'

"Don't think so. I think it's just hard to open," Caroline answered, tugging harder. Stephen reached down and helped. It opened, and they lifted the lid.

Caroline peered into the trunk. "Yuk! Someone put a dirty old brick in there. That wasn't there last night. I would have noticed."

"Wohl," Hannah said, looking in, "there is so much dust, grime and grit in there, an old brick could not much matter." She learned down to get a closer look. The brick, with bits of cement still clinging to it, was heavily stained with dark red. Hannah shot upright. "Do not touch it, Carrie! It does not look like dirt on that brick. Unless I miss my guess, it is blood." She dropped the lid down with a bang, and all of them took a step back as if the brick could suddenly jump out at them and hit one of them on the head.

"Damn it all!" Stephen said. "This we don't need. A bloody brick. What the hell next? Maybe it isn't blood. I'm going to get a pair of the disposable gloves the auction people wear," he said. "We need to get a better look before we fly off calling the cops. We will get laughed out of town if we call them to remove an innocuous brick. "

"We can hope, already," Hannah said, not looking very hopeful. "Better bring a pair for all of us, Stephen, and maybe a flashlight so we can see better."

"No gloves for me," said Jennet. "I'm not getting near a potential murder weapon."

"It wasn't the brick that killed Denny; it was the poison. The police shared that with us," Caroline added. "It could be paint or maybe it's just dirt. After all, our soil is pretty red."

Hannah's eyebrow shot up. "Wohl, could be; anything is possible. If it is blood, it isn't mine," Hannah said. "The blow I got did not break the skin. Still and all, it could have been used on me. The police took my bonnet and cape away so I could not examine them, but if something like a brick was used to hit me, there would be traces of it... dust or smudges. My hair or skin flakes might be on the weapon. All sorts of forensic tests could provide a connection. The DNA might well tell the story."

"Granny, did they take any samples of your hair last night when you were examined?" Caroline asked, realizing she didn't really know, nor had she thought to ask before. Some fine lawyer she was. Where Granny was concerned, Caroline was better at being a relative than an attorney.

"Yes. According to my reading, that is standard procedure now."

"You know more about crime than I do, Granny."

"Yah, wohl, you are not a criminal lawyer are you? I read about murder all the time, know the latest procedures from *CSI*. Not that I watch it, exactly," Hannah said, a shade too quickly, "but I do know these things."

"You are so busted," Stephen said.

He and Caroline had discovered Granny, who was babysitting; sound asleep in front of the TV at Caroline's condominium. The final minutes of *CSI* were being played out. Caroline knew Granny saw nothing wrong with watching TV at an English house, anymore than she found anything wrong with her fascination for gadgets and appliances in an English household. She wouldn't have any, nor use any, at her house, but she carried on the pretense that she wasn't susceptible to their lure somewhere else.

"Wohl, I ride in English cars, but do not own them, so what is the difference if I watch television, but do not own one?" Hannah asked.

"You tell me," Stephen said.

"Go get the gloves," Hannah ordered. "But, Stephen, we are going to have to report this."

"Yeah, I know," Stephen said glumly.

While he was gone, Jennet took a few pictures of the outside of the trunk.

"It doesn't matter what we think about the brick," Hannah said. "Maybe it is not blood; maybe it was not used on Denny, or me; but what is it doing in this trunk? Are we all in agreement it was not there when you bid on the piece?"

"One of us would have seen it. Jennet and I both looked at the inside very carefully,"

Jen nodded in agreement. "I even looked under the tray. Other than the dust of the years, there was nothing in that trunk except a key in the tray."

"None of this speculation matters. I agree; we have no choice but to call the police about it. Stephen is in denial. He doesn't want this to interfere with our wedding," Caroline said. " I couldn't care less if the police laugh at us. That's preferable to take the chance we might be withholding evidence."

When Stephen returned with the flashlight and gloves, everyone, even Jennet, pulled on a pair. "What did Jack say when you asked for gloves?" Caroline asked.

"He wasn't there. Laverna just handed them to me. People ask for gloves all the time to handle the textiles. I got the flashlight from my van."

Carefully, Stephen and Caroline tugged the lid open. Stephen fixed the light on the offending brick, but no one wanted to touch it.

"Maybe we should leave it alone until Benton gets here," Stephen said. "We can't decide on our own if the brick has any significance."

Caroline was glad Stephen was calming down and thinking logically. The blasted brick wasn't going to go away, and their involvement in the case was deepening. "Like it or not, we have to report it. If it's nothing, they can tell us that." With the light shining on it, the substance on the brick looked more like blood than ever, but maybe it was because they had blood in mind.

"I don't see the key. I know it was there," Caroline said. "It was in that little tray."

"It could be under the brick," Jennet suggested.

"Let's leave well enough alone. I don't think any of us should poke around in there, We are not going to learn anything, and the key will be found eventually," Stephen said, sounding hopeful. He was looking at Caroline. "We shouldn't have even opened it the second time, gloves or not."

"Who suggested gloves in the first place? Who hesitated contacting the police?" Caroline retorted.

Jennet played peacemaker. "Come on you two; we're all a bit overwrought. Not without good cause, but don't say something you will regret."

Caroline felt very sheepish. "Sorry," she said to Stephen.

"It's my fault," he said.

"I wasn't thinking. I..."

"Oh, just change the subject," Hannah broke in. "No mushy make-up scenes. Call Benton. Let him take care of it."

"This is all we need," Stephen muttered as he pulled out his cell phone and dialed the Chelsea Township police.

"Two encounters with Benton in one day," Caroline commented. "Maybe I better start praying for patience, Granny."

"Would not hurt," Hannah said.

Benton and Lee were there in a half an hour. Caroline was surprised Benton didn't snap to judgment and make any comments about the brick being unimportant like she would have expected, given her previous experiences with him. Instead, he called for a team to remove the brick, along with the trunk. Caroline hoped they wouldn't do anything to ruin her beautiful painted piece, although she would never look at it again without remembering the brick, and all the commotion it caused.

Benton's seriousness about the brick made her wonder if he was privy to some evidence he hadn't shared with them, something which connected a brick to the murder. Why would someone put a brick in her trunk? Obvious answer: to hide it. If it was connected with the murder or the attack on Granny, was someone trying to confuse the police by planting evidence on the most unlikely of suspects, Caroline, who had an airtight alibi? It was as ludicrous as putting the poison in the pie Hannah had made. No one would believe Granny would poison anyone.

"You'll get your trunk back," Benton told Caroline. "We'll take good care of it."

"It is a valuable antique," Caroline added, wishing she hadn't said anything when she saw Benton's expression of obvious annoyance.

"Yes, Ms. Miller. Since it's at an auction house, I figured that out."

Oh-oh, she thought. My comment was more than a little condescending. She wasn't going to make things worse by explaining that it was handmade or how much it cost, or that it was more of a hope chest than a trunk "Are you interested in antiques, Chief Benton?"

"Only when they might contain evidence," he said.

Caroline considered shutting up. Probably a wise move since she couldn't say the right thing anyhow. Her annoyance for Benton's past behaviors and inexperience was showing. She really had to try harder to be even-handed. Benton walked away to supervise the two deputies who were removing the trunk to a police van that had pulled up at the loading dock door.

"Careful," he ordered. "That is Ms. Miller's hope chest."

Now, Caroline felt really chagrined. Benton was being nice, which made her feel like she had been surly and unfair. Perhaps she was misjudging Benton. Stephen, who had heard the whole exchange, came over to her and put his arm around her shoulders. He seemed to be able to read her moods and thoughts better than she did his.

"I'm not a very nice person, Stephen," she said in a whisper.

"Hey, I only marry nice people."

Benton returned from the dock. "We have to do tests. Let you know when you can get the trunk; if it's clean, shouldn't be too long. We will be finished with your grandmother's clothing tomorrow. Someone will call you," he said crisply.

"Thank you, Chief Benton," Caroline said.

She expected him to reply with, "Just doing my job," but for the second time, she was surprised.

"You're welcome," he said. "I appreciate your cooperation." He sounded very sincere.

Caroline had a fleeting suspicion that Benton's new attitude had something to do with possible media coverage. An anomaly like murder in Amish country, even if the victim wasn't Amish, would put him under added scrutiny. If he ever hoped to be the permanent Chief, he could ill afford any missteps. He would need to quickly solve the crime, go by the book and not irritate anyone who might be of help to his investigation.

After he left, Caroline remembered she wanted to mention the key. It would give her reason to call him and she could ask if they had found any traces of brick on either Denny or Granny's clothing, but would he choose to tell her. She would soon know anyway. News got out fast in Chelsea Township, in more of a flood than a leak.

CHAPTER NINE

Hannah was actually tired enough that night to sleep her usual four hours without waking. She rose and worked on Jennet's quilt, which was almost finished. Jennet had gone back to Caroline's house. A body like Jennet could only live without a hair dryer so long, Hannah thought, as she dried her own freshly washed, waist length hair with a succession of hand towels, each a bit less wet than its predecessor. Hannah's hair had never been cut, and although there was more white than blonde in it now, it was still luxuriantly thick and lustrous.

Today was not a church Sunday; Amish families only attended church every two weeks. This week, Sunday would be for visiting, bible reading and quiet pursuits with the family.

Hannah was planning to spend the day at Caroline's helping with her wedding preparations. They had agreed to not mention Denny Brody's murder when they were working on the wedding. Like it would go away, Hannah thought, a bit gloomily. Oh, didn't she wish it was that easy. Today, Hannah was going to hand letter the place cards for the wedding reception. It would also be the day Hannah would see Caroline's wedding dress for the first time. Caroline, who was a fine seamstress, had found time to make her own dress. She had gone to New York, and with Jennet's help, chosen the fabric. Like Hannah, Caroline loved surprises and she wanted Hannah to be surprised when the dress was finished. Jennet's gift to Caroline was a beautiful antique lace veil she had found in Italy.

Sunday or no Sunday, Caroline and Stephen were going to pick up their wedding rings from Copious Clay. He had a shop in his home and turned out some wonderful pieces. The jeweler had designed their rings with some of the gold from the couple's first rings. It had been Stephen's idea. It would show they were not superstitious, and Caroline loved the thought. She decided it would be appropriate and show how positive she was this time. These were the rings they would wear forever. They were part of the past, the present and the future.

Of course Hannah would tag along. She would be the first to get a peek at the rings after the couple saw them. She would not interfere with their moment, but talk to Matilda while they tried the rings on. And, it would not hurt to ask Matilda a few questions about where she was when Denny was being killed. Hannah had only agreed not to speak of the murder with Caroline today. After all, she had to talk about something, and the murder was the most interesting subject. How she might slip in a private word with Copious was more problematic. An opportunity might present itself. Matilda was not on Hannah's prime suspect list, but like almost everyone else who knew Denny, Matilda disliked him. To know Denny Brody was to detest him. What an epitaph!

Matilda and her first husband, Ed King, had lived on property that was surrounded on three sides by land which Denny owned. Matilda and Ed bought their large lot from Denny's father shortly before he died. The Kings, like most of the Pennsylvania Dutch, kept their property immaculate. The house was painted pristine white, as was the picket fence, and the lawn was crisply trimmed. With a vengeance, Ed went after any weed bold enough to sprout in his yard. Their summer produce looked like photographs on seed packets. Matilda and Ed's perennial garden grew more luxuriant as time went by.

When the Kings bought the land and built their house, Denny was living in a trailer in the southern part of Lancaster County. After his father died, he and Pet moved their trailer to his father's property, which Denny had inherited. They built a house with an attached garage and barn on the largest parcel, and then built another barn, then added a free- standing garage. Pet did her best to try to keep up the house and the surrounding property, but Denny was uninterested in it, and Pet could just do so much. Denny was said to have told her she could not afford to hire someone to do what she could do herself. It became a hopeless task. After a few years, Pet left Denny, and then the place began to deteriorate more quickly. Denny moved back into the trailer and it wasn't long until the property began to look like an abandoned junkyard with old cars and clutter piled high against the buildings. It was said Denny had filled every available structure on the place with his purchases at auctions and estate sales.

An exasperated Ed King and a group of neighborhood residents complained to Denny. Denny just shrugged and said he was working on it. When he did nothing, the neighbors complained to the police, the fire company, township officials, all to no avail. There were no restrictions or covenants on what could be done with one's own property. Ed and Matilda decided to move and tried for two years to sell their own property without any luck. No one wanted to buy it; they would have to live next door to the Brody junkyard. The Kings could not afford to buy another house without selling the one they had. In desperation, Ed offered the property to Denny at the lowest price he could afford to sell for, and still buy a decent home. As the story went, Denny told him to put it up for auction, and Denny would buy it then for nothing. Ed fell into a deep depression at the thought of spending the rest of his life in the midst of Denny Brody's ever- accumulating rubbish dump. One day, Matilda returned from her cleaning job and found Ed slumped over, dead. Rumor had it he had committed suicide, but the police report listed his death as a cerebral hemorrhage. A few months later, Denny made good on his boast and bought the King property at auction for a rock bottom price.

Anyway you looked at it; it was a sad story and reason enough to want to get revenge on Denny Brody. Still in all, Hannah thought, Matilda was a gentle soul, not a person to resort to violence no matter what the provocation. If she wanted Denny dead, she could have found a way long before now. She seemed very content with Copious Clay despite the disparity in their looks and backgrounds. Hannah did wonder, though, why Matilda stopped going to church. Was it because of Ed's death, or because she married Copious just a few months afterwards? None of my business, Hannah told herself sternly. Curiosity, and speculation, along with a streak of rumor could cloud a person's perspective. Hannah was more interested in what Matilda observed the night of the murder than some farfetched notion she had anything to do with it.

It was Jennet who came to pick Hannah up that morning. The quilt wasn't covered and Hannah hurried out of the house before Jennet came in. "I will be right with you, Jennet. You do not have to come in."

Jennet looked surprised. No Amish woman ever let a visitor go without inviting him in and trying to feed him. Hannah dashed into the house again, threw a sheet across the quilt and came out. "Come in, Jen, and have a bite. I have some coffee and shoofly pie."

This time, a look of horror flickered across Jennet's face. "Uh, no-o, uh, thanks, Hannah."

Hannah realized what she had said and how she was acting, and dissolved into laughter. Jennet was now staring at her open-mouthed. Oh fine, Hannah thought. Jen probably thinks I'm insane. A mad, Amish poisoner, pushing tainted shoofly pie on unsuspecting innocents.

"Just come in a minute, Jen. I promise I won't kill you with kindness, or shoofly pie."

Now it was Jennet's turn to laugh. "I wasn't worried, Hannah, just taken back a bit."

Jennet followed Hannah into the house, stepping over Bear, who knew he was in the presence of familiar scents, so other than to open one eye and close it again, he didn't react. "Would you like some coffee, Jen, or something?"

"No, thank you, Hannah. I just ate. I'm meeting with the realtor today, so we can list Nettie's house and business. I just want to get it on the market. It will take me forever to sell it, I know. Good thing I can afford to wait for the right offer on the property."

Hannah thought again about poor Ed King who died trying to sell his property.

After Jennet had dropped her off at Caroline's, Hannah got to work on the place cards. She needed some distraction and this was a good task. Hannah had sketched a wildflower at the top of each card and now she was coloring them with strokes of watercolor paints.

"When are you going to pick up the rings?" Hannah asked, turning to call in the direction Caroline had gone.

Caroline answered from the open door of her bedroom. "Just a minute, Granny. I'll be right out." Hannah resumed her painting.

"Okay, Granny, are you ready?"

"For what?"

Caroline was now behind Hannah. "Turn around, Granny."

Hannah did, and saw Caroline standing in the doorway. "Oh, o. my! Carrie..."

Caroline's wedding dress suited her perfectly. It was a simple design of ivory silk faille with long, fitted sleeves and tiny buttons down the front. Its full skirt was floor length, but did not have a train. Hannah thought that if the Amish had fancy wedding dresses, this one would suit fine. It was simple and modest. It was the fabric and cut which made it so elegant. The only real ornamentation, other than the buttons, was a soft ruffle at the wrists and around the hem. Her veil, attached by two combs, and falling to her shoulders, was fine, elegantly crafted, delicate antique lace.

"Oh my. Perfect," Hannah said, for once at a loss for words.

"I saw a similar designer dress in a magazine. You wouldn't have believed the price! I knew I could make it for a fraction of the cost. Which I did! Jen was a huge help in finding the fabric. She knows everyone and every place in New York."

"You must have spent hours and hours on the making," Hannah said.

"Really, it wasn't too bad. I was a bit worried about having to rip out anything with this fabric, but it is very sturdy. Someday Molly may want to wear it. If she does, the dress should have held up well. I cheated a bit and didn't do button holes. There are snaps hidden under the placket. The buttons are already sewn on. It won't take forever to get dressed, and I'm not apt to lose one."

Caroline might be English now, but her Amish practicality and frugalness was still very apparent. Not a bad thing at all, Hannah thought with satisfaction. Of course there was that trunk she overbid on. Her grandmother wasn't about to mention it, especially today.

"Stephen is due to pick us up in a few minutes. I'm not superstitious about the groom seeing the bride in her dress before the wedding, but I want to surprise him on our wedding day. I need to change."

She had barely left the room when Stephen rang the bell. Hannah knew he had a key, but he knew she was there and didn't want to look like he was on such a familiar basis with Caroline before they were married. Hannah thought it ridiculous but sweet, and she didn't let on. It cost her dearly not to tease him about it. It was so tempting.

After a quick sandwich, they were on their way to the Clay house. The hamlet of Doylesview was still in Chelsea Township. Hannah had often thought every wide spot in the road was named after someone or something. Unless you had been born in the area, it made for much confusion. Many of the small places had been swallowed up by slightly larger areas, but the old name was still used, and local memories ran long.

Tourists were frequently seen driving around looking for some obscure place, and they weren't helped by directions from the locals: "Yous jus' take you self to where Elmendorfer Church used to be, and turn down aside Brink Crick, not North Brink Crick, now. She really runs east, not north. But that's no matter, already. Jus' go 'bout two mile down. Watch that, them run together, like." After the visitors' eyes glazed over in incomprehension, they wandered on muttering, and more confused than ever.

Stephen's car pulled up into an asphalt parking area between the tidy, one-story ranch house and the garage. Neat rows of red and yellow tulips bordered the parking area.

They are expecting us," Stephen said, nodding towards the carport, where a dark gray sedan and a gold van were parked. Partially to placate Matilda, who, despite not attending church, did not want strangers coming into her house on Sundays; Copious had turned the two-car

garage into his retail shop. His actual workshop was in the basement of the house. A professionally lettered sign said: "Clay Jewelry Designs - From Vintage to Modern." Copious had installed a burglar alarm system, and a large red bell was prominently placed on the shop front. Other than the sign and the alarm, it was a very modest appearing business for a jewelry shop.

"Doesn't appear fitting to local folks if I look too uppity. They'd think I charge too much." He had told Hannah it didn't look good to appear too prosperous. "And worse," he said, "I would be inviting a break-in. I keep the real valuables in the basement," he whispered to her at an auction. Hannah hoped he didn't whisper to too many people in such a public place as the auction house, and she told Copious exactly that. He responded that only people he trusted knew about the basement. To the public in general, it appeared he had a workshop in the garage. To further throw strangers off, he kept an old safe in plain view. Privately, Hannah considered that a bad move. A lure like a safe might tempt a thief, not deter one. Hannah had heard complaint after complaint from Copious about Denny Brody scarfing up all the vintage pieces that Copious depended on for his one-of-a-kind jewelry designs. He wasn't selling a whole lot of jewelry to the Amish or the conservative Mennonites, except maybe pocket watches, Hannah thought, fingering hers deep in her skirt pocket. Many of the area residents were very frugal, but all it took were a few prosperous customers and tourists interested in unique products. Combined with a reputation for honest dealings, a craftsman like Copious could turn a good profit with his jewelry. Hannah knew all about making money with unique designs.

It wasn't until Stephen pulled in behind the shop that he saw a third car, parked in the shade. "Looks like Copious has another customer," he said.

"Oh, that's just Petula, come to visit her brother on a Sunday," Hannah commented. She knew the car. Hannah hoped Petula had regained her composure after her distinctly distracted behavior of yesterday. Well, she reckoned, even if two people have been divorced for years, and were barely speaking, it had to be a shock to have Denny end up like he did.

Hannah hoped Pet's presence wasn't going to play havoc with her plans to talk to Matilda. She sure did not want to set off poor Pet again.

"Short period of mourning," Caroline commented.

"Nobody is mourning Denny. Relief seems to be the order of the day," Stephen said.

"Please, let's not let Denny Body ruin our perfect time," Caroline requested. "We agreed not to talk about this. Remember?"

"Hard to do that when everybody we see is connected to him," Stephen said, "but we can try our best." He reached over and touched Caroline's face in a protective gesture. "Okay?"

She flashed him a smile.

Talking to Matilda turned out to be easier than Hannah had anticipated. Pet, who had been deep in conversation with Copious when they arrived, offered to watch the shop while Copious went into the house, and down to the basement workshop with Stephen and Caroline.

Hannah was relieved to see that Pet seemed her usually friendly self, although a bit subdued.

Hannah found Matilda in the living room, sitting with her cat, a huge, fluffy, black and white creature, named Daynight, purring loudly in her lap. It was dim in the room; no one had bothered to open the drapes. Without asking, Hannah pulled open the drapes so a bit of April sunlight illuminated the area.

The room was, as Hannah had noticed on a previous visit, very feminine for a living room. The walls were a pale pink, and the braided rug on the floor was predominantly pink and green. Two dark green-blue plush recliners flanked a pink and white floral, slip-covered love seat. There was very little other ornamentation. Matilda sat upright in one of the chairs. She was a tall woman and her feet rested on the floor. Nearby, a patched quilt top sat stretched out on a frame. "How is the quilt coming?" Hannah asked, although she could see for herself it was untouched except by a goodly amount of cat hair.

"Oh, I need to get going on it," Matilda answered without enthusiasm.

"Maybe after the wedding, I could come over and work on it with you," Hannah offered.

"I suppose. That would be nice," Matilda answered, pulling the sleeves of her pink sweater over her wrists as if she was cold.

Not knowing how long it would take to get the rings, Hannah jumped in without further small talk. "A real shock Friday wasn't it?" she asked, perching on the love seat and turning to look at Matilda.

"Can't see Pet without having it bring back the whole nightmare of Denny," Matilda said in a tired voice.

Poor Petula, rejected by association. And she was a relative; too bad.

"It has been a long time since they were married. Years, isn't it?

"Some," Matilda answered, frowning in either concentration or consternation. "What did you think when Pet married Denny?"

"Not a lot; was no business of mine. Why should it be? I didn't know Copious's family, including Pet, except by sight. She wasn't a Mennonite, you know.

"Copious left here when I was barely thirteen. He is a lot older than me, you know. Then, he lived in Hawaii for years," Matilda said, pronouncing the word like "How-i-yah."

"How did Copious end up in Hawaii?" Hannah asked.

"Was there in the Navy and stayed on."

"Ever been there, Matilda?"

"Oh, no; I wouldn't go there. No, it is a place for pleasure. Life is too easy."

How would she know, Hannah wondered, if she had never been there? It was a peculiarly rigid attitude, even for a religious person. Why did some folks think life on Earth had to be a trial, without joy or pleasure, and their only reward would be in Heaven?

Hannah knew from her reading that Matilda's concept of Hawaii was totally unrealistic.

"Why did Copious come back if life there is so idyllic?"

"Dunno; it is not anything we talk about. I guess he would tell me if he wanted me to know," Matilda answered. "Got tired of it, I guess. Wanted to come home."

Seemed odd she didn't know for sure why he had returned. Did she really not know, or was she being evasive? Hannah decided to open another door with Matilda.

"How is Pet taking this? After all, she and Denny were married once."

"This may sound terrible, Hannah." Matilda leaned closer, dislodging Daynight from her lap. "I think we are all relieved to have Denny taken."

Hannah was taken aback by Matilda actually putting into words what so many people must have been thinking, but were hesitant to say. "He was a cruel, crazy man," Matilda continued. "No normal person lives such a selfish life. You must know the German word *schadenfreude?*"

"Sure," Hannah said. "It means taking perverse pleasure in someone else's misery."

"Well, that was Denny. He hounded my Ed into an early grave. When the Lord took Denny out of the way, Denny was working on doing the same to Copious."

"Oh, now, Matilda, aren't you being a bit dramatic? Copious complained about Denny, but his jewelry business looks prosperous to me."

"It is a good enough living," Matilda allowed, and picked up the cat and redeposited it in her lap. "Hannah, I just worry a lot. I'm afraid something will happen to Copious." She sighed.

"For goodness sakes, why? He looks real healthy to me."

"Oh, he has some kind of bad heart rhythm. His doc has him on blood thinner, so as he won't have a stroke," Matilda said. "But he says that can't happen with the blood thinner and Copious's heart is okay; it just the rhythm what's not regular. There is medicine for it, and Copious is taking it. I dunno, Hannah. Maybe doctors are too quick to experiment on folks. What next, I always say."

"Well, Matilda, it does sound like the doctor has things under control. Got to expect a few problems as we get older."

"I suppose," Matilda said.

If Matilda's concerns had been more trivial, Hannah would have quipped that the things you worry about don't happen, but in Matilda's case, maybe they did. It wasn't from lack of worrying that Ed died. But Copious looked far from being ill. Matilda was all alone except for Copious, an unusual position for someone from a Mennonite family. She had been an only child and so had both her parents. Matilda was a born worrier. With Denny out of their life, that was one worry gone, but Matilda would probably soon find another. Her perpetual frown line was a long time in the making and it looked permanent.

"So, you knew Pet and Denny when they were married?" Hannah asked, getting back to what she wanted to know.

"Not very well. They were living down the country, far end of Lancaster County. Denny's dad was alive then. He was a good neighbor. Not like Denny."

"How did Denny get along with his father?"

"All right. He left Denny everything, so I guess they were getting along okay. I'd see Denny and Petula visiting once in a while."

"Do you know if Mr. Brody approved of Pet?"

"Why wouldn't he?" She looked thoughtful. "She was a real pretty girl and always nice to everybody. I do remember Denny's dad said he was disappointed when Denny and Pet eloped. Denny's dad said 'he wanted to dance at the wedding.' I remembered that because we were Mennonites and they don't do any dancing at weddings."

"Yes, I know." Hannah noticed the past tense. She had wondered why Matilda still dressed as a Mennonite despite not attending church. Now was an opening to ask.

"Matilda, it may be none of my business, but why don't you go to the Mennonite church anymore?"

"I don't mind you asking, Hannah. I married out of the faith, so it doesn't seem fitting."

"I see, but then why do you still dress like a Mennonite?"

"Hannah, I don't know any other way to dress. It is too late for me to change my ways, already."

Hannah felt a tinge of embarrassment for prying. It had nothing to do with investigating the murder.

"Matilda, did you notice anything odd at the auction Friday? Either in the kitchen or generally?" she asked, trying to return to her purpose for questioning Matilda.

"Well, I don't think so. Other than you leaving, and then coming back and... you know, hearing about Denny's body and all."

"Did you notice anyone else leaving, or coming back?"

"Hannah, it would be hard to say. Folks move themselves around. Someone is always getting up, eating, or visiting, coming back and staying for a bit. Then, they do it again. You know what an auction is like."

Hannah knew all right. Who could have kept track of everyone, even if they knew ahead of time, that being more observant might be very important?

Matilda began again, furrowing her brown in concentration. "About the only thing I could say for sure, that the only people who hardly ever get up would be Dorcas and Swayne Hess. They are pretty spry for folks in their nineties, but once they sit down, they pretty much stay put. You might ask them if you are so curious. Why are you so curious anyways, Hannah?"

So, Matilda didn't know about the pie. Or, if she did, she wasn't saying so. Maybe she doesn't want to hurt my feelings, Hannah thought.

"Just my way, Matilda. Some might even call me snoopy."

Matilda nodded in agreement and made a shrill noise that Hannah would describe as somewhere between a guffaw and a giggle. "It's the books, Hannah. Everyone round here knows you read those mystery thriller books."

Hannah still wanted to see Pet, and it wouldn't be long before Caroline and Stephen came back. She told Matilda she would be back, and before Matilda could accompany her, went to the shop to see Petula Brody.

As she approached the door, she saw Petula cleaning a glass display case with a bottle of blue liquid and a towel. It was time for direct questions. Beating around the proverbial bush had to stop. Hannah didn't have time to methodically conduct an investigation. She would never get this thing solved before the wedding. Despite Caroline and Stephen wanting to ignore Denny's murder, the pie and then the brick had inextricably involved them all in the case. It was solve and solve quickly, or the specter of Denny Brody would be hanging over the wedding, whether or not they liked it.

"Hi, Hannah," Pet said in a bright voice.

"Help out here often?" Hannah said, dispensing with a greeting.

"Not really; I have my own business to take care of. But since I'm here, might as well be of some help."

"Yes," Hannah said. "Pet, did you notice anything 'different' in the auction kitchen Friday?"

"The police already asked me that, Hannah."

"Well, I am not the police and they don't tell me anything much.

"There were a lot of people and lots of activity, and no, I didn't see anything different. You were there. We were real busy. The police asked me if I saw anyone acting suspicious around the food, and I told them I didn't."

"Did you see Denny buying my shoofly pie?"

"No, but I am not surprised he bought the whole thing. Everyone knew he liked shoofly pie, and everyone knows you make the best in the township. Everybody wants your pie."

"Wanted," Hannah corrected. "Do not think there will be much call for it now."

"Oh, Hannah, that is silly. Who would think you could do anything like that? Maybe Denny put something in the pie, like more sugar, and the sugar was poisoned."

"Maybe," Hannah said. But not even Denny would sweeten the pie. Pet's theory, such as it was, was unlikely. The pie was already cloyingly sweet, and full of molasses. The molasses would disguise the taste of almonds. It was the perfect vehicle for poison.

"Pet, who do you think did this?'

"I don't know, Hannah. Lots of people had something against Denny. But poisoning him? It seems so... I dunno, weird. Why not just shoot him? Doesn't everybody shoot people they want to get rid of? Matilda says God struck him down. In a way that is true, isn't it?"

"So Matilda thinks," Hannah said. She wasn't going to learn anything more from Petula. Probably because she didn't know anything more, or if she did, she was not sharing. Yet. Maybe later, but Hannah didn't have time to wait until Pet got inspired to say more.

Hannah would love to question Copious, but it didn't look like she would have a chance today. Tomorrow, she could take the buggy and come back. He would be in the shop, and hopefully, alone. She had an excuse; her pocket watch was running slow. Copious could take a look at it, couldn't he? Not only a good excuse, but the truth, she thought. Hannah stuck to the truth whenever possible. It was much easier to remember than some flimsy, contrived prevarication.

She also didn't like the way Matilda was acting. Hannah did not fancy herself as a psychologist, but she did know a bit about depression. Matilda was showing classic symptoms. Whether Copious was inclined to take Hannah's suspicions seriously was another thing. Folks in these parts, and men in particular, didn't believe in depression. They figured it was a malingerer's excuse. In any case, she would talk to Copious tomorrow.

If she only had some faith in Benton's ability to solve this, she would not be so obsessed in investigating it herself. The expression on Benton's face when she mentioned how many people were in the auction kitchen was akin to a kid spun around too many times — a combination of dizzy and nauseous. It was going to take him forever just to finish the interviews. Who knew when he would find the killer? Nothing was going to ruin this wedding. That she, and now Caroline, were already tainted by their unwitting connection to the murder was unnerving enough. What was worrying Hannah even more was the reason. Was it really only to cast suspicion on them as a diversion, knowing no one would think them really involved? Or, was there something else going on? Could the killer wish them harm? Hannah wasn't ready to make any assumptions when it came to her family's safety. The only way to guarantee that was to have Denny Body's killer safely in jail.

If she talked to enough people, some piece of information would turn up to shed light on the case. It had to. Caroline and Stephen's wedding was a week from Friday.

Matilda may have thought Denny's death was the Lord's will, but the hand of man, or woman, was the instrument of Denny Brody's death.

Hannah had twelve days to find out who that was.

CHAPTER TEN

"What a well organized workbench, Copious," commented Stephen, who was well-known for being organized in his own business, albeit on a larger scale.

"Thanks, Steve, I can't find anything elseways."

Caroline knew Stephen did not like being called "Steve," but Copious, who had no nickname himself, shortened everyone else's name.

Caroline looked at the vast array of drills, chisels and other jeweler's tools that she could not name. Copious must have hundreds, and all were mounted on the walls, or in racks on his bench in the square basement room. There were dozens of drills alone, everything from miniatures to large, corded and cordless. The bench where Copious worked was a three- sided affair containing an array of drawers within easy reach of a swivel chair. Several types of gooseneck magnifiers and lights were poised above, ready for instant use. Jewelry that had been repaired and was ready to be picked up hung in tagged plastic bags from hooks, in another area. A large sink stood on one side, surrounded by mysterious jars and pots and cans. Wonder if he uses cyanide or maybe it is arsenic that is used by jewelers. Caroline couldn't help but wonder how many and what kind of dangerous chemicals were in this room. Then, she consciously pulled her focus away from thoughts of Denny Brody and back to why they were here.

"Rings are all ready. Came out real fine. Wait until you see," Copious said, pulling a bag down and laying the contents on a deep blue velvet-covered pad.

"Oh," Caroline caught her breath. The two wedding rings were a blend of bands of white, yellow and pink textured gold that gave them a burnished appearance. "They are engraved just like you wanted. Wish more folks wanted engraving. I do all mine by hand," he said, pointing at a nearby turntable of what must be engraver's tools. "None of that machine engraving. That doesn't take any skill a'tall."

Caroline had not wanted an engagement ring when she was married to Stephen the first time. Even though Stephen could easily afford it, she had thought it frivolous and unnecessary. This time she understood its reason and importance to Stephen. In this respect, she had changed from Amish sensibilities to English ones, at lest where diamonds were concerned. Caroline's engagement ring was a beautiful, but simple diamond set in platinum which they had picked out at Tiffany's in New York. As different as the individual materials in the engagement and wedding ring were, they were perfect together. Somehow, the wedding rings, made in Chelsea Township and the New York diamond represented their life together much as the past, present and future symbolism of the wedding ring materials.

"Try them on," Copious ordered. "Would be a hell of a note if they didn't fit and you had to jam 'em on at the wedding." He laughed like it was the funniest thing he could imagine. His laugh was hearty enough to make the delicate jeweler's tools in front of him to clink together

They fit. "Just like they were made for you." Copious roared at his own lame joke. They dutifully joined in his laughter. "You know what I say?" Caroline mentally ran through all the clichés and metaphors she could think of.

"Eat, drink and be merry, for tomorrow you die," he said. That was one Caroline hadn't considered, and would prefer not to. Copious sense of humor had taken a darker tone than she would have expected.

He continued. "Now, for the real funny part; you owe me exactly three thousand bucks. It turned out to be more time than I thought. Now, if that is not okay..." Stephen looked a bit taken back, but pulled out his checkbook. "Hey, Steve, I'm kidding," Copious said, pulling a bill from a clipboard on his wall. "It is still the amount we agreed on."

Stephen smiled, fielding the lame joke neatly, Caroline thought. Without saying anything, he began to write the check. "Hope you didn't want cash," Stephen said. Without waiting for an answer from Copious, he added. "I postdated it. Be sure to hold this until after the wedding. If Caroline backs out on me, I'll return the rings for a refund."

Now that, Caroline thought, was humorous, and all three of them were laughing. Copious could appreciate a joke, even on himself. What a nice man, Caroline thought.

Caroline and Stephen climbed the stairs to the first floor. Caroline said, "Matilda and Granny are going to wonder what was going on with all that hysterical laughter."

"Maybe," Stephen said. "I doubt if Matilda does all that much laughing with Copious. She seems like sober-sides to me."

"I agree, but I bet it doesn't stop Copious from trying," she said, quietly. Caroline felt sorry for the sad life Matilda had led with Ed King, but surely being married to a happy person like Copious was a far different matter. What had ever brought two such completely different people like Matilda and Copious together? He did not marry her for her money. Rumor had it that Ed King had a big insurance policy on his life. Rumor was all it was. The rumor mongers were forgetting that Mennonites, like the Amish, did not believe in insurance of any kind, trusting in the Lord's will. Maybe Copious was a rescuer type, a self-appointed Knight in Shining Armor saving a poor maiden from.... whatever. Matilda was not a maiden. Caroline had other things to think about than the unlikely pairing of Copious and Ed King's widow.

They found Granny waiting by the car. "Well?" she asked. Stephen showed her the rings now nestled in blue velvet boxes. "Looks real nice," Hannah pronounced.

"Coupious is good at what he does," Hannah said. Caroline knew that was high praise from an Amish person.

Caroline had bought Stephen's wedding present from Copious, too. He had designed some square cufflinks of similar brushed gold with an edge of a shinier gold. Caroline had arranged to drop by and pick them up tomorrow afternoon, when neither Stephen nor Granny would be with her. The Clays' house wasn't very far from Rose Mill Inn where the reception was going to be taking place. She was taking Jen there for lunch. Later in the day, Caroline was meeting the florist to confirm the final decision on flowers for the reception. There would be time in between to drop by the Clays.

They took Hannah to her house, and Caroline and Stephen decided not to go in with her. Hannah had told Caroline and Stephen about how she tried to keep Jennet from seeing the quilt in progress, and when they let her out, they were all still laughing. "I'd better get Jennet's quilt finished and out of the way before I have to go through an exercise like that again. Jennet would think I had finally gone over the edge," Hannah said.

After Stephen dropped her off at her condo, Caroline let herself in and went to the answering machine. It blinked with several new messages. The first was from Jennet's cell telling Caroline not to expect her for dinner. She would be working with the realtor until later in the evening. The second was from Molly, asking to spend one more night with her friend, Emily, whose mother said she would take them to school. Emily's mother was heard in the background, reiterating the invitation. Caroline returned that call and accepted the offer. The third call was from the Chelsea Township Offices. "What now?" she thought, momentarily imaging a worst-case scenario. Taking a deep breath, she told herself, it was probably Benton telling her the trunk could be returned not an announcement of another problem.

When she got through with a return call, she found it was neither good news, nor bad.

"Ms. Miller," I'm sorry to have to ask you this; I know it's inconvenient, but I would like to look around your grandmother's house. We don't need a warrant; it is not that official. I just want to make sure we have done this by the book." Benton sounded apologetic. "I know she is not responsible for the tainted pie, but..."

"Of course she's not. While we're at it, you know and I know, the 'book' you refer to would tell you, Chief Benton, that you don't have enough evidence to get a warrant. It is ridiculous that we are even discussing this. However, if you want to waste our time and yours, fine, look around her house. You won't find anything." Caroline saw no reason he shouldn't look around Granny's house.

"It can't be today." She was about to add it was Sunday, but since she and Hannah had been gallivanting all over the county, she couldn't sound sincerely pious. Her main reason to delay him was to prepare her parents, not let the police come barreling in multiple police cars. She hardly thought they would be using sirens or any dramatic devices that would be employed in another instance. Benton had some discretion. After all, he was asking her, not warning her. Unless he had a lot more evidence, no way would any judge give them a warrant. On the other hand, cooperating with him was to their benefit; it was only smart.

Tomorrow her sister would be at school and the neighbors going about their normal business. It would keep talk down, although Caroline had no doubt word would get out eventually.

"No, no, it won't be today and we'll keep it low key– one car and we could just be there to clear up some points in her statement if anybody should ask. That would be a good reason for being there, should any of the neighbors need an explanation."

Caroline was happy to see Benton's attitude change to a less confrontational one. Maybe Granny was wrong; perhaps Benton did have a handle on the how to conduct a proper investigation. Oh, I hope so, she thought fervently.

"Would nine o'clock be convenient?" he asked.

"That's fine," Caroline responded. "But I'll call you to confirm after I've checked with my grandmother."

"If I'm already gone, just leave a message," Benton said.

"By the way, Chief Benton, I forgot to mention something yesterday. There was a key in my trunk when I bid on it. I didn't see it yesterday, but we didn't want to disturb possible evidence looking for it."

"Key? We didn't find a key. Except for the brick, that trunk was empty. I'm sure. I was there when it was opened and the brick removed."

"Why would anyone take the key? It doesn't make sense. The trunk was open. If whoever put the brick in the trunk didn't want it found, then it would be understandable to lock it and take the key, or throw it away. That might delay discovering the brick for who knows how long."

"Hmm, "Benton said. "True. But it wouldn't be too hard to pick the lock. Old keys are everywhere; you could easily find one to fit. Kind of weird, but don't make too much of it. Maybe it will turn up."

Caroline thought not. Either someone wanted the brick found, or taking the key was inadvertent. Whoever took the key might still have it. Finding it would be akin to finding the needle in the haystack. In this case, it would be better, because at the moment, they didn't know where the haystack was.

"I can tell you... confidentially of course," Benton said, pausing, obviously waiting for her assurance.

"Yes, of course," she said. "Anything you tell me will be confidential." He certainly was trusting, and sharing details with her was irregular, but she was hardly going to remind him of that.

"Your Grandmother was right. It was blood on the brick, and it was a positive match to the victim's. That brick was used to bash Denny Brody. The coroner found traces in his head wound. Whoever used the brick on him didn't have an opportunity to really get rid of it permanently and stashed it in the trunk. They probably didn't know there was a key or they would have locked it in."

"Did you find any brick dust on my grandmother's clothes?"

"We did. Both on her bonnet and her cloak."

"How about blood?"

"Minute traces of Denny Brody's blood on her bonnet."

"So, Denny was hit before Granny."

"Seems so."

"How about prints, Chief Benton? Were there fingerprints on the trunk or the brick?"

"No, nothing."

"I can't say I'm an expert on fingerprints, Chief, but isn't that odd?"

"Not really. Could have been washed off. They'd be superficial; the blood was soaked in. We are sending it on to the State Crime Lab to get a better analysis. Might take a couple of weeks. As I told you, the brick wasn't the murder weapon. It didn't kill Brody."

Caroline decided Benton wasn't going to be of any further help. He'd decided to write off the brick as "not being the murder weapon," and therefore unimportant. He also wasn't going to consider the key's absence worthy of his attention. His attitude was better, but his sleuthing skills were still woefully inadequate. As Granny had said, no doubt getting the saying from some fictional detective, "considering the impossibilities was as important as assuming the possibilities."

After Caroline hung up, she grabbed one of the leftover lunch sandwiches, crammed it in her purse, and went to see Hannah.

When she got to the Miller farm, she walked around to the rear porch and tapped on the door. Hannah, looking a bit surprised, let her in.

Caroline relayed the gist of Benton's call.

"Wohl, Carrie, Benton may be getting more polite, but he is still a dummkopf," Hannah said. "Of course, the key's disappearance is important. There are no unimportant details.

"As for searching here, they can look around all day and will not find anything," Hannah said, resuming her work on Jennet's quilt. "Just better not make a mess," she added, looking up through the half glasses she wore for close work. "There! The quilt it is finished! What do you think?"

"Gorgeous!" Caroline said. "Jen and Ian are going to love it!"

"Got to remember to get some photos of it," Hannah said. Hannah kept albums filled with photos of her work.

Caroline took her cell phone from her purse to call Benton's number. She had memorized it; in fact, as she told Hannah, it was programmed into the phone as #9, after 911, her house, her office, Stephen's home,

The Crossroads, the phone outside her parents' house, Stephen's cell phone, and Molly's school.

"How does that work? Show me," Hannah requested. As usual, Hannah had to know about technology, despite not wanting to use it herself. Caroline showed her. "It's easy; just remember the single digit and hit it; then punch the larger 'send' button."

"Is it always on? How do you stop it from ringing?"

Caroline went on to show Hannah the basics of the cell phone. Amazingly, to Caroline, Hannah always understood technological directions immediately. It had taken Caroline a week of referring to the twenty- page instruction book and constant repetition to get the hang of the cell phone's multiple features.

"Don't those gadgets run on batteries? What if it runs down? What do you do then?" Hannah said, examining it.

"I have an extended life battery and I recharge it every night. The charger plugs into an outlet. Now you are all set to get a cell of your own," Caroline teased.

"No, thanks. I have survived 'til now without one." Hannah said, smiling.

Caroline, thinking of Hannah's experience at Spooky Nook Covered Bridge, murmured, "Yes, but..."

"Now," Hannah said, ignoring Caroline's tentative last words. "I have to straighten up for the police."

"Straighten what up?" Caroline asked, looking around the immaculate room.

"Wohl, for one thing, I am going to put Jennet's quilt away. They might get it dirty."

"Granny, I have a feeling they are mainly interested in the kitchen and that will be a pretty perfunctory search. Benton is covering...uh, following procedures. He doesn't expect to find anything."

"He might. I used to use rat poison! He might think that is relevant."

"You are kidding, aren't you?"

"Of course, I am, Carrie. I have not put out rodent poison for years. I have never had cyanide in the house. When we did keep dangerous substances, they were always in a locked cupboard in the shed."

"You better not clean too well, Granny. Benton might find that suspicious."

Hannah stared at her for a second, and then laughed. "So, now you are kidding a kidder. Glad to know you have some sense of funning left. Dealing with murder tends to make a person lose their sense of humor, already.

"Bring Jennet with you tomorrow. She would not want to miss the excitement. By the way," Hannah asked, as she accompanied Caroline to her car, "are you leaving it to me to tell your mom and daat about the Keystone Cops' visit in the morning?"

"Granny, you are the one whose pie is suspect, and it is your house they want to search. I'm leaving the pleasure of telling the folks to you."

"Coward," Hannah called, as Caroline drove away.

The next morning, Caroline and Jennet arrived at the Miller farm shortly before nine.

Hannah was waiting for them. "I put out a little food, just in case you are hungry, or the policemen are. They must get tired of stale donuts," Hannah said. "You and Jen can show them it is not poisoned."

"We are taste testers, now?" Caroline asked. "If we drop dead, the police will get the idea and not eat?"

"I was thinking more like, you eat, and do not drop dead, and they will eat," Hannah said. "Be positive."

Jennet sat down, laughing. "Glad I didn't miss this." Immediately, she had two of the three cats in her lap. Daisy, the eldest cat, was still staring at Jennet with unblinking green eyes, considering the wisdom of jumping into her already full lap.

"About all they are going to find is cat hair on Jen," Caroline commented, looking around the shining kitchen. Jennet was wearing a pale pink linen pantsuit and even across the room, Caroline could see it was gathering black and white fur from the kittens.

"Qwill and Arch are still kittens. They do not shed much," Hannah said, in her usual precise English that usually eschewed contractions, making her sometimes sound both prim and serious. "I brush them every day. Do not want cat hair floating around the quilts."

"What did Daat say when you told them about the search?"

"Nothing. I did not tell them."

"Granny!"

"Before I could say anything, your daat told me they were going over to your Aunt Gwen's in Lebanon County right after chores this morning. They are putting up a new dairy barn, and needed his know-how. I figured I would tell them later."

"Now who's the coward? I don't blame you." Any further discussion was stopped by Bear's barking from the porch, indicating Benton had arrived.

Benton and Lee were by themselves, in an unmarked car. Benton kept his promise to make the visit low-key. Caroline expected at least a couple of deputies and two vehicles. But, come to think of it, two more deputies and the Chelsea Township police would be fairly well depleted of personnel.

They made a desultory search of Hannah's cupboards and kitchen pantry, asking a string of useless questions like: "What poisons do you keep in the house?"

It took all Hannah's patience to answer them politely. However difficult it was, she remained business-like.

"Sure, I would keep cyanide on my shelf, next to the molasses. Who knows when I might need to do away with someone?" Hannah quipped after they were gone.

As expected, the police search was perfunctory, and proved futile, and the other questions amounted to nothing at all to do with the murder, but queries about her unconventional house. Benton and Lee had no qualms about eating several sticky buns each, or drinking her coffee.

"Ladies," Chief Benton said to Caroline and Jen when the search was complete. "I'd like to talk to Mrs. Miller alone for a moment, if it's okay with you."

Hannah watched as Caroline shot him a look of disbelief.

"Oh, it's nothing she needs her lawyer for," he replied. "Really, I'd just like to talk to her about something."

Caroline glanced at Hannah, who felt a pang of concern, but nodded her assent. After all, Hannah thought, Carrie understands I know my rights, and I can take care of myself.

When Caroline and Jen had left the room, Chief Benton continued. "Mrs. Miller - may I call you Hannah?"

"I suppose." Hannah shrugged. "Everyone else does."

"Okay, Hannah. We know that you've been doing a little bit of your own investigating on this case."

Hannah's mouth opened to dispute his remark.

"Don't look so surprised, " Benton said. "I'm not as dumb as I look. Okay, it's like this- with all the big auctions and shows going on, we're a bit stretched on manpower. We could use some help from a local, someone well connected with Amish and Mennonite ways. You might be able to get folks to tell you things that they would just as soon not talk to us about. You were a big help with those other murder cases and besides, we both know you're going to do it anyway."

Hannah smiled. Benton must be really needing my help, she thought. He is trying a combination of flattery and joshing. Not too good at either, poor fellow.

"And, I imagine you would like to know who hit you on the head just as much as we do," he continued.

Hannah nodded. "I will do what I can, Chief. But, Caroline is getting married, and I am pretty busy right now. I am not sure how much I can help."

Well," Benton continued, "I don't mean you would have to do our work - no interviews or dangerous stuff, just consult. We'd keep it on the QT, of course."

Hannah knew what that meant. She probably would do the work and Benton would take the credit. But he was right about something she'd known from the minute she'd seen Denny's body - she couldn't resist investigating a murder, especially one she was involved in without wanting to be.

"But we want you to be careful, and stay in touch with us constantly," Benton added, as to further convince her. "Whoever did this is obviously trying to implicate you somehow, and may have it in for you and your family. So, if anything the least bit suspicious happens, you need to let us know immediately."

"Wohl," she said. "I suppose I could do that much." Hannah didn't exactly agree to help, but neither did she turn him down. She supposed that was tantamount to tacit agreement to help the police.

"Well, thank you for letting us into your home," Chief Benton said, a little loudly, as he stood to leave. .

As Benton and Lee pulled out of the driveway, Caroline and Jen came back into the kitchen.

"They were very courteous," Jennet said. "Not at all like the Keystone Cops Caroline promised, but more like a rerun of Columbo, except they didn't have Columbo's brains. But what did they want to talk to you about that we couldn't hear?"

"Wohl, he said what they really came here for was that his wife wants to borrow my recipe for shoofly pie - without the poison of course," Hannah quickly quipped.

They all laughed, but Caroline's knowing glance at her grandmother told Hannah she knew that was not what Chief Benton had wanted. However, she must have decided to wait until later to try to find out the truth about their private conversation, for she said nothing.

Two hours later, Caroline and Jennet were driving though Lancaster County's gently rolling hills towards the reception site, The Rose Mill Inn. Behind them, loomed the densely forested "Welsh" Mountains, dark and forbidding even in the daylight. They had been so named by homesick early settlers from Wales, an exception to the proliferation of English and German names in the area.

"Why did you decide to have the reception at the Inn?" Jennet asked. The day had turned out beautifully, with a cerulean blue sky and not a cloud to be seen. A brilliant sun reflected off the car's surface. Jennet pulled out a pair of what Caroline assumed to be the latest style in designer sunglasses. The narrow rims of pink were a perfect match for her linen pants suit.

Caroline squinted against the glare and pulled down the visor. She wasn't sure where her supermarket sunglasses were. They were last seen dwarfing the face on one of Molly's dolls.

"To answer your question, Jen, Rose Mill Inn was the first place Stephen took me when I came back to Lancaster County. I was here from New York to try and help get my brother out of jail. As you may remember, Joshua had been accused of killing Abel Schueler in a barn fire. My family didn't know whom else to turn to. Granny got on the train, came to Manhattan and charged into my very staid law offices. I don't think they have recovered yet. She demanded I come home. Not knowing what kind of a welcome I'd get, or even if my folks would accept my help, I was hesitant. I knew Stephen was In Lancaster, and there was Molly to consider. As far as I knew, he was completely uninterested in her, or me."

"Wrong on three counts," Jennet said. "No one says no to Hannah; your family desperately needed and accepted your legal help; and as for Stephen, we know how that turned out," she added, looking at the ring on Caroline's left hand.

"Well, all of it took a bit of time and doing,"

They drove down a small hill and across another of the area's picturesque covered bridges. Unlike the Spooky Nook Bridge, this one was in beautiful restored condition.

A rapidly flowing stream foamed over huge boulders and curved out of sight. Alongside the stream, sat the three-story, slump-stone Rose Mill Inn, the site of an eighteenth century flour mill. Windows with the irregular texture of hand blown glass glinted from the reflection of sun on the stream's water. Rose bushes clambered over a low stone wall bordering the drive.

"They're gorgeous when they are in bloom," Caroline said.

"What color?" Jennet asked, with her journalist's eye for detail.

"Scarlet," Caroline answered, her mind flitting back to her first look at the Inn.

The interior was furnished in keeping with the building's Colonial origins. It was divided into several rooms with random plank floors and cozy, low beamed ceilings, and looked very authentic. Candles in clear, hobnail hurricane lamps cast golden coins of light on the natural colored tablecloths.

"Look at all the antiques, Carrie," Stephen said. "Everything is genuine; not a reproduction in the place. Must have cost them plenty, but it makes all the difference."

She had to admit he knew his stuff when it came to authenticity. Ironic, she thought. Caroline was surprised at Stephen's drink order, mineral water. His hard drinking, party days were over, or maybe he was just on guard.

"The music is nice, don't you think?" Stephen commented, making small talk. A pianist was playing Chopin. Caroline was grateful to Stephen for introducing her to classical music. It had comforted her many times in the intervening years.

She nodded, suddenly not wanting to remember any of the good times with him in the past.

Even then, Caroline knew she still had feelings for Stephen. But she didn't want to admit them, especially when she considered him one of the main suspects in the death of Abel Schueler, and the subsequent effort to let her nineteen-year-old brother take the blame. Her own experience as Stephen's wife had clouded her objectivity, making it possible to think him a likely suspect. To gain information from him, she had to appear to be cautiously friendly.

She had not wanted to remember any of good times in their marriage.

Caroline wanted to know more about Stephen's job. Stephen practiced what was politely called contingency law, but what Caroline privately and derogatorily, called "ambulance chasing." There might be a connection between it and Abel Schueler's death. Perhaps Stephen needed Abel to testify for a client, something an Amish man would never voluntarily do. The Amish had as little to do with English laws as they could. So many of those laws conflicted with religious teachings. What could an Amish buggy maker have that Stephen needed? Surely nothing which would be a reason *for a violent confrontation, one that could result in death? Stephen Brown might be a heel, but he couldn't be a murderer, could he? Anyone could be under provocative enough circumstances. Caroline had to know, not hope, the father of her child was not a suspect.*

"You said you're leaving next week? Going to plea bargain Joshua?" Stephen asked.

He should have known better than to expect her to divulge anything about the case.

She continued cautiously, "As you must know, we've pretty much exhausted the options. We've interviewed everyone even remotely connected with Abel, checked into every facet of his life. We found nothing. The local attorney I've asked to help can do whatever else needs to be done. There's not much I can do here, other than hold my family's collective hand. I have to get back to New York; I have my first important solo case coming up."

"I really am sorry, Carrie. I hope you don't feel like you let your family down. I'm sure you've done everything you could. I understand how frustrating it is to have people count on your ability to work miracles, when there are none to be worked."

In the dim light, his expression was unreadable. If he was relieved, she was at an impasse, she could not tell. He sounded so sincere, so empathetic. He's good, really good. I'd like to see him in front of a jury, playing them like a Stradivarius.

Caroline tried to switch the subject. As she recalled, nothing interested Stephen Brown more than to talk about himself. "Tell me about your practice."

"Well, if you've been listening to my dad, he thinks I'm a shyster."

She waited for him to continue. She certainly wasn't saying anything to put him on the defensive.

"People have the wrong idea about personal injury, Carrie. Their perception is that we are all money-hungry profiteers, prospering on the *tragedies of our clients. That isn't true. Sure there are a few bad apples who thrive on publicity, but the real truth is, that if it were not for what we do, a lot of little guys would get hurt You must know, those mega buck judgment amounts the press throws around, don't happen. Juries substantially reduce the award. Most of the time, we settle out of court. People don't realize how little the attorney really gets."*

She leaned forward, trying to encourage him to keep talking. He continued to seem sincere.

"When some poor guy is disabled for life and can't support his family, what's he supposed to do without ambulance chasers like us?"

Caroline wanted to tell him that all law firms of any repute took on a certain amount of pro bono cases for which they didn't charge a fee. He must know that and know she did, too. Stephen was trying to prove he was not an unsavory shyster. She didn't care if he was or wasn't; all she cared about was finding out if he knew anything which could help clear Joshua.

"Now if the rest of the world was more like the Amish, I would be in another specialty of the law. They are one group who would never ask for redress against anyone."

She stirred her coffee into a whirlpool. "They believe in turning the other cheek and helping each other...very effective in their order of things, Stephen."

"You have forgiven them for turning their backs on you?"

"I left them, remember? Now, I have contact with my family, which is good." She had almost said for Molly, but that was one subject she would not broach with Stephen Brown. He had not asked and she would not bring it up. It was his choice to walk away from his responsibilities, and he could not walk right back in, even if he wanted to. Of course he showed no indication of wanting to do so.

"Guess you will be back now and then?"

"I have my own life now, a very satisfying one," she said, without really answering his question. Even to herself, she sounded prissy.

Stephen didn't seem to notice. "You're smart to put the past behind you, Carrie. Would that we all would be able to do that. Unfortunately, the past is too much with us. One impulsive moment and life is never the same again," he said, and motioned for the check.

What did he mean? Was he talking about Abel Schueler's murder? Did Stephen have some knowledge of Abel's death? Or, did she just think that because she was still too involved with memories of the Stephen Brown of years ago? There was no way she could impartially assess the meaning of his words. Despite the warm night, she shivered.

Now, when Caroline thought about that first meal with Stephen at Rose Mill Inn, she saw the humor in suspecting him of anything concerned with Joshua's predicament. How wrong she had been about Stephen and her own feelings for him.

Like the wedding rings, Caroline and Stephen's decision to hold their reception at the Inn was another they had made to face the past and replace old memories with new ones. It was turning out to be a love story with more than a few twists. In the interim, Caroline and Stephen had become realists. They dealt with each problem, old or new, with a decision to resolve it in a way that would not undermine their love and commitment, but strengthen it. This marriage wouldn't be a righting of past wrongs. The young people they had been were very different from the people they now were. The past was put into perspective. This marriage would be based on their determination and commitment. It had nothing to do with forgetting, but much to do with forgiving.

Caroline and Jennet met with the Inn's manager and went over the reception plans. He looked a bit askance at Caroline's estimate of 200 and her request for bus parking. They had decided one bus full of

Amish guests was preferable to mixing dozens of carriages and horses with the parking of cars.

Caroline and Jennet sampled some of the dishes that would be served at the reception. I'm going with the specialties," Caroline said. "Starting with the appetizers --- shrimp en brochette, petite Gouda and spinach quiches; salad is mixed baby greens with sun-dried tomatoes and fresh artichoke hearts; entree --- beef sirloin and crab cakes with lobster sauce. Dessert, besides wedding cake, is miniature lemon sponge tarts with California strawberries. Then there will be Molly's Jordan almonds and sugar and spice pecans, both served in nut cups. The nuts cups, like the tarts, are very Amish."

"Oh, does that sound heavenly," Jennet said. "What are the Amish guests going to say about both the unusual food and how elegant it is? Not very 'Plain'," Jennet said, smiling.

"I'm sure every mouth will be too full to talk," Caroline said.

Don't you think you should add scrapple?" Jennet asked. "A delicacy not to be missed. Think of the treat," she said, wrinkling up her small nose.

"Well, Jen, considering you married a Scot who eats haggis, you shouldn't be talking," Caroline laughed. "Our New York friends will have quite enough Central Pennsylvania ambiance meeting my Amish family. And the other way around, too.

Jen was glancing at her watch. "I know you have to get back to the realtor's, Jen. I'll drop you off at the condo to get your car. How is it going?" Caroline had seen Jen's discouragement last night, but she hadn't mentioned it, hoping their lunch would be a lift for Jen.

"You want the bad news or the bad news? It is awful and worse. The shop I might be able to eventually sell, if I'm in no hurry. The realtor wants me to think of renting it, but then I'd be a long distance landlord. It never works, but I may have no choice. As for the house...

who wants a house where three people died? Bad luck, ghosts and God only knows what else."

"How about selling to an Amish family? They don't believe in superstition or ghosts."

"Not enough land. I might be able to rent it to an Amish family, but I'd still have the landlord issue. Also, an Amish family might think the house a bit grand. I don't know...I'm going to keep trying, I guess," she said, sighing.

"It will all work out; give it time," Caroline said, in what she hoped was an optimistic tone.

CHAPTER ELEVEN

After lunch, Hannah prepared for her planned trip to see Copious Clay. She would hitch up Clara and take the buggy. In Hannah's estimation, her horse Clara was the perfect age. She was twenty, which in equine years, just about translated to Hannah's age. Like Hannah, Clara had plenty of spunk and pep, but was disciplined enough to know where she was going without too many diversions from her mission.

Hannah took out her slow running watch, and attached one of her quilt tags to it. Copious could add his own tag, but no harm in this added insurance. Never hurt to advertise, she thought with a smile, despite quilts having absolutely nothing to do with watches. She had plenty of tags; might as well use them up. Probably the only person to see it would be Copious, and Hannah could bet he would have no use for a quilt. If he did, he knew where to find Hannah, all right. She carefully packaged the watch in a piece of tissue paper and put it in her black tote bag.

Gathering up two jars of last fall's Concord grape jelly, she held them up to the window. They were the deep purple of royal raiments. She nestled each jar in a bed of tissue, then placed it each in its own paper sack, and added them to the bag. If she did say so, that grape jelly with homemade peanut butter, made a lunch fit for any queen. No visit from Hannah was without a gift of food or flowers.

As she had been readying herself to leave, she decided to combine the visit to Copious with a "drop-by" at the home of Dorcas and Swayne Hess. It was, after all, on the way. Only seemed practical. Swayne and Dorcas had no family since the tragedy that took their only son. Hannah tried to see them once a week or so, just to make sure all was well. A person should not postpone a visit to ninety year-olds.

If Hannah had any qualms about an ulterior motive for the visit, she pushed them aside.

This was not really investigating, just being neighborly. Of course, the only topic of conversation would be the discovery of Denny's body. Even if Hannah wanted to talk about something else, no one else would.

It was a beautiful spring day, which helped to lighten Hannah's mood. The Millers had put up bluebird boxes along the driveway bordering the pasture. Today, the birds were gathering materials for their nests. Higher up, blue-black barn swallows dipped and dove in and out from the barn's eaves.

As Hannah drove down the long driveway and out onto the road, she was grateful there didn't seem to be much traffic. No matter how many times she took a buggy out, there was always a flicker of worry in Hannah's mind about automobile traffic. She kept as much off the road as was possible to do, but cars buzzed by her in a blur, too fast for her to hear or see them until they passed. Clara was placidly unconcerned and showed no reaction to anything but the pull of the reins. Hannah was beginning to suspect Clara's hearing wasn't as good as it had once been.

"If one of us has to go deaf," Hannah told the horse, "better you than me, Clara. When I'm investigating, I get some of my best information from eavesdropping. I would hate to lose my hearing." Clara whinnied softly, so she must have heard something.

Dorcas and Swayne Hess's house was built of red-brown brick, two stories and straight and square, with a porch at the front and at the rear. Hannah knew it had been built the year Swayne had been born. He was quite proud of the fact his parents managed to produce a house and a child two weeks apart at their advanced age of 48. Swayne came along twenty years after his older sister, who never married, so he was the last surviving member of his family.

Hannah tied up the buggy around the side of the house where there had been a hitching post since the house was built. Now, an enormous maple tree shaded it, as well as the rear porch of the house.

Hannah knocked at the back door, and without waiting for someone to answer, opened it and called in. "Just me, do not get up." She knew at this hour, she would find Dorcas and Swayne in front of their television set watching soap operas. For antique dealers, the inside decor of the house was curiously bereft of antiques. Everything in the place was circa 1950. These days, some folks claimed things from that era were antique. Maybe a person could use the term vintage, but antique? Privately Hannah thought plastic and Formica were junk.

Unlike Amish houses, built with as many windows as there was room for, the Hess home was dark, and what windows there were, were heavily hung with draperies, ordered when Sears was Sears and Roebuck, and still had a catalog. As long as they looked clean and neat, they were fine with Swayne and Dorcas. It was difficult to tell what the furniture looked like, anyhow. The two chairs, footstools and long couch were covered with crocheted throws, executed in various dark colored yarns. With the exception of a large screen television that Swayne had found at the Best-Stoltzfus household auction, the living room was bereft of anything new. When Hannah had suggested a recliner might help Swayne's leg problems, he answered, "Nope; too complicated --that lever and all."

"He seems to manage the remote control on the TV okay," Dorcas told Hannah. "I liked our old television; it was more ... you know, intimate."

"Dorcas, it was black and white," Swayne said in a bemused voice. "This TV was a bargain, anyhows."

Before Hannah got completely sidetracked by the Hess's banter, she knew she better steer the conversation to the recent past. "I put some of my standby cole slaw in the ice box and a jar of grape jelly on the kitchen counter. The slaw lasts two weeks, already."

"That's real kind of you, Hannah, but at our age we might not have time to eat all the jelly and preserves you already gave us," Dorcas said.

"Hell, we might not have time to let that cantaloupe on the counter ripen." Swayne laughed heartily, sending him into a spasm of coughing. He picked up a bottle of cough syrup from the table next to him and took a gulp.

"That stuff can make you a dope addict," Dorcas said, without taking her eyes from the television. She tottered to her feet. Today she was wearing high-heeled pink bedroom slippers trimmed in some kind of feathers, that Hannah thought was called marabou. Dorcas picked up a navy blue throw and tossed it over the TV. Beneath the lacy covering, the picture flickered surrealistically.

"Program's over, Swayne. Turn it off," she ordered. "We have company."

After pulling out the remote he had been sitting on, he did as she had requested. The room was immediately as dark as dusk.

Hannah switched on a lamp next to the couch. "Since I'm here, can I do anything for you?"

"No, thanks, Hannah. The girl will be here tomorrow," Dorcas answered. The "girl," was sent by the Hess's church and was somewhere around sixty.

"What do you hear about the murder?" Swayne asked.

"I should have killed that terrible man," Dorcas piped up. "Nobody would figure a 93 year-old as a cold blooded killer. If I did get caught, what's a life sentence to me? Free room and board! Just one thing, if I went to jail, would I have to work in one of those prison laundries?"

Although Hannah tried not to think of murder as humorous, the picture of Dorcas unsteadily crossing Spooky Nook Bridge dragging a dead body, followed by a second image of Dorcas in prison stripes and marabou toiling in the prison laundry was almost too much. Then, she remembered the excellent motive for murder the Hesses had. They could have hired someone to kill Denny. It still sounded beyond belief. It would take more than cough syrup for Swayne to be part of such a far- fetched plot. Hannah had known the Hesses for her entire life. They were inherently kind, and despite their own tragedy, not vindictive.

Swayne said, "She's like you know... wandering." He tapped his head. "Every year, round the time Haney died, she gets cobwebby-like. "But, even if'n I believe in the Lord doing the punishing, I'm sure glad I lasted long enough to see that bastard Denny get his."

"Haney was a wonderful son, a change of life baby," Dorcas offered, in a monotone. "They are the best. Swayne was a change of life baby, too. It runs in our family, like. He was a beautiful child." Hannah wasn't sure who Dorcas meant. Dorcas was, as Swayne said, "cobwebby."

Haney had been the only Hess child, an antiques dealer like his father, with an amazing memory and a keen eye for values. When Denny Brody began appearing at every auction Haney did, it soon became apparent that Denny regarded Haney as real competition. Denny made it plain that Haney Hess was never going to overbid him. Denny Brody was not easily intimidated. It didn't take long for Haney to decide he would never keep a business going in Chelsea Township, or even in the area. With his wife, he packed up his van and made his way to New Orleans where he had a job with a major antiques' dealer waiting for him. A few miles from his destination, Haney's van was hit by a speeding truck and was catapulted, landing upside down in Lake Pontchatrain. By the time the emergency personnel got to them, it was too late. Haney Hess and his wife were dead.

It may have been an excellent motive for the Hesses to hate Denny, even wish him dead, but years had gone by. It didn't make any sense to extract vengeance at this late stage. Still, Hannah thought, people do stew. Sometimes the pot goes from simmer to boil with just a little heat added. What could have happened to add that heat where the Hesses were concerned? Hannah was pretty sure the Hesses were as innocent as she was, but she had to be sure. Poisoning someone did not take muscle, although getting rid of the body did. And there was the brick and the blow to Denny's head, and her attack.

Dorcas sat up straighter, focused her eyes and looked brightly and steadily at Hannah. Hopefully, Dorcas was back from mental memory lane.

"Dorcas, could I ask you some questions about Friday night?" Hannah began. The elderly woman nodded. "Did you notice anyone leaving the auction room either before or after I did?"

"Denny did; before you. He was carrying a whole, entire pie. Like a pig he was. I just bet it was your pie, Hannah."

"Who else did you see?"

"Lots of folks, but nobody I knew would hurt Denny so permanent."

That is one way to describe murder, Hannah thought. Permanent hurting.

"You know," Dorcas said in an undertone, leaning Hannah's way, "the police came here and asked the same thing."

"I see. What did you tell them?"

"Nothing. I told them you were my friend and if you killed Denny, hurrah for you and good riddance to him." Nothing like a friend in need, Hannah almost said aloud.

"Leastways them cops is trying to do their job. Too bad they don't know how. Bunch of doofusses," Swayne said. "I hope they never find who done it. The guy who did deserves a frigging medal! Meritorious service."

What ever happened to Swayne's verbal censor? The man says whatever is on his mind. Maybe it shuts down in folks at a certain age. I can see what I have to look forward to, Hannah inwardly groaned.

"Time for *General Hospital*," Swayne said, using his cane to whip the afghan from the TV. "Want to stay and watch, Hannah?"

Hannah made her escape. Before she went to see them, she had doubted she would get any information from the Hesses, and she was right.

She could hardly wait to see Copious. At least the man seemed normal and might make sense. She really did need to discuss Matilda's depression with him. She was beginning to think this entire township was a few degrees off kilter. So far, everyone else on her suspect list was suspect alright, but suspect only of a mental or emotional disorder. None of them looked like either the murderer or her assailant.

As she pulled into to the Clays' driveway, she saw both of the Clays' vehicles in their usual places. Hopefully, Matilda was in the house and Copious in his store. She was going over how she would approach him about Matilda. Depression was a serious disorder, but in Chelsea

Township, it was still regarded as something a person could just "get over" if they tried to cheer up. Old concepts were hard to change. One of the good things about being a benign-appearing Amish grandma was built-in believability. People listened to you. Whether they chose to take your advice seemed to Hannah to depend on whether or not you could get them to ask for it. Copious was a sensible man, even a worldly man. He also had a doctor. If anybody would listen, he would.

The door to the store was unlocked, but no one was around. Copious must be inside the house. Hannah sat down in the shop to wait. After fifteen minutes, he still hadn't returned. Very peculiar. Copious was usually so careful about leaving a sign saying: "Be Back In A Few Minutes," and locking up. Hannah walked to the small back room where Copious did quick fixes like checking to see if stones were tight in their settings, and changing watch batteries. It seemed odd these days not to see a vast array of electronic gear. Matilda did not approve of radios or televisions, and certainly not computers or video monitors. Copious had told Hannah, he was one of the last remaining jewelers who conducted his business the old fashioned way. That is to his credit, Hannah thought. She laid her watch with her name tag on it at the rear of the bench, then picked up a pencil from the counter, took one of his business cards, and wrote on the back. "Left watch; running slow. Door open. Closed it. Be back. "

She laid the card on the counter. She was certain Copious would be back soon. He surely would not leave the store unattended for long.

If it weren't for the problem of running into Matilda and not being able to talk to Copious alone, she would go to the house. She finally decided to do that anyhow. Copious would want to know he had forgotten to lock the store. She would simply follow him back when he returned to lock it.

Hannah walked to the back door of the Clays' house, stopping to give the patient Clara a pat. The horse was going to need water soon. "Hang on, Girl; we will get this over quick like and go home," Hannah told the animal.

Vines and tendrils threaded their way through the lattice on the covered porch. Looks like clematis, Hannah thought. It will be beautiful in a month or so with big, dark pink flowers. She knocked at the door, but no one answered. She tried the door; it was locked. It was the same story when she went around to the front. She tried to think of all the places they might be. Maybe they took a walk. They could be visiting a nearby neighbor. Could be someone came by and took them out for lunch. Anyone might forget to lock up, but she kept thinking how unlike Copious it was to leave his shop during the hours he was supposed to be open. Maybe they were just napping and didn't hear her knocking. She would wait a little longer and then call Petula, who had been here yesterday. Perhaps Copious had told her where he was going. Somebody could have given them a ride. But as she thought about them, none of these scenarios made sense to Hannah and her worry was escalating as time wore on.

She searched the store for extra keys to the house. She knew Copious owned a handgun, but it was nowhere in the shop. He either had it with him or it was locked in the safe. Maybe the keys were there, too. She turned to the safe and tried pulling it open. The heavy door swung outward. It was not locked. No gun in it and no keys to the house; those locks were modern deadbolt types. In the safe's drawer, all she found was a key ring with keys to the jewelry cases, one to the front store door, and another, larger key. It was a large, old-fashioned key to a lock unlike the type of locks she noticed on the house doors. Could be some kind of shed key, she surmised. Hannah locked the store and turned the sign in the window over so it read closed instead of open.

She sat down to wait a few more minutes. If Copious hadn't returned, she was going to have to call Pet and if she couldn't shed any light on where the Clays were, she would call 911.

It was then that Hannah remembered the cellar door. Copious had trained a vine over another section of lattice to camouflage the entrance. He'd shown Hannah how clever he thought it was. Maybe he was in his shop and Matilda was napping. It was logical. Once more, Hannah returned to the house, knocked and called.

When she still didn't hear any response, she made her way to the hidden door. She pushed her way around the vines and pulled the lattice aside. There were three steep cement steps leading down toward the old planked door. Hannah knocked and called, this time putting her ear to the door. Not a sound. She looked at the lock. It was a large, old-fashioned one. The key in the shop! It is for this door, she thought. A few minutes later, she was trying it. The door opened easily and Hannah looked in, calling "Copious? Matilda?" All she heard was the piteous howling of the cat, Daynight.

Suddenly, something or someone came hurtling out of the darkened cellar and rushed by Hannah. She lost her footing and went crashing to the floor. Her last conscious memory was the foul, pervasive odor of sudden death.

A soft mewling and rough, wet tongue licking her face brought her to. "Daynight," Hannah said, hugging the cat's quivering body. Daynight began to purr loudly and rub enthusiastically against Hannah's face. Hannah was slumped against the bottom step. She hadn't fallen far and she thought her arms and legs were all in one piece. She didn't hurt anywhere, so gingerly, holding the handrail, she regained her feet. The cat who had jumped down, watched, looking concerned. The stench was coming from the direction of Copious's workshop. Hannah's heart sank; she knew from the odor what she'd find there. From previous visits, she remembered the closest phone was in the shop. As she turned the corner, she saw that the lights were on. In the brighter illumination, Hannah saw that the cat's little white feet were covered with blood. Hannah scooped her up and saw that Daynight wasn't hurt, only traumatized. It appeared the cat had stepped in blood. With what she hoped was a reassuring pat, she put the cat down again. Hannah listened, but heard no indication of another human sound. Another few steps and Hannah could reach the phone, but first she had to see the body. Whoever it was might still be breathing, clinging to a thread of life. When she got a full view of the victim, she stifled a scream. It was Copious, slumped against his jeweler's workbench. There was blood everywhere, seemingly spattered on every surface in the once pristine shop, and streaking Copious's pale yellow print shirt. He was beyond any human help. A large, highly honed jeweler's tool was stuck in his throat.

Hannah tried to stay focused, and tried not to gag as she turned to the black wall phone to dial 911. Oh, my Gott, she breathed. Matilda. Where was Matilda? If she had been in the house, the killer might have gotten to her, too. Hannah heard a noise behind her and, this time she instinctively screamed. Daynight let out a blood-curdling howl and flew under Hannah's skirt.

CHAPTER TWELVE

After dropping Jennet off at the realtor's office, Caroline pulled over and checked her array of electronic devices. First, the cell phone. Nothing from Molly's school or Stephen; the rest were calls from her office. She had taken a month off, but it was nice to know they couldn't seem to get along without her. She would listen to the messages later. Then it was to the organizer, her worldly version of Hannah's ever-present "To Do" list. At the top of the list was the reminder to pick up Stephen's cuff links from Copious.

She also had to visit the florist, but she thought Granny would enjoy going along, too, so she would do that later. Hannah was really into this English wedding stuff. Caroline would be the last one to spoil her grandmother's fun. Watching Hannah enjoy the preparations was a vicarious pleasure for Caroline. It kept her from being too intense about her quest for the "perfect" wedding. Seeing Hannah's delight in the smallest detail also helped alleviate any traces of guilt Caroline felt about denying her family the excitement of an Amish wedding. Being Amish was both so long ago and far away, yet so ingrained in her that she faced an ongoing battle to reconcile the two; she probably always would. Coming back to the area, accepted by her family, and being of some use to her community with her legal expertise was enough to help her come to terms with the disparity in the two parts of her life.

She reached the Clay house quickly, zipping over back roads she knew so well, slowing around each bend in case an Amish buggy was sharing the space.

The first thing she saw was Clara and Granny's buggy. Caroline had little doubt her grandmother was up to the collar of her black cloak in investigating Denny Brody's murder. Damn, after they'd agreed to let the police take care of this. What was it they had agreed on? Caroline thought back. The only thing Hannah had really said was that they would not discuss the murder on Sunday, and today was Monday. Hannah hadn't exactly said she would never ask questions. Caroline was thinking like a lawyer. She tried to give her grandmother the benefit of the doubt. She might be here for a perfectly normal visit. Maybe. Hopefully. Oh, well, she was not Hannah's keeper, or as Molly put it before her last time-out, "You are not the boss of the world, Mommy." So true, and Caroline was most definitely not the boss of Hannah Miller.

Copious's shop was closed, with the sign out and the door locked. Guess I was too quick to cross that item off my list, Caroline thought, a bit dismayed. Both cars were there, so the Clays must be in the house with Granny. But, no one answered the bell or her repeated knocks at the front door, so she tried the back door. She had no better luck there in rousing someone. They must be in Copious's basement workshop; maybe they can't hear the bell. She was torn between coming back, waiting or walking around the yard. She chose the latter, stopping first to have a word with Clara. Too bad the horse couldn't answer her when she asked, "Where is everyone, old girl?" All she got in return was a soft whinny and an attempt at a nuzzle from the honey-colored horse. "You thirsty, Clara? Let me see if I can find a bucket and get you a drink." She found the bucket straight away, but there was no faucet. Looking around, Caroline spotted a hose lying on the ground. She followed it, looking for the water source. It snaked around the corner of the house to the far side. Caroline spotted the faucet at the same time she saw what must be the basement door. The door, down a couple of steps, was wide open. Must be an entrance to Copious's shop, Caroline supposed. She called down into the doorway, "Copious? Granny?" Her own voice echoed back at her, but that was all. "Matilda?" she tried. "Anybody there?" They probably couldn't hear her back in the shop. She peered into the opening. It was dark, with the only light coming from the doorway and a few window slits. There must be a switch somewhere. Cautiously, she descended the steps, and just inside on the concrete wall, found a light switch. It lit only a dim bulb outside the door, but by then, her eyes had acclimated themselves to the dimness, and she saw a light coming from what she remembered from the previous day as the workshop area. She started to call again, but some instinct stopped her. She didn't know if she was being fanciful or smart, but there was something wrong; she knew it. All her senses told her so. It felt wrong and it looked wrong and it smelled wrong. It smelled like blood. If she was right and she rushed in like a fool, it might be her blood next.

Quickly and quietly, she retraced her steps until she was well out of the basement. She reached into her bag and dialed Stephen's number. He was no more than five minutes away. She tersely described the situation.

He didn't argue or suggest she was imaging things. "Carrie, don't go in there," he said. "Get back in the car and lock your doors. I'll call Benton and be right there." He broke the connection.

She returned to the car. Where was Hannah? She had to find out, but if something was wrong, what could she do? She had no weapon. Caroline had noticed a tool shed near where Clara was waiting. She ran back to find it padlocked. The hose! It had one of the new adjustable sprayers connected to it. She would drag it with her and it would throw anyone off kilter to be sprayed in the face with a sharp stream of water. She was going from dumb to dumber. Water would be a temporary deterrent.

Quickly, she assessed the situation, flitting from being perfectly reasonable to highly illogical, jumping from calm to near panic. She fought to think clearly. If someone was down there, they would have had to come on foot; there was no other vehicle in sight. How likely was that? Why was she being so quick to panic? Denny's murder had her nervous. Her gut feeling and instincts made her wary. Why didn't anyone answer her? The workshop was within earshot, but she didn't hear anything coming from the shop. Maybe the damn bell was just broken and they were in the house, eating Granny's grape jelly. Perhaps the smell she was sensing was some chemical Copious used. What chemical would a jeweler use that smelled like a dead animal? She hadn't smelled anything like that yesterday. Maybe they've been overcome by fumes. She had read too many of Granny's mysteries; her imagination was at full gallop now.

She was being hysterical and ridiculous; some dispassionate lawyer she was. She was in no danger. Stephen would arrive, followed by the cops and Granny and the Clays would saunter out from the house perfectly fine. Oh, God, she hoped so. In another minute she had convinced herself of it. Stephen would be here momentarily; it would be fine to walk into the cellar, and see if they were in there. Worrying about Hannah all the time was unhinging her. It was unnecessary and unwarranted.

But it wouldn't hurt to be cautious. The thought of one of Granny's Gothic mystery heroines, stupidly walking into danger flitted through her mind. This wasn't an old castle and it wasn't the middle of the night, and she was being fanciful. She got out of her car, and heard Stephen's van glide into the driveway and pull over next to her. Together, they waited for Benton. After ten minutes, he hadn't arrived. They hadn't seen or heard anything coming from the house. Stephen put in another call to the police dispatcher. She heard him swear under his breath.

When he got off the phone, he said, "There's a huge mess on Route 30; they're going to be delayed. I'm going in there, Carrie. There is probably some simple explanation."

"We could sneak around the house, staying close to the foundation," she suggested. "Go in, carefully and quietly this time, and cautiously get closer to the workshop until we can see the door. Then, quietly call, so we won't scare them all into heart attacks."

"I have a better idea. You stay here; wait for Benton and I'll go in," Stephen said.

"You are not leaving me here! I'll make myself into a loony for sure with worrying and concocting improbable scenarios."

"God, Caroline, how do you and Hannah find yourselves in these situations?"

"That's not fair, Stephen; the situations find us."

He groaned. "Okay, okay. Come on, but if anything is wrong, you get the hell out of there, pronto. Where's your cell? Bring it! You have a decent size flashlight? Bring it, too."

She told him her idea about the garden hose. Aloud, it sounded completely stupid, even to her. Nancy Drew at her worst. Next she'd be talking about throwing a cat at the supposed intruder.

"Forget it. I have a gun."

"A gun? I hate guns."

"Fine. I have one anyway. If you think I'm taking you, or myself in there unarmed, you are loony."

With Stephen in the lead, holding the gun, they descended the cellar steps. Caroline, holding his free hand, felt him tense when he caught a whiff of the air. He pushed her behind him and the two of them stealthily proceeded toward the workshop.

Caroline heard nothing until they were almost at the door; then she heard a human scream followed by the terrified howl of a cat. "Stephen, it's Granny. Don't shoot. Granny!" she screamed.

"Of course I'm not going to shoot," Stephen called, stepping into the workshop. "Oh, my God! Hannah, are you hurt? Carrie, don't come in!" he shouted, pushing her back so hard she had to grab the wall to keep from falling.

She heard Hannah's voice. "I am okay; I'm not hurt. There is no one here. Just poor Copious. I got here too late. I think he killed himself. There is a note."

Caroline stood in the doorway, looking at the scene. "Oh," she said, weakly. "Oh, no."

Hannah's only concern was for Matilda, and she was nowhere to be found when Stephen searched the house. "All I know is someone or some thing rushed by me, and I have no idea who it was. Why would Matilda run away from me? Why would Matilda leave through the cellar at all and not go through the house? It makes no sense," she said firmly.

"Maybe someone else found the body and was afraid they would be found and somehow blamed, or accused. Maybe whoever it was didn't see the suicide note. They heard you open the cellar door and saw a quick way out."

"You didn't see anything when you went in?" Stephen asked.

"It was too dark," Hannah said. "What I felt must have been Daynight; poor cat was terrified."

It took still another phone call before the police finally arrived.

Benton and Lee were both all business. By the time they arrived, Hannah and Caroline, along with Matilda's cat, who seemed desperate to stay with Hannah, were waiting in Stephen's van. Hannah had not touched anything. There had been no need to. She had seen the suicide note, which was lying on the bench opposite the body.

It was typed in large letters, obviously on a computer, Caroline noticed. The type was at least a 16- point, much too big a type to be from a typewriter. It said: "I couldn't live with the guilt. Copious Clay." It was dated. The thing that Caroline found so strange was the date. Why would he date the note? Did people date suicide notes? She asked Hannah.

"I do not think it is usual to date a note, but I have not run across that in my reading," Hannah said, her brow furrowed in concentration. "Not that I can remember. I will have to think about it. "

"What's the difference? He's dead; there is a note. That is that. Obviously, he was not in his right mind," Deputy Wayne Lee had commented, unnecessarily. He had climbed into the van to take a preliminary statement from Hannah.

"You can go," he said when he was through. "Same drill as last time; we'll stop by to get you to sign the statement tomorrow." He looked at Caroline. "Yes; we'll call you first."

Benton walked across the drive to the van. "Sad business," he said. "Sorry, you keep finding the dead guys, Mrs. Miller."

"Me, too," murmured Hannah.

"But, you know this clears you. Not that we ever thought you were anything but a scapegoat anyway."

Doesn't he have a way with words? Caroline thought. Such finesse.

"Chief Benton," Caroline said. "Where do you think Matilda Clay is? Both cars are here."

"I don't have any idea; figure she has gone somewhere with a friend. We'll station an officer here to break the news when she gets back."

"Would you call us?" Hannah said. "I do not think she should be alone when she hears."

"No problem. We won't release the name until we tell her. You have any idea who she might have gone somewhere with? I suppose you have a list by now?"

If he was trying to be cute, Caroline thought, it wasn't funny.

"No, I do not," Hannah said, with no trace of a smile. The look Hannah shot Benton reminded Caroline of her least favorite college professor when he was doling out failing grades. "I would suggest you call Petula Brody, Copious' sister and Laverna Best, to start. They both did things with Matilda. You think her date book could help, already?"

Benton didn't answer, but by his chagrined expression, the answer was obvious. He hadn't thought of it. "I'll let you know when we locate her," was all Benton said, and walked back towards the house.

"I'll call Josh and get him to bring Clara home," Caroline said. "I'll drive you home."

"No, you will not. I am perfectly fine to drive the few minutes home."

Caroline knew the futility of arguing with Hannah.

Obviously, Stephen hadn't learned. "No, Hannah. I'll drive the buggy home; Carrie will take you home, and then bring me back, and I'll get my van.

"I hope you two are more efficient planning your own lives, than planning mine. I am going to take my buggy home. You two can do whatever you like. Drive around in circles if you like. I am going home."

"If you want to do something, find some water for Clara," she added. "They have a bucket and a hose around here somewhere."

Caroline knew all too well where the bucket and the hose were. Her temporary insanity of thinking she could confront an intruder with a hose was one thing Hannah didn't need to hear about. She doubted if Stephen would tell her grandmother, either.

"I sure would feel better if I knew where Matilda was," Hannah said. "This is going to be a terrible blow. You know her first husband took his own life? There are times when accepting God's will is very hard."

CHAPTER THIRTEEN

Stephen took Daynight to his house, and then he was going back to the store.

"Temporary custody, until Matilda claims her," Caroline had told him. Just don't tell Molly the cat is there. It will give her ideas. You know how she wants a cat."

Caroline had no more gotten through the front door when the phone rang.

"Caroline, it's Claire Sutton."

"Hi, Claire." Claire Sutton was not only Emily's mother, but she and Caroline were room mothers at the girls' school. Claire had become a good friend.

"I know you have a million things to do for the wedding, and we'd love it if Molly could stay the week, or even longer, if you like. I promise I'll make sure she does her homework and no TV, no matter how much the girls beg," she added, laughing.

Caroline breathed a sigh of relief. She would just as soon not have Molly home, hearing all the details of Copious' suicide and Matilda's disappearance. The Sutton's was the best place for her for now. She accepted gratefully.

Caroline checked her messages. The florist had called to reschedule. The church had called about the music, and the third message was from Best-Stoltzfus. "What now?" she muttered, as she hit the 'Play Message' button.

"Carrie, this is Laverna. I am sorry to bother you, but you still have a box of purchases waiting for you here. We can't be responsible for storage, you know. If you don't mind, could you pick them up next time you are by? We are not here all the time; be sure to remember our business hours." No matter what Laverna Best said, she had this annoying way of flip-flopping from apologetic to autocratic and back. "Kind of passive-aggressive, aren't we, Laverna?" Caroline asked the answering machine.

I might as well get it over with, Caroline thought. Her joy in the auction purchases, including the small things she had bought, had been diluted by the shock of Copious' death, and the knowledge he had killed Denny Brody. It was so hard to believe; Copious seemed like the happiest of men when they had seen him Sunday. Did anyone, even Matilda, know how tormented Copious was? She was reminded of a country western song she'd heard recently. Some discordant whine about the "demons and gremlins clawing to get outside my mind." She remembered it because it sounded nothing like the usual lyrics heard in CW music. It was more like a line of dialogue from an "Alien" film.

As she changed clothes, Caroline turned on her computer to get her emails. "You Have Mail," it announced. She always had mail; why didn't they just say: "You Have No Mail?" It would make a lot more sense. At least she would never have to hear that annoying announcement. She hopped over to the computer, pulling on a shoe as she went.

She sat down and emailed Stephen that Molly was going to spend the remainder of the school week with the Suttons, and reminded him they were meeting at six o'clock for dinner. Then she scrolled through the junk mail, deleting as she went. Her total number of messages plummeted to a few, all of which could wait. She printed out one from a mutual friend of Stephen and hers from college. She could have forwarded it to him, but she wanted to see his face when he read their friend was "Bringing live chicken from Australia; Beware." It was part of their zany college code for letting someone know they were bringing beer to a party in their apartment house. The landlord only rented to college students who did not drink, and all the tenants were asked to pledge they didn't. They had been tossing the phrase back and forth for years with much hilarity. Caroline thought it was wearing a bit thin, but as long as it made Stephen smile, it was enough. They, along with Jen, were going to meet for dinner at Gibraltar, a favorite restaurant in downtown Lancaster, across from Franklin and Marshall College.

As the note printed out, she couldn't help but think of Copious' suicide note. It was printed so large, one could see it across the room. Maybe in some twisted way, he thought by making the print so large, Matilda would not have to get too close to the body, and still be able to read the note.

It was nearly five o'clock when Caroline got to Best-Stoltzfus and parked at the side door. With the exception of a forest green station wagon, the parking lot was empty. Caroline recognized the car as Laverna's. She hoped Laverna already knew about Copious. She didn't want to be the one to break the news, but if she had to, she would. With any luck, Matilda had been found by now. If so, no one had called her to let her know, but it had only been a couple of hours; it just seemed like longer. If Matilda had gone shopping with someone, they might not be back for hours. All the local outlet malls, which Matilda frequented, were open late.

Laverna was in the office, preparing to close for the day. Seeing Caroline standing in the doorway, Laverna looked at her blankly, obviously not thinking about the phone message. One look at her face and

Caroline knew Laverna had heard about Copious. Her usual flawless makeup was streaked and her eyes were puffy.

"The police called," Laverna said, thickly. "What is happening, Carrie? This used to be such a peaceful place."

"It still is, Laverna. Tragedies happen everywhere." Caroline knew she was grabbing at clichés, but isn't that what people do when they don't know what to say? "Have they located Matilda?"

"No, and I'm real worried. What if she is wandering around in shock, having found him like that. And, after Ed and all. It would unhinge anyone."

"I thought of that. Granny has, too. It is a terrible thing for Matilda. Have you talked to Pet yet?"

"No, Carrie; she isn't home. The police told me they went there, her being a relative and all."

"Well, they must be together; gone shopping or something."

"I guess," Laverna said. "That is what that Deputy Lee told me, but he was just trying to make me feel better," she said, dabbing at her nose with a tissue. "And I don't; I am worried. Can't they send out a search party?" Her voice was rising.

"Laverna," Caroline said, trying to get her off the path to hysterics. "Where is Jack?"

"I don't know. He's missing, too."

"What? Missing?"

"Well, I don't know where he is. I haven't seen him all afternoon and he is supposed to let me know where he goes. I depend on him. What is the matter with everybody?" She paced in a tight circle.

Caroline didn't know how to answer. She didn't think Laverna liked to be touched, but she tried anyway. She put her arm around the older woman's shoulders. Laverna didn't pull away, but she didn't respond either. How thin she is, Caroline thought. Her shoulders are so bony; I can feel them right through the fabric of her jacket.

"I'm here," Jack Best said, heartily, opening the door behind them. Both women jumped. "Sorry I didn't mean to startle you." When he saw Laverna, all traces of joviality left his face. "Honey, what's wrong?"

Immediately, Laverna burst into tears. Jack put his arms around her. "Carrie, what the Hell is going on?"

"Copious...he killed himself," Laverna blubbered, and added a moaning sound to her tears. "M-M atilda is missing."

Caroline explained, or tried to, over the noise of Laverna's sobbing.

"I can't believe it," Jack said, his face grim. "Copious, kill someone? No way!"

"There was a note, Jack."

"Is anybody out looking for Matilda?"

"The police are, but other than to check with Petula, nobody has any idea where she might be," Caroline said.

"Anybody look at the graveyard?' Laverna, who had now stopped sobbing, suggested. "She visits Ed's grave pretty regularly."

"I'll call Benton and suggest they look there. The puzzling thing is, her car is still at her house."

"Then she's gotta be with someone. She does a lot with Pet."

"Laverna, who else might Matilda be with?"

"She still has friends from her church and, there are other neighbors"

When Caroline called Benton, they put her though to him. "I put you on the speaker phone here, Chief, so the Bests can hear you, too."

"We just left Petula Brody's shop," he said. "It's shut on Mondays, and she's not home, either. I put a policewoman at the Clays'. The body has gone to the morgue."

Caroline told Benton what Laverna had said about who Matilda might be with. "Did you locate her date book?" Caroline asked.

"Couldn't find anything but a wall calendar with medical appointments and auctions. None for today. Maybe that's all she keeps; maybe she has a good memory, or has a pocket calendar with her," Benton answered. "We'll just wait for her to come home."

After Caroline had paid for the items she bought and put the box in her car, she drove into Lancaster. This was supposed to be a happy time, but it was turning out to be sadness piled on shock. Matilda was very much in her thoughts. How could anyone get through two tragedies so eerily the same? In spite of Matilda not attending church, Caroline hoped friends and faith would help get Copious' widow through this. There would still be shock and sadness, but the unwavering Anabaptist belief in the certainty of God's will, would surely be of comfort. Caroline had seen the Amish demonstrate their faith often at such tragic times.

She parked at the restaurant. Both Stephen's van and Jennet's rented car were already in the parking lot. Jennet was returning to New York in the morning and Caroline was determined to send her home with a few happy memories of her week. That meant they wouldn't talk about the auction, or finding the body, or how hard it was becoming to sell Annette's properties. Caroline knew exactly how to lighten the mood. She would ask Stephen to tell the humorous incidents which happened almost daily at his hardware store. Between the tourists and the customers, he had plenty of them, and was a natural born storyteller. Jen would leave laughing.

Early the next day, after Jennet left, Caroline was on the phone. She had rescheduled the florist. She was going out to tell Hannah to let her know, but first she wanted to see if there was any news about

Matilda. She called the police. She'd called so many times, the dispatcher recognized her voice.

"He's in," the dispatcher said, without waiting for Caroline to ask for Benton.

"Chief Benton, good morning," Caroline said, when he picked up. "Any news on
Matilda Clay?"

"No," he said. "We reached Petula Brody first thing this morning. She said she had been at a tag sale all day. She was pretty shook up at her brother's death."

"I would think so," Caroline said. She waited for Benton to continue.

"I offered to get someone to stay with her, but she said she would be fine. She told me she had seen her brother and sister-in-law on Sunday, but Mrs. Clay didn't say anything about going anywhere Monday. However, Mrs. Brody mentioned Matilda Clay occasionally goes away with other friends.

"Mrs. Brody said she offered to take Mrs. Clay to the tag sale, but Mrs. Clay said she'd pass. Must have had grocery shopping to do. We found a lot of groceries on the counter. Guess she left again before she had time to put 'em away. Wonder where she went?"

Caroline tried not to say, "Duh, don't we all!" Instead she said, "It is strange she went grocery shopping."

"Maybe she needed something. Why would you think that's strange?"

"Because people around here are pretty regimented. Monday isn't a market day. Friday, yes. Tuesday or Saturday, even Thursday, but not Wednesday or Monday. Matilda was raised as a Mennonite. It is very unusual for older Mennonite or Amish woman to deviate from tradition."

"I see, I guess, but she did. The groceries were still all over the kitchen counter."

"I have a hard time imaging a neat person like Matilda leaving her groceries 'all over the place.' It's out of character."

"Chief Benton, were did Mrs. Clay shop? Did you see any grocery bags from Fisher's?"

"Yeah, the bags were from Fisher's Supermarket. How did you guess?"

"I didn't guess. I told you Matilda was traditional. Fisher's is where all the Mennonites and Amish shop, but not usually on Mondays."

"Why do you keep bringing up what day it was? So this time she shopped on Monday."

Fine, Caroline thought. "Did you ask anyone at the market if they had seen her and how many times?'

"Uh, no, Ms. Miller --- Caroline, okay, if I call you that? Call me Kiel. Matilda Clay is not a missing person – not officially. We don't know where she is, but there is no sign of foul play, no reason to think she has done anything more than taken a trip, for whatever reason," he finished, unconvincingly.

"Chief," she said. She wasn't about to get on a buddy-to-buddy basis with him. "Let's suppose Matilda Clay went to the store and when she came home, she found her husband dead. She has now been missing overnight. She was so terrified, she ran away, leaving her groceries strewn all over the counter. She is not of sound mind. Caroline paused, to let her hypothesis sink in. "Let's suppose she has wandered away. Shouldn't we be thinking it's important to find her before she comes to harm?"

"She didn't take her car," he said. "She couldn't get too far."

"She has been gone overnight! " Caroline repeated.

"As I told you, she is an adult. There is no sign of foul play. I only have so much manpower; I've already used a deputy to station at the house," he said, answering her, in an irritated voice and clipped sentences. "Unless I have some proof Matilda Clay was abducted, which I don't, we can't call in the feds yet."

"I see," Caroline said, matching his annoyance.

Benton seemed not to notice. "Look, there are reasonable explanations for all of this. Could be Mrs. Clay went somewhere with a friend for any number of reasons. You don't have any grounds to think she knows her husband is dead. Like maybe it was Copious who went to the store."

"Then came home and killed himself?" Caroline asked, trying to keep the derision she felt out of her voice.

"Well, we have to think of every possibility."

Time to start doing it, she almost said.

"I will go over to Fishers; ask around."

"Good start," she answered, as if she was praising a child. "Tell me, what kinds of groceries were on the counter."

"I didn't pay a whole lot of attention. Nothing that would spoil. Fancy crackers and tins of those gross things like smoked oysters and stuffed olives. Some sparkling apple cider stuff in a fake champagne bottle. Does it matter?"

"I just thought there might be a clue as to what Matilda was planning, which might point to where she is now."

"Look, Caroline, you told me Mennonite women rarely shop on Mondays. So here's what I figure: Mrs. Clay went on a little trip with a friend. Mr. Clay decided to indulge in some goodies while she was gone. He bought the stuff and brought it home."

"A pre-suicide celebration?"

The irony escaped Benton. "Well, maybe he thought of it as a last meal."

Caroline stifled a groan.

"I'd still like to go out there and look at the food."

"Sounds far out to me, but the stuff is still there. We're through there. If you don't think Mrs. Clay would care if you snooped around, you can go look at it if you want. Just don't move anything, okay? She might not like that. I have another call, Caroline. I'll get back to you. Okay?"

All she said was, "Thank you," hoping the insincerity in her voice wasn't apparent.

CHAPTER FOURTEEN

"Sounds like that Benton fellow would be happy if you did his work for him," Hannah said, when Caroline told her of the phone conversation. "He would do well to try a bit of snooping around himself." She had told Caroline last night about Benton's request for her help, but that didn't mean she wanted to do it all. While she talked, she was straightening up her kitchen, energetically wiping off and drying the shiny, bright blue tile counters.

"I can't shake the feeling something has happened to Matilda," Caroline said. "If Pet hasn't seen her, who has? It amazes me we haven't seen more out-of-town media nosing around. I suppose Copious' confession ended any interest there might be in the case." Caroline then told Hannah about Laverna Best. "High strung, isn't she? Has she always been that way?"

"Rumor has it Laverna couldn't have kids, something about an old boy friend and a botched abortion. Sordid stuff, I would not repeat."

"You just did, Granny."

"Wohl, you know what I mean. You are not just anybody. I can trust you with a rumor. Who knows if there is any truth in it?"

"Sorry, Gran, I don't get it. Even if it was true, that shouldn't account for Laverna's excessive reaction now. It must have been years and years ago."

"I didn't say it made her high strung; she was always that way, even as a little kid. She got worse when she was just out of high school, real nervous like. That was when the rumor started. People have way too much time to talk about others, if you ask me. It is one thing to gossip and pass the news around, but ruining a girl's reputation is an evil thing to do," Hannah said, whipping her drying towel around.

"Any idea who the boyfriend was?"

"I never noticed her keeping company with any one boy; that is why I suspect it was only rumor. Kids can be real malicious, and Laverna's father was a rich man. Lots of envy from the other girls, I'd be willing to imagine."

Jack Best married her and he seems crazy about her. He was very sweet to her when she was so upset."

"Whatever the reason she is the way she is, she certainly reacted strongly to Copious' suicide."

"And who would not? Some folks show it more than others. She is probably concerned about Matilda. But, we all are, with maybe the exception of the police. If the Clays had the 'redial' feature on their phone, we could find out who Matilda called last."

"I did that once when I was looking for someone," Caroline said. "I'm sure you remember. You had disappeared and I was trying to find out where you went."

"Wohl, it will not work at the Clay house. They have outdated phones; not as much as a hold button on 'em. Call Petula on your cell phone. Please," she added.

Caroline pulled out her organizer. "Home or shop?"

"It's too early for her to be at the shop. Try her at home"

Caroline punched in the number. "She's not answering; the machine just picked up.

"Pet, this is Carrie Miller. We are all really sorry about Copious; no one has seen Matilda, and we are getting frantic. Please call me. Maybe we can figure out where she is. I'll leave my cell phone on; it is 439-5118; please call me," she repeated.

"Carrie," Hannah said. "We are not going to hang around waiting for Petula to call. Oh, that is right --- that cell phone can go with. Handy, I say. Let's go; we need to find Matilda before something happens. She was really depressed on Sunday. The Lord only knows what state she is in now."

"The graveyard! Granny, let's go there and look for her. It is a start."

"She puts fresh flowers on Ed's grave every week; every Monday. If there are new flowers, we will know she put them there."

"One small step closer to where she is."

"Small steps are not goot enough --- we need giant strides, if we are not already too late," Hannah said, reaching for her bonnet.

Caroline was surprised when Hannah guided her to a non-denominational graveyard. "I wondered about flowers on graves, knowing Ed was a Mennonite," Caroline said. "I knew the Amish didn't decorate graves, but I wasn't sure about all the Plain sects."

"Some do, some don't," Hannah said.

The graveyard was located very close to a busy interstate highway, and cars and trucks whizzed by, filling the air with fumes and noise. "Not exactly a peaceful spot for eternal rest," Caroline commented. "Why isn't Ed buried in a Mennonite Cemetery?"

"Ed King wasn't a Mennonite when he married Matilda; he converted for her. His folks are buried in this graveyard, so Matilda thought it fitting he be here, too."

Despite its proximity to the highway, the small graveyard with straight headstones was neatly kept, with nary a weed. A narrow stone path wound in and out between the graves. Small American flags fluttered on a few of the graves. Hannah noticed there were none of the usual plastic wreaths or faded bunches of artificial flowers she had seen in other English graveyards. It always struck her as sad and odd, that folks would offer up plastic so the decorations would last longer. At least fresh flowers died and dried up naturally, eventually disappearing altogether in a fitting manner.

Only one of the graves currently had fresh blooms on it. A small bunch of slightly wilted daffodils sat on a grave against a headstone marked simply: "Edward David King" and the dates of birth and death; nothing else.

"Very interesting," Caroline said. "So, Matilda was here, but we don't know when yesterday. It must have been before Copious died and she couldn't have known. You don't think she would go about her normal business if she knew, do you?"

"I doubt it; in fact I cannot imagine it. On Sunday, Matilda was at odds and ends – withdrawn more than usual --real down in the mouth. She was not interested in doing anything, not even quilting. She told me she worried all the time," Hannah said, sadly. She walked back towards the car.

Caroline caught up with her. "Granny, if Matilda didn't use her car, she couldn't have gotten here. She must have been here either on her way to or from the store. Has anyone looked in her car?"

"I don't know, but I'd like to. I also want to see the things she bought at the store. It doesn't sound like she bought staples from what you told me Benton said was not put away."

"No, it sure doesn't. Let's go do what Benton suggested. Let's go to the Clays' and 'snoop around.'"

Hannah got in the car, thinking. If Matilda was depressed on Sunday and suddenly preparing for a celebration on Monday, what could have happened in between?

As they drove to the Clay house, she asked Caroline the same question.

Maybe Matilda is a manic-depressive, given to mood swings," Caroline said.

"Sounds far-fetched to me. I never saw any sign of manic mood in her. She is always quiet, if not actually depressed "There might be something at the house, meds or a prescription."

"Um," Hannah said, distracted. "I am trying to remember who Matilda's doctor is if I ever knew; I do not remember now. Do not suppose he would tell us anything, but if she was being treated for depression, her doctor might be able to get the police to take her disappearance more seriously. Matilda had to have an address book, or maybe she marked down numbers in the phone book."

They had reached the house, and true to Benton's promise, a police car was discreetly parked behind the Clay vehicles.

They knocked at the back door and a female deputy with red hair, who introduced herself as Kayla Bradley, let them in. "Chief Benton said you were worried about where Mrs. Clay is, and would probably want to look around. If you need to borrow anything, I'll have to sign it out for you."

"Right," Caroline said. "I don't think we'll need to borrow anything. We do want to look for an address book to get an idea of who Matilda Clay might be with."

"That's a good idea; it'd be a real shame to hear about her husband without being prepared," the deputy said.

As if one could ever be prepared for such news, Hannah thought

"I'll be right here if you need me," Deputy Bradley said, sitting down at the dining room table where she could see both entrances.

She had been reading a book, and Hannah sneaked a look at its title: <u>Benjamin Franklin</u>. Well, Hannah thought, at least someone on this police force has a brain. Wonder how she stands the rest of them?

Caroline and Hannah began a systematic search of the Clay house.

First, they looked for Matilda's handbag. They looked in the bedroom, which was dark, with curtains drawn, but it was neat and the bed was made. No sign of it there, or anywhere else they looked.

"Matilda probably has her purse with her," Caroline said.

"And that means she was of sound enough mind to remember her purse, or purposely take it," Hannah said.

They looked at the groceries strewn over the kitchen counters. "Look at all of this," Caroline said, her hand pointing to the counters. "It is party stuff. Is that weird, or what? Matilda and Copious having a party? Was it someone's birthday?"

"That is an explanation, I suppose," Hannah said, opening the refrigerator, then the freezer section. "Wohl, there is no ice cream and no sign of a cake." Hannah had no idea when either Copious' or Matilda's birthdays were. Pet would know. She would ask her. The refrigerator did contain unopened packages of fancy cheeses and fresh fruit out of season, a treat Hannah knew that frugal Matilda would only have indulged in for a special occasion. "She put all the perishables away."

"But she left all this mess? Otherwise this house is immaculate. She must have left in a hurry. But why? It makes no sense."

"Maybe she had to go somewhere with a friend. No one else is missing are they?" Hannah asked the deputy.

"No, Ma'am. Not that we have heard about. No one has been reported missing."

Hannah and Caroline continued to look for an appointment book or an address book. It didn't take them long to find an address book. Between the kitchen and living room, in a small alcove, they found a small telephone table with a drawer and a bench. A 1960's model black telephone was perched on top of a phone book, too thick to put in the table's drawer. In the drawer they found a neatly arranged assortment of paper, pencils, rubber bands and paperclips. Underneath it all, was Matilda's small address book.

Hannah flipped through it. "Oh, no, she has been using this book for years. I recognize names of people who died twenty years ago. This will take forever to go through. Hannah slipped it into her pocket.

"Granny..." Caroline whispered. "You're not going to take it?"

"Of course not; I will check it out with the deputy, just like a library book. Do not want to misplace it in the meantime. Maybe the phone book will be a better source," Hannah said, sitting down at the bench and riffling through the thick volume. Close to the front she found what she was looking for, a page which said "Notes."

Caroline peered over Hannah's shoulder and saw neat entries of names and phone numbers.

"Too bad Matilda would not let Copious have electronic gadgets. We, you, I mean, could make a photocopy. Now we have to haul out this whole thing."

"Granny, it's only one page. I'll copy it down, and you continue looking around."

"Okay," Hannah readily agreed. "I'll go look in her medicine cabinet."

When Hannah got to the pink tiled bathroom, she opened the large cabinet over the sink. There was a bottle of aspirin, a bottle of an antacid preparation and a vast array of vitamins and supplements, but not one prescription for Matilda. Hannah knew the Plain People in general were enthusiastic customers for what used to be called patent medicines and folk remedies, but Matilda took it to a new level; her cabinet was packed with bottles from the health food store. There wasn't even room for the toothpaste which was perched on a wall mounted toothbrush holder. Other essentials --- hair brushes, a jar of pins, shampoo and soap --- filled a tray on the sides of the sink. Pink towels were piled high on the opposite side.

On the nightstand, she found a bottle of a well know blood thinner, Warfarin – rat poison, thought Hannah. They just gave people a little bit; she knew folks who took it. That was what Matilda had said Copious was taking. In the drawer were prescriptions for Copious from Garden General Hospital Pharmacy. One Hannah thought was a blood pressure medication; the other something to slow down the heart rate.

Hannah wrote down the names and returned to the medicine cupboard to jot down the names on the products from the health food store. Picking up one of the bottles, Hannah read: "Acetyl-l-carmainite-hydrocloride. I am never going to know what all this stuff is for. This bottle sounds like some kind of cleaning fluid," she told Caroline, who by now had finished copying the list from the phone book and had come into the bathroom. "I'll have to make a list and go to the health food store and ask. But, maybe we will not have to go to that extreme; we may be able to locate Matilda from the phone book list."

"Why don't you start calling and I'll look at the cars," Caroline suggested. "I have to get to the florist today, or I won't have a florist. If I cancel our appointment one more time, she will take my deposit and go to ... Holland, or wherever frustrated florists run away to."

Hannah sat down at the telephone table, and using the original list, began to make calls. First she called the neighbors, none of whom knew where Matilda was, but all of whom were concerned. Then she tried the rest. Thank goodness most of the Mennonites in Matilda's former church have phones, Hannah thought, or it would take her forever to contact her friends. There were a few who didn't answer, including the name Hannah thought she recognized as that of the bishop.

Despite the police withholding the story, two facts quickly became evident: almost everyone Hannah reached knew about Copious' death, and they knew it was a suicide. The gossip mill was grinding away. No one knew where Matilda was, nor had they seen her recently. As might be expected, each was appropriately shocked and everyone was concerned about Matilda's disappearance. When they offered to help, Hannah could only say, "Ask around, and let the police know if you hear anything."

Caroline came into the kitchen, shaking her head. "Except for a receipt from Fishers, which I found on the seat of Matilda's car, neither car has a sign of anything to help find Matilda.

"Deputy Bradley, could I look in the trunk of Mrs. Clay's car?"

The woman looked blank. "You could, Miss Miller, but I don't have a key. Can't you open the trunk from the inside?"

"It's like fifteen years old, Deputy. You have to open the trunk the old-fashioned way; with a key."

The deputy put her book down on the table. "Maybe there is a key around somewhere. I'll help you look. They turned up Copious' keys, but he didn't have one to fit Matilda's car. There was a key to his store.

"Okay if we look in the store? I left my watch to be repaired before I... found Copious Clay. There is a tag on it identifying it as mine. I'd like to take it back."

"I guess that would be fine, Mrs. Miller, but unlike the address book you pocketed, we really do have to sign it out. I'll go along."

Caroline couldn't help but laugh to see Hannah looking nonplused.

"Sorry, I forgot," Hannah said. Smart girl, that deputy. Hannah also thought the deputy was more curious than she was concerned about them taking anything. Must get boring with old Ben Franklin as your only company.

Deputy Bradley opened the door to the store. To Hannah it looked much the same as it had the day before –sparse and still. But today, it looked sad, as if its breath had been sucked out by Copious' death and Matilda's disappearance. I am getting fanciful she thought.

Her watch was where she had left it. They also found Caroline's present for Stephen in a small box, carefully tied with a red bow, at the back of another drawer, marked with her name and a small hand printed note saying: "Carrie Monday." There was a bill as well.

The keys to both cars were also in the drawer.

Sadly, Caroline wrote a check made out to Matilda Clay and put it into the drawer.

"Let's sign out, Granny, and go to Pet's."

CHAPTER FIFTEEN

They found nothing in the trunk of Matilda's car. Seeing the carefully wrapped package Copious had left for her was heart rending for Caroline. She fought down tears, as determined as Granny to find Matilda. They had time to go to Petula's house before the florist. Caroline wondered how she could think about flowers now. Her mind was full of thoughts of the dead daffodils on Ed King's grave.

At the Clay's, Hannah had tried calling Pet at both the house and her shop with no success.

"Want to stop at Pet's shop first? It's on the way to her house."

"Yes. She should be there, or would be under usual circumstances."

It was a ten minute drive to Petula's consignment shop. Her hours were 10-5 Tuesday, Thursday and Saturday. It was now a few minutes after 11. Pet's shop, called "The Consignment Boutique" was located at the end of a small strip mall. Only a few cars were parked in the lot.

"I am glad Benton talked to her, or I would begin to worry that Petula was missing along with Matilda," Hannah said. "Seems strange she isn't answering the phones."

"Maybe it's just bad timing."

"Maybe," Hannah responded. "But I keep leaving messages, and she is not calling me back."

"She's probably getting a lot of messages. She can't get back to everyone. Or, maybe sympathy upsets her too much and she needs some time," Caroline ventured.

"Yes, but we are trying to find Matilda. What could be more important than that?"

Hannah asked. "Nothing!" she said, answering her own question. "Petula cannot hide out, mourning in some corner. She must face this, trust in God's will and help us find Matilda!"

Caroline knew Hannah's mood would brook no disagreement. Hannah was becoming a bit testy, but not without reason.

It didn't take long to realize that Pet hadn't opened her shop yet. They tried the door, knocked and called out. Neither Caroline nor Hannah could remember what Petula's car looked like.

"I think it is some kind of station wagon," Hannah said. "Maybe dark green. I think it might be one of those minivans, or an AWD or an SUB."

"SUV," Caroline corrected. "A sports utility vehicle."

"I do not always pay attention to English cars. Unless I ride in them," Hannah admitted. "What is the difference?"

"One is bigger, one taller; one can go in the mud, or off-road."

"Oh? Wohl, an Amish buggy with a good horse can do all that."

"We're getting off the track, Granny," Caroline said.

"Off-track? Are you trying to be funny? "

"Unintentionally, if I am," she said, looking around the parking lot. "Let's drive around back. Maybe Pet parked behind the store."

"Would not count on it. Business people park in front, so it looks busier. Unless they are loading something."

They made a circle around the building, stopping at the rear of Pet's shop. Except for a cleaner's delivery truck, the rear of the strip mall was deserted.

"We can ask at the other stores; maybe someone has seen her," Hannah said. You take Poppy's gift shop and Shear Bliss; I will check the cleaners and the sandwich shop."

A matter of minutes later, Hannah came out of the second place, and Caroline, leaving the hair salon, saw Hannah shaking her head from side to side.

"Nope," Hannah said when Caroline was in earshot. "Nobody has seen her; nobody has heard from her, or has any idea where either one of them might be."

"I got the same story," Caroline said, getting into the car, "although Poppy did suggest Matilda might have gone to an out-of-town sale. She might not have told Pet."

"Nope," Hannah said, firmly. "I am getting a sick feeling about Matilda. No good has come to her."

"Granny, be positive."

"I am being realistic, Carrie, and looking at the evidence. It is not good, not a bit good." "Pet is probably home, but not picking up the phone; it must be ringing off the hook. She and Copious were close, even for a brother and sister, weren't they?"

"Yes," Hannah said. "Far as I could see, they were. Petula must be taking this real hard."

A short while later, Caroline wound the car along Spooky Nook Creek Road, a few miles upstream from Best-Stoltzfus Auction House and the spot where Denny Brody's body had been found. It was another soft Spring day, and along the creek, grass was pushing its way up through the remains of last autumn's fallen leaves. Hannah lowered her window. The water level of the creek was high and the sound of the creek burbling was soothing.

Caroline had gotten used to Hannah lowering the car windows and waving to every passerby as if she was riding in a parade. So far she had not adopted the subdued royal hand flutter, but retained the enthusiastic free flinging wave of a preschooler.

"It even smells fresh, earthy. Like Spring should," Hannah said, inhaling deeply. "I smell cherry blossoms, already. This is the kind of day we will have for the wedding," she said, as if she could somehow will it so. No matter how bad things got, how deep into others' despair Hannah's investigations brought her, her combination of belief in God's will combined with her natural buoyancy and optimism got her, and those around her, through.

Caroline didn't comment. Her mind was not on the wedding. It would be once they found Matilda. She had pretty much decided something had happened to the gentle woman. Either she was not in her right mind and was wandering around somewhere, a scary thought. Or, she was seeking refuge somewhere she felt safe. What was the celebration for? Caroline felt that was the key to where Matilda might now be. If Matilda was celebrating Denny's death, she was mentally ill. It was one thing to be relieved he died, quite another to have a party. Mennonites, or even former Mennonites, did not have wakes as did Catholics. Death, like life, was an understatement, part of a God-ordained plan, not a party.

Deep in her thoughts, Caroline almost drove by the turn off into Petula's driveway. A neat, white, oversized mailbox was painted with the name Petula Brody. If Pet was so embittered by her time with Denny, wonder why she didn't take her maiden name back? There were no kids, no reason to not be called Petula Clay. Maybe she kept the name because Denny couldn't stop her. It might be the one thing he wanted he could not get by bidding higher than anyone else. Small victory for Pet, but perhaps enough.

The driveway was paved and rose steeply to the top of a rise overlooking the creek. It was an isolated, picturesque location without another house in sight. The house itself was undistinguished. It was a manufactured house, not exactly a trailer, or even a prefabricated home, but a bit of each with brushed gray aluminum siding, warmed by a deep red shade of shutters and a dark red door. Pet had done what she could to disguise its origins with rose covered trellises at either side of the door and heavily budded rhododendrons and azaleas mounded under the windows. Tulips of various types, in a riotous mix of yellow and purple bloomed in drifts and curves across the graveled walkway. Pet's Blue Toyota Sienna was parked at the end of the driveway, near but not in, a sturdy carport. It appeared she was home.

Hannah slid off the pillow she normally sat on so she could see better and agilely hopped down from the car.

"Hello! Pet?" she called, in a startlingly loud voice for a woman her size.

The front door opened and Pet Brody stood in it, dressed in a school-bus yellow chenille bathrobe and matching scuffs. Caroline thought she looked like Big Bird, but without his benign expression. Pet's small eyes, usually as bright as a sparrow, were red rimmed, and bloodshot, either from lack of sleep or crying, or both.

"Oh, Hannah, I am all alone. My family is all gone."

"No, they are not," said Hannah, in a no- nonsense manner. Caroline could see that if either she or Hannah were too sympathetic, Pet might completely fall apart. "You have Matilda. Copious would want you two to take care of each other."

Other than sniffing into the tissue she clutched in one hand, Petula didn't comment. She smoothed out the tissue and blew her nose.

"Pet, we cannot find Matilda," Hannah continued.

"I know; the police called me. Hannah, I can't think of where she would take herself off to. You gotta call all the women from her old church. Maybe one of them took her in. Not everybody has a phone.

Most, but not all. And lots of them don't have answering machines. With one of them is where she has gotta be," Pet said, eyeing an errant weed in her flower bed. She reached down, pulled it, and stuck it in the pocket of her robe.

"Did you suggest this to the police?"

"No, but I will now that she still hasn't showed up."

Caroline wondered how long it would be before the police would actually follow through. Other than her car being at the house, there was still no reason to think Matilda hadn't voluntarily left. Maybe Pet was right and she was staying with a friend. But who? Hannah had called almost everyone in Matilda's address book and came away with nary a clue as to her whereabouts.

"Can we come in, Pet?" Caroline asked.

"Oh, sorry," Pet said and stepped inside the partly open door, pulling it all the way open "Sure; come on in."

She ushered them in to a bright, neat room. Unlike the frozen in time, retro style of Swayne and Dorcas Hess's home, which Caroline had seen many times, everything in Pet's living room looked new. It was very stylishly decorated. There were subtle plaid slipcovers, candles, leopard print faux fur pillows, and still more candles, two in antique silver candlesticks that reflected the colors in the glossy, apple green painted walls. The wooden coffee table was neatly stacked with *Martha Stewart, Country Living* and *Victoria* magazines.

"Sit down," Pet said, pointing to a loveseat. "You, Carrie, sit next to Hannah. Can I get something for you to drink? Soda? Water? I could make coffee. I could make lemonade, or..."

"No, thanks anyway, Pet. We can't stay long," Caroline interrupted before Pet ran down the list of every available liquid she could think of. Poor thing, trying to be a proper hostess, under these circumstances. Caroline wanted to hug the older woman, but knew it wouldn't be the right thing to do. Petula had encased her emotions in glass with very fragile walls.

Hannah looked around. "Oh, you re-did? Very pretty," Hannah said.

"I think so," Pet said. "Decorated it myself. I got all the ideas from the H&G channel." She pointed at the large television set.

Hannah looked blank.

"It's a television channel that has house and garden ideas," Caroline explained. Granny must have missed it in her channel surfing at Caroline's house.

"What will they think of next?" Hannah commented. Caroline heard the interest in her grandmother's voice. She expected to find Hannah checking the television listings when next she came to visit.

Petula didn't seem to notice, but concentrated on folding and unfolding the tissue and examining it for a spot not already soaked by her tears.

"How are you taking all this, Petula?" Hannah asked, direct as usual.

It was obvious the answer was, not very well, but Petula just shrugged. "I'll sort it out later. Guess I have to say it is God's will."

Caroline couldn't help but think that was a much overused explanation for such tragedies. She felt it was often used to excuse man's incorrectly directed free will.

"Is there a minister we could call for you, Pet?" Caroline asked.

"No, I'm not a churchgoer. Too many hypocrites running around church. They just want your money and to mess around in your life. I talk directly to the Lord. Don't need a minister to do that."

Caroline felt Hannah stiffen slightly, but Pet's philosophy was so widespread, even in this area of the country, that Caroline wasn't surprised to hear someone verbalize it.

"Is there a friend you would like to stay with?"

No, I'll be fine. I have to stay here in case Matilda decides to call or come here," Pet said.

"Exactly when did you last see Matilda, Pet?"

"When you'uns was there, Carrie. Sunday. I left pretty much directly after you did. We had dinner already and I had to go to a sale the next day. It was real unusual to have one on Monday, but this is the busy season for sales and the like. I asked them, Copious and Matilda, if they wanted to go with, but they didn't and..." Pet began to sniffle again; then actual tears splashed onto her robe. "My brother," she said thickly. "He was all I had."

"You have Matilda, and a lot of friends," Caroline countered, reaching for the box of tissues which sat on an end table, and handing it to Pet who clutched it to her chest.

"I suppose," Petula said through her crying. She began to sob, hiccoughing with the intake of air.

Hannah, her own eyes moist by now, moved to the chair where Petula sat, looking so desolate, perched on the arm, and patted the younger woman gently on the back. "There now," she murmured.

Hannah's touch seemed to calm Pet. "Why don't you take a little rest?"

Petula shook her head in assent. Hannah, who was much too short to put her arm around the tall woman, took her hand like a child and led her into the bedroom. They stayed until Petula fell asleep.

"Each person has to mourn in his own way," Hannah commented as they drove towards the Miller farm. "I don't like to think of her being out there alone, but I cannot make her come home with me. She kept saying, when Matilda comes back, she will need to be with her.

"I will send your mom over with some food. Being a midwife, she is very good with women in distress, whether it is a woman in labor, or not."

Caroline commented, "Pet said she was going to 'think on' where Matilda might be. Something might occur to her."

"She promised to call Benton if it did, but I think she is too upset to 'think on' much besides Copious being dead."

"I don't think the idea of Matilda coming to harm is a concept she is ready to consider."

"I am praying she will not need to," Hannah said with a sigh. "Too much has happened, already."

CHAPTER SIXTEEN

"You go to the florist, Carrie. As much as I would like to go, I need to decide on what to do next," Hannah said after they were in the car. "I will go home and talk to your mom about taking some food over to Petula."

Carrie probably was not too enthusiastic about seeing the florist either, Hannah thought, but she needed to think about something else, even if it was only briefly. Hannah had seen tears in Caroline's eyes from the minute they picked up the note and package from Copious. This time before her wedding should be full of joy, not such sadness.

Hannah and Caroline had a whole pile of broken promises, to Stephen, to Daniel and to each other, not to be involved, but how could they not be? Through no fault of their own, they were part and parcel of this whole sorry mess. Now, the only way open to putting it behind them was to find Matilda before another tragedy clouded their happiness.

"I will just quilt; nothing like quilting to help a person relax," Hannah said. "What else are you doing today?"

"Other than placating Stephen, nothing much. I was going to confirm Molly and my hair appointments and rough-up our new shoes."

"Do what to shoes?"

" Take them out on the patio and scratch up the bottoms, so we won't slip and fall walking down the aisle in them."

"Carrie, I am thinking you are over planning. Isn't this called obsessive?"

Hannah smiled for the first time in an hour.

"It's called a lot worse than that, but I'll spare you the reference."

"Oh, I have heard it," Hannah said, still smiling. "I do not care for references to body parts; I see them in my mind," she said. "As the English say, 'It is not a pretty picture'."

Caroline left Hannah at her door. "At least I left her laughing," Hannah thought.

In Hannah's kitchen, as well as in daughter-in-law Rebecca's house, was a blackboard. That way the busy family kept track of each other by leaving a note on each other's blackboard. Today, Hannah's was full. "Delivering baby at Mary Zinn's; should be home by early this evening. Bethy is doing supper." It wasn't signed, but it wasn't necessary.

Below it was a note from ten- year-old Bethany. "Granny-Susa said we all shud eat at there house at five. Went over early to help. Dad is with me. You shud come, too. If you want. Carrie if she wants, or anybody else to is fine." Hannah made a mental note to help Bethy with her spelling and punctuation.

She looked at the wall clock. It was nearly two now. Her grandson, Josh and his wife, Susannah, lived three miles away. Hannah had walked there many times, but if she was in a hurry, took her buggy and Clara. She had plans before she went to Josh's house, before Caroline returned.

She would take the buggy to Fisher's and see if anyone there could shed light on Matilda's unusual purchases on Monday. At the same time, she would buy some fresh things to take to Petula. Rebecca wasn't home and Hannah didn't have time to cook and investigate all in the same day. She might run by the frozen food lockers and pull out some casserole and drop it by Petula's, too. Their family used commercial freezers or "Frozen Food Lockers" since freezers needed more than the gas power the refrigerators they used did. It was especially helpful for storing meat and casseroles made in quantity, as well as vegetables and fruits in season, although having freezers didn't interfere with canning. Hannah always thought that canning ought to be spelled with a capital C since it was such an event every year. There was fall, winter, spring, and summer canning. There was a summer kitchen at the edge of Hannah's patio, complete with a large sink and a big wood stove. It was there that the canning went on, so they wouldn't heat up the main kitchen. Thank goodness for the commercial freezers, Hannah often said, or the canning would be going on day and night. The Amish really believed in waste not, want not. If they grew it or raised it, they tried to can it. Most English couldn't remember back to when they, too, utilized commercial walk-in freezers. The tourists gawked at the signs along the road in the Amish areas marked: "Frozen Food Lockers."

Hannah readied Clara for the trip. The horse liked nothing better than taking Hannah somewhere; at least Hannah liked to think so. Clara always seemed perkier than usual when she saw Hannah coming, all dressed and ready to go out. It must be boring being a horse Hannah thought, a thought she could appreciate. She didn't want to be put out to pasture anymore than Clara did.

It was a beautiful day, and despite the sadness of the morning, Hannah's spirits lifted as she and Clara set out the few miles to Fisher's Grocery.

Fisher's Grocery, despite its prosaic sounding name, was a large supermarket. It had grown over the years from one room into multiple structures of interconnected wings. Compared to the new supermarkets, in Hannah's opinion, it was exasperating to shop there, even if you knew the layout of the store. They kept changing the location of their stock and it took some backtracking to find everything. Its appeal was folksy friendliness and to the frugal, its lower prices. The frills were few and the amenities scarce. However, like almost everything in the Amish areas, they did provide a hitching rail for horses and buggies.

Hannah left Clara with her usual explanation, "Just be a few minutes." The horse always looked like she understood, Hannah thought.

Since every clerk at Fisher's knew everyone in the district, Hannah did not have to describe Matilda. Not only did they all know her, they knew about Copious, and they knew no one could find Matilda. As Hannah had feared, the police had not yet been there to question them. Hannah tried hard not to misdirect her irritation with the shoddy police procedures at anyone at Fisher's. They were concerned about Matilda, too.

She found the specific clerk who had checked Matilda out, an older woman named Josie.

"Yes, Hannah, I did kind of think her purchases were unusual. Still and all, it is not my place to pry," Josie said, apologetically.

"She didn't say why she was planning a party, and since I wasn't invited, I did not ask. I thought maybe a birthday, or an anniversary, but then I remembered Matilda's birthday and Copious' too, is sometime in the summer. They celebrated together; had a cookout last summer."

When she was reminded, Hannah recalled being invited, but she had been too busy getting Caroline back to Lancaster County to go.

"Josie, do you remember when their anniversary was?"

"No, but I know who would for sure. Laverna would know. She and Jack stood up for them when they was married."

Now Hannah had another place to go. Best-Stoltzfus was on her way home and she could find some reason to stop. The key to the trunk! She could ask if Jack had found it or heard anything. It was a flimsy reason, and she didn't really need a reason to be trying to locate Matilda, but some cautionary instinct told her to… to, what? Copious had killed himself and confessed in a note. But it seemed so pat, so convenient. He confessed to Denny's murder just like that, in a note, and so it was all over? How did he get the poison in Denny's pie, hit him over the head, drag him to the creek and get back to the auction before Hannah left to go sketch. No one saw him leave. Matilda would have had to see him leave, and return. Now she was gone. The shock of Copious' death had subsided and Hannah was starting to think harder. What had brushed by her in the Clay's basement? Was it really Daynight, or Matilda? Who, or what? Over and over in her mind, one line reverberated: Why was Matilda still missing?

Hannah decided to postpone her visit to the health food store. They might know who Matilda's doctor was, but she could ask Laverna. She probably knew. The doctor, whoever he or she was, would not be sharing information with Hannah. Even if Matilda was gone without a trace, there was doctor- patient confidentiality. Now, there was some privacy law, too. They wouldn't tell relatives, if someone was hospital-ized, how the patient was doing. Caroline told her even the police had trouble getting medical information.

Hannah bought the groceries she needed for Petula and drove the buggy to the auction house. Laverna's car was parked behind the office, along with Jack's string of Blue Best-Stoltzfus trucks and vans. They were open and accepting auction items today, and she found both Jack and Laverna in the office. Hannah stood in the doorway, waiting for them to notice her.

Laverna, looking her elegant self once again with every hair in place, stood over Jack, who was seated at his computer, surrounded by piles of paper, looking a bit harassed. "Computer is supposed to make life easier. Some paperless society; don't trust the thing not to crash, so I have to print out everything," he muttered, darkly.

"Jack, I keep telling you, put it on those CD disk things and store it that way," Laverna said.

"You do it, if you are so smart," he said.

"Not me," she protested. "I am too old to learn.'

"And I'm not?"

Hannah cleared her throat and both the Bests jumped.

"Hannah, I hope you are here to tell us Matilda has come back," Laverna said.

"I am not, but wish I was," Hannah answered.

"Any news at all?" Jack asked.

"None. If she stays gone longer, we can report her as a missing person."

"Oh, dear, dear," Laverna said.

"Laverna, who is Matilda's doctor?"

"I don't think she has one, Hannah. She is one of those health food fanatics."

"Well she surely must have gone to a doctor at some point."

"When Ed died, I think Matilda swore off church and doctors at the same time," Laverna said. "She thought both had failed Ed."

"I see," said Hannah, although she did not.

"Oh, I hope Matilda comes home. We could all help her get through this," Laverna said.

"She left a bunch of things on her kitchen counter," Hannah said. "Looked like party fixings. Was it their anniversary?"

"Oh my, no; their anniversary was New Year's Day," Laverna said, her eyes brimming once again. "Matilda, come back," Laverna called softly towards the window.

Jack looked alarmed. "It's okay, Sweetheart," he whispered, as he guided Laverna to a chair.

"It is not all right," she said, sadly.

"The police will soon be helping us find Matilda," Hannah said.

"Lot of help they've been. They can't even find the key to Carrie's trunk," Laverna said, neatly saving Hannah from having to mention it.

"It hasn't turned up here, either?"

Jack shook his head. "It may still, Hannah. This is a big place. She can get a locksmith to make a new one. Then, it will turn up," Jack said, flashing a small smile.

"Wohl, it doesn't matter; I do not know why I even asked. Guess none of us are thinking straight. I think the key is the least important thing right now."

"Why did you stop by, Hannah?" Jack asked.

"I was driving right by. Had to go to Fisher's," Hannah said.

"Oh," Jack said. "Better let you go; it's a warm day to let groceries sit around." He was neatly dismissing her.

Hannah took the hint and left the office. Talk of the warm day, made her thirsty and she stopped at the soft drink machine in the lobby, fished some money out of her pocketbook and was feeding it into the slot to buy water, thinking, I'm so old I remember when water was free. We are so dumb, we are paying for tap water now. Her reverie was interrupted with raised voices coming from the office. She knew she shouldn't listen, but years of habitual eavesdropping got the better of her resolve.

"Snooping...that's what it was." It was Laverna "She knows something, Jack. You are going to have to..."

The phone in the office rang, shutting off further conversation.

Hannah left as fast as she could, leaving her water still in the machine.

After stopping at the Frozen Food Locker, distractedly pulling out a couple of smaller casseroles, and adding a few packages of frozen vegetables, she continued towards home. Her mind was occupied with mulling over the snatches of Jack and Laverna's conversation. It could have been about anyone or anything. Maybe. As Hannah drove, she tried to fit the bits of conversation into various scenarios. Were they hiding Matilda? Did Matilda swear them to secrecy? Was she afraid of someone? Did she have a nervous collapse, and didn't want anyone else to know?

One by one, Hannah discarded her theories. If Matilda was in her right mind, she would not worry Petula, or any of her other friends by hiding, nor would the Bests let Hannah search in vain for Matilda. Surely Jack would not want his flawless reputation ruined by lying to the police when they asked about Matilda, or had he said they asked? Laverna said they had, Hannah recalled. The worst thing a detective could do was drift off into fanciful scenarios unsupported by any facts. It was one thing to follow your gut instincts, another to concoct plots and motives without any reasonable basis to do so.

Hannah was a half mile or so from home, on a particularly winding stretch of road. She hadn't been paying much attention as Clara knew the way. Still, this was a tricky patch, so she urged Clara further onto the road's graveled shoulder. Clara was not fond of loose gravel, and she slowed to a walk. Hannah suddenly heard the roar of an engine, followed by squealing brakes. She was aware of a thud, a blur of a vehicle speeding away, her own voice screaming "Clara!" and then, nothing but blackness.

The next thing she remembered was being poked, rather vigorously by something damp.

She lay on the ground and opened her eyes to see Clara's damp nose inches from her. She forced her eyes open and squinted into the hazy sun, looked away and blinked. Her vision cleared. The horse, still attached to the upright carriage, looked unhurt. Hannah didn't feel any pain and scrambled to her feet. She, too, seemed to be in one piece.

Carefully, she took stock. First, she examined the horse; Clara looked perfectly fine. "Oh, Clara, you could have been killed," Hannah said through tears of relief.

The buggy looked unscathed as well. The wheels were straight and the body square as ever. Whoever hit her was going mercifully slow. The blow which hit the buggy was so glancing that Hannah simply toppled out. Maybe we should have seat belts in buggies, she thought. Most of the fatalities are from folks getting dumped out of the buggies; sometimes they are run over. She shivered with the thought. It happened all too often.

"They could have stopped, the *dummkopfs*," she told Clara, who tilted her head. She tried to think what the vehicle looked like. She had just a glimpse, but her impression was that it was a van and it was red or maybe maroon, or was the red she remembered, from regaining consciousness with the sun in her eyes? It didn't matter. Whoever it was, was long gone and she, Clara and the buggy were fine. She brushed herself off, climbed back into the buggy, and drove home, watching even more carefully. She had already decided to tell no one. There was no reason to get the family, especially Caroline and Stephen, upset.

When she got home, she unhitched Clara, fed and watered her, then for some added attention, brushed her and gave her an extra apple. She was so grateful nothing had happened to the horse, she would have brought her into the house if she could have. Clara probably would bolt if she did and Hannah laughed aloud at her silliness.

Although it seemed like hours since she had last been home, it was not yet five o'clock. She thought of going back to Petula's, but Rebecca would go when she arrived and that would be best. She took the casseroles to Rebecca's kitchen, left a note on the blackboard and returned home. Hannah, who never took naps, lay down on her couch to rest her eyes. Immediately, three cats appeared and climbed onboard. The kitten's settled down at Hannah's stocking feet. They both liked feet. Feet with shoelaces were their favorites, but in a pinch, they'd settle for toes to bat at. Hannah tucked her toes under a pillow, which the kittens promptly settled down on. The older cat, Daisy, sat on the back of the couch, standing guard. Hannah drifted off almost immediately.

It was Bear's insistent barking which awakened her. She heard Caroline's voice calling from the porch. "Granny, you home?"

"Coming, Carrie," Hannah answered. She opened the door.

Caroline stood with a large bouquet of spring flowers in her arms. "Gran, I.... What on earth happened to your eye?".

Whoops, thought Hannah, so much for the tell-no-one idea. She left Caroline standing there and went to the kitchen, sneaking a look at her eye in the kitchen mirror. Oh, no, she had a black eye, or the beginnings of one. Her left eye was bruised and slightly discolored. She should have looked at herself sooner. She could have put one of the bags of cold food on it. Now she would have to tell Caroline. She grabbed a large glass vase from the walk-in pantry and turned to face Caroline who had followed her. "Here," Hannah said, pushing the vase at her.

Caroline didn't say a word until she had filled the vase with water and unceremoniously stuffed the flowers into it.

"What happened? You ran into a door, right? Or did someone punch you for snooping?" Each time Caroline looked at her grandmother, Hannah saw she wanted to laugh. She obviously knew Hannah wasn't hurt otherwise.

"How did the quilting go? Do tell me about your afternoon, Granny," Caroline sat down on a kitchen chair, and glanced at the blackboard. It is after three. Aren't you going over to Susa's?"

"I haven't decided. I was waiting for you," Hannah said. "I have a lot to tell you."

CHAPTER SEVENTEEN

Hannah filled Caroline in on the afternoon's events, as Caroline went through a myriad of emotions including surprise at the Best's conversations and anger at the idiot who could have killed Granny, then fear at what might have been the outcome, relief that it wasn't, and finally amusement at Hannah's painless, but unsightly, black eye.

"Exactly how are you going to explain the shiner?" Caroline asked.

"Allergy?"

"Try again."

"It doesn't even hurt?"

"Only when I look at myself in the mirror. Guess I will have to borrow some dark glasses from you. Do you have any of those rhinestone jobs?"

"Sorry, Granny, not my style."

"Ray Bans, maybe?"

"No designer frames, but I do have an extra pair of plain black ones; I think they would be much more fitting."

"I suppose," Hannah said. "Too bad Jen left; she would have had something jazzier."

"The idea is to underplay this. Remember? And last time I looked, weren't you Amish?"

Hannah got up from the table and opened the refrigerator. "Let's eat, Carrie. I think better on a full stomach." She pulled out a dish of baked chicken, a bowl of green beans and bacon, and some chunky yellow potatoes. Then, she opened the breadbox and pulled out a loaf of white bread. "Don't worry, this is sourdough, not that white gluey stuff everybody eats,' Hannah said. "Fisher's is getting real upscale."

Since Caroline had been away from the Amish so much in the past few years, she had forgotten how fast they ate. While Caroline was still daintily buttering her bread, Hannah had downed her entire dinner.

"Good heavens, Granny, how can you eat so fast? I'd choke if I tried it."

"Remember I had nine kids. If I ate slow, they would have eaten all the food before I got started. Besides, eating slow takes too much time. I know the English think it is a social occasion. The Amish think it is engine stoking time.

"Good thing you do not have much of an appetite; we would never get to discussing what to do," she said and cleared Caroline's half-full plate along with hers. "I will fix you a bag to take home. Do not want to waste anything."

As they sat with a plate of cookies in front of them and sipped coffee, Caroline said, "Here is where it stands. Still no Matilda; I called Benton. He is dragging his feet. You found out he hadn't asked any questions at Fisher's and he told me he is taking the deputy off Matilda's house starting tomorrow. If she hasn't appeared by tomorrow afternoon, we can report her as a missing person and the FBI will get involved."

"Then maybe we can get people with smartz on the case, besides us, that is."

"If we were smart, we would have figured out where she is by now," Caroline countered.

166

"I don't know which I find more curious, the Bests' peculiar conversation or the coincidence of you talking to them and then virtually minutes later, being run off the road."

"Why would anyone want to run me down? No, if they wanted me dead, they could have really smashed into me."

"I wish you wouldn't be so graphic," Caroline said.

"Sorry. But it was only a glancing blow."

"So you think it was a warning?"

"I thought of that, already."

"One of the Bests?"

"Don't know that they would have had time. Besides, I think the truck or van or whatever was red, a dark red, but I am not positive. The Bests or the auction house do not have any red vehicles. I've seen them all, lined up at the auction for years. I know what Jack and Laverna drive and there is nothing of any shade of red."

"But, you're not sure it was red."

"No, just the best guess," Hannah said, setting down her mug of coffee.

"Okay, Granny, let's run with it for the moment. It's all we have. Who around here has a red van, truck, whatever? Not the Hesses, not the Kings, not Petula. Actually I can't think of anyone I know."

Hannah reached for the cookies; the plate was empty. "Carrie you ate all the cookies. Oh, my Gott!" Hannah's face blanched.

"What?" Caroline asked. She knew it was not the absence of cookies Hannah was reacting to.

"Denny Brody's truck was red. It _is_ red!"

"Where is it?"

"Back at Denny's house, I suppose."

"Either that or the police still have it," Caroline said. "I'll call Benton," she said, reaching for her purse and her cell phone.

"He's not there, but I talked to Lee," she said a few minutes later. "Lee said all the evidence was released. Denny's van was returned to his property and secured. Which means locked."

"The car keys, who has those?"

"The set which was found in the ignition was kept by the police. There is probably another set somewhere at Denny's house," Caroline said. "Wouldn't you think?"

"What do I know about keys for automobiles? If it is like a house key, there would be a second one in Denny's house, I guess."

"Carrie, what harm would it be to look there? Maybe we could tell if it was what I thought I saw if I see the car again."

"The police might have garaged it,"

"Not the way I hear it. I hear there is no room in any of Denny's garages. He leaves his truck outside. I have been by that property. It is so ratty looking, I try not to look. It is like looking at someone with a real bad scar – a polite person averts her eyes if she can, and pretends everything is normal."

"I suppose it wouldn't be out of the question to take a quick look," Caroline said, somewhat hesitantly. "But, Granny, as you say, if someone wanted to hurt you, they would have. It has to have been an accident. Who would be driving Denny's van? Why? There must be hundreds of red vans, and red vehicles around. It was probably a tourist. That makes a lot more sense. Why can't we let it go? You know, everything that happens isn't a mystery, or at least not a potential crime to be investigated."

"Your point is well taken, lawyer Caroline." Hannah smiled. "Maybe I have been reading too many mysteries as Matilda said." At the mention of Matilda's name Hannah felt swept by sadness.

"I have to say it. If Matilda has not come home by now, she is not going to. She is gone somewhere else," Hannah said, serious again.

"Something has frightened her, or shock has sent her away. Gott im Himmel!" Hannah stood up. "Why didn't I think of this before?

"Carrie, what if Matilda has gone to Denny's place? She used to live there with Ed King!"

"We should have thought of that sooner. You may be right, but I don't think we should go alone. Matilda could be ill, or ..." At that moment, Caroline's cell phone rang. "It's Stephen. I'm going to have him meet us there, Granny. If Matilda is there, we may need help with her."

Stephen had called to tell Caroline her trunk had been returned by the township police and there was no key with it. When he heard the theory as to where Matilda might be, he readily agreed to meet them there.

"Think we should call the police?" Caroline asked him.

"They won't come. I can hear Benton now, 'Where is the crime?' " Stephen answered. "Well call them if there's a problem. Carrie, don't you and Hannah get your hopes up; Matilda could be anywhere."

"I know, but we need to look where she used to live. We will see you there,"

"Wait for me."

"Well I can tell you, we are not about to knowingly walk into a dangerous situation. Or rush in where angels fear to tread," she said.

"Clever saying; where did you hear that one? Not from Hannah; it's not her mantra for sure. Actually, I wanted to warn you about rats, skunks, who knows what at Denny's place."

"We'll wait," she said.

"Maybe we should take the cats," Hannah said when Caroline relayed Stephen's warning "Really, Carrie. You were raised on a farm; you are not afraid of a few vermin. They are more afraid of you than the other way 'round"

"Wanna bet?"

"Come on, Granny. Let's get over there before it gets any later. I don't want to poke around in that place after dark. Let's take some flashlights."

It didn't take long to get to the Brody property. The place had more of a junk yard look than Caroline had remembered. A dense copse of evergreens half hid the two houses. Maples and oaks and holly grew thickly along the street. A mailbox at the end of the drive hung tipped, its door opened. She could see there was only a lone advertising circular in it. A single lane driveway, lined with boxwood gone wildly untrimmed, led between the clusters of buildings. It looked like there were three barns, several trailers and a couple of storage sheds, in addition to a smaller and a larger house. Boxes and tarps covering who-knew-what, were piled against the sheds. There were also three garages. In front of one was a red van.

"What a disaster! While we wait for Stephen, let's walk around and call for her," Caroline said. "We are not breaking in! No matter what."

Hannah did not answer her, which in Caroline's experience, meant she had heard, but didn't necessarily agree with her. The flatter the statement, or the more it sounded like an order, the less attention Hannah paid to it. Caroline wished she'd been a bit less strident. Too late now; she decided not to press it.

They made a large circle around the two houses, calling out Matilda's name. First, Hannah shouted, then Caroline; sometimes both of them called at the same time, sounding like an off-key Greek chorus. The only noise they heard in response was a scattering of birds, the squawk of blue jays, and alarmed cries of squirrels high in the trees. Hannah made her circle smaller and smaller until she was calling at the windows. "I cannot see in; shades are down."

"Disappointing, I'm sure," Caroline said.

"Wait, I can see in here, just a crack," Hannah was peering in a side window of the larger house. "Oh, it needs a lot of redding up. It is a terrible mess, already."

Caroline joined her at the window, shining her flashlight in, too. It looked like a bedroom. Under piles of clothing, papers, and paper bags, the wooden posters of a bed could be seen. One would have to clamber over all the junk just to get to the bed, and burrow in like a giant chipmunk to get near the mattress.

"Oh, my, how awful," Caroline said. "Matilda wouldn't be caught dead in a place like this," then immediately regretted her words.

Hannah appeared not to have heard. She was already on her way to the smaller house.

Next they circled the out buildings, again calling and still hearing nothing in return. It was getting darker. Caroline and Hannah both had flashlights and Caroline had a cell phone in her pocket, but they had locked their purses in the car.

"Where's Stephen? We're going to need more than these wimpy flashlights, and soon!" The sky was fading from the pinkish hue of a spring sunset to pearl gray with the encroaching darkness.

"Or, we will have to go into one of the buildings where there is electric light, already," Hannah said, mildly.

"I'm calling him," Caroline said. Stephen was not at any of the numbers she tried. He did not answer his cell phone, the phone at the store, or his house. The only responses were voice mail, a recording, and an answering machine. "He must be on his way," she said.

"Why don't we see if the houses are locked? If they're open, we can turn on some lights," Hannah said.

"Okay, Granny. I suppose that's a good idea. If they are un-locked".

Nothing was unlocked, including the trailer and the storage sheds. However, the side door of the oldest-looking barn was unlocked.

"Oh, good," Hannah said. "We can get some light." Inside the door was a metal switch plate. Caroline flipped up the switch. A high wattage light bulb suspended from the rafters lit up the area under it, and cast shadows in the corners.

"It is terrible!," she breathed. "What a horrendous mess!"

Cardboard boxes and plastic bags were heaped and stacked everywhere. Furniture of every vintage from antique to modern held more bags and boxes. Rudimentary aisles were left between the clutter, which in places reached five or six feet high. The air was foul with the odor of mold and decay.

Caroline pointed. "Don't look, but there's a dead mouse in that trap," she said, indicating a shriveled rodent in a trap near the door. "No wonder it stinks. There are probably dead rodents everywhere."

For once Hannah was silent, but not for long. "I had no idea it was this bad," she said. "This is chust terrible, already."

In the middle of a stack of cardboard boxes sat a 1950's model red convertible with the top down. "Even a car in here. What a waste. Someone could drive that, or sell it and put the money to good use."

"I suppose there's no harm in walking around while we wait for Stephen, but stay in the aisles. Something might fall on us if we start climbing around. And watch out for live mice!"

"They will be more frightened of you than you are of them."

"Yeah, right," Caroline answered, her hand over her nose and breathing through her mouth to avoid some of the foul stench. "Dod bed on id."

"What are we supposed to be doing in here, anyhow?" she said, abandoning the attempt not to smell anything. With fresh air coming in through the open door, it was better. "Besides being grossed out?"

"Matilda," Hannah called out loudly.

"What? Do you think she would be in here? She couldn't stand this disaster for a minute."

"Maybe something fell on her and she is trapped. Look at that mess in the corner; anybody could be in here. You would never see them," Hannah said.

"Kind of unlikely she's anywhere in here, Granny. The 'leaving no stone unturned' theory won't work in this place. It would take an army to find anything, or anyone in here."

"I know," Hannah said, quietly.

"Yow!" What is that?" A flutter from the rafters caused both of the women to jump. "A bat?"

It was not a bat, but a piece of cardboard the size of a dress box. They both shone their flashlights toward the rafters.

"There is all sorts of paper stacked up there,"

"More like shoved and piled," Caroline, said sweeping her light over the area. "It might have been dislodged by the reverberations of calling for Matilda. Let's not shout anymore."

"Good thought," Hannah agreed. We should look for a light switch to light the outside. Wouldn't you think there might be one?"

"Granny, I was raised on an Amish farm, remember? What do I know about floodlights?"

"Wohl, Stephen has a barn and you see movies. I figured you might have learned about such things."

"There could be floodlights. Maybe there's a switch on the other wall. But I don't like poking around in here; we could easily dislodge something. I'm concerned about things falling on us. Be very careful."

"Of course; I am always careful," Hannah said, already making her way down the middle aisle toward the car. "We could turn on the car lights."

"It's probably dead – the battery I mean. Cars don't need keys to turn on the lights, I don't think, so if the battery isn't dead...."

By then Hannah had reached the car. "There is no key in the ignition; I was hoping there would be, and some other keys along with it. Maybe house keys, already. Then we would not have to break in, just go in."

Caroline did not bother to get into the finer points of breaking and entering. In this case, who would care? Denny was owner of this place and Denny was dead. But it was a moot point. There were no keys in the ignition.

"Carrie," Hannah suddenly said, her voice shaking.

"What? What's wrong?" Caroline asked, alarmed.

"Look," Hannah was pointing at something caught on the edge of the car's front bumper. As she came closer, she could see it was a woman's pink sweater.

"Oh, Carrie. Matilda has been here and not long ago. She was wearing this sweater on Sunday."

"Are you sure?" Caroline bent closer, and then recoiled. "Oh, no! Granny, there's blood all over it. She shined the light still closer. "The blood is still wet!"

CHAPTER EIGHTEEN

Hannah took a deep breath to steady herself, and quickly said a prayer for Matilda. Then she turned her flashlight into the car itself. The upholstery was red; the carpeting was red. She needed to see if there was blood anywhere else. Why hadn't she brought her reading glasses?

"Carrie, your eyes are better than mine. Do you see any blood in the car? I cannot tell. Caroline climbed in on the opposite side, trying not to touch anything. "I don't see any in here,"

"Keep checking. I'll walk around the car and look on the ground," Hannah said.

"Be careful," Caroline said, from the back seat.

"Of course," Hannah said automatically. She walked around the back of the car. "Oh, Carrie, the keys are in the trunk lock, just hanging there. Looks like to a whole bunch of things," she called. Even though she knew she should not touch anything, she reached out for the keys and turned them to pull them out. The trunk lid came open; she had to jump back to keep from being hit as it rose. She briefly flicked her flashlight into its interior.

Later, she didn't know which of the ensuing events happened first. Was it her own ear piercing scream as she saw the bloodied body of Matilda Clay, staring back at her, or the rafters above them raining down a storm of debris?

It must have all happened in a matter of seconds, but to Hannah it seemed like eons. Instinctively, she dove under the car for protection and called out to warn Caroline. When the deluge from the rafters stopped, Hannah tried to free herself while calling Caroline's name over and over. There was no answer. Finally, Hannah stopped calling, worried about dislodging more of what seemed like a ton of cardboard, newspaper rags, and dust. The light hanging from the rafters showed air thick with dust swirling around in a whirling-dervish cloud. By now, she had managed to climb out through a stack of debris a couple of feet high. "Carrie," she coughed, and called again, and again.

There was no answer, and it took Hannah a few more minutes to see Caroline in the back seat. She had her head down and Hannah could see her back rising and falling. She was breathing, thank God. She was also unconscious, and it did not take Hannah more than a moment to see the probable cause. A piece of thick particle board was suspiciously close to her head. It looked like it had fallen on her and bounced off, lodging in the seat. Hannah couldn't see a mark on Caroline, or any sign of blood.

She had to get help, and quickly. Where was Stephen? She couldn't risk moving Caroline in case she had a neck or a head injury. And, how far could she get? The interior of the barn was impassable now that the path was full of debris. Even with the brief look Hannah had at Matilda, she knew she was beyond anything Hannah could do for her. Hannah had seen enough bodies to know that Matilda hadn't been dead long, but she was definitely gone.

Hannah still had the keys clutched in her hand and she slipped them into her pocket.

Carefully she climbed into the car with Caroline, a task made easier by the pile of cardboard which had settled next to the car. She checked Caroline's pulse and found it strong and regular. Closer up, she saw a welt rising from the front of her granddaughter's head. She had, as Hannah thought, been knocked out by the particle board. What she couldn't locate was Caroline's cell phone. She gently frisked Caroline, searching where she could reach. She couldn't find it; the phone was lost in the mess.

Stephen wasn't there yet either, or else he didn't hear the cave-in and didn't know where they were. Pulling the offending particle board over Caroline and herself as some protection, she tried calling out for Stephen. On the third call, more stuff tumbled down. She couldn't risk it.

What could she do? Praying for inspiration didn't seem to be helping much. Calling out was no good, and could make things worse.

Suddenly, she remembered the keys in her pocket. Caroline had warned her that the car battery might be dead. Even if it wasn't, she couldn't risk the noise of honking the horn. It might finish off the cave-in and them with it. She wasn't sure you needed a battery to honk. But if the car battery was not dead, could she drive out? This was one terrible time to learn how to drive. The furthest thing from her mind was to worry about being chastised by the bishop for driving. Even he would understand the urgency of the situation. As if in affirmation of her decision, several small pieces of particle board tumbled down, one narrowly missing her. She listened and heard an even more ominous sound, a groaning, wrenching noise from overhead. It could mean the whole place was caving in.

Slowly and cautiously she climbed into the front seat and tried the keys. It took her just one try to get the right key to fit in the ignition. She turned it and the engine turned over. Without any help from her, the car had started.

Now, what next? She had to drive about thirty feet. And, go fast enough to propel the car through the debri and barn door without crashing and careening off of it. Going too slowly might not do anything but knock the whole place down on them. It was a terribly risky thing to do, but she couldn't just stay here and wait for it to happen, anyway. She wished she knew how to get the top up to protect them, but it was cloth and could not afford them much in the way of safety. At least the car was heading in the right direction. Carefully, she looked at the controls and the gas pedal. Thank God, there seemed to be only two pedals. Stop and go, she guessed. There did not seem to be one of those clutch things. That was what stalled cars as she knew from something she had read. She reached cautiously into the glove box. There was a manual, but there wasn't time to read it. On its cover it read: "1955 Dynaflow", whatever that meant. A further groan came from the rafters. It sounded very threatening.

Hannah tried the left pedal, but nothing happened. That must be what is called the brake; the right must be go, but nothing happened when she gently pushed that. She was so short she could barely see over the wheel. She knew where she wanted to get to without being able to see. Getting there was the problem. What if she didn't have enough gas? She looked at the other things on the control panel. There was a gauge marked "Fuel", and a needle indicating it was full. Quickly she looked at the instruction book. Thank goodness she had taught herself to speed-read. She had neglected to take off the brake, and then there was the lever thing. It had to get into "D" for drive. Then she should be able to push the go pedal all the way down and if God was willing, get them out of this horrible place before it came down around their heads.

Ever so slowly she tried the lever to put in into drive and it went there easily. She reached down and pulled at the brake release. It, too, cooperated. She craned her head back and glanced back at Carrie, who was still half on the floor and had not moved from under the protective covering of the particle board. Her color looked okay and Hannah could see her chest moving. Hannah hadn't shut the trunk after the shock of seeing Matilda there, but that didn't seem to matter. Even if Matilda flew out, it was only her body. Her soul was far beyond this place.

Hannah turned around, put her hands firmly on the wheel and said a final prayer. It was now or never time. She scooted down to get her small foot firmly planted on the accelerator, and then pushed it with all her might. The car bumped and bolted down the pathway and shot through the door with a loud splitting of wood. As soon as it had cleared the door, Hannah turned off the key. The car shuddered to a stop inches from a tree.

The next thing she saw was Stephen's van turning into the driveway. He had a look of absolute horror on his face. Simultaneously, she heard the earsplitting noise of the barn collapsing behind them.

CHAPTER NINETEEN

"I missed Granny driving?" Caroline asked, after she regained consciousness. She was sitting next to Stephen, her head on his shoulder, holding a plaid ice bag on her right eye. They were at her condominium, and it was almost nine o'clock.

Caroline had regained consciousness in time to see the barn collapsing, and the police arrive, led by Wayne Lee, looking mightily chagrined, and later, to see his head going from side to side as Hannah related what had happened.

After being looked at by an EMT, Caroline had been taken to Meadow Community Hospital, examined and given the okay to go home. She had a bump on the head, but no severe concussion. When she gave her name, the emergency room nurse commented that the Millers "sure are specializing in bumps on the head lately." She eyed Hannah's shiner, but seeing it wasn't recent and probably received earlier than that evening, said nothing.

"Wohl," Hannah said, "you also missed finding Matilda's body. Believe me, it was a good time to be knocked out cold. Thank God you were spared that discovery. It is easier for me; I am old and used to finding dead bodies," Hannah said matter-of-factly.

"Unfortunately," Stephen concurred. He pulled back and held Caroline at arm's length, scrutinizing her discolored and bruised eye.

"If this was less serious, I would say the hers-and-hers matching shiners are very rakish – a family trait which I hope Molly will not be developing."

"Black and blue humor, Stephen?" Hannah asked.

"Sorry, Hannah; I guess that was inappropriate," Stephen apologized.

"Being sad and shocked Matilda died is one thing, but she would not want us to sit around crying," Hannah said. "Much as we might wish to, we cannot bring her back, except to remember her when she was here. She would want us to celebrate her life and, I might add, find her killer.

"The thought of all of this being coincidence is nonsense. It is all connected and we must find the link, or no one will feel safe."

"By all of this, you mean --- what, Hannah?"

"Wohl, Stephen, while we sat at the hospital waiting, I had time to think this out. I have been incubating some on a thought I had earlier when Carrie and I were at the Clays. When she found her present to you..."

"Gran!" Caroline said.

"I know how to keep a secret, Carrie. I will not say what it is."

"Good," Caroline responded, and repositioned the ice bag she was holding against her eye.

"Copious left the package and a note along with the bill. And it occurred to me how careful and neat his printing was, and that was good because he did it without a computer; then I wondered on and I thought how much time it took nowadays to do business, billing and the like, without a computer.

"Wohl, I put that in the back of my mind and did not think on it again until it came to me at the hospital. Maybe Matilda's death made me wonder again, hard."

"I'm not following you, Granny," Caroline said.

"I am getting to it, Carrie. What I am thinking is that if Copious did not have a computer, how did he write the suicide note? And why was the printing so big?"

Caroline dropped the ice bag as she stood up. "Good God, Granny, it was right there all the time!"

Caroline was following Granny's train of thought and it was even more horrific as she brought it to its logical conclusion. "Matilda was murdered. If Copious' suicide was staged and he didn't kill himself, maybe he didn't kill Denny, either."

Now Stephen was standing. "What the hell is going on around here, and how could we not have seen it sooner?"

"Maybe we did, but it was too awful to think possible," Hannah said. " So we jumped to the easy solution. We did not think smartz."

"Now, there are three killings and not even a glimmer as to of who the killer is," Caroline added.

"I need to step up the detecting," Hannah said.

Caroline sat down, trying to think what she could possibly say that would make Hannah leave matters entirely to the police, no matter what they had asked of her. Granted their track record was bad, but the danger was becoming too great for Caroline's comfort. Trying to get Hannah to give up on the case was going to be some job!

If she tried to tell Hannah flat out, she shouldn't or couldn't take the chance, it would make her grandmother more determined. Hannah would still do it, but would not share what she was up to and it would be more dangerous, and Caroline would obsess on what Hannah was doing without her.

The thought of running off to be married somewhere else and taking the family, to get them all away briefly, crossed her mind. Her head hurt and her eye smarted. She had to talk to Stephen alone. Together they had to formulate a plan to keep Hannah out of this, before something else happened.

"Hannah," Stephen said, quietly, but firmly, "You realize, don't you, that the so-called accident with the buggy today was most likely a warning to you? You have been asking questions all over town. You simply have to pull out of this. Right now! For your sake, for Carrie's sake, for the rest of your family's sake, you have to let this go!"

He had said the right thing, Caroline knew, by Hannah's face. Determination was replaced by disappointment, and then acceptance.

"You are right, Stephen. Matilda does not need us to find the murderer. Neither do Copious or Denny. They are in the Lord's hands, now."

That speech was as much of an apology from Hannah as they were going to get. And as far as Caroline cared, an apology wasn't needed, just an assurance.

Whoever the killer was, didn't want Hannah dead or she wouldn't have received warnings. It was high time to heed them.

"I'm calling Benton now," Stephen said, fishing in his pocket for the policeman's card. I don't think he's going to blow me off this time. He sure can't say Matilda committed suicide, not unless she's a contortionist, shot herself in the back of the head and climbed into a trunk and locked it from the outside."

Magician would be more like it, Caroline thought.

Stephen dialed the number and was put on hold to wait for Benton. He put the call on speaker phone, so Hannah and Caroline could hear.

Caroline warned Hannah that Benton would be able to hear them, too, so watch her comments. She had visions of Hannah muttering "Dumassel." or some equally flattering remark, in Pennsylvania Dutch, German, or even English. She had very little tolerance for Benton as it was. If he started acting like he usually did, woe was he, Caroline thought. Granny would not hesitate in taking him on.

There was only one thing that annoyed Hannah more than inept-ness, and that was being called "dear," even by someone her own age, let alone a younger person. Caroline thought Hannah was safe from Chief Benton calling her anything like "dear," "sweetie," "honey," or other demeaning, insipid terms used for older people. After seeing how irritatingly direct Hannah could be, Benton probably had some other, not so innocuous, names in mind for her.

"Benton," the voice of the chief came on the line.

"Chief, this is Stephen Brown. I have Mrs. Miller and Caroline Miller here with me. Okay to put you on speaker phone?"

"Yeah, sure," Benton said. Caroline thought he sounded harassed, or maybe she just thought he should be. "How they doing?"

"They're fine, thanks"

Stephen then related their suspicion about Copious Clay's note.

"Maybe Clay knew someone with a computer; been planning it a while."

"Why would he write a note with a computer at all? Why not just write it by hand?

When you think about it, none of it makes much sense. We saw him the day before. He didn't act suicidal. He seemed to be perfectly normal," Stephen added.

"I've heard that when a guy decides to off himself, he gets in a good mood; like he's made the decision and then gets real calm ... even happy."

Hannah looked as disgusted as if she had tasted moldy food or lemon pith, but she didn't say anything.

Stephen went on. "What is the coroner saying about the wound?"

"Clay's or Mrs. Clay's?"

"Both."

Benton hesitated. "They just got to Mrs. Clay."

"Okay, then tell me about Clay's." Caroline heard an annoyed note in Stephen's voice, but Benton, or anyone else who didn't know him, would probably miss it. She always paid attention when she heard it. It was the precursor of his courtroom tenacity, and tougher questions would be next.

"Are the ladies still listening? Do you think they...?"

"Yes, go ahead."

"He died from blood loss. From a wound to the left carotid artery. We figure he had to have done it himself. If someone else did, he would have had time to fight or stumble around, which he didn't."

"Any alcohol or drugs in his system?"

"No alcohol; labs on drugs aren't back yet. We figured for a suicide with a note, there was no rush, if you know what I mean."

"I'm not sure I do know what you mean, Chief."

"Well, it's on the back burner, now that Mrs. Clay was found."

"She couldn't have been a suicide."

"Well, it's possible, except there isn't a weapon; least not that we found. Nothing in the car. It is going to take days and days to get into that pile of crap... sorry, ladies, I forgot you were on the squawk box. The barn; we have to sift through that whole place."

"You are calling this a homicide, a possible homicide, what?"

"Well, it could be either, or could be another suicide."

"How convenient," Hannah said in a whisper.

"Excuse me," Benton said. "I didn't get that."

"Have you found the sweater I mentioned in my statement, Chief?" Caroline asked.

"The one you thought you saw?"

Hannah had enough. "The one we both saw, with the fresh blood. It was in front of the car, caught on the bumper."

"No sign of it. You probably drove over it. We don't know where to start looking for it now."

"I was not thinking of evidence at the time, Chief. I was trying to get us out before the place caved in." Hannah's face was getting red.

"Too bad you had to scream," Benton said.

Hannah looked up. Praying for patience, Caroline thought. Hope it works.

"This is getting us nowhere, Chief," Stephen broke in. "I'd appreciate knowing what the labs and the coroner come up with. You can depend on our discretion. Anything you tell us will be kept in confidence."

"I think we can handle this, Mr. Brown. We might have to eventually call in some help with the barn. Right now, we are calling Mrs. Clay a possible homicide. All depends if we can find the gun."

"And Copious?"

"Still a suicide. As I said, he stabbed himself in the carotid artery with a jeweler's engraver; the jewelers call it a 'graver'. Coroner found a bracelet, one of those medical alert things, on him. It said he was taking a blood thinner. So he'd bleed out pretty damn fast."

"I see."

Stephen's mild comment didn't match the fierce look on his face. "We'll keep in touch."

Stephen hung up the phone without saying thank you, or goodbye or any of the usual niceties.

"Good control, Stephen," Hannah said. "I was expecting you to throw the whole phone, squawking box and all, clean across the room."

"Wouldn't do us much good, Hannah."

"You didn't tell him Granny's buggy was hit. Why?" Caroline looked puzzled.

"Really, Love, do you think he would even take it a bit seriously? With all he has on his plate? The jerk isn't even taking a murder, no, make that three murders, seriously.

"I can envision the scenario forming in Benton's mind. He would like nothing better than to say Matilda was depressed; she found Copious, who had committed suicide, with a jewelry tool for God's sake, because he was remorseful over poisoning, then smashing Denny Brody in the head. For the already depressed Matilda, that was the final straw. After all, her first husband was said to have been a suicide. So she went to the place she was once happy, where she lived with Ed King, got in an old car trunk, shot herself, tossed the gun somewhere in the barn, threw her bloody sweater clear over the car, lay down with a bullet hole in her head, pulled the trunk lid down and conveniently died."

By now, Stephen was pacing around the room like an inmate at the zoo, and growling under his breath to spare Hannah the expletives he was undoubtedly thinking.

Caroline glanced at Granny who sat, looking stunned by Stephen's words. Laying out the whole thing made it look horrific. It wasn't only the mishandling that was so crystallized in Stephen's summation; it was the gravity of what had happened and how it had escalated. Caroline didn't want to say aloud what she was thinking. What now?

As if he had read her mind, Stephen said, "I'm calling Tom Palo at the FBI Field Office in Philadelphia. I need to see what can be done before that damn fool Benton sits around long enough for someone else to get killed. He will fool around until the media attention forces him to do something."

187

"Can't the FBI just come in and take over?" Hannah asked. "I do not know that much about the FBI."

"Only under certain circumstances. The state has primary jurisdiction. I want Tom's advice," Stephen answered. He was still pacing, but, now, with a plan in mind, he looked less angry.

"If there is a reasonable assumption Matilda was kidnapped, they can step in," he continued. "No question about jurisdiction," he said, addressing Hannah. "Kidnapping is a federal crime."

"There are several vehicles on Denny's property, including the red truck," Stephen continued. "Matilda may have been brought to the barn in that. If she was abducted, whoever did it wouldn't want to have their car seen. What better cover than a truck that belonged to a dead guy?"

"Keys?" Caroline asked. "How would someone get the keys? I suppose anybody who knew anything could hot wire it or break into Denny's house and find a second set."

"Not if both houses on the place were as messy as the one we saw into," Hannah said. "Less they knew where to look, or got lucky."

"Granny, weren't there other keys with the ignition key?"

"I think," Hannah paused, "Yes! There was a set of keys. I was not exactly thinking of the other keys. I was too busy trying to get us out of there."

I wish Stephen would stop pacing, Caroline thought. He's wearing off the finish on my hardwood floor.

"Hannah, you think you were hit by a red truck? Who knows what car was used to transport Matilda? It could have been the car you drove out of the garage, although I very much doubt if anyone, unless they didn't have anything else, would use that one if they were trying to keep a low profile. Everybody would notice it. It's not like there are a lot of 1955 Buicks around. Besides, that barn was so full of debris, no one could have gotten the car back in and rearranged the junk without a fair amount of time. Why bother, with any number of other vehicles available?" Stephen was considerably less agitated than he had been, and he stopped pacing, but didn't sit down.

"Before Benton and his people paw around and possibly compromise any evidence, I'd like to see that truck examined," he continued. "All we need to find there is one link to Matilda."

"DNA?" Hannah said, sounding interested.

"Right, or any physical evidence."

"Realistically, Denny's property, even without the evidence buried in the barn, is more than Chelsea Township can handle. Won't Benton have to call in the State Police?" Caroline asked. Her head was throbbing and she transferred the ice bag to press it against her forehead, rattling the ice into place.

"He is going to grandstand as long as he can. But he will have to call for help eventually. Let's see what Tom advises," Stephen added. He turned and eyed Caroline. "You look awful."

"Thanks," she said. "And, I love you, too."

"I'm serious, Carrie; you need to get some rest. My head is starting to hurt, thinking of the day you two have had. Hannah, are you staying here tonight, or do you want me to take you home? Then I'll come back. In case Carrie needs anything in the night."

"Maybe I'd better stay; who is going to chaperone the two of you?" Hannah said, with what Caroline recognized as a mock-serious tone.

"Why, Granny, there is a bundling board down the middle of my bed."

"Good, then you won't kick me," Hannah said.

"Very amusing, Granny; you are sleeping in the guest room. No way am I going to share a room with someone who only sleeps a couple of hours, and then starts 'redding-up' the house."

Wohl, you know," Hannah said. "Redding-up around here goes lots faster than at my house. You have all sorts of electric cleaning gadgets."

Hannah, who often stayed over, kept extra clothes and toiletries in Caroline's guest room, so it wasn't a problem for her to spend a night without anyone at the Miller house worrying, but after a day like they'd had, Stephen decided to stop by and fill the family in.

"I'm not looking forward to telling your family about today, or about Matilda."

"You might leave out the part about me driving," Hannah suggested.

"Oh, sure, Granny, dream on. They'll hear about it fast enough."

"Poor, poor Matilda," Hannah said, serious once more. "And Petula; now she is really all alone. I'll go home first thing in the morning and Rebecca and I will go over to Petula's with some food. Maybe now, Petula will come stay with me for a while."

Don't count on it, Caroline thought. Pet was a very independent woman, and could be very stubborn.

"Later, I'll go with you to see Laverna and Jack," Caroline said. "Laverna is going to be a basket case. Matilda was a good friend; it will be a big loss to her, too."

"Least she has Jack to comfort her. He is a blessing – steady as Clara in a crisis. "

CHAPTER TWENTY

Hannah got up at 4 a.m. and peeked in Caroline's door. She was sleeping peacefully beneath the covers, and Stephen, who was still dressed, minus shoes and jacket, lay on his side, on top of the blanket, with one arm around her. Hannah felt like waking him and suggesting he at least cover up. Instead she brought an extra quilt from the guest room and covered him. Neither Caroline nor Stephen moved. They must be exhausted, Hannah thought.

Stephen had come back at eleven, looking completely drained. Caroline had already gone to bed, and Hannah only asked him, "Okay at the farm?"

"Yes. What could they say?"

"Not much, I suppose. Thank you, Stephen. Go to bed; I'll talk to you in the morning."

He nodded, bent down, and gave her a hug. "Good night, Hannah," he said and went into Caroline's room, leaving the door open.

By five o'clock, Hannah had quietly showered and dressed. Her eye felt fine, but looked dreadful. It would worry Rebecca and Daniel something awful if they saw that eye. Caroline could maybe hide hers, Hannah thought, but she could not. On Caroline's vanity lay an array of cosmetics. Maybe later she would try to cover up the worst of the bruise with that little stick marked "concealer." It was more of a medicine than a cosmetic, she supposed. Better to put that on her eye than walk around with dark glasses, bumping into things because she couldn't see.

She looked around for something to do, and going into Molly's bright, jonquil yellow room, saw the perfect chore for a quiet time.

On the chair, covered by a light piece of plastic, lay the dress Caroline had made for Molly, the one she would be wearing as a flower girl. It was cream colored, silk moiré with puffed sleeves, and scattered with pastel flowers made by hand from silk satin ribbon. When Jennet had seen it, she had told Caroline she should be a designer. It was so light, it almost floated, Hannah thought, picking it up carefully. A roll of matching thread and the sewing basket were nearby. The hem had been basted, but Caroline hadn't had time to finish it. Hannah spent the next hour, carefully hand hemming it with almost invisible, tiny stitches.

She took the sewing basket and put it in the guest room closet where she knew Caroline kept it and saw all the extra fabric and scraps Caroline had left over from sewing her dress and Molly's. Hannah wondered if Caroline would part with the smaller scraps. She could make a wall hanging for Caroline and for Molly as of some sort as a keepsake of the wedding. She'd ask about it later. Maybe she could sketch something while it was on her mind. It was then she remembered her sketchpad, the one she'd dropped the day of Denny's killing. The police must have found it, but she never got it back. She would call as soon as she thought someone who might know about it was there.

Molly's window faced east and Hannah watched the black sky lighten to pearly gray, then a few minutes later to pink. Rain, she thought. In Hannah's experience of forecasting the weather on a farm without a weather report, a red sky in the morning foretold rain. It might as well rain today. Even from the sky, tears would be appropriate. Wash everything fresh, and then the sun could shine until after Caroline's wedding.

Molly's shoes were nearby. How sweet these are, Hannah said to herself, as she examined the soft creamy leather shoes. She turned them over. They were slick on the bottom. No wonder Caroline said they needed to be roughed up on the soles. Another chore to keep Hannah occupied until she fixed breakfast. She walked through the kitchen and let herself out through the sliding glass door to the aggregate patio. Good thing she was dressed, she observed. The patio was clearly visible from the street. Caroline's condo was only a year old and the shrubbery was still new and kind of *strubly*, Hannah thought, using the "Dutch" word for unkempt. Could use a gardener around here. If Caroline and Molly weren't waiting to move to Stephen's house, she thought, and then stopped herself. No, she was going to ease off the interference. Caroline and Stephen were about to be a family. She would wait until asked to help. Or at least try to. Cannot change an old dog into a pussycat all at once, or whatever the English saying was.

She reached down and roughed up one, then the other sole, checking to make sure it was enough to keep them from slipping, but not so much they would be worn out too fast. Knowing Caroline's sense of frugality, Molly would wear them many times until she outgrew them.

As she straightened up, she had an instinctive, wary sense of being watched. Going back into the house, she switched off the patio lights and the kitchen lights as well. Her eyes adjusted and she saw a dark colored car parked across the street. She could see there was someone in the driver's seat, but she couldn't see the driver well enough to tell more. Maybe waiting to pick up somebody for work, for one of those car pools? Why would anyone watch Caroline's house? It was nonsensical. The experiences she had finding dead people was making her jumpy and worse, fanciful. Guess it could not be helped. She just had to let logic settle her nerves, she told herself sternly.

Well, it would not hurt to take a better look. She knew Caroline had a strong pair of binoculars for watching birds. As Hannah recalled, they were with the bird guide in the bookcase on a low shelf so Molly could reach them. She found them and went, not to the patio door, but to the kitchen window where she could see across the street but wouldn't be so vulnerable to being seen herself. It was not a van, not a truck, but she couldn't be sure about the color. If it stayed a while longer, it would be light enough to tell; she tried to focus on the driver, but the windows must be tinted. She could see movement, but no other details. This was silly; she put the binoculars back along with the bird book. Maybe she did read too many mysteries.

She picked up the white shoes. There was a noise behind her, and she clutched Molly's shoes tighter. "Oh?" she said.

"Good morning, Granny. Did I startle you?" Caroline stood in the kitchen doorway, in her blue nightgown. Its color unintentionally matched her slightly bruised eye..

"Not really; I did not hear you coming. Good morning, Carrie. How are you feeling?"

"Okay. My head is fine and my eye is hardly bruised. All that ice helped, I guess."

"Stephen is still asleep. Are those Molly's shoes?"

"I roughed them, like you wanted. Had to do something. I also hemmed Molly's dress," Hannah said. "I will do your shoes if you want to get them." Hannah was chattering, something she did when she felt guilty. Right now, she felt chagrined about her clandestine activity of watching a perfectly innocent car. Worrying about being observed, indeed. What was she thinking?

"How about moving in? I might be able to get everything done before the wedding." Caroline smiled.

Hannah thought everyone was trying very hard to be lighthearted. She hoped Stephen wouldn't come out of the bedroom singing some corny English show tune.

"Maybe. But, if I stayed, you'd soon throw me out. I am pretty bossy," Hannah said.

"Really? I wouldn't have known that if you hadn't told me."

"Go make the coffee; I do not know how to use that new electric percolator, but you can show me."

"Yes; right away," Caroline said, padding into the kitchen. "Come on, Boss Lady," she called over her shoulder. "I also have a new electric waffle iron you haven't seen."

Hannah sneaked a look out the window, but the vehicle was gone.

After breakfast, Stephen left to go to the store to call his friend, Tom, at the FBI. He hadn't said a word to either Hannah or Caroline about being careful, but he knew their errands today had nothing to do with investigation, but everything to do with sympathy and mourning.

Neither one of them was thinking about much else. Hannah wondered if Petula had someone with her. Despite repeated attempts to get her on the phone, it was busy every time Hannah had tried calling. Either Petula was getting a lot of condolence calls or she had taken the phone off the hook, Probably the latter, Hannah thought.

Hannah tried calling the Bests at home. Jack answered on the first ring.

"Laverna and I spent the night out there, Carrie. The doctor had to be called for Petula and didn't want her left alone," he said. "Laverna is pretty torn up about it, too."

Caroline and Hannah drove to the Miller farm to pick up Rebecca, and the food Hannah had purchased. Rebecca was waiting for them. "Hmm," she said, looking at the two discolored eyes. "Pretty picture you both will make at the wedding."

"Don't you think they will be gone by then?" Caroline asked.

"Doesn't matter none; you will be able to powder it over."

"Now, as for you, Granny," Rebecca looked sternly at Hannah. "Since you are not supposed to wear cosmetics ... you will just have to pray hard it fades fast."

Hannah knew her daughter-in-law's sense of humor, and that she was "funning."

"Wohl, I better start praying right this minute; it is going to take a lot of praying time," Hannah said, starting to get down on her knees.

"Come on, you two, we have a lot to do," Caroline said. "Sometimes, I think I'm the only one with any dignity around here."

"Lighten up, Carrie," Hannah said. "There are too many tears already." Hannah understood Caroline's seriousness. She was so like her father; even as a little child she was solemn. Must be inherited, Hannah thought. Although Caroline had a sense of fun, she kept it in check most of the time. Having Molly was helping. You can't raise a child unless you have a sense of humor. Molly was a merry little girl, like her grandfather, Gil Brown, and like Stephen. And like me, Hannah thought with some satisfaction.

They carried the food Hannah had bought to the car. Rebecca had put together an additional basketful. She had also picked a big bouquet of daffodils and hyacinths. The heady fragrance filled the interior of Caroline's car. "We are maybe going to have to help Petula arrange for the funerals. That is one place I cannot help much," Hannah said.

"I'll do what I can; maybe the Kings can help," Caroline said. "The funeral is either going to have to wait until the coroner releases the bodies, or just be a memorial service. That would certainly be easier on Pet. Let's see what she wants."

When they reached Pet's house, several cars sat in the drive. A non-descript looking gray sedan was parked next to Laverna and Jack's cars, along with a black sedan which Hannah recognized as that of Carl Osgood, the funeral director whom Jennet had used when her sister, Nettie, died. The license plate frame discreetly advertised its business: "Osgood Funeral Home."

"May be the Bests have already arranged things," Caroline observed, a hopeful note in her voice. "Who does that gray car belong to?"

"I do not think if I have ever seen it, but there are lots of gray cars around. They all look the same," Rebecca commented.

"It is as not as bad as Amish buggies. The only way you can tell whose is whose, is if you know the horse. Even then ..." Hannah said, her voice trailing off as the door to the house opened. A small woman dressed in a black skirt and gray turtleneck sweater stood, waiting. Her most distinguishing characteristic was her long dark hair, streaked with gray.

At Caroline's quizzical look, Hannah shook her head. Rebecca didn't seem to recognize her either. Hannah knew her daughter-in-law's habit of tilting her head when she was puzzled. It was tilted as she glanced at the woman beckoning them in.

"Need help?" The woman shouted as she saw them unloading the trunk. Hannah walked around Caroline's car in a big circle, trying to get a better look at the gray car, as if she'd know much by just looking; Rebecca was right; darn things all looked alike.

"No, thanks," Caroline called back.

"I'm Boots Osgood," she said when they got closer. "Think you know my husband, Carl."

Caroline introduced herself, Hannah and Rebecca.

197

Hannah thought "Boots" was an unlikely name for a woman who was at least fifty. "Is 'Boots' short for something?" The Amish were fond of nicknames themselves, but mostly to distinguish people with the same Amish name. Hannah knew men named John Yoder, with nicknames like Shorty Yoder or Johnny Yoder or Butcher Yoder. The nickname was often based on a physical characteristic or occupation. Hannah saw no boots on "Boots."

"Yes," Boots said. "It is short for Bernedetta."

"Oh, I see," Hannah said, politely.

Boots laughed gleefully. "Yes, everyone 'sees' when they hear my real name. My mom was reading some romance novel when she was expecting me." She glanced towards the house and lowered her voice. "Petula is inside with the pastor, and the Bests."

"Petula has a pastor?" Hannah asked. As far as she knew, Petula wasn't a churchgoer. She was usually at a weekend flea market like The Black Angus where she had shares in a booth on Sundays.

"I guess; he is in there. Could be Laverna called him," Boots answered.

"Your husband?" Caroline asked. "Is he here, too?"

"He's doing a funeral today, so he sent me with condolences. The Clay remains are still resting with the police, you know," she said in a hushed voice, and bowed her head slightly.

Hannah thought Boots presence a bit of an intrusion, but maybe Pet had called her, so she tried to be polite. "Pretty pin you are wearing," Hannah said, noticing an unusual leaping dolphin in front of a small rock design.

"Thank you," Boots answered. "It's the cremains of my mother."

"What is 'cremains'?" Hannah asked.

Out of the corner of her eye, Hannah saw an appalled look on Caroline's face.

"Oh, some call it ashes; what's left when someone is cremated," Boots said. "It's the style now, to remember the departed. You can even have faux diamonds made from the cremains. Sure beats cutting their hair like the Victorians did and weaving it into a brooch."

It was Hannah's turn to look aghast. For once she was struck dumb.

Boots chattered on. "We even had our dog, Fleabag's, cremains made into a little bone; he loved bones. It's on our mantle."

Remind me not to visit Boots, Hannah thought. Her whole house is probably filled with cremains.

"Petula will be happy to see you," Boots added, carefully wiping her feet on Pet's doormat, and beckoning them in. "She's in the bedroom with Laverna."

Just what Pet needs, Hannah thought an unofficial greeter, mourner and saleswoman, hovering like a turkey buzzard waiting for the "cremains." I am becoming a cynic, she chided herself. Could be Boots is a friend of Petula's.

Juggling the food, they walked into Pet's house to see a strange man draping black cloth over Pet's lampshades.

"Who might you be and what is it you are doing?" Hannah asked directly.

"Pastor Ben Samuels," he said, answering half of Hannah's question. He stuck out his hand, not observing that all three women's hands were full of containers He was very short and thirty or so, but already balding, with a shiny, high forehead and sandy colored hair badly in need of a trim.

Hannah was not to be deterred. "What are you doing to Petula's lamps?"

He reached down and swept Petula's carefully arranged decorating magazines off her coffee table and unceremoniously stuffed them under the couch. Oh my, Hannah thought, I do not like this man at all. "Our faith calls for a strict climate of reverential mourning," he intoned.

Sackcloth and ashes? Hannah wondered. "What faith might that be?" she asked.

"First Faith Free Will Tabernacle Church; the FFFWTC."

For a minute, no one said anything. Hannah hadn't heard of the church, and she doubted Caroline or Rebecca had either. "Has your church been around long?"

"Oh, years," Pastor Ben said

"How many years?" Hannah asked.

"Several."

"How many do you mean by several?"

He stopped his redecorating efforts and glared at Hannah. "Almost two," he answered.

"I see," Hannah said. "The Amish church has been around for five hundred years," she couldn't resist adding. She didn't trust this man, and she always listened to her instincts.

Hannah was beginning to enjoy his discomfort. She often thought if she hadn't been born Amish, she would make a good lawyer.

"You have a church in Lancaster County?" she continued her interrogation.

"Not quite yet. We are like the Amish; we meet in our members' homes. We are in the midst of a worldwide fund campaign. For church expansion."

"Worldwide? How many churches do you boast?" She couldn't resist using the word boast; it seemed so appropriate. She glanced at Caroline who was looking at the pastor with what Hannah recognized as a look of distaste. Rebecca had gone into the kitchen and Hannah heard the refrigerator door opening and closing as her daughter-in law put the food away. The back door opened, and she could hear Jack Best's booming voice greeting Rebecca.

The pastor was edging toward the front door. "Many," he mumbled.

"How many?" Hannah asked again. Out of the corner of her eye, she saw Jack standing in the doorway to the living room.

"I'd have to look it up," he said. "It is growing all the time."

"Sit down, Reverend," Jack said, coming into the room. He indicated a loveseat. "Make yourself comfortable." Jack towered over the pastor, who sat rather promptly, Hannah thought.

"Tell me," Jack asked. "How do you know Petula?" Jack was inches from the little man "She go to your church?"

"No, Jack," came the answer from the doorway into the hall. It was Laverna. "I met Pastor at the health food store when I was shopping with Matilda. He seemed to be very caring, very concerned about Matilda's welfare, so I called him to comfort Petula."

"In her time of need." Now that he had a supporter, the pastor spoke up.

"And has he comforted her?" Hannah asked.

"No, Pet doesn't seem to want to see him ... yet," Laverna answered.

"Then go, Parson," Jack ordered. "And take your black whatchamacallits with you. We will call you if we need you.

"Jack," Laverna protested. "I told you, I called the pastor."

"Then you have his number," Jack said. "We all have his number. Bye now, Parson or Pastor, or whatever you call yourself." Jack picked up the box of black draperies and grabbing the cloths Pastor Ben had distributed over Pet's lamps and tables thrust the whole thing at the little man.

The pastor scurried to the door, trailing cloths. "Call if you need me," he said.

"Right," Jack said.

"Jack," Laverna said after the man had gone. "How could you have been so rude?"

"Honey, you must not have been there, but I tossed that guy out of the auction a few weeks ago for trying to find converts in the middle of bidding. He is scum."

She put her hand to her mouth. "Oh, dear, but he seemed so nice."

"Good eye for creeps, Hannah," Jack said. "I don't know what he was up to, but he sure didn't belong here now."

"I guess," Hannah answered. "I do hate to make a fuss, but my instincts told me that man was up to no good. No one was watching him; he could have stolen things."

"I do not think we gave him time, Hannah."

Hannah was rearranging Pet's magazines and straightening lampshades. She finished just as a small, nasal voice came from the hallway.

"Where are my pretty candlesticks, the ones with the fat pastel candles?" Pet stood in the doorway, dressed in a flannel nightgown. Bony ankles and large, bare feet stuck out from under her gown. Her face was a devastated mask - swollen, red eyes and tear marks down her cheeks. She held a soggy handkerchief clutched in her hand. "I want my candlesticks. Who messed things up? It was that preacher person, wasn't it?" she rattled on. "My candlesticks, my pretty candles."

"We will find them, Petula," Laverna said. "They're probably just out of place."

Rebecca came in from the kitchen. "Come on, Petula, I'll take you back to bed and fix some nice soup and then get some custard for you," she said soothingly, putting her arm around Pet's shoulders.

"The doctor left her a sedative, but I thought she might want to see Pastor Ben first, so I didn't give it to her, yet," Laverna said.

Jack said, quietly. "Where is it, Laverna?"

Laverna looked on the verge of tears herself. "Here, in my pocket." She pulled out a physician's sample packet and handed it to Jack. There is a prescription for more on the kitchen table. I didn't think I should leave the medicine with Pet. She might forget what she took."

Laverna at least used her head there, Hannah thought. In her present state, Pet might take all the sedative.

"Could Hannah come with me?" Pet asked like a child.

"Of course she can, Petula," Rebecca said, soothingly. "After we give you your medicine and get you all comfy, I'll fix your food and Hannah will stay with you until you fall asleep."

"Thank you," Petula said, and Rebecca took her hand, and led her down the hall.

"I'll look for the candlesticks," Boots said, brightly. Her high voice fell on the room like a discordant soprano, off key and reading the wrong music, Hannah thought uncharitably.

She didn't belong here, and Hannah wasted no time in firmly telling her so. "Go along now, Boots. We do not need you here. We will call you, if and when." One of the blessings about being of a certain age was that you could speak your mind, and everyone forgave you. Boots was probably used to being dismissed, for she recovered nicely.

"Nice to meet you all, even under these tragic circumstances." She bowed her head again.

Jack opened the door and didn't waste any time in closing it behind her. He threw the deadbolt. "God only knows what pest will walk in

203

next. We won't open the door until we see who it is," he said. "I'm going to look for Petula's candles. What am I looking for, anyhow?"

All of them looked, but there was no sign of the fat candlesticks or candles.

"They were fairly expensive looking," Caroline said. "Silver, I'd say. I got similar ones for a wedding gift from a store in King of Prussia."

"Oh, dear," said Laverna. "Maybe Pastor Ben took them by mistake."

There was a collective groan from the others, whether from the thought of having to call him to ask if he'd seen them, or the fact that he might have stolen them, Hannah thought. She was a bit irritated at Laverna's naïveté. At her age and with her experience at the auction with all sorts of people, she ought to know better. She always seemed so controlled and efficient, if somewhat hard to get to know. That was before people she knew began to turn up murdered. It was enough to muddle anyone's calm.

"What are we going to do? Pet loved those candles," Laverna began to sniffle. "What have I done, calling that Pastor? I was only trying to help."

"We are either going to find them here, or I'll buy her some more," Jack said, patting Laverna's hand. "Let Pastor What's-His-Face take them, if he did. It is not worth upsetting anyone more," he said, mostly to comfort Laverna, Hannah thought.

"Don't expect to see his flock expand any time soon."

Hannah didn't want any more details. Laverna was beginning to look like she could use a sedative herself. She was frantically opening cupboards in the kitchen, calling out, "Not here; nothing here."

The candlesticks had not turned up, and it began to be obvious they weren't in the living room or the adjacent areas.

"I'm taking Laverna home," Jack quietly told Hannah. "She's not doing any good here, at least not tonight."

"Does she have a prescribed sedative on hand, Jack?" Rebecca asked.

Laverna was opening drawers in the small bathroom.

"Her doc prescribed some Valium a while back, when she was having a rough patch."

"Give her something to eat and then give her one, but keep an eye on her. If she doesn't calm down, call her doctor, and don't let her have the bottle of pills. When people are this upset, they forget when they had their last dose."

"Take one of these containers of soup. You both need to eat something," Hannah said, bagging the container and handing it to Jack.

"It will be okay," Hannah said, looking at his worried face. She wanted to say, "The Lord will see you through," but she knew Jack was not a religious man and she respected his feelings. Didn't understand them, but it was his choice.

"Oh, it's not me; I'm fine. Laverna is so emotional and high strung. She has trouble with this kind of thing."

"Take her home, Jack," Hannah said. "She will be better away from this for now. I'll call you tomorrow."

"Thank you, Hannah." And he bent down to hug her, something he had never done before. Not for the first time this week, she felt tears prickle her eyes.

CHAPTER TWENTY ONE

All that day, Rebecca, Hannah and Caroline took turns staying with Petula. Caroline was glad the distances between Pet's house and theirs weren't any greater. Between driving back and forth, talking to Stephen on her cell phone from the car, and tending to Petula, Caroline was wearing out. Neither Rebecca nor Hannah looked the slightest bit fatigued. I'm really out of shape, Caroline thought. She hadn't been to the gym in days. Amish women didn't need gyms, she thought. What a wimp I've become! She vowed to walk more and drive less, knowing she had made that vow many times before, and broken it for convenience. Once car-dependent, always car-dependent, she mused.

Rebecca had consulted with Pet's doctor by phone and the two agreed Pet shouldn't be left alone until she was calmer. But, by evening, Pet's initial shock had given way to quiet sadness, and even that seemed to be lifting. Pet agreed to spend the night at Rebecca's house. If Petula continued to improve, she could go home tomorrow, the doctor said.

Hannah asked Caroline to drive her to the Best house because the auction house was closed for the day. She wanted to see how Laverna was faring. "Or I could just take Clara," Hannah suggested.

That afternoon, it had begun to drizzle and Pet's television said it would rain off and on for the next two days before it improved.

"No, Granny, I'll take you; it is wanting rain," she said, unintentionally lapsing into "Dutchified English," the slang the Amish used among themselves. When she was tired or around her family, she occasionally fell into Amish jargon.

"I'll pick you up at nine," Caroline said. "If Petula is ready to go home, I'll take her, then, or when I bring you back." Occasionally Caroline felt like an Amish taxi, but usually she didn't mind driving her family around when she could. When she was at work, they managed fine on their own.

She was in her car when Hannah ran out, calling, "Oh, wait, Carrie; I almost forgot to tell you. I wrote down the license number for that Pastor Samuels fellow's car. Just in case ..." She pressed a scrap of paper into Caroline's hand and Caroline dropped it into her purse.

When Caroline got home shortly before six, she saw Stephen's car was already there.

Just seeing his car buoyed her spirits, which were definitely soggy from absorbing the sadness of the day.

As she opened the door, she was greeted by the wonderful fragrance of Stephen's cooking and the off-key sound of his attempt at singing a snatch of an opera. Must be Italian food, she thought. Stephen telegraphed the type of food he cooked by what he was singing. The commonality was that all the food was delicious and all the singing awful. Given the choice, Caroline could listen to discordant music forever in exchange for the delicious meals from such a cook. How lucky she was to get a man who cooks. No Amish man ever entered a kitchen except to eat.

"Hi," she said, trying not to start tearing up from the built up tension of the day. He turned down the heat on the pan in front of him, and wrapped her in his arms, caressing her neck and back. "Um, I might melt right into you." She could feel herself relaxing.

"Sounds good to me," he answered.

By unspoken agreement, their dinner conversation centered on Molly and the wedding. After dinner, they opened the presents which had arrived that day.

It was then that Caroline remembered the missing candlesticks. "They just disappeared, Stephen," she said, telling him about Pastor Ben's sympathy visit.

"The guy sounds like a weasel at best and a con man at worst. I would love to have seen Hannah toss him out."

"That awful little man was the only one who could have taken Pet's candlesticks."

"What could Laverna have been thinking, to let that jerk in?" Stephen asked.

"She thought she was helping," Caroline said. "She was as upset about the missing things as Pet was. Well, almost."

"Jack had the right idea. Get Pet some new ones. It is a good thing they are selling the business and moving to Florida. Laverna sounds stressed out."

"I can tell you, Stephen, it was a blessing Mom was there. Between Pet, Laverna and that funeral director's wife, Boots, of all the weird names, it was very surreal. Mom didn't seem at all bothered by it. I guess after seeing Amish women through labor, and without as much as an epidural, she has a lot of experience at being calming. She was completely cool, did and said all the right things."

"I'll call Osgood and tell him to let Petula decide if, and when, to call him, and not to bother her in the meantime."

"Good idea; he'll listen to you."

"I'd hope so; Carl is a pretty nice guy, despite the Digger O'Dell mentality. Besides, his potential 'clients' are my customers. Everything around here depends on word-of-mouth recommendations. Good Will is Good Business is our slogan."

"It is? I mean, I didn't know Crossroads had a slogan."

"We don't, but maybe we should." Stephen smiled, showing the same dimple Molly had.

"We can work on it." Caroline smiled back. "Hey, who is Digger O'Dell?"

After dinner, she and Stephen sat in the living room with their coffee, laughing while he explained who Digger O'Dell was and how he sounded on the old radio tapes of The *Life of Reilly* and *Jack Benny* comedy shows his dad had left him.

That led into one of the many discussions about Stephen's father, Gilbert Brown, and what a wonderful man he had been. He had encouraged Caroline when she wanted more education, even loaning her the money to pursue her goals, when she was estranged from her family, after she left the Amish to attend college. After Caroline and Stephen ended their marriage, it was Gil who insisted on supporting Caroline and Molly, and with Hannah, became their family. When Caroline could, she paid back the money, but could never repay him for his affection and belief in her, and his love for his granddaughter.

Sadly, he had been a gambler all his life. It was one thing to gamble in business and succeed, but Gil couldn't stop. He borrowed money from people he would not have associated with otherwise. It wasn't long before he was in over his head.

"Dad was irreparably flawed, Carrie." It had taken a lot for Stephen to be able to talk about his father without intense pain. "All his wonderful qualities wasted," Stephen said.

"No, his love was not wasted. We loved him; he saved Molly's life and Bethany's, perhaps even Granny's."

"Someday we will have to explain it to Molly; how he gave his own life rather than see the girls and Hannah hurt."

"When she's older. You know, neither of the girls remembers any of it, and for now, it is just as well.

I remember way too vividly, Caroline thought back. Gil wanted to stop gambling, to quit helping the syndicate, but he still owed money and had nothing left to borrow on. Two thugs hired to get their money from Gil, took the girls and Granny. Now, it seems like a nightmare; like it didn't really happen. Gil went after the thugs, and rather than see the girls harmed, got shot saving them. It was worse than awful, but if it wasn't for that, she thought, I might have thought Stephen was the one who was responsible for the arson-murder Joshua was falsely accused of.

And if it hadn't been for the unfortunate killing, she would never have had the chance to know Stephen again, and fallen in love, this time for the right reasons.

"Tell me about your friend Tom at the FBI. What is he saying?"

"Unofficially, it sounds to him like Matilda was probably kidnapped, then murdered. He is going to pursue it."

"Benton won't like this," Caroline said.

"Who the hell cares what Benton likes?" Stephen said. There is a murderer running around while Benton sucks his thumb and worries about whether he is made chief, not acting chief. One well-placed call to a major television network would blow Benton's aspirations for making chief. Would they love a story like this! "

"No, Carrie, don't look alarmed. You know, no matter how strong the provocation is, I wouldn't do anything like that. All we need around here is a feeding frenzy of media attention."

"What are the odds of Benton making chief?"

"Zero! If I have anything to say about it."

"How about Lee?"

"Carrie, he is twenty years old, or thereabouts. His chances are zero, too. But at least he's just green, not purposely obstructive, like Benton."

"How fast do you think the FBI will move?"

"As soon as they have the facts, or, as Granny would say, 'as fast as greased lightning.'"

"In the meantime, I'd like to call in a private investigator to find out what she can about the esteemed reverend."

"Who are you thinking of using?'

"My friend, Ellerie March."

"Good choice." Stephen answered. "Speaking of Benton, another thing you won't like, Carrie. When I talked to him this afternoon, I found out he hasn't interviewed Petula; he hasn't checked her alibi for the time of either killing. He has not interviewed the Hesses, the Bests or anyone else."

"What is he doing? What could he be thinking of?" Caroline could feel herself flushing with suppressed anger.

"Nothing and nothing are the answers. Honey, he is in way over his head and floundering. He should have called in the State Police at the very beginning. That Copious died a couple of days later, leaving the oh-so-convenient suicide note, brought any thought Benton had of calling in the experts to a grinding halt. Damn fool! Now he's full of excuses: 'waiting for test results; wanting to give Petula Brody time to absorb the shock.' Stupid, stupid, stupid," Stephen said and muttered some saltier obscenities.

Caroline didn't blame him. It was pure frustration. "Matilda might still be alive if Benton had moved sooner."

"Maybe, but I doubt it. You and Granny figured it out, but if Benton had been looking, he probably wouldn't have thought of Denny's place."

"Her fate was probably sealed when she discovered Copious' body."

"You think she saw the murderer?" Caroline asked. "Then he took her to kill her away from the scene of the 'suicide?' "

"I do," Stephen said.

"Okay. But why would he take her to Denny's? He would have to know about Denny's, and that no one was likely to look for her there," Caroline said.

"And, Stephen, she hadn't been dead long. Her body was still warm. Why hold her for so long if he was planning to kill her? Why wait?"

"Good questions, Honey. Maybe Matilda somehow mentioned Denny's place, or that she lived there once, or maybe he already knew. The place was a disaster, the perfect place to hide a body. It could lie around for months. Unpleasant thought, that. We could guess, but only the killer knows that answer."

"Stephen, if I had to guess, I'd say, the killer was reluctant to kill Matilda at first, but realized she could identify him and finally got up the nerve."

"It also could mean the killer left Matilda there, tied up, and left himself to establish an alibi, then returned and shot her."

"As Granny might say, too many scenarios, too many suspects and way too much supposing."

"I'd like Granny's take on this. She has always had the ability to distill the theories and clarify the facts."

"I'm sure she is doing that right now instead of sleeping." Caroline couldn't help wondering if the killer was sleeping and where he was. He could be hundred of miles away, or right in their midst. She sat closer to Stephen.

At eight the next morning, she called Ellerie at home, gave her the license number Hannah had copied down and the other scanty information they had about the FFFWTC church.

Ellerie agreed it sounded like some kind of scam. "Petula didn't even know the guy, but her friend met him at the Health Food Store? Sure, great place to find congregants. I love to nail these creeps," Ellerie said with relish. "We have a new investigator on staff. He specializes in rooting out cons like this. I'll get him right on it."

When she hung up, Caroline thought about the pastor's visit. Whether they could prove he had the candlesticks or not was unimportant. As Jack said, they could buy Pet some more. If the man had had more time and they hadn't arrived when they did, he might have cleaned Pet out. Who knew what else he might have been up to? It was unconscionable.

Hannah was waiting outside her house, despite the threat of imminent rain. She came armed with her gigantic umbrella. Caroline thought it looked big enough to have a sword concealed in it. When she mentioned that to Hannah, her grandmother laughed. "Ah, yes, she said. "There is a heroine in a series of mysteries set in Egypt who has a device like that. Very handy for foiling villains. I do not believe she has to use it much, but it is a wonderful deterrent."

The only problem with Hannah brandishing any weapon was that no one would believe an Amish woman capable of violence. Hannah's best defenses were a piercing intellect and a razor-sharp mind.

Hannah was no more in the car than it began pouring. Wind blew sheets of rain across the windshield and the wipers had a hard time keeping up. When the storm abated a bit, Caroline asked, "How is it going, with Pet, I mean?"

"Rebecca thinks Pet is doing well enough to go home," Hannah said. "Pet is fussing about Pastor Ben Samuels coming back, if the house looks unoccupied."

"I doubt if that happens. I think between you and Jack, we've seen Ben's tail feathers."

"I think maybe you are right," Hannah said with satisfaction. "Rebecca thinks Pet will be better off at her own house where she feels she has some kind of control. Now, if we can keep the Osgoods away. She is not ready to think about a funeral."

"Stephen said he would call Osgood. I can pretty much guarantee Carl will back off."

They had arrived at the Best's home. An open gate stood between two ornate stone posts. Caroline wound the car up the steep driveway. The house stood at the top of the hill on a flat piece of land. The view of the valley and the creek in the distance was almost as impressive as the stone house. Jack had it built for Laverna when she inherited the business and had added onto it several times in the intervening years.

"What a shame only two people live there," Caroline said. "It is big enough for a large family."

"Noisy pride," Hannah said, using a term for showy. Caroline used to think it was an Amish saying, but she had only heard Granny use it and she used it sparingly. It wasn't charitable and Hannah tried her best to be kind and charitable. Caroline thought she succeeded – most of the time.

"Poor Laverna, having to substitute an inanimate object for what she really wanted, a family. But, then again, a body has to live some-where," Hannah said, remembering the charity part.

Caroline had her finger on the doorbell when Jack pulled the door open, a wan smile on his rugged face. "Sh-h-h," he cautioned. "Laverna is lying down a while. She is taking this real hard. She and Matilda had been pretty close ... going to sales, already, and all that kind of thing, I guess." He glanced up the curving stairway. "She mostly has no time to *dopple*, but is still not dressed, and lying down so soon."

Caroline waded through Jack's verbiage, which included colloquialism, slang, and what Stephen referred to as Amish-isms, like "dopple" for wasting time. She thought it very sweet that Jack was so concerned about his wife. Laverna's all-business attitude must have been severely adjusted by the shock of three deaths of people she knew.

He led them past the formal living room. The room was sparsely furnished, but the few pieces in it were costly 18th Century antiques. Caroline was amazed to see the upholstered Colonial furniture slip-covered with semi-fitted plastic covers. I'm surprised Laverna doesn't just rope it off, Caroline thought. Despite the plastic, it was a beautiful room, and as far as Caroline could tell, authentically decorated. The only more modern note was a portrait, which hung over the fireplace. It was Laverna's Father, Amos Stoltzfus, in a vested business suit, complete with a gold watch chain hanging across his ample stomach. It looked to be of 1940's vintage. She noted the painter's style. Amos looked a lot like Milton Hershey. Caroline wondered if the same artist responsible for the well-known Hershey portrait, painted Amos' portrait.

Past the living room was a dining room, its chair seats also protected by plastic.

"Laverna is one for plastic on upholstery," Jack said, seeing her look at the seats. "I make her take it off when we have people visit. Otherwise, they stick to the plastic; makes an awful noise when they get up, already." Caroline glanced at him. Was he joking, or serious? Considering his concern about his wife, she thought he was serious, so she stifled her desire to giggle at the thought of the Best's guests literally sticking around.

"Come, we can sit in here," he said as they reached the end of the hall. "I won't let Laverna decorate here. It nettles her some, but I have to have some place to put my big feet up, already. I got me a great room," Jack said.

Caroline wasn't sure of his meaning, but she soon saw for herself. Jack's room could have been called a huge room, for although it probably had as many square feet as Granny's great room, this room looked like an eighteenth century tavern with heavily beamed ceiling and dark, rustic, barn siding covering its walls. Random planked wooden floors were covered here and there with red hooked rugs. Not an inch of plastic was in evidence. Two oversized plaid couches were set on one end and a red leather club chair and matching footstool was obviously where Jack put up his big feet.

Politely, he waited for them to sit down before flopping down in his club chair, sighing as he did so. As the grayed daylight fell across his face, Caroline realized it wasn't only the light that caused the lines around Jack's mouth to deepen. She felt a pang of empathy for him. He looked like he'd been hiking up a long hill.

Hannah had no problem with unvarnished frankness. "You look terrible, Jack. You getting any sleep?"

"Some. I'm fine," Jack said predictably.

"Wohl, a person would never know it to look at you. You've been fretting way too much about Laverna."

"I'm kind of helpless when it comes to making women feel better, Hannah."

"Laverna is very strong. Give her a bit of time. Get her busy with something."

"I thought we should go down to Florida and start hunting for a place. Getting away from here sooner would be a good thing for Laverna."

"Did you get a buyer for the auction house?"

"We got 'em lined up, soon as I say the word. Having a murder in the place makes the buyers even more anxious. Bunch of ghouls," Jack said, almost spitting out the last words.

"What is it they say? Bad publicity is better than no publicity," Caroline said. Unlike Jennet's problem of selling a house where someone died violently and potential buyers worried about a ghost haunting the place, a murder at a business only peaked curiosity.

"What are you going to do with the house?"

"Keep it for a while. Florida might not be a good fit for us," Jack said, looking around at the room.

All three of them jumped like kids caught playing with matches when Laverna padded quietly into the room.

Caroline thought she looked like her old self. She was dressed in a bright green sweater and matching pants. Her hair was gathered at the neck by a gold clip. She was in her stocking feet.

"How is Petula?" she asked without the usual polite preamble.

"Much better," Hannah said. "Rebecca thinks Pet can go home like she wants to.

"You look better, Laverna; such a shock *greisles* you, already."

Despite Hannah's use of term for being ill, in Caroline's opinion, Laverna was a person who snapped back. She was more bendable than breakable.

"You are very charitable, Hannah, especially after what I did." Laverna sat in one of the straight back chairs.

"What you did?" Hannah asked.

"Yes. I called that creepy Ben Samuels and upset Petula even more. What was I thinking?"

"Do not be so hard on yourself, Laverna. You were trying to help. Trying to comfort a friend is not a terrible thing. It is a good deed."

"Ben Samuels was the one who helped himself to Petula's beautiful candlesticks. She worked so hard turning that tiny house into a little jewel. Everything has a special place."

Caroline was getting weary of all this breast beating and blaming.

Obviously, so was Jack, for he broke in. "Laverna, forget it; let's move on. Carrie knows where to get some just like them, so we will replace them." His gentleness with her had turned into a not so subtle annoyance at her harping on the subject.

"You are right, Jack. Let's do move on. Matilda and Copious," she said, with a catch in her voice, "would want us to move on. So we will move on. Now!" She popped up from her chair like she had been sprung.

Caroline hoped she would not hear the phrase "move on" again. Laverna might be more resilient than Caroline had thought, but like crystal, it wouldn't take much of a blow for her to crack.

"I'm going to make coffee, a nice big pot."

Just what Laverna needs - a big pot of caffeine, Caroline thought. She glanced over at Granny; an unspoken thought passed between them.

"We need to go," Hannah said. "Carrie has things to do. For the wedding." Caroline knew that when Hannah was trying to extract herself from people, her sentences got shorter and shorter. "Keeping busy."

"It's stopped making down," Jack said as he opened the front door for them. "Just spritizing now; looks to clear up." It was obvious he was going to take the "move on" mantra to heart. After Caroline and Hannah were in the car and on the way to meet Stephen at the hardware store, Hannah was the first one to speak.

"Wohl that was a fun visit!"

"Maybe it would be for a psychologist. But for an ordinary person, it was darn depressing."

"Did you notice Jack does what I do when I am stressed? Falls into using a lot of Dutch words?"

"Sure; it wonders me not," Caroline answered, trying not to laugh, but not succeeding. Hannah joined in.

"A good laugh would do the Bests some good," Hannah said. "By the way, where are you taking me?"

"Sorry. We're meeting Stephen at the hardware store. Guess I forgot to mention it. I told Stephen we'd have a meeting at the store to lay out a strategy, or was it him that suggested it? Oh, well," she said. "It was one of us. He especially asked for you. Benton is doing nothing. We need to brainstorm; do you mind? "

"Mind? No; it will help me see things clear-like, get the theories worked out. We can use his computer. That will do it quick as a cat getting across the street."

"Right, Granny. After we get the solution to the case on the computer..."

"All right, Carrie, tease me. I do not mind. I am just a poor, little, dumb Amish granny," Hannah said, almost managing to keep the laughter out of her voice.

"Seriously, Granny, we have to come up with something. I simply cannot have this black cloud hanging over our wedding." As if she could just wish it gone, she thought. "I'm hoping something Ellerie March turns up may help. At least we can exhaust the possibilities for information. I have a feeling we are very close."

"Hmm," Hannah said. "I hope and pray so, but no matter what happens, we will keep your wedding a separate and joyful event from all this."

Hearing Hannah's words, Caroline caught the optimism and determination in her grandmother's voice, and she began to believe it could be true. Her wedding day would be okay; no, not just okay, but wonderful!

The fog was increasing and Caroline drove carefully. Still, she almost passed Stephen's hardware store. It loomed, large and well lit out of the morning fog. The weather hadn't deterred the customers. The lot was full of a mixture of cars with Pennsylvania and out of state license plates. The Amish parking area was empty. It was dangerous enough to drive a buggy in good weather, let alone a thick fog.

When they arrived, Hannah saw the Amish teen employees who were daughters of several families in her church district. She motioned for Caroline to go up to Stephen's office. "I'll have to say hello to Mary and Katie. Would not be neighborly, not to."

Caroline nodded and went up the stairs.

Stephen was pacing his office, a sheaf of computer printouts in his hand.

"Hi," he said. "Where's Hannah?"

"She'll be right up."

"Caroline," he said. "I'm glad Hannah isn't here yet. I need to talk to you alone for a minute." He closed the heavy door to the room.

"What's wrong?" Caroline didn't like his tone. She had heard that same ultra serious sound before, in court. She unexpectedly felt her knees trembling.

"I think we should postpone the wedding," Stephen said. "There is no way on Earth you can plan a wedding and play detective at the same time. It's dangerous; it's ludicrous; and as my mother would say, it is unseemly."

"Unseemly?" she countered. "Your mother? Since when are you quoting your mother to me? You are telling me what to do. Oh no,

Stephen. You are not telling me what to do! What about the flowers? The invitations? The restaurant?"

Even to her own ears, she sounded childish. Stephen sounded stiff and controlling, but that was no excuse for her to revert from a grown woman to a surly teenager, she chided herself. Where is your rational, considered, legal training? Oh, God, I'm so stressed, I'm a nervous, illogical basket case. To prove it, she felt herself about to cry. Damn, I can't fall apart; that won't help a bit. Despite all, a tear slid down the side of the nose.

Stephen did not race over to comfort her, nor give any indication he had even noticed her distress. Instead, he said: "Sit down, Caroline." He poured each of them a glass of water from a carafe sitting on the table. "I said, postpone, delay, not call it off. I love you; I want to marry you."

Instantly, she felt better. "I didn't mean to sound so hysterical, Stephen, or needy or ..."

"Caroline, I am not trying to tell you what to do, I'm worried. And, Carrie, no one, especially not me, expects you to be perfect. You are way too hard on yourself.

"There is no reason why we couldn't postpone and every reason why we should. If for no other reason than this murder business is spoiling your plans. How many appointments with the florist, the church, and the caterer have you had to change?"

"A lot," she admitted. But, Stephen, I did work it in."

"That's not the point. I don't want you and Hannah to be in any danger. So far, I haven't thought so, or I wouldn't have let it go on this long. Whoever the killer is, he isn't after you or Hannah. Yet. But if you get too close, that could change. You could be caught in the crossfire."

"But ...,"she started to counter.

"There is also the matter of how stressed this is making you. Can you honestly tell me you are calm, cool and collected?"

Caroline hadn't really analyzed her feelings. She knew she was tired, even edgy and emotional, but aren't all brides to be? There is even a name for the condition: Pre-wedding Jitters. Still, she couldn't truthfully say being in the middle of a series of murders was not affecting her and exacerbating her stress. If she hadn't been so stressed, she would not have reacted so strongly and irrationally to Stephen's perfectly reasonable suggestion to postpone.

Another thought hit her. "Stephen, a lot of what you're saying makes sense. But," she continued, "just because we postpone is not going to stop the investigation. The killer isn't suddenly going to turn himself in because we delay the wedding until May, or June, or whenever. He'd still be out there and still a menace and still dangerous and, at the rate the investigation is going, will still be at large, with his shadow looming over our wedding, and everyone's potential safety. On the other hand, he might never be caught and we'll keep postponing. Who's in charge here? Are we, or is some murderer?"

Stephen looked thoughtful. "Well, you do have a point. Even if we eloped, we'd be married, but not necessarily safe."

"I've eloped with you once, Fen," she said, using her pet name for him. "Running away for the wrong reasons is not going to happen again."

"Okay, how about a compromise? I know I'm not going to do much about you being a perfectionist where the wedding plans are concerned, but you have to let people help you more. I'll ask Jennet to come as soon as she can, instead of next week. She can handle more of the last minute details."

"And?"

"And, I'll work with you and Hannah to lay out a plan for taking care of some of the details. Following through with Ellerie, talking further to Pet, that kind of stuff. None of that looks too time consuming or potentially dangerous. In three days, if nothing breaks, I'll try to nudge Tom into expediting the FBI's involvement. It is in their laps then. As soon as that happens, you and Hannah will no longer be involved. We'll go on with the wedding and that is that."

Surprisingly, Caroline was relieved. This mess wasn't anything she ever wanted to be in; neither did Hannah, although she relished the puzzle aspect of any investigation. Maybe her grandmother did read too many mysteries. Caroline vowed to start buying her books on cats or roses, or some such safe subject.

After Stephen's insistent and normal concern had sunk in, Caroline had no compunction about just laying down the case right now and leaving it, but three days surely wouldn't hurt anything and they might have it taken out of their hands by the FBI before then. They could gather interviews; see what Ellerie came up with on the background checks. There couldn't be anything dangerous there, surely.

Hannah's timing was perfect. She found Caroline and Stephen in an embrace. If she noticed Stephen's face and Caroline's eyes a bit red, she didn't say anything. In fact, Hannah looked a bit ferhexed and ruffled herself.

"The nerve," she sputtered. "Some folks have no manners."

"Don't tell me; let me guess," Caroline said. "One of the tourists asked you a question you didn't appreciate. Not something about your underwear, was it?"

"Not this time," Hannah said. "This woman asked me if I was an Amish cult member.

"Cult!"

"Great," Stephen said, wrinkling his face in disgust. "What an ignoramus she was. I assume we won't be seeing her around here again, after you finished answering her."

"Actually, I was very restrained," Hannah said. "I simply informed her quietly."

"Granny, I have seen the recipients of your answers to stupid questions. They couldn't leave the premises fast enough."

"Wohl, I am a lot more controlled these days. Soft spoken, already. I have been praying for patience a lot; trying to work with Benton has given me more opportunities to ask for the Lord's help."

"So, what was your restrained answer to such a nervy question?" Stephen asked.

"I said the Amish were a religion, not a cult."

"That's all you said?" Caroline asked, narrowing her eyes in disbelief. She knew Granny too well.

"Wohl, that was all I said in English," Hannah admitted.

"But, you had some choice comments in Pennsylvania Dutch?" Stephen also knew Hannah well.

"Wohl, yes. Part Dutch and part German. There are not Dutch words for some of what I said. I felt much better afterwards, too." Hannah sat down on one of the comfortable leather chairs around Stephen's conference table, and folded her hands primly in front of her.

"Come on, Hannah; don't make us beg to hear what you said. And, translation, please. My Dutch is not that good."

"Wohl," Hannah said, looking as if she was savoring the moment. "I said: 'No, we are not members of a cult; are you? Or do you call your cult a coven? Then with great dignity, I very sweetly turned my back on her and walked away. I heard her saying, 'Well I never,' but I did not look back. Guess she is probably gone by now. Sorry if I drove your customer off."

Despite herself, Caroline was convulsed in giggles. Hannah had provided the perfect antidote for the remains of tension in Stephen's office. Hannah and Stephen joined in the laughter.

"I hope she didn't speak German," he said when things quieted down.

"The German part was mainly the two words," Hannah answered, smiling broadly. "We Amish do not have a Pennsylvania Dutch word for 'cult' or 'coven,' not believing in all that stupidity. Besides, the woman did not appear like someone who was literate already, let alone trilingual, yet."

That sent Caroline back into peals of laughter. She knew perfectly well the German words for 'cult' and 'coven' were 'kult' and 'koven', and pronounced the same as in English, but Stephen didn't. She would tell him later when she could say something without giggling.

She turned to the papers Stephen was putting on the conference table. Her light mood quickly evaporated into gravity. She had agreed to put the investigation on hold in just three days. Three days was a short time to discover out who had committed three murders.

CHAPTER TWENTY TWO

Caroline told Hannah of the agreement she had made with Stephen. Many of Stephen's observations about the amount of stress on Caroline were things which had been worrying Hannah, too. Hannah's belief that everything, even the weather, would be fine by the day of the wedding was being severely tested by forces neither she nor Caroline could control. Hannah's prayers had become fervent that God would show her the right way to work through this muddle before it spoiled the wedding. She felt a bit selfish about asking for the Lord's help. It made the prayers sound like begging instead of requesting He would show her the way to help herself and her family. Well, no one expected her to be perfect. Unlike Carrie, Hannah didn't aim for perfection, only to do as well as she could.

Right now, Stephen's case papers glared at them from the conference table. In lawyerly fashion, they were neat and organized, and even combined a time line with the unfolding of events. Perry Mason could not have done it better. But poor Perry and Della didn't have all those electronic gadgets. Della had to do everything with a typewriter and a telephone.

Hannah laid out her own papers, with facts and suspects written in a most old-fashioned way on a lined pad with a pencil.

"We need to talk to everyone again," Hannah said. "This time, with the shock of murder not so fresh in their minds, they might remember some little detail they did not mention the first time."

They went over every loose thread in the three murders.

"I still feel uneasy that the key to my blanket chest is missing," Caroline said. "Whoever put that brick in there, must have taken it. If we could only find it."

"Give up on that one, Honey," Stephen said. "Chelsea County doesn't have a C.S.I. to painstakingly collect evidence. Denny Brody's murder scene, in fact the entire auction property, was contaminated by size, scope and sightseers. Any clues were trampled or washed down stream."

"I guess," agreed Hannah. "Still and all, I too, wish we could find the key. Whoever hid the brick might not have been trying to implicate any of us. The chest may have simply been the handiest place to dump it. He might have been planning to come back later to get rid of it. He probably lost the key before he could get back. If he took the key, why? The chest wasn't locked. Unless, he was interrupted before he could try to lock the brick in, and pocketed the key for later use."

"Let's not waste any more time thinking about a lost key," Stephen said. "It is minutia. You don't have time for every little unimportant, trivial detail."

Stephen's use of the word "you," not "we," didn't escape Hannah's notice. If it was up to Stephen, they would have long ago washed their hands of investigating the murders. Hannah felt like Caroline did: it might be that one small, nagging bit of minutiae, which might lead to the solution. She had been involved in too many investigations not to know that.

"Okay," Caroline said. "You are right; we don't have enough time to go over every aspect in detail."

Hannah and Carrie knew they had to assemble the larger pieces of the puzzle before they could use their intuition. The key was unimportant for now. Maybe Carrie is hung up on the word "key," as if it was a metaphor to finding the murderer, not just an old rusted piece of metal, accidentally lost beneath the floor boards of such never-to-be-found bits and pieces of debris.

Two hours later, the combination of efforts was paying off. Small memories and omissions came to light. One thing the women agreed on was that Denny's truck, as usual, had been illegally parked at the very back of the auction property. There was a sign posted: "No Parking at Any Time." Jack didn't like anyone parking so close to the creek. The ground was loose and besides, it made it hard for turns onto the main driveway. Hannah knew Denny always ignored the sign. She was annoyed at not being able to remember more about her attack at Spooky Nook Creek. One of the things they decided to do was to revisit the scene.

"It would serve more than one purpose if I go back there," Hannah said. "Might jog my memory and we just might find something the police overlooked. By the time they got there, the light was gone, and who knows how well they searched.

"It is a given, the local authorities are not doing their job. If they were, we wouldn't be here, playing cops," Stephen added.

"We could run out there this afternoon," Caroline said. "The rain has let up for now, but it's supposed to get bad again later. It will be messy enough as is."

Stephen said. "At the very least, you'll need boots to slog through the mud. Maybe I should come with you," he suggested.

"We do not need you, Stephen," Hannah said. "You would quick get bored, already. We are closer to the ground; easy to look for clues."

She waited for him to take the opening for saying that she was especially closer to the ground, but his mind was occupied with more important things. Even Hannah could see that, when he once again began to pace.

"Too bad we don't have more of my drawings; not that I saw any people, but it might help me remember," Hannah mused aloud.

It was then that Caroline remembered the photos Jennet was snapping at the auction. "They might provide some clues. I'll call her now," she said picking up the phone. Jennet answered on the first ring. Caroline asked her if it would be possible for her to come earlier to help with wedding details, which she was glad to do. "Do you have the photos from the auction yet? Great! Could you bring them?" Caroline asked, wishing Jennet had used a digital camera to take them.

"I mailed them; you should have them today," Jennet said. She would fly in from New York the next day, and Caroline would pick her up as soon as Jen emailed her the time and flight. She wanted the time alone with Jennet to fill her in on both what was going on with the case and with the wedding plans.

Stephen and Caroline discussed who would inherit Denny Brody's estate. Since Denny and Pet were divorced, it was unlikely Pet would get anything. So, who would? Denny had no kids, no relatives. Did he even have a will? Perhaps he left the estate to some charity, although Denny Brody hardly seemed the generous philanthropist. As far as Caroline knew, he wasn't a client of her firm, but Caroline could phone her law firm and get her paralegal, Susan, to look into it.

"This is going to take too long; I'm going to have Ellerie do a background check on everyone connected with this case. Maybe something will turn up. We can hope, anyway,"

Caroline said, scribbling notes on the yellow legal pad.

"Okay," Stephen said. "Now we're going to discuss safety. Hannah, we want you to carry Caroline's cell phone." At Hannah's look of surprise, he added. "I didn't say use it; just carry it in case of a life or death emergency. We'll show you how to use it. It's very simple. Keep it on and if you do have to call for help, just push buttons."

"I know how it works; I asked Carrie, already. I was ... curious," Hannah said, trying not to think of the old adage of what curiosity did to the cat. "But what about Carrie? What is she supposed to use?"

"I've already bought her another," Stephen said. "One which even takes pictures; thought it would be nice for our honeymoon. We can send pictures back to Molly, at least when we're still in the U.S." After the wedding, Stephen and Caroline were going to New York for a few days, and then flying to London and Paris for ten days.

"Anyhow, that's beside the point," Stephen said, handing Hannah the phone.

Hannah wanted to know how that was possible, taking pictures with a cell phone. Imagine! However, this wasn't the time to ask. As it was, she was way too nosey for an Amish woman and way too interested in technology. She would accept Carrie's phone, but more to please them than that she thought she would ever need to use it. No one was apt to want to hurt her; scare her, maybe, but that was all. Then she thought of the incident with Clara in the buggy and involuntarily shivered. Neither Carrie nor Stephen seemed to notice.

"I want you to promise to wear the phone around your neck, Granny," Caroline said. "It isn't going to do you any good if you carry it in your handbag, if for some reason you can't get to the handbag. I put it on a strong, black ribbon. You can tuck it in to your undergarments and be able to reach it in an emergency. Let's go over it again," Caroline said, producing the small phone. "It's very uncomplicated. Even Molly can use it."

"Molly uses a computer, too," Hannah answered wryly.

Caroline programmed the phone so Hannah could call 911, Caroline's new cell phone, Stephen's cell, Stephen's office, Caroline's house and Jennet's cell. "Just don't forget to keep it on. In case it should run down, there's an extra battery." Caroline showed her how to change it if it became necessary. You probably won't need it. I'll recharge the phone in the car when I'm with you, so it should be fine."

"Do you want any other numbers on it?" Stephen asked, in a teasing voice.

"No, thank you. I am wired enough to the English world as it is."

While Stephen made coffee, Caroline called Ellerie March, and put her on the speakerphone so Hannah could hear. Briefly, she outlined what she wanted to do with background checks on the suspects. "Unless the federal and state authorities come in sooner, I'm giving this three days max. If nothing turns up, I'll let Benton and the FBI worry about it."

On the other end of the phone, Ellerie groaned audibly. "Kiel Benton couldn't find out anything if he wanted to, and he is too lazy to want to. All he does is posture and play cop. He reminds me of a puffer fish, full of hot air."

That Ellerie is my kind of woman, Hannah thought. Not only speaks her mind, but agrees with us as to what kind of policeman Benton is.

Ellerie continued, "You know, Caroline, three days is not much time. Thank God for the Internet. I can find out a lot in a couple of hours from records."

"I'll fax you a list of the people we need checked out," Caroline said.

"The sooner the better," Ellerie answered. "I'll stick the esteemed Reverend Samuels on the back burner. I think he can wait."

Caroline agreed.

"I'd ask you why the three day deadline, but I can guess. Your wedding, right?"

"Yes," Caroline answered with a small sigh.

Ellerie said, "As the kids say, I totally understand. Priorities."

By noon, they were finished with the meeting.

"How much we've accomplished, I'm not sure," Caroline said. "But something's better than sitting on our hands."

Hannah looked at her original list of suspects and motives. She had crossed out half her suspects. The Clays were dead. It was impossible to see any way Swayne and Dorcas were involved. The list of everyone who disliked Denny would fill the phonebook. Hannah knew a lot of gossip about the man, but no links with anyone who had a motive substantial enough for murder. Her list now consisted of the Bests and Petula. She could imagine one of them being able to poison Denny Brody, but not kill Copious and Matilda. Besides, Petula was at the auction, as were the Bests, when Denny's body was found.

She verbalized her thoughts to Caroline and Stephen.

Maybe Copious did kill Denny, although again, it was hard for Hannah to picture it. Perhaps he did commit suicide, but stab himself to death? How painful! And no guarantee he'd die; someone might have found him, still alive. He could have chosen from a vast array of poisons used in jewelry making to die less painfully. And why would he have wanted Matilda to find him?

Hannah felt both frustrated and discouraged, and could not suppress a sigh.

"Could be we need a break from this, Granny," Caroline suggested. "Let's go have lunch and then slog through the Spooky Nook area."

"That is your idea of a break?" Stephen said, lightly. He's probably smiling at the thought that the time is now down to two and a half days, Hannah thought. Part of her was ready to quit now, but the other part wanted to solve the murders. Even if they ignored them, they'd be hanging over the wedding like mourning drapes.

"Just be careful," Stephen said, as he put the yellow knee boots in Caroline's car.

Hannah saw Caroline's mouth open as if she was about to retort he was overprotecting her, when he added, "Don't get muddy, or fall in the creek; it's cold this time of year."

Hannah shot Stephen a look, to see if he was joking. He looked completely serious, but then winked conspiratorially.

"Very funny, you two," Caroline said. "Stephen, get out of here before I throw a boot at you. And, Granny, your punishment is to be taken to a restaurant where the menu is in French and I'm going to order for you."

"Perdone moi, Mademoiselle? Je parle francais. Ooh, la, la."

"And where did you learn that?" Caroline was laughing.

"I get around," Hannah answered in what she thought was a French accent.

"It was very convincing until you got to the 'Ooh, la, la' part." Caroline laughed harder.

"Guess that was a bit too much whipped cream on the éclair," Hannah said, with a giggle of her own.

Nothing like a good laugh to make things go better, she thought.

The menu at Le Suisse turned out to be in French, but also German, Italian and English, so Hannah was saved from Caroline trying to order something like snails for her. The restaurant was so new Hannah hadn't heard of it. It was perched on a ridge with a spectacular 360 degree view of the Lancaster Valley. Surrounded by a deck, even on a partly cloudy day, it was a beautiful setting. Caroline ordered in French.

"Show-off," Hannah said, jokingly. Being called a show-off by an Amish person was akin to an insult, but Caroline knew Hannah was teasing.

Actually, Hannah was delighted that Caroline had added French to her mastery of English and German, not to mention Pennsylvania Dutch, which she already spoke, but which, of course was not a written language. Hannah always thought the variety in spellings folks used in trying to write "Dutch" was very amusing. Most folks don't realize how many languages the Amish speak, she often mused.

"Stephen speaks French thanks to having a French mother. Anne-Marie is fluent in five languages. A lot of Europeans are. Even Molly, who learned French at her ballet class, is more fluent than I was. So, I decided to take lessons," Caroline said. "I'm going to surprise Stephen with a little speech at our wedding."

"Just don't say 'Ooh, la, la'," Hannah said between bites of delicious veal roulade stuffed with spinach and mushrooms. "A person could get real soon *sprecky* like a pig eating this kind of food," she said.

As they ate, they watched the sky clear to partly cloudy. An hour later, they were on their way to Best-Stoltzfus Auction House.

"We are going to need those boots," Hannah said, looking at the mud surrounding the parking lot. "I want to find my sketchbook, if it hasn't been washed away by now." Hannah was thinking of hiking up her dress and cloak and tucking them into the boots. It messed the clothes up some, but for sure, not as bad and dragging them in mud.

"I see a car in the lot," Hannah said. "Think it may belong to one of the auctioneers, Popeye Lewis."

"I don't know him. How did he get that nickname?"

"Wohl, his real name is John, but Jack Best started calling him Popeye because he has big muscles in his arms from lifting furniture and the like."

"I think I know who you mean," Caroline said. "I guess we'd better tell him we're here and that we want to look around, not that he would object. Jack and Laverna wouldn't mind."

The outside door to the auction room was open, and they found Popeye in the office.

Popeye was muscular, not only in his arms, but his shoulders and tall with it. Hannah wondered if he ever played English football. He'd be pretty intimidating if he didn't want some fellow to run away with the ball. She thought the sport, what she knew of it, to be a bit violent. But, she liked the idea of baseball; even Amish boys played baseball.

"Just wanted you to know, Popeye, Carrie and I are going to look around the covered bridge area. We have boots in case it is muddy."

"It is muddy alright, That crick is way up the bank; you don't fall now. Gonna need them boots. Better take some of them slickers from the hook here, too." He pointed to a row of thick plastic slickers the staff used for working outside on rainy days. "Got us all sizes. We can hose 'em off if need be. Got them big boxes of gloves, too —them doctor ones Jack keeps so as we don't dirty up the fancies. Youse don't want to dirty up those nice clean clothes. Pennsylvania mud don't soon come off."

"Thanks, Popeye," Caroline said, smiling at him. Hannah saw that the infectious grin Carrie received in return was missing a few teeth, making Popeye look like a seven year-old who had an intimate relationship with the tooth fairy. Popeye needed more help than the tooth fairy could provide. He would have to get implants if he wanted new teeth. Hannah doubted he made enough money auctioneering and delivering goods to the winners to get any more teeth than he now had. But it didn't seem to be bothering him or his disposition a bit. He politely left so they could get dressed. Finding a slicker to fit Hannah wasn't impossible, but it took a while. She figured out a way to do it; she took a long jacket and pushed her skirts up into it, using the zippered front with a drawstring to keep them from falling. Then she topped that with a second, large pocketed slicker, which hung to her ankles. With boots added, she would be mud- ready, and rain impervious.

Caroline, who was dressed in jeans, got quickly into the rain gear. "Now, for the gloves. Small for you and medium for me."

"Okay, but bring a couple of pair each, in case. One could tear and we could drop or compromise evidence, or ..."

"I get it, Granny. Isn't 'the things you worry about don't happen' a mantra of yours?"

"No, Carrie, it is not a mantra; I do not believe in such nonsense. It is a truism. The downside of it is that it takes a lot of worrying for it to work. Some folks like to worry; it gives them something productive to do. As you very well know, I put the worrying in greater hands." She glanced heavenward, or in this case, ceiling-ward. Even to her own ears, she sounded a little excessively pious. Did I say that, she asked herself?

"Whatever," Caroline answered, and began to look in the glove boxes. "Here is a fit for me," she said, slipping one on. Next, she picked up one of the other boxes, tipping it on end to see the size. It rattled. "Something's in there, probably a coin," she said distractedly.

Hannah moved closer. She was trying to get the hang of shuffling along with everything she wore. "Wohl, if I fall in the creek, I'll either float like a beach ball or sink like a bag of rocks."

"Granny!" Carrie almost shouted, although Hannah was only a few feet away. "The thing in there is a key!" She fished it out wearing her latex glove, held it up and showed it to Hannah.

"It looks like your blanket chest key."

Caroline nodded, and took still another glove, dropped the key inside and tied the top shut with the fingers of a third glove.

They both jumped when a voice on the other side of the door called out. "Just a minute, Popeye, we are still tucking in some things."

Might say that, Hannah thought.

Caroline slipped the glove into her bra where it would be safe for now, and tucked her sweater tightly into her jeans waistband. A minute later she said, "Come in, Popeye. We're all ready."

He laughed broadly when he saw them, then chagrined, apologized. "Sorry, youse ladies look like youse is fixin' to catch a whale in Chesapeake Bay." He squinted at Hannah. "Maybe none of my beeswax, but ain't that a shiner you got there, Hannah?" Caroline's black eye was well hidden under her make-up.

"It is," Hannah answered, hoping he wouldn't pursue the matter further. She didn't mind the black eye as much as the questions about it.

Popeye wouldn't be deterred. "What did the other guy look like?" He laughed as if this was an original comment. "How did it happen?"

"Buggy went off the road."

"Lucky it weren't worse," Popeye said, suddenly serious. "Did your horse get hurt? Know you put lotta' stock in Clara."

"She was fine, and so am I. Just a little sensitive about the accident," Hannah said.

"Women don't much like being teased none about their driving, even when it's driving a buggy."

"Something like that, already," Hannah said as she waddled out in her double layer of slickers.

They got in Caroline's car and pulled on the boots over their shoes. "Wohl, we will be clean if we can maneuver in these getups," Hannah said. "What do you think about finding the key – in the box of gloves, of all places?"

"An excellent question. Someone hid it there on purpose, dropped it there accidentally, or put it in there and hasn't been back to retrieve it."

"I would not think it got there accidentally. 'Bout as likely as flew there, already. Maybe there are fingerprints, or DNA." Hannah said, looking doubtful. "A lot of folks probably handled that key. I doubt if there will be anything usable, but ..." She attempted to shrug her shoulders under layers of squeaking plastic.

"I handled it with a glove, so if there's any evidence, it did not get messed up. I think it's likely someone put the key there planning to lock the brick in the trunk, to at least delay it being found, but didn't get back to retrieve it. Once it was found, why bother?" Caroline asked.

"Why not lock the trunk as soon as they put the brick in it? Why walk away with the key? The only reasonable explanation I have is that the key would not lock the trunk. Remember how hard it was to open? We thought it was stuck, but maybe the lock was damaged. Once he had the key out, the trunk was stuck shut and he could not or did not have time to get the key back in, so just took it, maybe without thinking, and maybe on purpose. One less thing to connect him, or her, to the brick," Hannah said.

"Pretty stupid to stash the key in a box of gloves," Caroline said.

"Not really," Hannah said. "Who would ever look there? We found it accidentally. As far as I'm concerned, it is not the key which is important; it is the opportunity."

"What do you mean?" Caroline asked.

"Who had the opportunity to take the key, and who had the opportunity to hide the key in the box of gloves? We figure that out and we know who put the brick in the chest and who used the brick on Denny and on me. We maybe find the killer."

"Of course," Caroline answered. "We were way too focused on why the trunk was or wasn't locked."

"Wohl, sometimes clues are like a snow globe. Don't try to make too much of it until the snow settles down. Then, you can see it plain.

"Carrie, I am thinking we should put the key back where we found it."

"But it's my key," Caroline said. "We certainly can't put it back and watch the box to see if anyone ever comes back for it."

"I am not suggesting doing that. Only putting it back. Best we not give the killer any idea we found it until we find him. We will put it back right where we found it.

"We should think on the matter of opportunity while we move on. It wants rain again," she said, glancing at the sky. "Let's look at the bridge area before it gets any darker."

Caroline drove the car to the far side of the parking lot.

"As I said, I am only hoping this visit to the site will jog my memory some," Hannah said. "That bump on the head not only knocked me out, it may have temporarily unglued my memory. Anything I saw right before I was hit is a blur. Though chances are, there was nothing to see. I was hit without any warning. I sure remember everything else, clear as a just polished drinking glass, already."

A few minutes later, they were glad of their protection against the elements. It was wet and muddy along the pathway to the creek. It hadn't started to actually rain, but moisture was dripping off the trees, and as they made their way towards the spot where Hannah recalled she was standing, they brushed against wet bushes.

"Here!" Hannah said, "I was right here, looking at the bridge from this angle. I was trying to get a view without the warning sign in the way." She stopped and looked around. She was positive it was the place, although she wouldn't have known it except for the unique angle of foreground, creek and the Spooky Nook Bridge in the background. Today, the creek was running much faster, churning up white foam

239

as it dashed against the boulders on its path. The day was similarly overcast, but unlike the day of the murder, there was no sunset to lighten the sky. It was too early in the day and rain too imminent. The sky was a monochromatic smoke gray. There was enough light to see around, but Hannah saw nothing interesting. If she had dropped her sketchbook here, it was probably lost under layers of mud and leaves, beaten down by the recent rains. Briefly, she closed her eyes, trying to envision her exact position on the day of Denny's death. She recalled propping her sketchbook against her left arm. She squatted down closer to the ground.

"Carrie, you have younger eyes; come over here," she called to her granddaughter who was a bit ahead of her, moving low lying branches aside. "I'm trying to see if there is any sign of my book."

"Even if it turns up, Granny, it will be waterlogged and probably ruined," Caroline said.

"So, if we find it and it is ruined, we are no worse off than if we do not even look for it, yet."

"I suppose, if you don't count muddier as worse off." Carrie was plenty muddy already, Hannah noticed. Her slicker was splashed with an abstract pattern of mud.

"Oh, stop complaining, already. We are washable. Anyway, we are probably clean as a pin under all this plastic."

"Umm," Caroline muttered, close to the spot on the ground where Hannah indicated. "All right!" she yelled, popping up like a cork. "I see your book, Granny!"

Caroline had her gloves on, and she bobbed down again to pick up what Hannah recognized as her sketchbook. It was soggy, and slimy with mud.

"Hold on while I get these gloves on; I do not want to touch it with bare hands," Hannah said, although she was pretty sure the rain and mud had obliterated any usable evidence left on the book.

"It has to be ruined," Caroline said, holding the book at arm's length. "It's waterlogged."

She slogged through the mud towards her grandmother.

Hannah didn't hold out much hope it could be of any use, as she took it from Caroline, and slipped it into one of the plastic bags she had brought along.

"I will examine it later," Hannah said. "Now, we search the area around where we found it."

"Not for long," Caroline said. "It's starting to rain and I'd just as soon get out of here before the creek gets any higher."

It was starting to rain, but not heavily, and Hannah did not want to lose track of the spot where the book was found. She pulled her flashlight from the slicker pocket, switched it on and illuminated the area.

"Carrie, I see something else, way under that bush there."

Caroline groaned, looking at the spot Hannah indicated. "I know you want me to crawl under there and look."

"Wohl, we could come back," Hannah said.

"Oh, no! We're not coming back. This is it. I'll see if I can get under there. What is it I'm supposed to be looking for?"

"It looks like something shiny," she said, peering closer. "I think it might be a glove; a glove like we are wearing."

Caroline moved closer to get a better angle. "I see what you're looking at. It does look like a vinyl glove!" Without further complaining, she ducked under the bush, and a minute later, triumphantly dangled a surgical glove by its finger.

"Despite what you say, you have darned good eyes for your age, Granny."

"Thanks, I think," Hannah answered, giddy with the second find. Her excitement was short lived when she got a better look. It was encrusted with mud. Still it was possible evidence. Her mind was whirling with possible scenarios as to how the glove might, or might not prove useful in solving the crime.

"This glove might not have a thing to do with the murder, you know," Caroline said, voicing one of Hannah's own thoughts.

Hannah was holding it in the beam of light. "On the other hand," Hannah said. "And, I am not trying to be funny, it may prove very useful. It is inside out, like somebody was in one big hurry to discard it." She slipped it into another zip bag and added it to the slicker pocket.

"Well, don't even think of suggesting we look further for a second glove. It's really starting to rain," Caroline said. "What are you doing now?"

Hannah didn't answer. She had taken out another bag and was knotting it on an overhanging branch along their path. "This is just in case we decide to come back."

"You come back, it will be without me," Caroline said. "I'll still be getting the mud out of my hair." The hood of her slicker had been dislodged during her foray into the bushes. Her hair and face were streaked with mud.

"Oh, the rain will help," Hannah said, mock-serious. "Nothing better than rain for the shiny hair."

CHAPTER TWENTY THREE

By the time they returned to the auction house, it was pouring. The rain had done little to wash the mud from their slickers and boots. As Popeye had predicted, Pennsylvania mud didn't come off easily.

As they neared the main building, Caroline realized she was not only wet, muddy, and cold, but grouchy as well. Conversely, Hannah seemed downright cheerful, trudging along like a half-drowned duck, but looking upbeat despite her sodden condition. Caroline knew the reason. Granny had found two useless clues, but it was something, and enough to make her impervious to what must be similar discomforts to her own.

Caroline saw Popeye at the office window; he must have been watching for them. When they got to the door, he opened it before they could.

"I was about to come out looking for youse," he said, and then took at good look as they stood in the doorway. "Lordy, did you fall in Spooky Nook Crick?"

"We look like two hogs in a pen, right, Popeye?" Hannah asked cheerfully.

"Well, I… I wouldn't exactly, uh…" he stammered.

"I sure would," Hannah said, as she caught sight of herself in a mirror hung by the office door. "We would be cleaner if we had fallen in the creek. Now we are standing here dripping all over the auction house. We could use some newspapers and paper towels if you have them. We'll just roll these slickers up and take them home to wash off,"

"I can do it real easy."

"No," Hannah said. "I would feel more modest if I did it."

Popeye looked bewildered, but went off to get the papers.

"I wanted to stop at the car," Hannah whispered. "To unload the plastic bags, but he was at the window. Bad planning; a detective with smartz thinks of these things ahead of time. Just proves I am no professional. This is not good."

"You do okay," Caroline said. "Who'd have thought he'd be watching for us?"

"Now I have this muddy mess to clean up. Serves me right," Hannah said, lightly.

"You have to get into the office and put that annoying key back," Hannah whispered.

"Got any bright ideas how?"

"Sure, ask to use the phone. He doesn't know you have a cell phone."

Caroline knew she must be more tired than she thought; she should have thought of the use the phone excuse herself. Cells had pretty much made that maneuver obsolete. Time to haul the old ploy out again. "Who is going to put it back?" she asked. "Old Amish women do not use the phone."

Before they could figure out the details, Popeye came noisily though the swinging doors from the kitchen. His arms were piled high with towels, and newspapers.

"Found these towels. They are none too new; about to be rags, I'd say. Guess they look clean enough for muddying up," he wisecracked, laughing heartily. "They're from a household auction lot for next week;

you can wash 'em and return 'em later." He set them on a nearby table and spread newspapers near where they were standing, still dripping water. "Don't give the floor a mind. It's gonna get cleaned — one of these days. Nobody ever pays it no notice, anyhows."

"How about the gloves, Popeye? Do they get reused?" Hannah asked.

"No way!" he answered. "Them's cheap; more trouble than they are worth to red 'em up."

Caroline wondered where Hannah was going with this line of questioning. Of course they wouldn't clean up the gloves.

"They would be real handy for me, handling my quilts and all,"she continued. "Could we buy a box or two?"

"Couldn't sell you them gloves," Popeye said. Jack would have my hide for selling them to you." He stopped, waiting for a reaction. Caroline saw the punch line coming.

"Oh," Hannah said, seriously. "I should not have asked. We will find them somewhere."

"Jack would want me to give you some." Popeye laughed. "Whilst youse are changing, I'll go get some. I will let you know before I come back in. Don't do none for ladies to get interrupted whilst they are changing clothes.

"Am I seeing things, Carrie, or did you get yourself a shiner out there?"

The water must have washed off my concealing make-up, she thought.

"No, I had a barn come down on my head," she answered.

"You are a card," Popeye answered, smiling broadly, and showing his almost toothless grin.

As soon as he was gone, Caroline had the boots and slicker off and a towel around her head. "I get it, Granny; put the key back and if he comes back too soon, pretend I had to use the phone," she said, quickly drying her feet off with one of the towels.

"Right; go, already!" Hannah said, making no attempt to add further directions.

Barefooted, she scurried into the office, pulled the key from her bra and realized she had secured it so well in its glove in glove package; she could not get the confounded thing out. She didn't see scissors or a knife. Resorting to the most primitive of tools she bit the glove and felt the crunch of key against teeth. "Oh, damn," she muttered. Immediately her tongue confirmed she had chipped her tooth. Trying to ignore the implications of a chipped tooth a week before her wedding, she enlarged the hole in the glove, pulled the key out, and dropped it where she had found it.

Stuffing the gloves back into her pocket, she parked the bit of tooth between her jaw and her cheek and returned to the entryway where Hannah was back to being a harmless, albeit a bit damp around the edges, sweet-faced and innocent Amish Granny.

"Boots," Hannah said. "Put the boots back on."

Caroline complied, and just in time. Popeye was calling "OK in there?"

"Come on in," Hannah called, cheerily.

Easy for her, to be cheerful, Caroline thought. She didn't break her tooth.

While Hannah profusely thanked Popeye for the gloves, Caroline pulled a tissue out of her pocket and surreptitiously wrapped the bit of broken tooth in it.

She said goodbye to Popeye, but didn't smile, for fear he'd notice her newly broken tooth. He might comment, seeing a kindred set of teeth. She would feel obliged to come up with some fib for the recently broken tooth. He is so nice, and I feel lousy enough about being devious, she thought.

"What is with you?" Hannah asked, the minute they were out of sight of the auction house.

"Look," Caroline said, briefly flashing a grimace at her grandmother.

"Your tooth! Oh, Carrie, how did you manage to do that?"

"Biting that damn key!"

"You were checking it to see if it was made of pearl?"

"You are not the slightest bit amusing, Granny. I couldn't get it out of the glove I'd knotted it in, and I didn't have time to look for a tool, so..."

"I'm sorry, Dear. Sometimes my humor is inappropriately timed. I am so sorry you chipped your tooth. But what is done is done. You kept the piece I hope."

"Yes; it is in my pocket. Maybe we can super-glue it back, or something."

"Oh, no; that would not work," Hannah said. "Caroline Miller, now you are teasing me."

"It seems only fair. I'm sure the dentist can bond it or cap it, or something. I'll call him when I get home."

The wind had come up and the rain was blowing across the car in sheets, making it difficult for the wipers to keep up with the deluge.

"I'm glad we got out of there when we did or Popeye's worry about us ending up in the creek might have come true," Caroline said as she drove into the driveway leading to Hannah's house.

Later, at Hannah's house, they sat at the kitchen table, with steaming mugs of Hannah's comfort beverage, coffee with cinnamon and a bit of chocolate stirred in.

"Wohl, we better get to the book we found," Hannah said, seeming none too anxious to do so.

"It's a mess. Maybe we should wait until it isn't so wet. I could take it home and use the hair dryer. I want to get home, call the dentist and shower. Then check my messages before Stephen gets there". Caroline yawned. "A nap would be nice, too. My normal exercise program doesn't usually include mucking through the jungle."

Hannah stifled a yawn of her own. "Sounds like a good plan; dry out the sketchbook, and I will look at it tomorrow. I sure do not expect there will be much to see." There were splatters of dried mud on her sleeves.

"Better change before the folks see you," Caroline suggested. "All we need is to get them worried about what we're up to. Stephen is enough to reckon with; we don't need Mom and Daat fretting, too. "I have things to do tomorrow morning. I'll call Mom's phone and leave you a message. Okay?"

"I suppose," Hannah answered. "We are lucky to have reason for a phone with your mom being a midwife, and all."

"Otherwise I'd be driving over every time I needed to talk to you," Caroline said. She eyed the sketch pad. "You have any clean plastic bags? I'd just as soon not import any more mud into my car."

Later, on her way home, Caroline rehearsed what she'd say to Stephen about her tooth. Maybe he wouldn't notice? Unrealistic thought; as a former attorney, Stephen had a propensity for noticing everything. Oh, well, she would just 'fess up', as Hannah would say. The whole story might make him realize how stupid she'd been, but people were always telling her not to try to be perfect. Biting the key was an interesting way to begin her quest for imperfection.

Arriving home, she was relieved to see no sign of Stephen's car. Looking at her watch, she realized it was only five o'clock. A day with Granny sometimes seemed like it had gone on forever.

Ready for a shower, she took a look at herself. The tooth wasn't that bad and the shiner was fading quickly. The mud was another matter. Her hair was matted. Her jeans were already in the washer, along with the slickers, which she had first rinsed off under the shower spray. The sketchbook waited on top of the dryer where Caroline had put it on a towel.

Later, wrapped in a huge terry robe with a towel wound around her head, she had just finished returning and making phone calls. Susan, her paralegal, had called. Call her at home after six. Jennet would be flying in late tomorrow afternoon. Yes, the dentist could see her tomorrow morning. According to his nurse, it wouldn't take more than an hour to put a porcelain veneer on the chip. Super gluing on the broken part would not be part of the process, she laughingly assured Caroline, when she heard the details of how the accident happened. "Remember the old 'no tooth as tool' warning?"

"I tell Molly that all the time. It will be a 'don't do as I do, do as I say' story now."

Molly was the next on her call list. Caroline was feeling guilty that between her time spent with Hannah and the wedding preparations, she was not saving any Mommy and Me time for Molly.

Molly was an easy-going, adaptable child, yet always open to an adventure. She was thrilled to spend "an entire week" with Emily, who had a houseful of brothers and sisters and a stay-at-home mommy. After Stephen and Caroline were married, and moved into their new house, she planned on working mainly from a home office. As for the houseful of brothers and sisters, they would be working on that, too. Stephen was an amazing father, and Caroline could only dimly remember the time she thought he did not want to a part of Molly's life. She was so wrong, and when she found out he had been watching over Molly and her from as close a distance as she permitted, she vowed never to judge anyone so harshly and so subjectively again.

Molly was full of school news, stories about Emily's baby sister, and on and on until she finally said, "Well, Mom, it's been good talking to you, but I'm reading chapter books with Emily. I am clear through the Boxcar Children series, and now I'm letting Emily catch up, so we can be tied. Ties are fair," Molly declared. Caroline could see the mixture of miniature adult one minute and little girl the next. Glancing at the clock, and seeing it was almost six, she had a fleeting thought about dinner. Stephen would be there soon, and she couldn't ask him to cook again. She would thaw some of the leftovers. She started towards the bedroom to dress when the doorbell rang. It wasn't Stephen; he had a key, and never forgot anything.

She looked out the peephole to see an eye close to the other side. "Ellerie!" She pulled the door open.

"Hi, Caroline. I thought I'd come by and make your day. Is this a terrible time?" She held a fat legal size envelope in her hand. "I just tried your cell but it was taking messages, and I was close so ..." Ellerie March, Caroline's friend, advertised herself as a "Domestic Investigator." Caroline knew that mainly meant chasing down dead-beat dads for child support, but Ellerie's office did just about any kind of investigation as well.

"I wouldn't turn away anyone who said they would make my day," Caroline said, standing aside. "Come in. Sit down," she said, motioning her to a plaid sofa in the living room. "Would you like something to drink? Let me throw on my clothes; it'll only take a minute."

"Go, go, go," Ellerie said. "I can find my own glass of water."

Caroline dashed into the bedroom, pulled on a peach fleece warm-up outfit and wound a dry towel around her still wet head. She was too anxious to find out what Ellerie was talking about to take the time to dry her hair.

Ellerie was perched on one of the bar stools, water bottle in hand. Caroline thought Ellerie was one of the most natural beauties she had ever seen, with her thick, sun-streaked blond hair and casual grace. She was taller than Caroline by at least four or five inches. Yet it wasn't her good looks, but intelligence and humor, which were Ellerie March's defining characteristics.

"You better sit down," Ellerie said, moving to the couch. "Or, you are going to be blown away by what we found out."

Caroline sat on the couch facing Ellerie.

"Oh, this is fun," Ellerie said. "There are a lot of secrets in Chelsea Township."

"However, Jack Best is as clean as one can get; so is Laverna," she continued. Jimbo, my best investigator, found out that a year and a half before she married Jack Best, Laverna spent seven months near Roanoke 'visiting an aunt'. We couldn't find any record of an aunt, not here or in Roanoke. Why would anyone visit a non-existent relative for seven months? It's a no-brainer. Could Laverna have been waiting out a pregnancy? Bingo! She was living in the mountains at a home for unwed mothers."

Caroline was taken aback. Proper, controlled Laverna, of all people. "The baby?"

"Sad outcome there; it was a complicated delivery – the placenta separated and the baby died a few minutes after he was born. They almost lost Laverna, too. She was in the hospital for two weeks; they had to do a hysterectomy."

"Oh, how awful! Poor Laverna. How did you find out all this stuff so fast?"

"We start with the obvious, make a few suppositions, get to the gossip and it's not that hard. People tell Jimbo everything and anything. He knows the right questions to ask; has a very simpatico way about him."

"What did he find out about the father? Not Jack?"

Ellerie shook her head. "Nope."

"Oh, my God! Denny Brody?"

"Yep! It was on the birth certificate."

"I wonder why Laverna didn't make up a name for the father?" Caroline asked.

"Who knows? Maybe she was distraught, or too sick to think of it. Maybe she didn't want to lie. She was just a kid."

"How sad," Caroline said. "No more babies, either."

"Jack Best married her anyway. If I was a suspicious person, I might say it wasn't kids he was interested in, but the Stolzfus connection. But, I've met him a few times and he doesn't seem the grasping type."

"He isn't, or at least he sure doesn't seem to be. He is absolutely devoted to Laverna."

"I would say both Bests have now jumped to the top of the suspect list. They both must have good reason to detest Denny," Ellerie said.

"But we don't even know if Laverna ever told Jack about Denny fathering her baby," Caroline said.

"True; she might have kept it from him. I just assumed a husband would find out somewhere along the way, especially if there were no kids."

"Yeah, well, most men would figure it out, at least in today's world, but Jack and Laverna come from the generation where such things were either not talked about or hushed up."

"Ellerie, did Jimbo find out if Laverna was going to put the baby up for adoption, if it had lived?"

"Yes, she planned to. No one who went to that unwed mother's home kept her baby. Not in the 1960's."

"Where is it buried? Did Jimbo find out?"

"They told him they didn't keep records on that since most of the babies were adopted. They said the mothers made their own arrangements.

"Hmm," Caroline said, thinking. "Someone must have helped Laverna. Most likely her father. That baby had to be buried close by. But I don't think his final resting place has any bearing on the case. He died and he's buried somewhere."

"If you change your mind, I can have Jimbo follow up. If the baby is buried in the area, he will find the grave."

"I don't think it's important. What else do you have?" Caroline asked, still caught up in Laverna's long ago tragedy.

Ellerie took another paper-clipped sheath of papers from the fat manila envelope. "Denny Brody and Petula Brody were never divorced." She paused, pulling the clip off the top sheet. "Because they were never married in the first place."

"You are kidding!"

"No record of a marriage; no record of a divorce. But, there was a license issued in Maryland. It was never filed. No record of a divorce filed anywhere in the US, but that makes sense. Don't need a divorce if there was never a marriage."

"It was issued, but not filed?" Caroline said, truly shocked. "But everyone thought they were married; she uses his name. Would she have known?"

"You'd think!"

"She would have had to be drunk or duped not to."

"I'd go for duped, but why?" Ellerie asked. "I mean, guys go to extremes to get a girl in bed, but a sham marriage? Didn't they live together for years? And neither were married previously, or since. At least, the public records don't show any other marriages for either of them."

"I can think of two scenarios. Maybe they got the license, and for some reason, decided to postpone the marriage itself, and never got around to it. Or, they did get married and the wedding chapel, minister, whoever, didn't file the license."

"Well," Ellerie said. "Didn't it occur to them they should have gotten a copy after it was filed. Isn't that the procedure?"

"I got married in New York, and that's the way it works there. It's the same in Pennsylvania. Usually, the bride and groom get a signed copy from the minister and then he files the original, and a copy of the filed document is sent to the couple by the county where they were married."

"Maybe Denny and Petula were too naive to know they should have an official copy so they never missed it."

"I suppose anything is possible," Caroline answered, thinking there was more than naiveté, or even stupidity involved. It would be an interesting question to ask Petula when she and Granny talked to her. There was something nagging at her. Say Pet thought they were married, and when she wanted a divorce, Denny told her if she divorced him, she'd never get a dime. Why would he do that?"

She ran her top-of-the-head supposition by Ellerie.

"Denny was a hoarder, someone who wanted to keep everything he got; maybe he wanted to "own" Petula on his terms, but he knew if he married her legally, she would own half his stuff and be entitled to half his money, so there was no 'real' marriage. He gets a 'wife' for nothing. She leaves him when she can't take it. Later, when she tries to divorce him, she finds out there was not a valid marriage. That would give her a motive. Pet finds out that she couldn't collect alimony or even inherit. She couldn't even have the satisfaction of divorcing him. That would leave a bitter taste in anyone's mouth."

"Wouldn't it though?" Ellerie replied. "Wait until Granny Hanny hears this!"

Caroline and Ellerie were so intent on their conversation that neither one heard the front door open, so they both jumped when a familiar voice said: "Wait until Granny Hanny hears what, Ellerie March?"

Hannah came into the room, an inquisitive expression on her face, and carrying what Caroline recognized as a quilt wrapped in Hannah's usual method of string-tied butcher paper.

Behind her came Stephen, laden down with three shopping bags.

"Stephen stopped by to bring a new set of side curtains for the buggy," Hannah said, by way of explanation. "I asked him to bring Jennet's quilt over since she is coming tomorrow."

"And I suggested we stop by the store, get something for dinner and she bring the quilt along," Stephen chimed in. "Since I knew Jen was coming tomorrow, I picked up a few extra things at the grocery store," he said, looking sheepish.

Caroline had reminded him dozens of times that she had a very small refrigerator-freezer and not to keep bringing food until they used up what was already in there. It did no good; he kept the appliance full to overflowing.

"Hi, Ellerie," he said, going into the kitchen to put the groceries down.

"Hi, Stephen," Ellerie answered, getting up to greet Hannah with a hug. Everyone in Lancaster County who knew Caroline, had also met Hannah.

As usual, Hannah was direct. "Guess you must have some news or you would not be here, and Carrie would not be talking to you with her hair wrapped in a towel."

"And I wouldn't have been saying, 'Wait until Granny Hanny hears this'."

"That, too," Hannah said, divesting herself of her cloak and placing it behind her on a chair. "Well, what should I hear?"

"Stephen," Caroline called. "You should hear this, too." The noise of cupboard doors being opened and closed abruptly ceased, and Stephen strode back into the room. He sat next to Hannah on the couch opposite Caroline.

As Ellerie and Caroline filled them in on Ellerie's reports, Caroline saw mirrored on their faces the same reactions she had had to the new information: incredulity and sadness, surprise and speculation.

When they had finished filling them in, Hannah was the first to speak.

"So much for people in Chelsea Township knowing everything going on. I had no idea! Never heard so much as a whisper about any of this. I would say we need to talk to Laverna and Jack, separately. Then we need to talk to Petula ..."

The ringing of Caroline's phone interrupted Hannah.

"Telemarketer, probably," said Caroline. "The no-call law doesn't stop them all." She took the call in the kitchen.

"We have an unlisted number at the farm," Hannah said. "Do not get many of those calls."

"How do you have an unlisted number, Hannah? How do Rebecca's clients in labor get hold of her?" Ellerie asked.

"The moms-to-be have it memorized. The midwife's number is the something they are not likely to be forgetting."

They could hear Caroline's voice, but not what she was saying. By the tone of her brief responses, she was doing the listening, not the talking.

She ended the call and returned. "Ready for another surprise, even if it's not such a startling one?" She continued, without waiting for an answer, "That was Susan, my paralegal. My firm, Bryce Jordan, does have a will on file for the late Dennis Quentin Brody. That's all she knows. I'll have to talk to Bryce tomorrow. He's at a banquet in Philadelphia tonight. I could call him on his cell, but it's probably off and I'd only get his voice mail. It can wait until morning."

"Interesting," Ellerie commented. "As goes the old advice: 'follow the money, follow the women, or both'."

"Looks like we will be doing both, already," Hannah said, this time with no trace of humor in her voice.

"God only knows what Denny has stashed away. He must have had a ton of money, the way he acquires all that junk, and sells little or none of it. We've thought of money as motive before. But, with no relatives to inherit, we kind of put money as a reason for murder on the back burner," Caroline said, getting up and changing seats so she could face everyone. "Then when Copious left a suicide note, it seemed even more muddied. Only after we found Matilda were we positive Copious was murdered, too. Financial gain seems an unlikely reason for any of the murders. What other reason looks likely in the three murders? Common denominators?"

"OK", Hannah said. "I have been thinking along the same lines. Ellerie and her investigator have turned up plenty of new bits to chew on. Let's take it one person at a time. First, Laverna. Yes, thirty-five years ago, it was a scandal to have a baby with no marriage first. But if it came out to today, who would care? The Bests are moving, anyway. I am sure Laverna is bitter; who wouldn't be? Sure is high strung, but I cannot see her killing Denny. It's like Dorcas and Swayne – it has been a long time ago."

She turned to Ellerie. "You did not find out anything about Dorcas and Swayne Hess, did you?"

"No secrets. They are comfortably well off. Haney left an insurance policy and they have retirement income. No drugs, no mention of drinking. They talk freely about Haney and how Denny drove him off, but more with sadness than bitterness."

"My deduction, exactly," Hannah answered. "You got all that information pretty darn quick, already."

"It wasn't too hard. I took the bits and pieces you gave me, verified them, made a quick check of public records, then meshed it all with a call to the chatty secretary at the Dorcas and Swaney's church," Ellerie said.

"It sounds easy when you are the expert," Hannah said. "OK. We pretty much decided the Hesses could not be involved unless they hired a hit man. A fellow has to know where to get such a person. Swayne would not. If he ever got mad enough to harm a fella, he'd do it himself. "Back to the secret life of Petula. There is a fair bit we did not know," Hannah said. "Now, what do we know?" Wohl, we know she never married Denny. We don't know if she was aware she did not legally do so, or even if he knew if wasn't official, or not. Could be it was one of those bureaucratic mix-ups where the license did not get filed. A young couple might not know about it. We would never find it in Denny's disaster of a house, even if there was a license.

"Now, after a time, Pet walks away. Asks Denny for a divorce, already. He either agrees, and then cannot find the license or any record of it. Or, he tells her it was a one of those unauthorized preacher-by-mail things, so it was not legal; thus they are not married. Either way, she has no claim on his money. But, either way, killing him would not get her the money; she wouldn't have a claim."

Stephen interrupted, "She could have filed a palimony suit. She might have a pretty good case if she could prove fraud."

"Then everyone would know there never was a marriage," Caroline said. "It would be the major topic of conversation in the district. She owns a business, has a life of sorts, uses Denny's last name."

"The name is the one thing Denny could not keep from her, or he would be the villain in the piece. He would be the one everyone would talk about," Ellerie added.

"Wohl, Ellerie, I do not think he would have cared if he was the subject of more gossip. He surely knew everybody talked about him as it was. He seemed to be oblivious."

"We found out he had no friends; none," Caroline added. The towel slipped from her head and she just left it off, well aware her curly, tousled hair made her look even younger. Another notch in my belt for imperfection, she thought.

"So, who would he leave his money to, assuming he had any left?"

No one answered. Hannah, deep in the cushions of the couch, struggled to sit up straighter.

"Back to Pet, I do not see a motive. We are more or less at one of those impasses my fictional detectives flounder around in."

"But they, unlike us, figure it out," Stephen said.

"Now, Stephen Brown, do not be such a pessimist. We will solve this yet. Look how much more information Ellerie has brought us," Hannah retorted.

Yes, more information, Caroline thought, but they were still not heading down a straight line to the solution. They were going around and around, getting nowhere fast, with two days left until the case was out of their hands. She looked down at her own hands and saw three broken nails. Oh well, she thought; they will add to my shabby-chic wedding look --- the remains of a shiner, a capped tooth and ragged fingernails.

"Maybe tomorrow when Carrie sees about the will, the solution will start to come together and it will all be clear. We will get straight to the end." Hannah said, optimistic once more.

Caroline was more of a realist; she still saw a circle with no end. Later, she would realize 'whirlpool' would have been a more apt description.

CHAPTER TWENTY FOUR

"Let's eat!" Hannah said, scooting off the couch. She didn't need to look at a clock to know it was past her dinner hour; her growling stomach told her. "We are going to need all the brain food we can get. There is plenty for you, too, Ellerie."

"By 'brain food', you mean fish, right?" Ellerie asked, suspiciously.

Hannah chortled. "Don't trust Amish cooking, huh? Do not worry; it is not brains from a cow. I will not eat that stuff. It is fish; nice, fresh bay scallops. And, Stephen is cooking."

When dinner was over, they all sat around the table.

"Why don't we go over the basic facts, just one more time, for Ellerie's benefit," Hannah suggested. " She is not as close as I am; she might have a new 'take,' like they say in mystery novels."

"Sure," Ellerie said. "Shoot. Sorry, I wasn't trying to be flip. Go ahead."

"I have been thinking," Hannah said. "We are maybe putting too much focus on Denny Brody. Nobody liked him. OK; lots of suspects. Copious – everybody liked him and he liked everybody. Who would want to kill him? Someone who needed him dead, trying to make it look like a suicide. Then there was poor Matilda. I see no reason anybody would want her dead, unless she saw Copious' murderer. There is no way she could have killed herself, already."

"You're on the right track, Granny. Denny's murder had a whole series of different elements. What do we know? He was poisoned. Your pie, which dozens of people knew was his favorite, and that his habit was to buy the whole pie, was the vehicle for the cyanide, which is fast acting. For some reason, he was also hit on the head; then someone tried to hide the body for later disposal," Caroline said. "That person, saw you and hit you to keep you from seeing him. But he or she was not trying to kill you, or he would have done more than just knock you out. I keep saying 'he' because it would take one strong person to get an unconscious man, even a slight one like Denny, across a rickety bridge. Whoever it was, surely was in a hurry, or he wouldn't have stashed the body to deal with it later.

"Copious was stabbed with a sharp jeweler's tool and basically bled to death, after leaving a suicide note written on a computer, although there was no computer at the house. If he wanted to kill himself, why didn't he just handwrite a note?"

"Because", Ellerie said, getting into the spirit of the discussion, "it wasn't a suicide. Someone else had to kill him; they couldn't copy his handwriting for a suicide note. That someone probably knew Copious was on a blood thinner; maybe, or maybe it was Copious' bad luck."

"Right," Caroline said. "I agree someone probably knew he was on a blood thinner."

"Ladies," Stephen said. "Lots of people knew Copious had a heart condition; I did."

"Well, I did not," Hannah said. "There are a few things I do not know. If he had been Amish, I probably would have known."

Hannah continued, "Getting back on topic, anyone who saw the bottle of pills could have known about it. Blood thinners are pretty widely prescribed for people who are at high risk of stroke, or other heart problems. Either Copious or Matilda could have mentioned it to any number of folks. Anyone could have heard the medication name mentioned at the drugstore, or overheard it at the doctor's office. And everybody perks right up when they hear a name mentioned. It is just the way it is around here – we call it 'nose trouble'."

Ellerie laughed. "That is a new term for snoopy to me."

"Matilda's murder seems plain enough," Caroline said. The murderer couldn't kill her at the Clays' house because it would blow the suicide angle. Whoever it was, took her at gunpoint to the place he or she thought least likely for her to be found, at least for a long time. We found her only because we knew the history of where she once lived."

"Just for supposition, say there is more than one person involved," Hannah said. "Anybody of any size can be a poisoner, or even hit a fella with a brick, but it takes someone strong to cart a body. Anybody of any size could also have stabbed Copious, but he was stabbed close-up, so whoever did it must have been someone he wasn't afraid of. Anybody could have pulled a gun on Matilda and forced her to Denny's barn, but I wonder what made her get into the trunk of that car. I don't think she would have unless they shot her and shoved her in. That person would have known that car was in the barn, and unlikely to be found for who knows how long."

"So", Hannah said, continuing, staring at her empty plate "Where does that leave us, Ellerie?"

"Well, Hannah, I don't know your cast of suspects personally, but offhand, I'd say it's looking like more than one person was involved in the killings. You say Petula Brody, Laverna Best and Jack Best all had alibis at the time of Denny Brody's murder, but who else is left? If all three were somehow involved, they could have taken part, in brief segments of time, and covered for each other. I don't know; it is possible, but a stretch for probability. From what you tell me about their behavior before and after the crimes, not a one of the three was acting like a guilty person. I am not the expert here, so take my opinion for what it's worth – not a lot. I've only run into one murder case in my work and it hardly qualifies me as an authority.

"If you can get the FBI into this, you will have at least some forensic evidence to work with." Ellerie sat back.

"Only one of the crime scenes, at the Clays', was uncompromised," Caroline said. "Spooky Nook Creek is overflowing in places and muddy as a swamp. We were there today and any evidence that might provide useful as proof would be hard to come by. There have been dozens of people walking around.

"I'll see what my firm has to say about Denny's will; as soon as it's read, it will be public. God only knows how long it could take to appraise his belongings. For all we know, he could have collected money like he collected things. If there is any money and any of the suspects inherited, it's going to be a powerful motive, but we would still have to prove it reason enough to kill," Caroline said.

"Wohl, money as a motive sure cannot apply to the Bests. They have plenty of money," Hannah said.

"Maybe," Stephen said, "to all appearances, they do, but you never know. Could be they have everything tied up in the business, or maybe it's all in Laverna's name. On the other hand, why the devil would Denny leave money to either of them?"

"Guilt? Look what he did to Laverna," Caroline said.

"We don't even know if he knew Laverna was pregnant. Maybe she didn't tell him."

"Knowing Laverna like I do, I think you could be right," Hannah said. "Her father probably wouldn't have let her marry Denny, even if he'd been willing."

"Wohl, we could sit here speculating all night ..." Hannah yawned. "I have things to do. I should be quilting. I am that far behind in my quilt orders."

"Could I run you home, Hannah?" Ellerie asked. "It's on my way and I'd love to see your place."

"Sure," Hannah said. "I like being hospitable."

Caroline knew what Hannah really liked was showing her quilt collection to a new visitor. Pride was a distinctly negative characteristic for an Amish person, but sharing was not only condoned, it was encouraged. Hannah did walk that fine line, her granddaughter thought, amused by Hannah's expertise, even at line-walking.

As they were leaving, Ellerie said, "Denny's will conversation made me wonder if he had any insurance policies."

"Darn, I should have thought of that." Caroline grimaced. "Is there a way to find out, other than looking in the house for a policy?"

"I do not plan to go near that house again," Hannah chimed in. "Leave it for the authorities."

"I have a faster and safer way to find out about an insurance policy. Jimbo can find out anything, either on the net or from his contacts. I'll get him on it tomorrow," Ellerie offered.

As Ellerie and Hannah walked away, Caroline heard Hannah's voice float back. "How does that Jimbo fella know all these contacts? This sounds real interesting."

After Ellerie and Hannah drove away, Stephen turned to Caroline.

"You are looking more like Molly every day,' he said, blandly.

"Don't you mean Molly looks more like me? Besides, she looks exactly like you."

"No. All my teeth are intact," he said, looking amused by his remark.

"At least no barn collapsed on me today," she answered, and told him about the key.

"I'm glad you put the blasted key back," he said. "Leave it there; we don't need it, don't want it. I'm even beginning to dislike that chest."

"Stephen!"

"Sorry, Honey. The chest is an inanimate object, I know, but I'm sick of discussing its damn key. Where it is, what significance it does or doesn't have. Enough, already!"

"I agree," she answered, rubbing the edge of the chipped tooth. "From now on, it's a *verboten* topic."

"You do look kind of cute. The hair-do is maybe a bit too Sharon Osbourne-y."

"Oh, no!" Her hand flew to her head and encountered tufts of hair sticking straight up. "I forgot about my hair. I must look like I'm wearing a fright wig. Who is Sharon Osbourne-y, anyway?"

Stephen smiled. "It is Sharon Osbourne," he corrected. "You don't know who she is?"

"Must be someone on TV, a celebrity. Right?"

Stephen was smiling broadly.

"Don't tease me, Stephen Brown. You know I don't watch TV. I am incredibly bad at pop culture."

"I do," he said, pulling her into his lap. "There's still a bit of Amish left in the old gal yet."

Early the next morning, Caroline tried drying out Hannah's sketchbook. The pages at the front and back looked worse dry than wet. However, the middle pages, where Hannah had been working on drawing the covered bridge, dried out fairly well. She couldn't see anything which would help anyone; no strangers in the bushes, no body in a barrel, just a tranquil scene of bridge and creek. Well, no one expected anything from the sodden book, so Hannah probably would be happy with what she did have. She could do another drawing from what remained. Caroline put it aside.

She decided to call her boss, Bryce Jordan. She knew he was an early riser and would be on his treadmill, especially on a rainy day, such as this one. There were flood warnings for low-lying creeks and streams. Caroline wondered how Rose Mill Inn was faring. The Inn itself was situated on an upper level, three stories above the creek, and built like a fortress. Still, the horrible thought of having to row to her reception was flitting through her mind. The wedding was a week away, so the weather had to turn before that.

Bryce answered on the first ring.

"Good morning, Bryce." Like almost everyone else in the area, he knew Hannah was investigating the three deaths.

"How is the Amish Miss Marple doing?" he asked.

Caroline told him, and as she did, she could hear a small change in his voice. She hoped it was from exertion on the treadmill and not irritation at her involvement in Hannah's "scrapes," as he referred to them. He hadn't realized the extent of Caroline's participation. But, she was on leave, and the firm wasn't involved. Until now.

"Bryce, I understand we have Denny Brody's will."

"We do. Next, you're going to ask me what's in it. Right?" The good humor had returned.

"Well?"

"Why don't you come in and look at it? I'd like to see your face when you do."

"I have a dentist appointment first thing this morning, can I come after that?"

"Anytime this morning is good. I have a late lunch meeting at one o'clock." Bryce's voice came through as coolly neutral. Caroline knew he wasn't going to tell her anything more on the phone. Worse yet, she wouldn't be able to tell anyone what was in the will. Not yet, and no exceptions, not even for Stephen or Granny. She almost wished she hadn't called Bryce until the will was probated. But, if there was something vital to solving the murder or murders, it might be too late by then.

Later, at the dentist, Caroline was relieved to find out how simple the procedure to repair the chipped tooth was. An hour in the chair and she was on her way. The only pain was paying the bill.

She drove to downtown Lancaster and parked behind her office. Bryce Jordan had taken an old building, which had originally started as a residence containing the owner's law office in the mid-1800s, evolved into a series of varied businesses in the 1900s, and rehabilitated it from its most recent use as a plumbing supply store. It was beautifully restored and while keeping its original character, was a thoroughly up-to-date law office. Bryce's decorator had done a masterful job, using leather furniture, natural cherry bookcases and cabinetry with framed vintage photographs, area memorabilia and folk art. A client knew he was in a law office, businesslike, yet welcoming.

Susan, her paralegal, was at lunch, but Bryce was in his office with the door open, waiting for her. A fat, legal-size file lay closed on the desk blotter. Caroline could hardly keep her eyes off it.

"Sit down, Caroline," Bryce said in a tone that was more invitation than order. "I would ask you how things are going with the wedding, but from what you said, it doesn't sound like you have had much time to plan a wedding. I'm not going to give you advice, suggest prioritizing, or give you time management techniques. I'm sure Stephen has taken care of those areas." Bryce at sixty years old had classically handsome features, which had evolved benignly as he got older. He smiled often and broadly, but no one could be tougher in the courtroom.

Privately, Caroline thought his comments about Stephen sounded a bit chauvinistic, as if she would take orders from Stephen. A relationship required negotiation, not domination. Caroline remembered the word domination in Latin meant master. That would be the day.

Bryce was a wonderful boss and a good friend, but a product of his age where women with families rarely worked, and were not expected to be assertive, but acquiescent when a husband "suggested."

"Denny Brody's will, will blow your socks off, Caroline. I thought nothing surprised me anymore, but I found out differently. Denny Brody might have been a bit compulsive, make that really compulsive, but despite that, he was smart. He was the kind of guy who did crossword puzzles in ink. The kindest thing I could say about Brody was that he was not a nice person, so I was amazed Denny had it in him to do such a thing. At first, it seemed generous. Now I wonder. Here, take a look." He slid the folder towards her, and sat back, watching her as she opened the file.

CHAPTER TWENTY FIVE

Despite the steady, light rain, Hannah tried to ignore the gloom and whistled a nameless tune as she pinned the binding to a quilt. This pattern was one of her own designs, which was ordered by a woman in Los Angeles. "Make it in sunny colors," was her only request. At the library, Hannah looked up some pictures of California scenes and chose to depict a sunset at the beach. It did perk up a dark day, she thought, looking at the vibrant pallet of pinks, reds and yellow predominating and the turquoise of the water contrasting. Privately, she thought it quite beautiful and kind of hated to give it up, but a thousand dollars would do a lot of good for folks in the community.

She had been up since before dawn. All three cats had nestled next to her all night, and after their breakfast, returned to her still warm bed. Hannah's fluffy down comforter was covered with a hand quilted duvet cover she had made. She didn't like the heaviness of two quilts on her legs, so she used a ready-made down comforter in place of polyester batting. It worked so well that she thought of making duvets for sale at "Flying Needles," despite the incongruity of the words "Duvet" and "Amish." Her own duvet was pieced and embroidered, but she envisioned appliquéd duvets, which might be even prettier. Maybe morning glory with trailing vines, she mused. Nettie's death and the potential sale of "Flying Needles" put the idea on hold. Hannah was busy enough as it was and about two months behind in the orders she had now. If only these murders hadn't happened. She had never seen Jessica Fletcher on TV, but she had read a book by someone using the fictional character's name. Of course Hannah had read Agatha Christie. Those were fictional characters; Hannah was not, but she empathized. Real people do get involved in such things; she was proof of that. "Right, Bear?" she said to the dog, who was snoring as loudly as a man. He thumped his tail, opened one eye and was asleep again in a minute. The animals were not fond of dreary, rainy days.

She finished the careful pinning. With bindings, she sometimes machine stitched one side, but this quilt had a wide binding, and she wanted every stitch to be done by hand. Hannah could hand-sew as sturdily as a machine. This quilt would be hung, not used on a bed, according to its new owner. The owners would not hang it in the sun if they followed Hannah's instructions on quilt care included with each of the pieces she sold.

Last night's conversation was much on her mind. No wonder Laverna carried sadness about her; no wonder she was overly controlling, yet often edgy. Hannah could never imagine herself in a similar predicament, but sometimes it happened to Amish girls. Once in a while, a courting Amish couple slipped and there was a quicker wedding than would otherwise be. In the Amish community, few counted the months and were only happy for the couple who married. Pregnancy was not a talked about event; the birth was considered God's gift to the family and the community, and that was that.

For Laverna and Jack, there were no babies, no one to take over the Best-Stoltzfus business. A real tragedy compounded by circumstance. The up side was that Laverna had a devoted husband and they had worked as a team at the auction for all these years. It was a shame they didn't adopt. Hannah shook off the thoughts of what might have been.

Petula's story was even more shocking and perplexing. No marriage? A sham marriage?

She must have been totally clueless, as the kids say now, Hannah thought. She couldn't see any reason why Denny would pull such a trick. All the suppositions they came up with last night around Caroline's table seemed ridiculous.

Hannah poured herself a second cup of coffee and sat down. Suddenly, a thought they hadn't considered, came to her --- Denny's father. Matilda said Denny's father was so happy about Denny marrying and settling down. The old man was crazy about Petula. She could hear Matilda's voice saying so. Could Denny have contrived the marriage just to please his father? People did strange and devious things to inherit money. If there had not been a legal marriage, Denny would not have to share anything with his non-wife. Terrible, and evil, if true. It was not Hannah's place to judge, she knew, but how could she not have an opinion?

"I need to think about something else," she told Bear, who didn't even bother to open an eye. His only response was a muffled thump of his tail on the braided rug where he sprawled. The rain had temporarily let up. She decided to take the buggy, with the new rain curtains Stephen had installed, and drop by Caroline's to pick up her sketchbook, or what remained of it. She had a key.

Then, she would stop at the auction house to see if she could talk to Jack privately. This was one of the days Laverna was usually at home, so it should be easy to get Jack aside. She wanted to know how deep Laverna's bitterness towards Denny was, or if she had forgiven him. Hannah relied on her intuition, and something told her this was important to know.

What excuse could she use for stopping by? She tried never to lie, but flimsy excuses didn't really fall into the outright lie category.

Bringing food was flimsy, and not a reason to take Jack aside. Then she thought of something better. She remembered the slickers. If I know Carrie, she thought, she has washed them off.

To get Jack alone, she could ask his advice about Florida. She was thinking about buying a "cottage" in Sarasota? She had the funds available and it would be some place to loan out to older Amish couples to get them out of the winter weather. Hannah, of course, did not consider herself old, but someday she may be. Her eldest sister, Grace, and her husband, Joe Weaver, both had bad arthritis, and she could let them use the cottage in the bad weather months. This was not a lie, but something she had been considering. She had thought of a newer place, or buying a "fixer-upper," and paying some of the retired Amish to get it into livable condition. It would give the retirees something to do if they wanted to, plus a bit of extra funds. So, she would mention the two options to Jack, and ask his business advice. It was a pretty poor excuse for a visit, but Jack might not think so. The Bests hadn't yet moved to Florida, but he and Laverna spent the month of December there every year, albeit nowhere near Sarasota.

From there, she could swing the conversation around to Laverna. People told Hannah things they would never discuss with others. Maybe because she was genuinely interested. Despite the Amish and small town propensity for gossip, Hannah was cautious. She knew the difference between betraying a confidence, and passing along harmless news.

Hannah dressed, and then eyed Caroline's cell phone attached to a piece of black ribbon. She told Carrie and Stephen she would wear it, and if there was any danger, use it. Hannah liked to keep promises whenever possible. She wasn't expecting danger. Wearing the phone was for Carrie's peace of mind. And, why not? Nobody would see it. As Carrie had shown her, she checked the battery, briefly re-examined the instructions, and made sure the ringer was off, but the phone was on stand-by mode. Calls could go out, but nothing would come in. Carrie said they would be stored like an answering machine. What will the world think of next? Hannah wondered, already knowing the answer was too vast to contemplate.

She slipped the phone over her head, tucking it securely into her undergarments. Lancaster County Amish women wore bras, although serviceable cotton ones. An occasional tourist seemed fixated on knowing what undergarments Amish wore. Hannah found the curiosity somewhat bizarre, but so were a few of the visitors. For security, she looped the cord around her bra strap nestling the phone to her left so if she needed it, it could be accessed with the right hand.

A half an hour later, she was at Caroline' house. Leaving Clara tied up to a post Stephen had provided near the driveway, she saw Caroline's car was not in the carport; she must still be at the dentist.

Letting herself in, Hannah went to Caroline's laundry. She saw the slickers washed and dried off and hanging near the washing machine. The sketchbook lay face down on top of Caroline's clothes dryer. Beside it lay a roll of paper towels and a hair dryer. The book was no longer soggy, but still damp. Glancing at it, she wasn't surprised to see how unenlightening her drawings were as to clues from the crime scene. They were bit smudged, but considering the weather conditions in which they had been discovered, she was amazed that there was anything left to see. It was lucky the book had landed flat and not on its side. She wrapped it in a towel she had brought and left the bundle, slipped into a big plastic bag, by the door.

Then she went to the guest room and found Jennet's quilt still in its package. She opened it and spread the creation out onto the bed. "Oh, my!" Hannah spoke out loud. Even in the subdued light, the quilt glowed with texture and color. "It is my favorite yet," she murmured.

She knew she said that about every quilt she designed, but this one was more special, as it was a gift for someone she loved. She decided to leave it spread out, covered with a sheet from Caroline's orderly linen closet, which smelled faintly of lavender. This closet is too pretty to need a door on it, and there are no cats to climb in and mess it up. Idly, she wondered how Daynight was doing at Stephen's hardware store. The cat was probably making a big hit with the customers. She decided Matilda would have approved.

Hannah found a large, flat sheet and took it out to cover the quilt. She planned to whip off the sheet like unveiling a painting. Kind of showy behavior for an Amish woman she knew, but what was the harm? The maneuver would delight Jennet, and making someone happy mitigated any qualms she had.

As she was preparing to leave, the mail came through the slot in the door. It floated down to the floor.

Hannah scooped it up and put it on the hall table. On top was an envelope, addressed to Caroline and Hannah. Jennet knew Hannah's curiosity would tempt her, but her manners would prevent her from opening it if it was addressed only to Caroline. She opened the packet and saw Jennet had made two copies of each photo. Hannah glanced through the pictures. Good for a magazine, but not much help at a crime scene, Hannah thought, looking them over. Both Pet and Laverna were plainly in sight in several of them, for all the good that would do. The Hesses were not in any of the crowd scenes, even though Hannah had not seen them moving around, And Dorcas would be hard to miss in any of the kitchen scenes. I guess they could have been there, but avoided the camera. Anyone could have left before or after the photos were taken. She slipped her set into her pocket.

Clara was patiently waiting, and as Hannah untied the reins, the horse whinnied softly, putting her head down to nuzzle Hannah.

"You are the world's sweetest horse," Hannah told her in Pennsylvania Dutch. Clara was also a smart horse who could understand commands in either Dutch or English. Wonder if she could learn more languages, Hannah though idly.

The rain was holding off as Hannah drove towards the auction house, and up the driveway. Only Jack's car was there. So much for worrying about getting him alone, Hannah thought.

She tied Clara up in the covered area especially set aside for Amish buggies and wagons. "Hasta la Vista, Clara," Hannah said. If she was going to teach Clara, she better learn herself, she thought. She didn't believe the phrase exactly meant "Stay!"

She picked up her bags and knocked softly at the door. There was no answer, but the knob turned on the door as she let herself in. Through the open door to the office she saw Jack was in his office, absorbed at his computer. He started when Hannah spoke, "Jack?"

"Oh, Hannah. I didn't hear you come in.," he said, swiveling his chair around, and rising. Hannah saw a screen headed "Florida Properties."

There was the excuse, and now she didn't need one. He was alone.

"I brought back the rain things," she said, figuring Popeye had told him of her visit yesterday.

"Rain things?" Jack asked. He hadn't risen, or asked Hannah to sit down, so they were eye to eye. His were puffy; from lack of sleep, Hannah surmised.

"Popeye did not tell you? Carrie and I came by to look at the creek, to see if we could find my sketchbook."

"Did you?"

"Yes, and I was surprised it was in as good a shape as it was, already. It was protected a bit, way under the bushes."

"That's good," Jack said, offhandedly. "No, I haven't seen Popeye, but it was fine he loaned you slickers, and such."

"Jack, how is Laverna?"

"She will be fine when we get to Florida. She needs sun."

Privately Hannah thought Laverna needed rest and a change of scene more than sun. By the look of him, it wouldn't hurt Jack to get away from all that had happened either.

"Have a buyer for the business?"

"Yeah, lots of interest, thanks to what happened here. Ghoulish reason, like."

Hannah decided to come right out with it. "Jack, we did a background investigation on everyone connected with Denny."

"*You* did?

"Wohl, we hired an investigator to do it."

"What did you learn about us? We surely must have been included as connected to Denny Brody, right?"

"We found out you two are crackerjack business people and have a spotless reputation."

"Come on, Hannah. There must be more than that."

"Wohl, about Laverna..." If Laverna hadn't told him, Hannah wasn't going to, but mentioning his wife's name might work if Jack did know.

Jack preempted her. "I know all about Laverna and Denny, Hannah. Laverna told me before we were married. It didn't matter. Laverna never had to apologize to me. She was an innocent kid and that rotten Denny seduced her. Her punishment was losing her baby and not ever having more. It broke her heart." Jack's eyes were filling with tears.

"I am sorry, Jack. No one will hear anything about Laverna's past from me. You know that."

I know," Jack said, softly. "God, Hannah, I am so sorry. It's just that I wanted to protect Laverna." He put his head in his hands and they were shaking. He stopped talking.

"Jack, we found a glove, the kind you have here. Since it was turned inside out, there are probably usable skin cells for a DNA test." She had no idea if that was possible, but neither did Jack.

"Hannah," he said. "I didn't kill Denny. He was dying when I found him. I knew it. God, you should have seen him; it was awful. But, he was saying, 'Laverna, Laverna' – and if anyone had heard him, they would have known Laverna poisoned him. I had to shut him up."

"So, you picked up a brick and hit him?"

"God forgive me; I did."

Now that Jack had started, he couldn't stop trying to rid himself of keeping the secret of what he'd done. "I picked him up, put the brick in my jacket pocket and figured I could hide the body across the covered bridge. It was about to rain and I figured nobody would be likely to go near the bridge. I could come back later and do something with the body. I didn't know what, but I'd think of something. It was stupid to stuff him into the barrel, but I never thought anybody would see him."

"And when you saw me, you were trapped. You thought I might see or hear you."

"You were too close to where I had to go to get back, so I wouldn't be missed. I knew I hadn't hit you hard enough to hurt you bad."

"I'm not sure how you knew that. You could have injured me worse than you did, already. You were lucky, Jack."

He looked at her. "I was *lucky*?"

"Wohl, you didn't hurt me worse and you did not kill Denny. The cyanide did!"

Jack looked dazed. "But, Laverna poisoned him; he was saying her name."

"Could it be he realized he was dying and was asking her forgiveness, or yours?"

"Oh, God, what have I done?" Jack asked, and Hannah looked away from his face; he was sobbing.

She gave him a minute. Then she went on. "After you hit me, you put the brick back in your pocket. Why did you hide it in the blanket chest?"

"He didn't; I did." Laverna said from the doorway. Neither Hannah nor Jack had heard her come in. "I found Jack's jacket with the brick. With blood on it. I figured if I hid it in the chest, nobody would think you or Carrie would have anything to do with it. It was dumb. We are not very good at criminal behavior, are we?" She laughed, shrilly. "He was trying to protect me and I him. Sort of a twisted *Gift of the Magi*, don't you think?"

Hannah knew the classic O. Henry story and thought it a stretch for Laverna to attempt a comparison.

Laverna walked over to Jack, who stood up and put his arms around her.

"None of it was necessary," Hannah said. "I know you didn't poison Denny, Laverna. You are not the kind of woman who would ruin your life to get revenge."

"No, Hannah, of course I didn't kill Denny," Laverna said, turning towards Hannah. "What good would that do? It wouldn't change anything. None of it could be undone. Why rehash the misery?"

In Jack's face, Hannah saw a mixture of resignation that he would have to take responsibility for what he had done, and relief that Laverna hadn't been involved.

"If you had a reason to kill Denny, you certainly had no reason to harm Copious or Matilda, nor did Jack."

"But, how did you know I didn't kill Denny?"

"Jennet took photos of the auction, remember?"

"I was too busy to pay much attention, but now that you mention it, I do remember."

"You are in a lot of them, but not in the kitchen. Never in the kitchen." Hannah knew that it still might have been possible for Laverna to sneak into the kitchen and poison the pie, but none of the women in the kitchen had seen her. It would have looked strange and been memorable if she had appeared in the kitchen. Everyone at the auction had his or her job. Laverna's was in the office, not in the kitchen.

"Whoever poisoned that pie did it in the time from when I left it, to the time Denny bought it," Hannah continued. "It was someone who had access, however brief, to the pie. Someone who knew Denny would buy the whole pie, like he always did."

"Everybody knew that," Laverna said, looking puzzled.

"Hannah, you think whoever killed Denny killed Matilda, too?" Jack asked.

"I do," Hannah said. "And I am pretty darn sure Copious did not commit suicide. Someone just made it look like a suicide and planted a note. He or she made two mistakes, at least. One: the Clays didn't have a computer; and two: letting Matilda see him or her. He had to get rid of her. The murderer probably had no intention of killing Matilda originally. She just got in the way."

"You think it's a woman? Or a man, or maybe a couple? Who lives around here? Are you eliminating Amish? How about Mennonites? They aren't violent and couldn't be killers, right? How 'bout that preacher feller? Maybe you should let me go along to protect you. Like a body guard?" Jack was starting to play twenty questions, a game Hannah had been peppered with before.

"I don't know, Jack. I'm working on it with a private investigator and Carrie. We will let you know if we need your help, as a bodyguard. She thought of his brick wielding. Well, he did that efficiently, but Bear would be a more reliable guard --- not that she needed one.

"Oh, poor gentle Matilda," Laverna began again. "She had such a tragic life from the time Denny took to destroying Ed Yost. After Ed died, when Copious came along, she was so much happier; even leaving the Mennonites did not bother her much. She used to say that the golden rule was the most important thing and trying to do what Jesus would do was the next most important thing. Going to church was not important to her, because she carried church in her heart. I really miss her, Hannah."

"I know you do, Laverna. You must believe what she did – she is in a better place with Copious, and there is no more sadness in her existence."

Hannah addressed Jack. "Knowing that you, Jack, put Denny's body where it was found, has focused our suspect list. Previously, we were thinking the killer couldn't have been a woman, unless she was strong enough to get the body from the truck to the bridge. Besides, why would anybody who poisoned him care where his body was found?"

"So, all along you thought more than one person might be involved?"

"We knew it was possible," she answered. "Although I could not figure out whom or why," Hannah answered a touch of irony obvious in her tone of voice.

"But the Clays, Hannah? Who would kill them? Everybody loved them," Laverna's voice broke.

"If Copious 'confessed', the killer was safe."

"Why would the killer choose Copious to throw the blame on? Why not anyone who hated Denny? God knows there were enough candidates, already, to choose from," Jack said.

"Oh, I get it; the killer had to be someone who had access to cyanide. Copious was a jeweler; don't they use all kinds of poisons in their work?" he asked.

"That is what I figured, Jack. The killer probably knew that would throw the police off, too. They would sure be quicker to believe Copious' suicide. They could close Denny's murder investigation without having to work too hard, already." Hannah didn't share her small doubt with the Bests that she hadn't completely ruled out the possibility, however unlikely, that if Copious had easy access to cyanide, so did Matilda. She certainly knew he was on blood thinners. But, try as she might, she could not imagine Matilda killing her husband, with whom by all accounts, she had a satisfying life. Depressed people almost never kill their mates without reason; they kill themselves. Even if she took the unlikely scenario further, there was the question of Matilda's death. She couldn't have shot herself, tossed the gun away, climbed into the trunk, gotten the top down and died. How would she have gotten to Denny's barn in the first place?

"The FBI won't be too quick to write off Matilda's death," Hannah told them. "The crime scene will take days, maybe weeks, to sift through. I would not be surprised if they move a little faster than Benton and boys.

"Jack, you know you should get a lawyer. I imagine he will advise you to turn yourself in. If you need to talk to someone about who to get, call Stephen. He will suggest someone he trusts."

"I will," Jack said.

Laverna put her hand in his. "Will it be all right, Hannah?"

"It is not up to me, Laverna, but I feel it won't be as bad as you are thinking. A little praying never hurts."

Jack smiled wanly, but relief was evident on his face and in his voice when he said, "I guess I got myself into a real pickle, huh, Hannah?"

"Jack Best," she answered. "That was the worst attempt at gallows humor I've ever heard in my life." They would get through this, she thought. Prayer and humor, along with each other's love and support were pretty potent antidotes for the Bests' problems.

Now what? Hannah wondered. Should she go back home, and wait for Carrie? Rebecca, and Daniel, along with half the Amish in the district were at a barn raising for a family who had lost their barn in a fire. They would be gone all day. She grew up watching barn raisings, but it was still a thrill, even after being at hundreds, to see the almost choreographed effort involved The speed at which the structure rose was phenomenal. To think, it took hundreds of years to build a cathedral and hours to raise a barn. Even Hannah had to admit, the cathedrals were a little bit fancier. Still and all, if the Amish were hired to raise a cathedral, they could probably shave a couple of hundred years off the finishing time.

Thinking of the ludicrous picture of Amish men crawling all over a cathedral lightened Hannah's mood, as that of the sky darkened.

She was anxious to share the results of her interview with the Bests, with Carrie, but she was not going to resort to calling Carrie's new cell phone number. Anybody could hear those conversations, shouted at each other like they were. She could go by Stephen's store and tell him. It could wait. If everything fell into place, she might have the crimes solved by the time she saw Carrie. She tried to remember Carrie's schedule. Oh, yes, today was the conference with Molly's teacher at one o'clock, and then Caroline was going to pick Jennet up at the airport mid-afternoon.

Hannah had a choice; she could go visit Petula or the Hesses first. She decided Pet first, then the Hesses. In case it rained hard, she would just as soon not be too far from home, nor too close to a creek in case it flooded and stranded her and Clara out in the weather. Clara was too old for these shenanigans. She should be warm and snug in the barn, not muddy to the knees. If Hannah was going to get these cases figured out in the two remaining days before they promised Stephen they'd stop investigating, even a race horse couldn't get Hannah around fast enough. Her light mood evaporated as she headed towards Petula's house.

All she was thinking about now was, that if she found Petula as emotionally drained as she had been the last time she'd seen her, it would be real hard to bring up the story of Denny and the sham marriage. The last thing she wanted to do was send Petula over some mental precipice into a total breakdown. Poor soul had undergone so many traumas in such a short time.

She started down the lane to Pet's house. "Okay, Clara, let's get this over with," she said, in a decidedly unenthusiastic voice, half wishing she had decided to see the Hesses first. Granted, they were a little like a box of assorted chocolates. You never knew what you were going to get until you took a bite; might be bitter or might be sweet, or might be a nut. Hannah broke off her thoughts of Swayne and Dorcas and pulled up to Pet's house. Her car was there.

Hannah turned the horse around to afford Clara some degree of protection from the rain and loosely looped the reins over the metal railing. Clara would be protected by the overhang, and the wind was driving the rain away from the carriage itself. It would only be a few steps for Hannah to get to the house. If this rain kept up, Petula would lose her flower garden, but the building had been here through higher creeks than this one, Hannah thought, venturing a look at the churning water. There were plenty of trees to anchor the bank, and the house, which was back and well above the bank, didn't look to be in any danger. Still, she wasn't about to subject herself or Clara to a long visit with Petula Brody.

It took a couple of sharp knocks before Pet opened the door.

"Hannah," she said. "Why are you here?" Despite Rebecca's assurance that Pet was doing better, she did not look so to Hannah. It was the middle of the day and Pet was still in her pajamas and barefooted. Her hair was a matted nest.

"May I come in?" Hannah asked, unnecessarily as by then she was in.

"Sure. Whatever," Pet mumbled. "I'm sorry, Hannah. Didn't mean to be rude. I was taking a nap."

"That explains why you opened the door in your nightclothes. You should be more careful, Pet. Do not open the door when there is ..." Hannah almost said, a murderer loose, but she thought better of it. She did not need to remind Pet of her loss. "Before you know who it is."

"Can I get you a cup of tea?" Pet asked, recovering a bit. "Just let me slip on a robe."

"I'll get the tea," Hannah said. "I see the kettle and the tea canister."

"Oh, okay," Pet said, and went into the other room, bare feet shuffling against the wood floor.

By the time she returned, in a bathrobe and slippers, the teakettle was boiling and Hannah had two mugs with tea bags waiting for the water. Pet shooed Hannah into the living room and busied herself playing unwilling hostess.

She brought them each a mug and sat opposite Hannah. Hannah had left her cloak on, a signal she was only dropping by and did not plan to stay for a long visit.

"How are you doing, Pet?" Hannah asked.

"Fine," Pet said.

Her eyes do look better, Hannah thought; not so swollen. She wondered if Rebecca had filled the doctor's prescription for more tranquilizers for Petula. That could be accounting for her behavior. "What can we do to help you, Pet?"

"There is nothing to be done. Bodies are still not released. We cannot have any services yet. I'm just going to let Mrs. Osgood handle it. Jack said he would take care of the arrangements. Laverna is real upset, too."

"I know," Hannah said.

"This wasn't supposed to happen, Hannah. All these poor people dead." She reached into one of the large patch pockets of her yellow robe and dragged out a pristine, folded handkerchief. "Matilda, Copious. It shouldn't have happened," Pet sniffed.

"Denny?" Hannah asked. "I know you do not want anyone to have died. Not even Denny, no matter what he had done."

"Well, of course I did not want him dead. But we'd been split for years, now. I didn't give a damn about him. Lots of people hated Denny."

"So I have heard tell," Hannah said, setting down her cup. It was still too hot to drink. "How long were you two married?"

"Too long," Pet spat out.

"It must have been hard," Hannah said, feeling ever so guilty for her devious line of questioning.

Pet sat back, and looked steadily at Hannah. "You know, don't you, Hannah?"

"That you and Denny were not legally married? Yes, Pet, I just found out. Who could blame you for being bitter?" Hannah wasn't about to start suggesting forgiveness.

"All those years, there I am thinking we were married and I had to stick it out. And I did, until I couldn't stand it any longer. I got me a lawyer and he said I couldn't get a divorce. There never had been a marriage certificate filed. Denny tricked me. It wasn't any clerical error, either. I told Denny he couldn't sleep with me unless we had it all legal. I was a good girl, Hannah," Petula said, her indignity as clear as it must have been all those years ago. She continued, "Denny told me it was so I never could get any money or any of his 'stuff.' I didn't want his stuff. But I sure as hell wanted alimony. The lawyer said I could sue him. But then the whole world would know."

"Pet," Hannah said, gently. "No one would have blamed you. You were an innocent victim." Trying to think of something to distract Pet, Hannah remembered the photos of the auction. In her current state, even a picture of the Clays together would only either distress Pet further or incense her. "No one will ever know from me," Hannah assured her, thinking it was the second secret she'd promised to keep in one day.

Pet seemed not to be listening. "Denny married me to sleep with me and have a wife to please his daddy, to make sure he'd get his daddy's money. Money, money, it's all about money!" Pet stood up, knocking over Hannah's cup which spilled hot liquid onto Hannah's cloak. The heat soaked through, but by the time it got to Hannah's skin, it wasn't hot enough to more than warm her.

Suddenly, Pet screamed at Hannah, "You know! You prying old snoop!"

And Hannah did know. Like at a certain point with a quilting design, the pattern became clear. If she had done more than taken a cursory look at the photos, she would have seen Pet in the kitchen, Pet at the pies. Who would better know Denny's habits? Copious was Pet's brother. She knew about the cyanide. And she killed Copious and

287

Matilda, too. "Oh, good God, Petula," Hannah said, half in prayer, half in shock

Petula reached her hand into her other pocket. When it emerged, it held a gun. Hannah wasn't surprised. The police hadn't found the gun that killed Matilda because it wasn't in the remains of the barn. Pet had taken Matilda to a place where she knew she might not be found for months, but she hadn't been about to leave the gun behind.

As if she was reading Hannah's mind, Petula said, "I didn't want to kill, Matilda, Hannah. Really, but she saw. She was supposed to be at the grocery store. She would have shared the money, but Copious wouldn't. I was going to burn down the barn, cremate poor Matilda, but you and Caroline came too soon. I had to get rid of Copious because he might have missed the poison I took from his shop. I would have had the insurance money from the barn fire."

She seems lucid, Hannah thought, but jumping from place to place, from one murder to another; the only common thread was money. Hannah was trying to stay calm, get herself out of this, and to do that she had to keep Pet talking.

"Pet, if I figured this out, someone else will, too. Do not make this any worse. You will never get away. There will be no place to hide."

Pet said, "Bet no one would ever find me at Denny's."

So much for lucidity, Hannah thought. "If you are going to kill me, what is the harm in explaining why you did it? Was it the money? If you weren't married to Denny, you couldn't inherit his money. Someone would find out. I did."

"No, Hannah, you don't get it. Denny told Matilda he was leaving everything to her! Some drivel about righting past wrongs! How about the wrong he did to me?!"

"How did you find out?"

"Matilda told me, and she would have shared the money with me. She said so. She showed me a copy of Denny's will, but Denny said she couldn't even tell Copious, and she didn't until after Denny was dead. I just helped everybody get their wish. I got Denny out of the way. Everybody's way."

"Copious?" Hannah asked. She wanted to say, 'he was your brother', but dared not. It might send Pet over the edge she was already teetering on.

"You didn't know him, Hannah. He was a mean spirited man. He wouldn't have shared that money. No matter what Matilda said. He would go off to Hawaii like he did when I was a kid. Then, he left me home to be raised by our drunken Pa.

"Besides, I needed someone to blame Denny's murder on. Copious wouldn't help me when I was down and out, and he knew about Denny and me not being married. Men stick together," she said, as she callously jerked Hannah to her feet.

"Ouch," Hannah protested. "It is raining," Hannah said, inanely. It was the only thing she could think of; a pretty lame stalling technique. She would have to do better than that if she was going to get out of this alive.

"Yeah, the harder the better," Petula sneered. "We are going to take a walk in the rain."

"I won't go!" Hannah said, defiantly, as the taller woman waved a gun at her.

"Look, Hannah, I could whack you with the gun so I wouldn't mess up the house, or just strong arm you out of here, or we could go for a walk. You choose."

Hannah knew her only chance lay outside where she might be able to outrun Petula, who would be instantly weighted down with a soggy chenille robe and unwieldy bedroom slippers. "Outside," she answered, trying to sound more frightened than she was. Then she remembered the two things that may yet save her.

"Good. I want you to go swimming," Petula said.

"I can't swim," squealed Hannah, lying without compunction.

"Yeah? I bet you can. Doesn't matter none; with that Amish get-up you're wearing, the creek will weigh you down like a piece of cement was attached to you"

Shoving Hannah in front of her, Petula opened the door and pushed her out onto the stoop and off into the entry yard which had already turned muddy. The younger woman was close behind. Rain was falling in a deluge and the creek was boiling and ripping noisily downstream.

Please, God, let this work, Hannah silently prayed.

"What about my horse? You are not going to drown Clara."

"No, I need her to go home, so they can think Granny has had a terrible accident. But if you don't get down that creek bank, I will drown her, too, or at least try to. She's such an old nag; she probably would drown or break a leg."

"I will go," said Hannah, sadly. "But please let me say goodbye to Clara. Please, Pet."

"Oh, all right, but I'm watching you and if you try anything, you and your horse are both in the creek. Say goodbye from here."

"Clara's deaf. I have to get closer or she won't hear me. Pet, we have shown you kindness," Hannah pleaded like she hadn't ever pleaded. When Pet paused before she answered, Hannah knew she'd won.

"Okay, okay, go tell the horse goodbye, but I'm watching you. Remember, if you want to save that old nag, don't touch her."

"I will n-n-ot," Hannah stammered.

She walked up to Clara, thankful for the sudden deluge and darkening sky. Even Clara, was hard to see from where Pet stood pointing the gun.

"Thirty seconds," Pet called.

"I have to say goodbye, Clara. I do not want to go, but you will be all right," Hannah shouted, making sure Pet heard, too. "Goodbye, Girl." And Hannah blew an elaborate series of kisses towards the horse. With her left hand, she pulled the looped reins free and turned quickly back towards Pet.

"You have stalled enough," Pet said, without hint of emotion.

Hannah moaned. "Oh, God!" she said and clutched at her chest with both hands. "My heart," she waved around, trying to slump without falling. She pushed and pressed at her chest so realistically that Pet's eyes widened in momentary surprise. For a moment, Hannah thought she saw a satisfied narrowing of those same eyes.

"You are either faking a heart attack or really having one. Either way, you are out of my way. I'll give you the benefit of the doubt and see if you die of natural causes. We will wait."

Hannah continued to weave, moving her feet around, and clutching her chest while moaning piteously. She began to alternate the moans with Pennsylvania Dutch and German phrases, while Pet stood stoically and watched, not moving a muscle. Hannah was beginning to lose her voice from the exerting performance, which must have made her sound like she was on her last breath.

"Scream, all day," Pet said. "There's no one to hear you and the road must be washed out by now."

Pet's feet, encased in their ankle high slippers, were unmoving. How could a human being just stand there? Hannah wondered through her moans. She can't shoot me, or Clara, or there would be bullets to explain. But, she is going to get tired of waiting through my death throes, and shove me in the creek. It is now or never.

Suddenly Hannah screamed, "Clara, Come!" in Dutch, and ran to the horse who had come running and was now between Hannah and Pet. As Hannah had hoped, Petula was mired in the mud. Before Petula could react or think of firing a shot, Hannah dove in through the curtains and Clara took off. Clara didn't need reins to know where to go. And Pet couldn't follow them. As she had said, the road was washed out. It was not passable by an English vehicle, but easily negotiated by a smart Amish horse, tri-lingual, yet.

CHAPTER TWENTY SIX

As Hannah reached the main road, a squadron of now unneeded rescuers met her. She had punched in almost every number Caroline had programmed on the cell phone and said enough; they had all heard her and knew Pet Brody was holding Hannah at gunpoint. Thanks to the storm and her nonstop performance, any noise from the cell phone had escaped Petula's notice and Hannah kept jumping from number to number before the respondent had a chance to say much.

Caroline and Stephen were there as were vehicles from, the fire department, the state police, the township police and rescue squads. Pet was still at large and Hannah supposed a helicopter would be joining them as soon as the weather cleared. The main part of the storm had moved through.

Stephen volunteered to drive the buggy and Clara home and give the horse a hero's rubdown and a meal in her own warm, dry barn. Caroline could bring him back for his car later. Hannah was checked over by one of the paramedics who had tended to her after the barn cave-in. She half expected him to mention that she seemed to be a frequent customer, but this was too serious and he was too professional. Nobody felt like joking, Hannah thought, and small wonder, already. She felt like crying. All this waste of precious life. Both Benton and Lee were at the scene. Benton had few questions for Hannah. Most of the information had come through during her overheard conversation with 911 and the other numbers.

"Any ideas where she might head?" Benton asked.

"Maybe Denny's place; she knew it well," Hannah answered. "There is her store, too; she might have gone there if she keeps any money on hand."

"Can you think of anyone who might help her?"

Hannah thought hard. *"Gott im Himmel!"* Hannah caught her breath. "What time is it?"

The policemen looked at each other, surprised by the strange question. "Almost 4:30. Why?"

"Are there soap operas on television now?" The policeman gave shrugs, bewildered as to why she would be asking such a question.

"No, they're over," called a voice at the edge of the barricade. It was one of the neighbors who had gathered when the sirens sounded began.

"Move those people back," Benton ordered. "They are too close if they can hear our conversation."

"Chief," Hannah said, "Petula could be headed towards the Hesses. They would take her in, and they are only down the road, but far enough not to have heard the commotion. They only watch the soap operas on television in the afternoon, so might not know about Pet and all."

Benton muttered something. "I know the house. Backup?" he asked the trooper. His tone was as grim as the situation was.

All Hannah could think of was how physically frail both Hesses were. She was more frightened for them than she had been for herself in confronting Petula. Now, she was praying in earnest for Swayne and Dorcas. Petula needed a car and the Hesses had one; they might have money in the house, and she'd want that, too. Hannah remembered how cold and unfeeling Petula had been with her.

"She would not hesitate to shoot them in cold blood, Chief."

"Don't doubt it for a minute, Mrs. Miller, but we're not going to let that happen. You can't help here right now. Let Caroline take you to your house."

"Please let us know."

"It's the least we can do," he said.

Just then, the senior of the State Police Troopers returned from his foray up to Petula's house. "She's gone; looks like she changed clothes in a hurry; left her slippers in the mud. No weapon there either. Her car is still there; she's not in it or anywhere on the premises. The house and immediate area are secured. We'll fan out. The creek is treacherous. If she tries to cross it ..." he shook his head, scattering droplets of water in an arc.

Quickly, Benton told the Trooper Hannah's theory.

Caroline helped Hannah, who was cocooned in blankets, into her car. Neither one of them said much on the way home. There would be time for discussions and explanations later. A police car led the way. Benton, efficient under the scrutiny of the State Police, had assigned a 24 hour guard on the Miller Farm. Road blocks were already set up along the road. Privately, Hannah had hoped Pet was still at the house. She couldn't get anywhere dressed as she was in sodden bathrobe and muddy slippers. She would have to change, which it seemed she had. Her fear for the Hesses escalated. Hannah shivered violently, not from cold or wet, but from reliving the experience, and worrying about Dorcas and Swayne's safety. Pet would not be deterred, that much Hannah was sure of if the Hesses got in her way.

"They will be all right, Granny. Have faith," Caroline said.

"I am trying," Hannah said, wearily.

The rain had stopped. Sunlight slanted from the western sky and glared into Caroline's face. They drove along in silence until the patrol car ahead of them signaled at the Miller's driveway and turned in.

Two burly deputies Hannah didn't know accompanied them. One took the key and opened the door to Hannah's house while the other one stood between the porch and the women still in the car.

"Remember my animals," Hannah called. She had warned them about Bear and the cats. Hannah didn't hear Bear barking. She had trained him to alert her when a stranger approached. She calmed herself. "Petula could not have gotten here by now," she called to the closer deputy.

"Procedure, Ma'am," he said politely, but firmly. The sound of his voice must have alerted Bear. He sounded like a junkyard dog, barking and jumping at the door. The deputy at the door looked taken aback.

"He won't bite," Hannah assured him. "Bear! Quiet!" she commanded and the commotion stopped.

The deputy opened the door and pawed at the wall. "We are Amish. No electricity," Hannah reminded him.

The deputy looked chagrined. "Forgot for a second," he said.

He pulled the flashlight from his belt and went inside, and from the car's open window, Caroline and Hannah could hear scuffling and yipping, meowing and mild cussing, all interspersed by the deputy calling. "It's okay; just the animals in the way."

After a few minutes, he emerged. "It's all clear." Bear was looping around him happily.

Hannah and Caroline got out of the car and went up the porch steps into the house. Now that the sun was out, there would still be plenty of light in the house.

When they were in the house, Caroline took over. "Granny, you look like some kind of a soggy sausage, wrapped in those blankets.

"I'll go upstairs and run you a bath. Then I'll light some lamps and fix you something warm to drink. Don't worry; if the cell rings, I'll call you." As she spoke, her phone did ring. It was Stephen calling from the barn, reporting on Clara. She was fine and he'd be there as soon as he finished.

A few minutes later, Hannah was bathed and dressed in dry clothes. Taking a bath while eyed by three cats and a dog was not exactly a relaxing experience. Bear tried to run off with the blanket she had been loaned, and the cats sniffed her shoes, trying to figure out where she had been to bring back such odd scents. She would have locked the animals out, but then they'd whine and meow at the door.

Who could relax, already? Hannah thought. She was too busy praying Petula would not harm Dorcas and Swayne, if she had gone there, as Hannah's instincts told her the woman had.

When Hannah came downstairs, and into the kitchen, she found Stephen and Caroline sipping coffee at the kitchen table. When Caroline saw Hannah, she jumped to her feet.

"Sit down, Granny, and let me wait on you for a change."

Hannah was in no mood to argue. Despite the warm bath, she ached from the exertion of her encounter with Petula, and the leap into the buggy.

The three of them brought each other up to date on the afternoon's events. Hannah was first, telling of her visit with the Bests, listening to Jack's confession. She went on to tell the details of her encounter with Petula. In Hannah's version, all the credit for her narrow escape went to Clara for acting as a barrier between Hannah and Petula.

"I'd say Clara was a secondary player in the drama," Stephen said.

Hannah was finally finished with her part of the story. She set down her coffee cup and looked at Caroline appraisingly.

"You are waiting to tell me something? Am I guessing right, already? I know that look."

"Yes," answered her granddaughter. "And, I guarantee it is something which will distract you while you are waiting to hear about the Hesses."

"You going to tell me, or do I have to guess? "Hannah snapped, uncharacteristically.

Caroline ignored Hannah's remark. "I discovered that Bryce Jordan does have Denny's will. Granny, he left everything to Matilda Clay, as you already know. The will said: 'to right an old wrong.'"

"Denny probably thought he was buying his way into heaven," Stephen commented.

"As if that could do it," Caroline said, caustically.

"What happens to Matilda's inheritance now? You know she hasn't a single living relative; at least none we know of. Guess there must be some distant relative," Hannah said.

"Wait. There's more," Caroline said. "Bryce also has Matilda's will, written after Denny's death. She left everything to Copious, but if he predeceased her, she left it all to you, Hannah Miller."

For one of the first times in her life, Hannah was momentarily speechless.

Caroline continued. "She said she knew you would use the money to do good for the community," Caroline finished.

"This is a lot of money?" Hannah asked.

"It will take a while to appraise all the real and personal property, but I can tell you, there is over three hundred thousand dollars in Denny's bank account, at least the one we have found."

"Good for the community?" Hannah asked, still a bit dazed, but already thinking of just how best the money could be used. Maybe some of the horror of the deaths could be forgotten with the ideas she already was formulating.

Bear leaped up from Hannah's side and bounded to the door; seconds later they heard a knock. Stephen went to answer it, followed by Hannah and Caroline.

A woman deputy in the uniform of Chelsea Township stood there. "Deputy Bradley," Hannah said. "You have news?" Hannah tried to read the deputy's impassive expression.

"Yes, and it is good. May I come in?"

"Sorry. Of course; come in," Hannah said, a wave of relief sweeping over her.

"Petula Brody is in custody – unharmed. You were right; she did go to the Hesses. The Hesses are fine ... actually, more than fine."

Hannah's sigh of relief was audible. Several minutes later, the deputy had joined the family at the table and was holding her own mug of coffee.

"I came to tell you because I was on the scene when she was taken into custody," she began.

"When we got to the Hess home, Ms. Brody was already in custody, so to speak. To tell the story briefly: she had gone there and, of course, they let her in. You were correct in assuming, Mr. and Mrs. Hess knew nothing about the incident at the Brody home. Well, it seemed she asked them if she could borrow their car. When Mr. Hess, who is a bit deaf, asked her to repeat herself, Ms. Brody pulled a gun. Mrs. Hess then threw a crocheted afghan of some sort over Ms. Brody, throwing her off balance. She knocked over a table and fell into the television set. When we got there, Mr. Hess was sitting on her and Mrs. Hess had the weapon Ms. Brody dropped pointed at her.

"Mr. Hess seemed quite upset about his television set, and his cough syrup being spilled, but even more annoyed about the fact his wife was none too steadily waving a gun about." Deputy Kayla Bradley managed to relate this tale without a smile, but the other three were in various stages of laughter. They knew Dorcas and Swayne, and could visualize the entire scene.

"So," the deputy said. "The paramedics say the Hesses look just fine, but we called a nurse to stay the night with them."

"Petula?" Hannah asked. "You said she was uninjured?"

"She was physically unhurt, according to the paramedics; but it took four deputies to get her into the patrol car."

Hannah did not mention Jack Best. She had already asked Stephen to recommend a criminal lawyer for Jack, if he hadn't already found one.

After the deputy and patrol cars had gone, Caroline spoke. "Come on, Granny; you are going home with me. You need to be with family now. Let someone take care of you for a change. We'll feed the animals before we go."

"No," Hannah started to say; then she remembered Jennet was coming and would see the quilt. She didn't want to miss that moment. Hannah also had to admit a bit of pampering under the circumstances would not be a selfish thing. She felt an immense sadness for all of them. Despite her trust in the Lord's will, and knowing Matilda and Copious were in a better place, she wasn't anxious to be alone to go over and over the scene at Petula's house. And the impact of Matilda's trusting Hannah with the responsibility of the money hadn't really sunk in. Caroline was right; she needed to be with her family.

"I'll get my bag," she said.

Caroline had called Ellerie and asked her to pick up Jennet at the airport, briefly explaining the circumstances. Ten minutes after Caroline, Stephen and Hannah arrived at Caroline's house, Ellerie was at the door with Jennet.

As Hannah had hoped to do, she unveiled Jennet's quilt. Jennet had tears in her eyes when she saw it. "Oh, Hannah, it is beautiful," she said, gazing at the quilt which lay glimmering on the bed in the subdued lighting. "How can I ever thank you?"

Hannah didn't need thanks; Jennet's reaction was enough.

A few minutes later, they all sat in Caroline's family room, while Caroline, this time, told the story of the afternoon's incredible events. Both Jennet and Ellerie, who hadn't heard all the details, were wide-eyed and silent, listening.

"Oh, in all the excitement, Caroline," Ellerie spoke up, "I forgot to tell you that the Delaware State Police, captured Pastor Ben Samuels. In his possession were all kinds of stolen items. Seems he made a habit of doing exactly what he did at Petula's house. He'd visit the bereaved and walk off with some small object of value. No wonder Petula was more than a little upset when she realized her silver candlesticks were missing. The police found a small space in the hollowed bottom of the candlesticks. There was cyanide powder in them. The police said they could smell it and so, removed the felt covered bottom."

Caroline said, "Why didn't she just get rid of the cyanide in the first place?"

"Good question," Stephen said. "She probably just didn't have the opportunity, or maybe she thought she would have further need of it."

"Thank God she did not," Hannah said.

"She was so paranoid, anything was possible," Caroline said.

It was quiet in the room. Each of them was thinking about the amazing events of the past week.

Suddenly, Hannah sat forward in her chair, a resolute look on her face. "This is out of our hands now. We need something happy to think about. I suggest a wedding. About a week from now. Anybody up to it, already?"

The room was a sea of smiles. Followed by a chorus of "I am!"

EPILOGUE

Just as Hannah had predicted, the day of Caroline and Stephen's wedding was a perfect day. This week of warm weather following the storms, prematurely brought about a full blown early spring. Flowers opened and trees leafed out almost overnight. Rose Mill Inn looked like an English inn in late May. What nature had not yet provided, Hart Florist, aided by Jennet's expert eye, had. Roses were added to the tendrils of vines around the arches and down the sides of the gazebo. It looked completely natural and very beautiful. Massed pots of pink and white freesias lined the paths, perfuming the air.

Inside, each round table was draped in white organza over solid pink cloths and edged in silk rose petals. The tables were centered with miniature nosegays of baby roses and white violets laid around fat white candles tied with green satin ribbon.

Caroline's family would not, of course, take place in the actual religious ceremony, but there was no objection to Amish attending English weddings and many of them did. Both the church and Rose Mill had provided places for tying up the horses in the shade and had hired Amish boys to water them.

The church was decorated with two white tree roses at each side of the altar.

Just before sunset, as the string quartet began playing, the guests were seated. The traditional selections were chosen to mean something to the bride and groom.

Then to the sound of "Pacabel's Canon", came the bridal party. Caroline was preceded down the aisle by Molly, who carried a miniature pastel spring bouquet and Jennet in a striking pale pink silk, ankle-length, column dress, with long sleeves. She was carrying white and pink long stemmed roses. Last, came Caroline, who was ethereal and beautiful in the dress she had so painstakingly made, worn with the simple lace veil Jennet had brought to her from Florence. She carried a large nosegay of white violets. Caroline did not need to be given away nor held up. Her march to the altar where Stephen waited with Jennet's husband, Ian Hunter, as his best man, was sure and resolute. The smiles on both their faces were contagious. The entire congregation smiled with, and on them.

The simple, but poignant service was short, and sealed with a chaste kiss, so as not to embarrass the Amish present who did not kiss at their weddings. As Caroline and Stephen proceeded down the aisle to the recessional, shafts of colored sunlight poured in through the colored glass windows at their backs, as if they had planned it, which, of course, Caroline had. Hannah looked at the scene with great satisfaction. Somehow, with a lot of help from her friends and from the Lord, Caroline's perfect day had been accomplished.

It was later at the reception dinner that Hannah got Jennet aside. "Jen, dear, you might think me crazy, but I since I have come into some money, I'd like to buy Nettie's house."

"Why, Hannah? As a home for one of your grandchildren?"

"In a manner of speaking. I plan to turn the pool house into a little house for Josh and Susanna. Josh can put in a truck garden and sell the produce at Roots and the Green Dragon," she said, naming two of the area's largest farmers' markets. That way he can save up until he finds a larger property.

"Meanwhile," Hannah continued, warming to her subject, "I'd turn the house into a maternity home and clinic for Rebecca. That way, a woman who was about to deliver, especially in the winter, could settle in there instead of having Rebecca make a breakneck carriage ride from miles away. If a complication arose, it's an easy trip to the hospital or for a doctor or ambulance to come to her. Rebecca could train midwives there too, kind of like a midwife school. If one of the moms needed bed rest, she could get it there rather than with a half dozen other kids swirling around her."

"Hannah, what a wonderful idea!"

"Now about Flying Needles," Hannah continued. "I want to buy that, too. Amish and Mennonite women need a place to sell their own work with no middle man taking the profits. It was a successful business for Nettie when she was running it. Guess we could make it the same, especially with less overhead."

"We would even be able to work on quilts on the third floor," Jennet said, becoming enthusiastic.

"We?"

"Yes, Hannah. Ian and I have been waiting to sell one or the other of the properties and build a small place in Lancaster County. Now, you have made that possible. It would just be for weekends and vacations now, and later for retirement. You promised to teach me to quilt someday. Seems like now is a good time.

"Speaking of resolution of problems, what's going to happen to Jack Best?" Jennet asked.

"Stephen says he will probably get a suspended sentence. Whatever happens, Jack and Laverna are going to Florida. Someone bought Best-Stoltzfus."

"Good heavens, not you, Hannah?!" Jennet looked shocked.

Hannah laughed heartily. "What a terrible thought, Jen! I have quite enough to do, already! No, it is not me. Nobody seems to know who it is yet."

"The local Amish telephone is slipping," Jennet teased.

Caroline and Stephen came over to their table. "I assume you've broken the news to Jen," Caroline said. She is glowing with happiness, Hannah thought with approval.

"It's a wonderful plan, don't you think? Matilda would approve," Jennet said.

"She would! When the rest of the estate gets straightened out, what is left will go to the Relief Society to help those in need in the community. It will be a lasting tribute to Matilda and Copious," Hannah said.

"It will keep you too busy to get into any trouble. Ever again," Caroline said.

"Never say never," Stephen whispered in his wife's ear, as he whirled her around for their first dance, *Time After Time*.

THE END

RECIPES

Standby Amish Cole Slaw

Ingredients:

3 pounds cabbage shredded

12 carrots shredded

1 red or mild white onion (like Walla, Walla or Vidalia), thinly sliced

1 green Bell, or red Bell pepper; halved and sliced thin

1 cup oil

2 cups sugar

1 cup apple cider or white vinegar

2 teaspoons celery seed

1 teaspoon white pepper

1 teaspoon salt

Directions:

Put shredded cabbage in large bowl. Layer onion, carrots and pepper on top. Boil oil, sugar, vinegar, celery seed and salt for 1 minute. Pour over cabbage mixture. Let stand at least 2 hours - (Best if let sit overnight) then mix well. Put in airtight container. Will last 2 weeks in refrigerator.

Strawberry-Rhubarb Shortcake

Ingredients

Sauce

8-10 stalks rhubarb, trimmed and chopped into one-inch lengths (no leaves, they are poisonous).

4 cups strawberries, hulled and sliced in half

Sugar or other sweetener, to taste.

Zest and juice of one orange

Zest of one lemon

One-half teaspoon ground ginger

Directions:

Combine all ingredients except for the sugar, in a heavy saucepan. Bring to a boil over medium heat, stirring occasionally. Once at a boil, reduce heat and simmer until rhubarb is tender. Stir in sugar to taste. Makes about eight cups.

Using your favorite shortcake, cut the shortcakes in half, top with a generous spoon of the sauce, cover with the other half of the short-cake piece, turned with cut side up, pour on more sauce and top with whipped cream or ice cream.

Serves 4-6

Shoofly Pie Coffee Cake

Ingredients

3 cups all-purpose flour

1 and 1/3 cups sour cream

1 cup sugar

3/4 cup butter - softened

1/2 cup brown sugar

1/2 cup light molasses

1/2 cup chopped walnuts --pecans are super, too

3 large eggs

2 teaspoons baking soda

1 and 1/2 teaspoon cinnamon

1 teaspoon nutmeg

1 and 1/2 teaspoon baking powder

1 and 1/2 teaspoons vanilla

¼ teaspoon salt

Directions:

In a large bowl, sift together flour, baking soda, baking powder and salt. Set aside.

In a separate medium bowl, mix together the butter, sugar, eggs, vanilla and molasses until you get a consistency of wet sand. It works best if you mix with fingers or two forks.

Add wet ingredients to dry ingredients and stir. Add sour cream and beat until smooth.

In a separate small bowl, mix brown sugar with walnuts, nutmeg and cinnamon.

In a separate small bowl, mix brown sugar with walnuts, nutmeg and cinnamon. Preheat oven to 350 degrees, bake for 35 minutes or until toothpick comes out clean.Preheat oven to 350 degrees.

Simply Delicious Lemon Sponge Pie

Ingredients

3 tablespoons butter, softened

1 1/4 cup sugar

4 eggs, separated

3 tablespoons flour

1 dash of salt

1 1/4 cup milk

2 lemons, juice and grated peel only

1 unbaked 9-inch pie shell

Preheat oven to 375.

Directions:

In large mixing bowl, cream together butter and sugar until light and fluffy. Beat in egg yolks, flour, salt, milk, lemon peel and lemon juice. In small bowl with clean beaters beat egg whites until stiff but not dry. Gently fold whites into the first mixture. Pour mixture into pie shell.

Bake in 375 oven for 5 minutes; reduce heat to 300 and bake for 45 minutes longer or until top is golden. A wooden pick inserted in center should come out clean. Cool lemon sponge pie on rack

Notes on Molly's Jordan Almonds

The tradition of Jordan Almonds served at weddings (simply large Spanish almonds coated with colored or white sugar coating) can be found in various European cultures. They are a reminder life is both bitter and sweet. Guests are given five sugared almonds signifying five wishes for the bride and groom. These wishes are for health, wealth, happiness, children and a long life

Jordan Almonds make delightful wedding favors. The Amish would serve them in decorated nut cups. Molly would add a little note explaining the almonds' meanings so guests would know not think they were only a candy treat.

ABOUT THE AUTHOR

In writing her two mysteries, Barbara Workinger, draws on her background as a research journalist and antiques dealer, as well as an interest in the art of quilting. She combines them with a fascination for the Amish area where she lived for over twenty years. Ten of those years were spent in researching the Amish.

The first series features irrepressible Amish quilter, Hannah Miller, AKA "Granny Hanny," and her formerly Amish granddaughter, Caroline, now a Lancaster attorney. In the first book, "*In Dutch Again*," Hannah's neighbor, antique dealer Annette Adams is found murdered, and Hannah is drawn into the investigation. "*In Dutch Again*," takes place against the colorful background of autumn in Central Pennsylvania.

The sequel, "*Shoofly Pie to Die*," Barbara's latest romp through Amish Country, is set in the spring. In each book in the series, well researched details of everyday Amish life and special events are woven into a fast paced mystery.

Barbara was a finalist in the Malice Domestic Best Unpublished First Mystery Contest.

A fourth generation Californian and University of California alumnus, Barbara now lives in suburban Portland, Oregon. She and her husband Paul have seven grown children and one very spoiled cat. She is a member of Mystery Writers of America, Sisters-in-Crime, and Pennwriters.